ABHIJNANASHAKUNTALAM

KALIDASA

ABHIJNANASHAKUNTALAM

The Recognition of Shakuntala

Translated from the Sanskrit and Prakrit
with an Afterword and Notes by
VINAY DHARWADKER

PENGUIN BOOKS
An imprint of Penguin Random House

PENGUIN BOOKS

USA | Canada | UK | Ireland | Australia
New Zealand | India | South Africa | China

Penguin Books is part of the Penguin Random House group of companies whose addresses can be found at global.penguinrandomhouse.com

Published by Penguin Random House India Pvt. Ltd
4th Floor, Capital Tower 1, MG Road,
Gurugram 122 002, Haryana, India

Penguin Random House India

First published by Penguin Books India 2016

Page 349 is an extension of the copyright page

10 9 8 7 6 5 4 3 2

The international boundaries on the maps of India are neither purported to be correct nor authentic by Survey of India directives.

ISBN 9780670087464

Typeset in Adobe Caslon Pro by Manipal Digital Systems, Manipal
Printed at Replika Press Pvt. Ltd, India

www.penguin.co.in

for
Aneesha Dharwadker,
architect,

and
Sachin Dharwadker,
film-maker

DUSHYANTA (*looking down*): In our descent at high speed, the world of human beings is a truly amazing sight. For—

The flat ground remains farther away
As the peaks of mountains zoom towards us;
Trees cease to be indistinguishable in a mass of green
As their branches become distinct to our sight;
Fine lines in the distance, without a trace of water,
Now acquire breadth and visibility, and become rivers.
Look, the earth seems to move closer and closer,
As though someone were heaving it up towards me.

MĀTALI: Your observation is exact. (*He gazes in awe and wonder.*) Oh, the earth's beauty is sublime!

Kālidāsa, *Shakuntalā*, Act VII
(circa 400 CE)

Contents

Preface

Kālidāsa's *Shakuntalā* is a play that dramatizes a love story. It is the earliest play in world drama and theatre to be centred on a comprehensive narrative about love, and it is the oldest of the complete, free-standing works in any genre of literature around the globe to be focused on this theme. It develops a vivid representation of the process of falling in love, of infatuation and passionate union, of separation and failed reunion, of finding and losing and regaining a soulmate, and of reuniting in a child and living happily ever after. In fact, it defines the paradigm of romantic comedy for future times, but it is an extended comedy with tragic and serious elements set in a heroic frame.

Shakuntalā is a full-bodied play that enacts the story of Dushyanta and Shakuntalā in seven acts, with a large cast of lively, memorable characters. It is composed in a combination of prose and verse in the Sanskrit and Prakrit languages, and most probably acquired its finished form around 400 CE. It belongs to Indian literature in its classical period (400–1200 CE, approximately), which coincides broadly with a period of extraordinary development in the dramatic and performing arts across the subcontinent. During the interval of about 1000 years between the third and thirteenth centuries—from the last Senecan tragedy to the earliest significant Chinese drama—India is the only place in the world with a vibrant, multilateral theatrical culture, and *Shakuntalā* is the finest of the Sanskrit–Prakrit plays to emerge in that environment.[1]

This dramatic work is traditionally attributed to Kālidāsa, who may have been a historical figure around the turn of the fifth century, a poet and a playwright working under the court patronage of Chandragupta Vikramaditya, the most famous of the imperial rulers of the Gupta dynasty in north India.[2] Over the past 200 years or so, modern international scholarship has arrived at a critical consensus, based on more than a millennium of scholarship and discourse in Sanskrit, that Kālidāsa was most likely the author of either six or seven works of drama and poetry belonging to different genres. The long poems ascribed to him include *Meghadūtam* (The Cloud-Messenger), *Kumārasaṁbhavam* (The Birth of the Young God), *Raghuvaṁsham* (The Dynasty of Raghu), and possibly *Ritusaṁhāram* (The Cycle of Seasons); and his three plays are *Vikramorvashīyam* (Vikrama and Urvashī, or Urvashī Won by Valour), *Mālavikāgnimitram* (Mālavikā and Agnimitra), and *Abhijñānashākuntalam* (The Recognition of Shakuntalā).[3] Despite the concerted efforts of dozens of scholars since the late eighteenth century, however, it is still not possible to formulate a single fact about Kālidāsa's career or personality, and everything that is said about him as a flesh-and-blood individual remains speculative in the end.

Nonetheless, the text of *Shakuntalā* has been transmitted to the modern period in determinate manuscript forms, and we can correlate it in a variety of ways with a stream of literary references, quotations, analyses, evaluations, critiques, and commentaries in Sanskrit since about the eighth century, the middle of the classical period.[4] The play has been preserved and circulated along three main lines of textual transmission, commonly known as the Devanagari, Bengal, and Kashmir recensions, which are distributed over three script systems and regions of the subcontinent, and diverge on several levels but are closely interrelated. Since the early nineteenth century, the Devanagari recension has proved to be the source that connoisseurs find the most satisfactory aesthetically, that scholars in India and abroad discuss most often, and that teachers and students in the modern Indian educational system study most widely. The Devanagari text of *Shakuntalā* has been edited with critical rigour by a succession of European and Indian scholars since the 1840s, and every word in it has been weighed, vetted, analysed, and annotated in a number of Indian and European languages. I have used the twelfth edition of the Devanagari text published by the Nirnay Sagar Press in 1958—edited by Narayan Ram, and commonly regarded as the most balanced version of the play—as the basis of my translation, notes, and critical commentary in this book.[5]

As one of the paradigmatic plays in world drama, and as the most famous individual dramatic work in the history of theatre outside Europe, *Shakuntalā* is the focus of a long, widespread, and distinguished tradition of translation. William Jones's inaugural rendering in English, based on an unedited form of the play in the Bengal recension, appears in England in 1789 (shortly before the French Revolution), and triggers other translations not only in the world's modern languages but also in those of India itself. In proximity and at a distance in time and space as well as language and culture, Jones's translation generates an unprecedented order of imaginative discovery and rediscovery around the globe until the mid-twentieth century, stimulating assessments and reassessments of the text, ideological appropriations and re-appropriations of classical India, and fresh production across the arts and media, together with renewed performance on the stage.[6]

In this worldwide web, however, a large number of the modern lines of transmission originate in indirect rather than direct translation. The pattern of indirect dissemination outside India is fully evident at its earliest stage: George Forster's German version of *Shakuntalā* of 1791, for instance, which alters the course of the *Sturm und Drang* movement and of Weimar classicism, is not a rendering of a Sanskrit–Prakrit source but a translation of Jones's English version, which is based on the latter's own intermediary interlinear rendition in Latin prose. What offsets the proliferation of indirect derivations in the long run is the periodic return to the classical text, especially among scholars and commentators in the modern Indian languages after the mid-nineteenth century—even though their access to the past is mediated thoroughly by Orientalism and modernity.[7]

For any translator of *Shakuntalā* today, the problem at the core of this intransigent web-work spills over in two directions at once. In one, he or she has to negotiate extensively with the intricacy of Sanskrit as a language (of which both Greek and Latin are virtual subsets), and of the Sanskrit–Prakrit literary system, its dramatic tradition, and its historical and aesthetic contexts. In the other direction, he or she has to fully accommodate the qualities of Kālidāsa's play, as a poem in prose and verse and as a superb performance vehicle, which require sustained immersion, not only in literary practice and theatre-craft across genres and periods, but also in the separate practice of poetic translation.

In this book, I offer twenty-first-century readers a brand-new translation of *Shakuntalā*, which balances multilingual scholarly access to the Sanskrit–Prakrit text and its discursive environment with literary representation in English that draws on a practitioner's experience in poetry, poetics, and translation spanning four decades. Unlike previous translations in this language, my rendering here attempts to reproduce Kālidāsa's poetic devices, figures, and effects in precise detail, and to transpose the shape as well as the substance of his primary and secondary plots and tertiary incidents on to this language without loss. At the same time, my version seeks to capture the liveliness of the dialogue, the dynamic evolution of three-dimensional characters, and the dramatic quality and thematic range of the whole with its fifty or more speaking parts onstage. My translation starts 'from scratch' with the Sanskrit–Prakrit texture of the Devanagari recension, and hence offers new interpretations of the larger and finer features of the play, resolves long-standing issues of syntax and semantics, and offers fresh solutions to persistent problems of interlingual and aesthetic representation.

If these methods and techniques are successful, then general readers should encounter a brisk, transparent English text that leaves them free to engage vigorously with the world of Kālidāsa and that of the play, without having to fret about outdatedness, obscurity, or unreliability. Scholars, specialists, and connoisseurs should be able to experience a renewed pleasure in the text, to discover what has been missing in the past, and to see a familiar work in a vivid, unprecedented mirror image. At the same time, directors, actors, and theatre professionals should discover a performance vehicle that gives the classical an edge of the experimental, and reverberates with unforeseen possibilities for the contemporary cosmopolitan stage.

Shakuntalā is a perpetually modern classic because it retains its freshness and renovates its significance in different historical periods, but it fixes its own location as an imaginative work in three distinct worlds. The love story of Dushyanta and Shakuntalā unfolds in epic time and space, in which human beings are larger than life, kings rule 'the whole earth / Bounded by the blue borders of the sea', and ascetics in enchanted forests acquire supernatural powers (Verse 45). The drama on the stage, however, unfolds in a world of beauty and taste, painting and poetry, palace and garden, courtier and merchant, and city and kingdom evidently set in the classical period of Indian literary history. At the same time, the meaning of the action—which Dante would call its anagogic meaning—unfolds in the celestial realm, where gods intervene in human affairs and human beings speak face-to-face with gods. As it traverses the celestial, epic, and classical worlds, *Shakuntalā* exceeds the limits of romantic comedy and heroic play and becomes an ancient, autonomous Asian prototype of cosmic drama.[8]

Most important, perhaps, *Shakuntalā* dramatizes a story that places an ideal of love between two individuals at the heart of the founding of a nation and the naming of a land. In the final analysis, Kālidāsa's play about Dushyanta and Shakuntalā reimagines the conception and birth of their son Bharata, whose divided descendants several generations later fight the great war of the Mahābhārata (and of the Bhagavad-gītā within it), and who gives his name in perpetuity to the land known as Bhārata—with which we are familiar otherwise as the *Indos* of the Greeks, the *al-Hind* of the Arabs, the *Hindostan* of the Mughals, and the 'India' of the British.[9] Bharata is the seven- or eight-year-old boy who appears only in Act VII, wrestling with his bare hands with a lion cub, and living up to his childhood epithet of Sarvadamana, 'the one who dominates everybody'. Kālidāsa's plot is specifically designed to project Bharata as the child of two ideal lovers, who choose each other freely on the basis of mutual attraction, passion, trust, compatibility, and respect, and learn to walk together as 'companions in morality' (Segment 189). Unlike the Mahābhārata in Sanskrit, the *One Thousand and One*

Nights in Arabic, and Boccaccio's *Decameron* in Italian, all of which give us smaller love stories set inside dialogic narratives, *Shakuntalā* offers us a full-fledged dramatic work for the stage that fuses myth and romance, the tragic and the heroic, comedy and fabulation, realism and idealism, the local and the national, earth and cosmos—a representation, at once, of things as they are and perhaps as they ought to be.

The Book

This book has a modular structure that readers can rearrange functionally to suit their individual needs and interests. The Guide to Pronunciation provides all the necessary information on my use of terms from various Indian, Asian, and Europhone languages. In general, for words and expressions that have been assimilated into English, I have followed the *Oxford English Dictionary*; for expressions that have not been assimilated or standardized, I have followed the practices in international scholarly discourse for spelling, italicization, and diacritical marks. For material from the Indian languages in my commentary and notes, I have mostly used the standard system of diacritics for Sanskrit as the common denominator. Technical terms in my critical discussion that are likely to be unfamiliar are glossed or translated at first occurrence, and also at subsequent occurrences, if necessary. The Guide will be particularly useful for theatre practitioners and readers interested in learning or reviewing the pronunciation of the names of the numerous characters in the play.

The Translator's Note, which appears just after the Guide to Pronunciation, offers a practical as well as general account of my methods and techniques of translation. The first two sections explain my rendering of the external form of the play, which proves to be complicated: the division into acts, the placement of the Prelude and various Interludes, the numbering of verses, and the identification of dramatic scenes and textual segments. The last three sections of the Note discuss the languages of the play and the multilayered process of translating Sanskrit and Prakrit prose and verse into contemporary literary English, concluding with an analysis of the tropes in a representative poetic passage in the text. Readers will find it helpful to review the first two sections before reading the translation, and may prefer to return to the final sections at a later stage.

My English version of *Shakuntalā* appears immediately after the Translator's Note. It is impossible to present a translation of the play to a modern reader without accompanying explanations, and it is impossible for a modern reader to read it, even in the original, as though it were a free-floating text without a history. Since any critical discussion that seeks to measure up to this work and its contexts inevitably has to cover a lot of ground, I have preferred to place my commentary in an Afterword that does not postpone the reader's encounter with the translation. In the final, abbreviated form in which it appears here, the Afterword focuses selectively on three features of the play: its manifold plot; its principal characters and their characterization; and its treatment of the ring that propels its dramatic action.

A number of Appendices, placed after the Afterword, provide information on particular aspects and contexts of *Shakuntalā* in condensed forms—such as lists and tables—for easy access and utility. Appendices A and B deal with the play's characters; C and D cover its settings and shifts in time and space; E, F, and G are concerned with genre, dramaturgy, and aesthetics; and H focuses on versification. The titles of the Appendices flag their contents clearly, and the reader can use them to chart a course through their territory, whether familiar or unfamiliar, as needed. Directors, dramaturges, and actors will find all the Appendices—except the last—of practical use in the theatre, since they touch on various aspects of performance, in the Sanskrit–Prakrit tradition in general or specifically in relation to *Shakuntalā*.

The Notes to the Play cover various expressions and statements, images and figures, formal features, allusions and references, unstated assumptions, and literary and dramatic conventions in the translation that require explanation or interpretation. Patient readers may prefer to read through the translation continuously on the first occasion, in order to gauge it as a self-sufficient play-script; and to return to it for a second reading, when they can pause periodically to consult the Notes to the Play. The separate Endnotes to the whole book identify the sources of my quotations and references, offer supplementary information, and sometimes expand on my commentary. The Select Bibliography at the end—which is selectively annotated—lists all the works that I cite, as well as other sources that readers may wish to explore on their own.

The basic conventions in the book follow international practice and are easy to follow. The acts and scenes in the play are numbered with upper and lower case Roman numerals, respectively; 'II.iii', for example, refers to Act II, Scene iii. Each act begins on a new page, and runs continuously to its end; the start of each scene is marked with its number in boldface along the left margin of the translation. The play's introductory and intermediate parts—the Invocation, the Prelude, and six Interludes—are placed at the beginning of the appropriate acts. This version of *Shakuntalā* contains 191 verses or poetic passages; they are numbered consecutively in a single series for ease of reference, and the numbers appear in brackets along the right margin of my translation. Each verse is located at the end of a well-defined segment of the text, and my commentary refers to the verses and the segments by the numbers they share. The Notes to the Play are keyed to the translation by segment number, verse number, and annotated word or phrase, as necessary.

In the translation of the play, the dialogue is printed in roman typeface, and the stage directions are given in italics. Some directions are specific to one character speaking at a particular moment in the action. These are embedded in his or her dialogue, and are placed in parentheses; some parts of them are formulaic, and hence are in a 'telegraphic' style, whereas other portions are more distinctive, and are expressed in full sentences. A range of embedded, parenthetical directions appears, for example, in the first scene of the main action (I.iii) before, between, and after Verses 10 and 11. Other stage directions in the play-script are more general, or pertain to more than one character: they cover exits and entrances, coordinated movements on the stage, or complex shifts in the dramatic situation. Directions of this kind are set in separate lines, apart from the dialogue, and appear without parentheses; see, for instance, the entrance of three new characters on p. 34, before Verse 10. All such stage directions in the play-script, with or without parentheses, are translated as precisely as possible from the directions in Sanskrit.

At a few junctures in the text, however, I have had to insert connective or explanatory statements in the dialogue, or additional stage directions, chiefly in the interests of clarity, coherence, and performability. All of my interpolations that go 'beyond' the play-script in the Narayan Ram edition are placed in (square) brackets. In I.iv, for example, new stage directions are required to streamline the asides among four characters on the stage (p. 44); and, in VII.i (before Verse 166) and VII.ii (after Verse 177), additions are necessary for the dialogue to be comprehensible in reading as well as performance (pp. 161,

168). My use of brackets in the translation is consistent with standard practice, in which brackets—as distinct from parentheses—indicate insertions and modifications in texts, quotations, and citations.

Finally, the presentation of poetry in the play-script and other parts of the book also follows familiar conventions. The first word in every 'poetic line' in a verse here begins with a capital letter. If a given poetic line is too long to fit into the page-width, it is 'run on' in an additional physical line; a run-on line is indented on the left, and does not begin with a capital. Readers as well as performers should treat a poetic line, including any run-on portion of it, as a single rhythmic unit. Examples of run-on lines appear at the beginning of the play-script, in the Invocation, where five poetic lines are too long to be accommodated. Ideally, an actor would capture the rhythm of Verse 1 by delivering each of its nine poetic lines as a unified, finely modulated measure of sound and meaning, regardless of its visual layout on the page.

Acknowledgements

I finished a full draft of my translation of *Shakuntalā* in Madison, Wisconsin, between October 2014 and June 2015. As I was teaching during the academic year, and had other institutional responsibilities at the University of Wisconsin–Madison, I had to concentrate my work on the Sanskrit–Prakrit text in long stretches on four or five days a week. The process of rendering Act I was slow, since I consulted four commentaries at each step (Rāghavabhaṭṭa's in Sanskrit, Shrikrishnamani Tripathi's and Yadunandan Mishra's in Hindi, and C.R. Devadhar's in English), and intermittently compared my evolving translation to the English versions by Barbara Stoler Miller, Michael Coulson, and W.J. Johnson, and to the Hindi translations by Mohan Rakesh and Rewaprasada Dwivedi.[10] However, once I had determined my overall orientation to the play's text, the commentaries, the other renderings in print, and the field of scholarship on *Shakuntalā*, I was able to fine-tune my strategies as well as my practical goals. Especially from Act III onwards in January 2015, I focused my attention primarily on Narayan Ram's 1958 edition, on Rāghavabhaṭṭa's fifteenth-century Sanskrit commentary included in it, and on Mishra's multilingual scholarly work (in Sanskrit, Prakrit, and Hindi), with periodic references to Miller and Dwivedi. I deliberately did not consult the older works by William Jones, Monier Monier-Williams, and M.R. Kale before I had completed a draft of my translation.[11]

In July 2015, I moved to Berlin on sabbatical leave, which enabled me to work on this book without interruption, though in unusually spartan conditions. During my first four months in Germany, I polished and finalized my translation; I also compared it at this stage to Jones's prose version and to Monier-Williams's edition and rendering, but neither source led to any changes in my text. At the same time, I prepared a large amount of material for my critical commentary on *Shakuntalā*; however, after a reassessment in November 2015, I decided to recast it completely. The Translator's Note, the Afterword, the eight Appendices, and the Notes to the Play that appear in these pages emerged from this late process of reconceptualization and rewriting.

As a poet, translator, and scholar, my encounter with *Shakuntalā* has had to be an act of single-minded and self-disciplined isolation over fifteen months, but I owe thanks to a number of people and institutions for making it possible. At Penguin India, R. Sivapriya took a great leap of faith and imagination in 2012, when she invited me to translate the play for Penguin's prestige edition of Kālidāsa's works, designed to set a standard in the global Anglophone market. Since R. Sivapriya's departure for other professional opportunities in mid-2015, Ambar Sahil Chatterjee has steered the project with great skill, tact, and enthusiasm, and has adjusted and readjusted his editorial and publication schedules to accommodate me. As before, the copyeditors, designers, and production staff at Penguin-Random House have been exemplary professionals in the art of making books, and have made sure that this volume meets the highest international standards. I am especially grateful to Arpita Basu for her meticulous work with me on every aspect of the text.

At the University of Wisconsin–Madison, my thanks to Professor Robert Glenn Howard, chair of the Department of Comparative and Folklore Studies, and Professor Ellen Rafferty, chair of the Department of Languages and Cultures of Asia, for supporting my sabbatical plans; and to Dean Karl Schultz and Associate Dean Susan Zaeske, College of Letters and Science, for their approval. My gratitude to the staff members at the university's Memorial Library, especially its interlibrary loan services, who obtained all the books and articles that I needed at the initial stages of this project. In Berlin, I am obliged to the International Research Center (Dr Erika Fischer-Lichte, director), Freie Universität, for providing me with guest privileges at the university library, without which I would not have been able to complete my manuscript. On a more personal note, my thanks go to Sandeep Kindo, doctoral candidate in Languages and Cultures of Asia at Wisconsin, for his generous help with securing some essential print and online research materials; and to Dr Narges Hashempour, scholar and theatre practitioner, Fellow at the International Research Center, for her perceptive feedback on the presentation of *Shakuntalā* to audiences outside India.

Most of all, my thanks to Aparna Dharwadker, scholar of Indian theatre and world drama and of various literatures, and colleague at the University of Wisconsin: our partnership now extends to four decades on three continents. In Madison, Aparna read each act as I completed it in my first draft of the translation, and offered her candid responses as a reader and spectator of plays; and, in Berlin, she read the revised translation as a whole as well as a long draft of my commentary, and offered her critical assessment as a scholar and theorist of drama. Over fifteen months, we also talked about numerous features of *Shakuntalā* and of classical Indian drama, poetics, and dramaturgy. My time in Europe would not have been possible without Aparna's tenure as a Fellow at the International Research Center and its focus on 'Interweaving Performance Cultures'. Our exchanges helped me to reshape the book until it acquired its finished form, and our ongoing conversation intersected at many points—in Chicago and New York, in Madison and Berlin—with the lives of our children, Aneesha and Sachin, to whom this volume is dedicated.

This project is intimately connected to my collaboration with Aparna on the translation of Mohan Rakesh's *Ashadh ka Ek Din* that Penguin India published in 2015. R. Sivapriya commissioned me to translate *Shakuntalā* after she had read that manuscript; and Ambar Sahil Chatterjee supervised its editing and production as a book under the title *One Day in the Season of Rain*. Rakesh's play is paradigmatic in modern Hindi drama, in post-Independence Indian theatre, and in postcolonial literature more generally: a work of modernist classicism, it imagines Kālidāsa's life and literary career comprehensively through the plots and characters of his poems and plays, and becomes a unique dramatic equivalent of a *Künstlerroman* on the world stage. Kālidāsa's *Shakuntalā* and Rakesh's *One Day in the Season of Rain* form a perfect pair of 'bookends' in India's literary history: one is a play that is 'the validating creation of a civilization' in the classical period, and the other is an experiment in intertextual modernism that refracts it, some 1500 years later, in 'the disorder of things'—the debris—of postcolonial times.[12]

Vinay Dharwadker

Berlin, Germany
15 January 2015

Guide to Spelling and Pronunciation

Terms from the classical and modern Europhone languages, such as Greek, Latin, French, and German, are printed in italics and spelt in their standard international forms (for example, *Künstlerroman*). Words from Europhone and Indian languages that have been naturalized in English are used without italics and without diacritical marks, following *The Oxford Dictionary of English*, third edition (2010) for orthography, spelling, grammatical forms, and so on. Thus, for example, the text consistently uses the style karma, rasa, brahmin, kshatriya, and Devanagari, without italics and diacritical marks. All borrowed words and uncommon naturalized terms are glossed in the main text at first and subsequent occurrences, as necessary.

All terms in Sanskrit and Prakrit are transliterated using the system defined in the following table. Besides common words and all characters' names, the transliterated material includes classical and premodern authors' names, place names, titles of works, names of languages and metrical verse-forms, and so on. Hence, the spellings with diacritical marks range from *aṅka* and *aprastuta-prashaṁsā* to Shakuntalā, Priyaṁvadā, Māḍhavya, and Shāraṅgarava; from Dhanañjaya and Vishvanātha to *Nāṭyashāstra* and *Shriṅgāra-prakāsha*;

and from Mahārāshṭrī and Hastināpura to *shārdūlavikrīḍita*. Important words in modern Indian languages, such as Hindi, Urdu, Marathi, and Bengali, also are transcribed here in the same system (for example, *bahurūpiyā*, *charaṇa*, and *chamelī*). However, commonly romanized modern Indian names and titles of works are spelt according to conventions in print and other contemporary media; thus, Narayan Ram rather than Nārāyaṇa Rāma, and Mohan Rakesh, *Ashadh ka Ek Din*, and Nirnay Sagar Press.

For readers as well as theatre personnel and performers, the following table provides the full list of alphabetical symbols with diacritical marks used in this system of transliteration, with notes on the standard pronunciation of vowels, consonants, semi-vowels, and other elements. Sanskrit and Prakrit words are pronounced as they are spelt, with each syllable (centred on a vowel) articulated clearly. The symbols appear in the conventional order of the Sanskrit alphabet: vowels, nasal and aspirate, velars, palatals, retroflexes, dentals, labials, semi-vowels, sibilants, and voiced aspirate. The semi-vowels are specified with terminal vowels, but consonantal elements are given in their 'bare' forms.

a	as *u* in b*u*t (short simple vowel)
ā	as *a* in f*a*ther (long simple vowel)
i	as *i* in s*i*t (short simple vowel)
ī	as *ee* in f*ee*t (long simple vowel)
u	as *u* in p*u*t (short simple vowel)
ū	as *oo* in b*oo*t (long simple vowel)
ri	as *ri* in *ri*p (short syllabic liquid), for the vowel *ṛ*
e	as *a* in m*a*ke (diphthong)
ai	a vowel glide that conjoins the short *a* and the long *e* (diphthong)
o	as *o* in g*o* (long simple vowel)

au a vowel glide that conjoins the short *a* and the short *u* (diphthong)

ṁ a nasal, and also a sound that nasalizes the vowel that precedes it, as *m* in hi*m* (nasal)

ḥ an aspiration or 'breathing vowel' that adds a separable *h* sound after the preceding vowel, as *h* in ba*h* (aspirate)

k as *ck* in lu*ck* (unvoiced unaspirated velar)

kh as *ckh* in blo*ckh*ead, or as *kh* in Indian-English la*kh* (unvoiced aspirated velar)

g as *g* in *g*ut (voiced unaspirated velar)

gh as *gh* in ho*gh*ead, or as in Indian-English *gh*ee (voiced aspirated velar)

ṅ as *n* in cli*n*k (velar nasal)

ch as *ch* in *ch*in (unvoiced unaspirated palatal)

chh as *ch-h* in pit*ch-h*ook (unvoiced aspirated palatal)

j as *j* in *j*oke (voiced unaspirated palatal)

jh approximately as *dge-h* in sle*dge-h*ammer (voiced aspirated palatal)

ñ as *ny* in English ca*ny*on, or *ñ* in Spanish se*ñ*or (palatal nasal)

ṭ as *t* in *t*op (unvoiced unaspirated retroflex)

ṭh as *th* in ho*th*ouse (unvoiced aspirated retroflex)

ḍ as *d* in *d*ay (voiced unaspirated retroflex)

ḍh as *d-h* in ma*d-h*ouse (voiced aspirated retroflex)

ṇ as *n* in ti*n*t (retroflex nasal)

t as *t* in French *t*out (unvoiced unaspirated dental)

th aspirated dental *t* with no English equivalent, but *not* pronounced like *th* in *th*ing (unvoiced aspirated dental)

d approximately as *th* in ba*th*e (voiced unaspirated dental)

dh aspirated *d*, with no English equivalent (voiced aspirated dental)

n as *n* in ski*n* (dental nasal)

p as *p* in *p*ill (unvoiced unaspirated labial)

ph as *ph* in u*ph*ill (unvoiced aspirated labial)
b as *b* in *b*ig (voiced unaspirated labial)
bh aspirated *b*, with no English equivalent (voiced aspirated labial)
m as *m* in *m*ap (labial nasal)
ya as *yu* in *yu*p (palatal semi-vowel)
ra as *ru* in *ru*n (retroflex semi-vowel)
la as *lu* in *lu*g (dental semi-vowel)
va approximately as *wo* in *wo*rld; between *wo* in *wo*rse and *ve* in *ve*rse (labial semi-vowel)
sh as *sh* in *sh*ut, used here to represent both ś (palatal sibilant) and ṣ (retroflex sibilant)
s as *s* in *s*ome (dental sibilant)
h as *h* in *h*at (voiced aspirate)

While keeping the various Indian languages distinct in their transcription, I have made one set of exceptions for specialized terminology. In Appendix G and elsewhere, I have replaced the long Sanskrit compounds for categories of *bhāva*s with more user-friendly forms common in Hindi and Marathi; for example, I have used *sthāyī bhāva* instead of *sthāyibhāva*.

Illustrations

1. SAMPLE OF SANSKRIT TEXT

Title and opening lines of play in three different scripts: Brahmi, Devanagari, Roman. In each panel, the play-title is followed by 'Act I' and the first two quarters of Verse 1; this portion of the Invocation corresponds to the first five lines of my English translation.

Top panel: Text in Brahmi script, as written most likely in Kālidāsa's time (400 CE).

Middle panel: Text in Devanagari script (evolving since late classical times), in mid-twentieth-century print form.

Bottom panel: Text in Roman transcription, with diacritical marks, early twenty-first century.

2. MAP OF NORTH INDIA

Map representing approximate locations of Kaṇva's Ashram, Indra's Ford, and Hastināpura (labelled in capital letters), projected onto north India in early twenty-first century. The River Mālinī, a real geographical feature, flows out of the lower Shivalik Mountains near contemporary Kotdwara, and merges with the Ganges near Bijnor. 'Indra's Ford' is a natural formation of islands and sandbars that breaks up the larger river into branches that can be crossed with relative ease. Kālidāsa's descriptions of the three locations (for example, white sand along the Mālinī, deer on the mountain slopes) remain 'poetically true' to the landscape today.

3. KAṆVA'S ASHRAM AND DUSHYANTA'S HUNTING CAMP

Schematic diagrams of physical settings, Acts I–IV. These diagrams only conceptualize locations of dramatic action, and do not represent stage sets. Location of main action in each scene is indicated by Roman numerals in parentheses.

Upper frame: Imagined layout of grounds of Kaṇva's Ashram, on west bank of River Mālinī, for main action of Acts I, III, and IV.

Lower frame: Rough plan of Dushyanta's hunting camp, also west of the Mālinī, at some distance from Kaṇva's Ashram, near edge of enchanted forest.

4. DUSHYANTA'S PALACE AND MOUNT MERU

Schematic diagrams of physical settings, Acts V–VII. These diagrams only conceptualize locations of dramatic action, and do not represent stage sets. Location of main action in each scene is indicated by Roman numerals in parentheses.

Upper frame: Possible layout of Dushyanta's palace grounds at Hastināpura. Main palace building on left, facing the gate; ancillary structures on right and at top.

Middle frame: City market in Hastināpura, at some distance from palace precinct.

Bottom frame: Kashyapa's celestial ashram on Mount Meru.

1. SAMPLE OF SANSKRIT TEXT

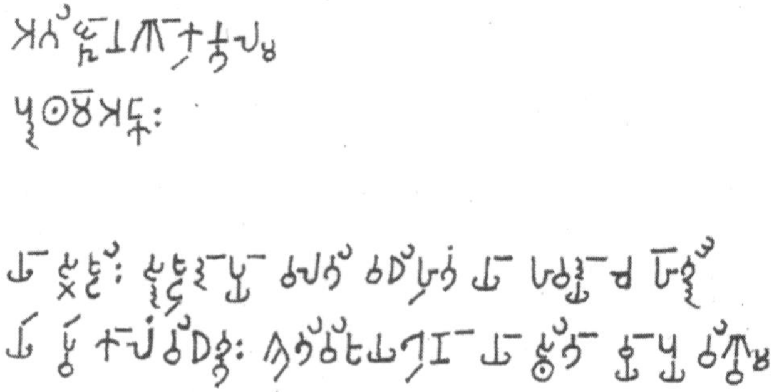

अभिज्ञानशाकुन्तलम्

प्रथमोऽङ्कः

या सृष्टिः स्रष्टुराद्या वहति विधिहुतं या हविर् या च होत्री
ये द्वे कालं विधत्तः श्रुतिविषयगुणा या स्थिता व्याप्य विश्वम्

abhijñānashākuntalam

prathamo-aṅkah

yā srishṭih srashṭurādyā vahati vidhihutaṁ yā havir yā cha hotrī
ye dve kālaṁ vidhattah shrutivishayaguṇā yā sthitā vyāpya vishvam

Title and opening lines of play in three different scripts: Brahmi, Devanagari, Roman.

2. MAP OF NORTH INDIA

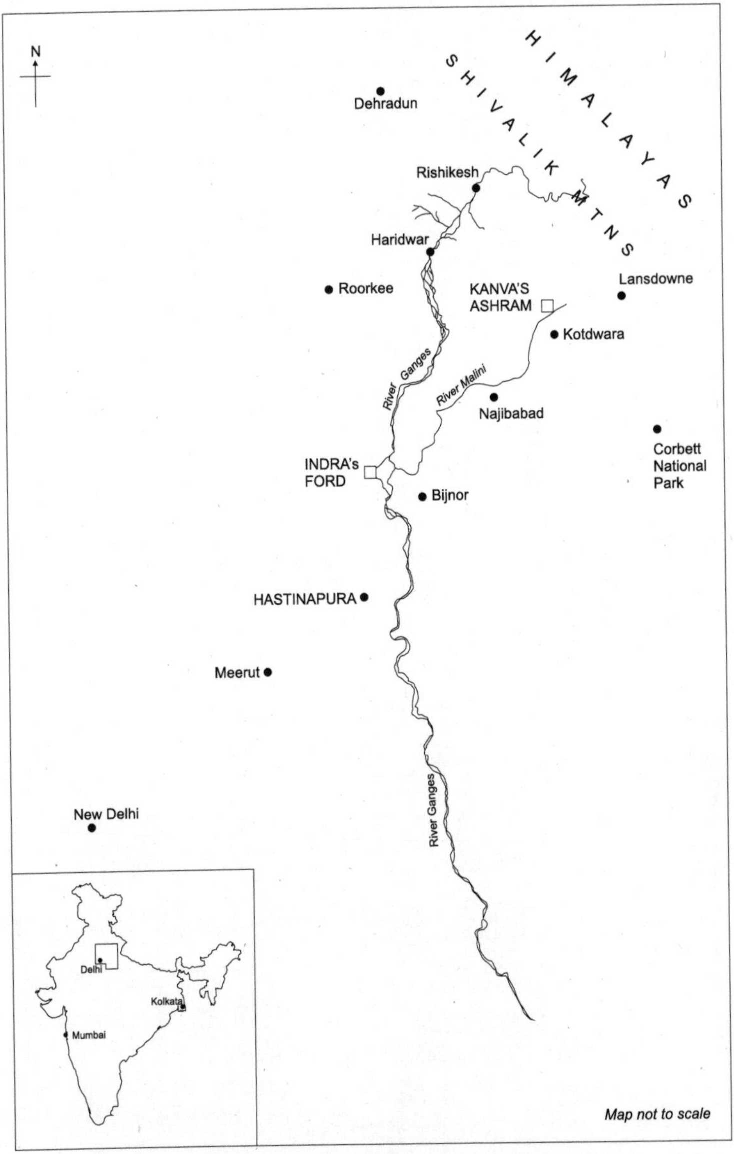

Map representing approximate locations of Kaṇva's Ashram, Indra's Ford, and Hastināpura (labelled in capital letters), projected onto north India in early twenty-first century.

3. KAṆVA'S ASHRAM AND DUSHYANTA'S HUNTING CAMP

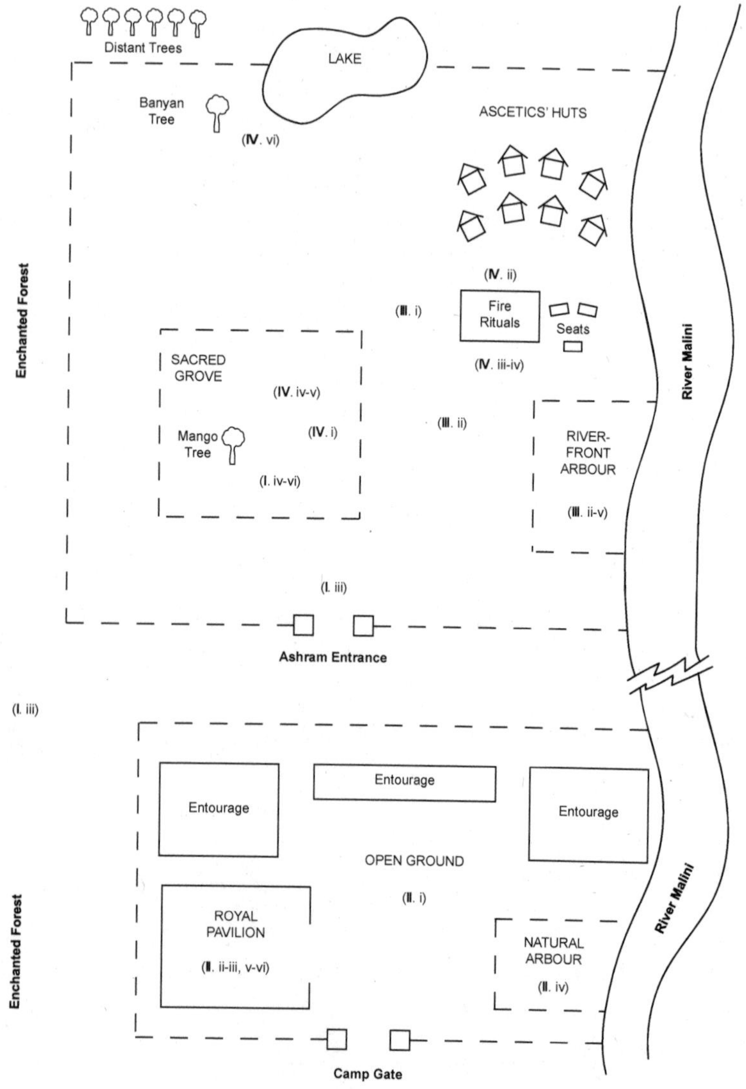

Schematic diagrams of physical settings, Acts I–IV.

4. DUSHYANTA'S PALACE AND MOUNT MERU

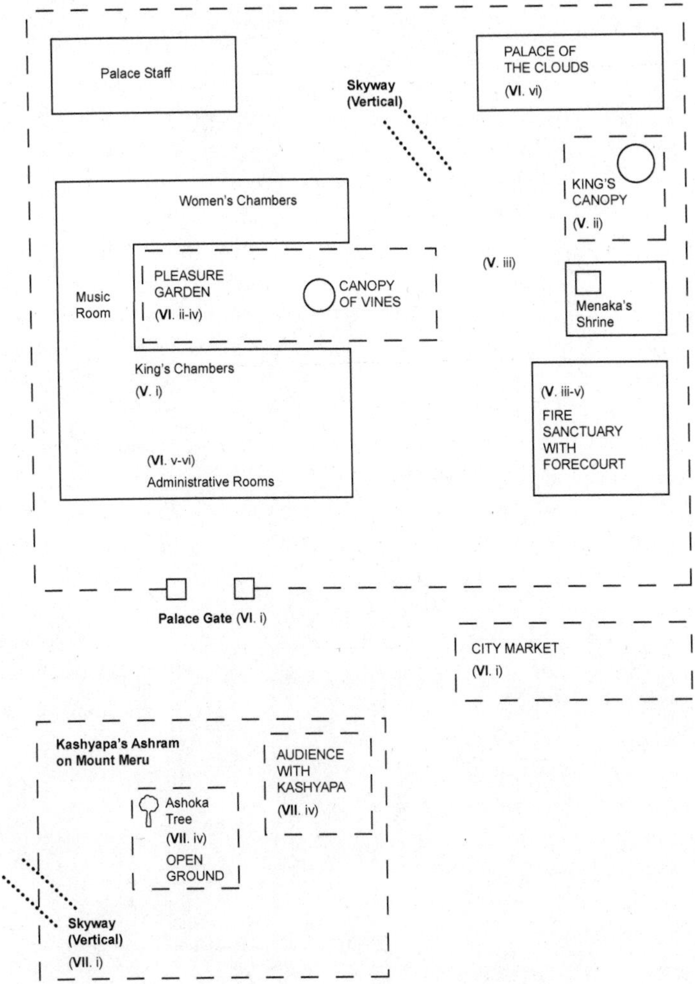

Schematic diagrams of physical settings, Acts V–VII.

Translator's Note

Acts and Interludes

A modern edition of the Devanagari recension of *Shakuntalā* leaves many readers with a strong impression of organic unity in its dramatic structure and its texture of words. Every part of the action is defined clearly, the parts are interrelated at multiple levels to constitute a balanced whole, and the whole is presented as a seamless continuum of events, characters, and meanings. Each portion of the story that threads the drama gets as much stage time and textual space as it needs—no less and no more—and the narrative sequence progresses from beginning to end with 'the best words in the best order' on a spectrum of languages and speech varieties.

The actual organization of the play-script, however, is more refractory than this impression suggests. The text transmitted from classical to modern times has fifteen separate parts that have to be assembled in a satisfactory order on the page: the seven pieces of the main dramatic action that comprise the bulk of the seven acts; the Invocation and the Prelude that frame the play, in its textual form and in the theatre; and the six Interludes that bridge the dramatic and narrative gaps, individually and in pairs, at the beginning of Acts II, III, IV, and VI. These components are separate because they differ in form, and are distinguished by the labels they have carried since the classical period; and the order in which they have to be placed is sequential as well as hierarchical, because they occupy positions that are different and of different kinds, even as they perform distinct functions in the whole.

The sequence of these fifteen parts is fixed, but their textual placement in relation to each other is variable, mainly because of uncertainties about the outer form of a play and the boundaries of its internal divisions. Logically, the Invocation and the Prelude together (I.i–ii) ought to appear outside the main action, especially since the Prelude foreshadows it and stands in a meta-theatrical relation to its drama.[1] Along the same lines, each of the Interludes should be placed in an intermediate space, between the end of one act and the beginning of the next one. But, by this logic, the opening Invocation should be separated from the Prelude also, because it plays a different rhetorical role with respect to the audience; and the pairs of Mixed Interludes (in Acts IV and VI of my version) ought to be broken up, since each of the nested scenes bears an independent relation to what precedes and follows.

Various manuscripts in the three recensions of *Shakuntalā*, and the modern print editions and translations based on them, collectively have experimented with the possibilities of textual arrangement that this reasoning suggests. In the case of the Bengal recension, for example, William Jones's English translation of 1789 places his renderings of the Invocation and the Prelude together under the label of a Prologue, and absorbs the Interludes into the acts without formally distinguishing between their varieties of action. While Jones uses an unedited source, Chandra Rajan's English translation exactly two centuries later reflects the textual organization of the play in the editions of Richard Pischel (1922) and D.K. Kanjilal (1980). In this instance, too, the Invocation and the Prelude are grouped into a Prologue, but the Interludes are clearly identified and located inside Acts III, IV, and VI. In each of the last two, only what I label as Part 1 is an Interlude, while Part 2 is absorbed into the main action; whereas the Interlude in Act II is not named as such, and an Interlude is specified in Act V, using some material that is not in the other regional traditions.

In the case of the Devanagari recension, Monier Monier-Williams's critical edition of 1853 situates the Invocation and the Prelude outside the dramatic action as a whole, and also places all its Interludes outside the acts: in Act III, the Interlude is as expected; in Acts IV and VI, only Part 1 is identified, and Part 2 is merged into the main action; but, in Act II, the Interlude is absorbed into the main action. The Narayan Ram edition of 1958, which is the text I translate here, follows Monier-Williams's pattern of identifying the Interludes, except that it places all the Interludes inside the acts, and also moves the Invocation and the Prelude into Act I.

In this vacillation over centuries, only Tripathi, Dwivedi, and Dwivedi's edition of 2008 embodies the logic of placement by structural function to its full extent. It draws on a new range of Devanagari manuscripts, clearly labels the fifteen parts of the text, and separates the Invocation, Prelude, and six Interludes from the main action in the seven acts; the Invocation and the Prelude appear as 'preliminaries to the play' before Act I, and each individual Interlude or pair of Interludes is placed between two consecutive acts, with the whole series in its proper sequence. Aesthetically, however, the Dwivedi edition is the least satisfactory, because its physical fragmentation on the page—seven acts with eight other units outside them—is antithetical to the play's impact of unity.

The irresolution about the verbal presentation of *Shakuntalā* that has persisted over the past several hundred years arises from uncertainties about the conception of an act in drama, and my translation adopts a solution suggested by the *Dasharūpaka*, Dhanañjaya's tenth-century Sanskrit compendium of classical dramatic theory. The *Nāṭyashāstra* (about 300 CE) is the earliest work in world literature to define an act or *aṅka* as the principal division of a play, and Dhanañjaya's summary of that definition highlights three features: 'an act is a repository of various kinds of meanings and objectives, arrangements of events, and aestheticized emotions'; it is a division of a play in which 'the protagonist's actions are directly perceptible, and the fullness of the principal plot is foregrounded'; and 'Acts ought to be fashioned with introductory material, etcetera, placed at their beginning'.[2] These features are a reminder that a play such as *Shakuntalā* is both a work of dramatic literature and a play-script, and an act hence is as much a unit of textual organization as of performance in the theatre; and that, in the Sanskrit dramaturgical tradition, an act is the largest division of a play, and there are no terms for any interstices between the acts that make up a play-script. My translation therefore places all the labelled 'introductory' and 'intermediate' material in *Shakuntalā* inside the appropriate acts and at their beginning, in the sequential order in which the Invocation, the Prelude, and the six Interludes ought to alternate with the successive portions of the main dramatic action. This placement inside the acts is aesthetically the most satisfactory, because the classical stage directions in the play strongly imply that, both in reading and in performance, its action flows without interruption from one kind of part to another, with the only designated breaks being the successive breaks between the seven acts.

Scenes, Segments, and Verses

In order to make the play more accessible to a range of users in the twenty-first century, including general readers and theatre practitioners unfamiliar with Indian literature and its classical period, I have introduced three practical features into the organization of my translation.

The first is the identification of well-defined scenes in each act. Sanskrit dramaturgy does not separate the scenes in a play, as it employs other means to analyse the plotted action into smaller units, moving from the principal and secondary plots to tertiary incidents in the 'spatial form' of the drama, and from the main stages to numerous sub-stages in its 'temporal form'.[3] In a practical perspective, however, it is easy to see that each act in *Shakuntalā* contains several scenes, the boundaries of which may be unmarked in the playscript, but are indicated nevertheless by changes of setting, exits and entrances of characters, inceptions and conclusions of events and situations, or thematic shifts in dialogue, or by combinations of two or more such transitions.

For contemporary readers, and especially for theatre personnel, the division of a classical dramatic work of this sort into circumscribed scenes is an effective aid to interpretation as well as performance. To avoid violating the integrity of the Sanskrit–Prakrit composition, especially its superb modulation of the appearance of continuous action in each act resembling a cinematic montage, I have matched the boundaries of scenes suggested by modern principles with 'junctures' or 'sub-junctures' identified routinely in Sanskrit and Indian analyses of the plot of *Shakuntalā*.[4] The beginning of each such scene is marked (in boldface) along the left margin of my translation, using standard notation in upper case and lower case Roman numerals: III.iv, for example, specifies Scene iv in Act III. This scene division is particularly useful in identifying changes of setting—the physical time and location of the action represented on the stage. Illustrations 3 and 4 offer diagrams of the scenes and settings at Kaṇva's ashram, Dushyanta's hunting camp and palace, and Mount Meru; and Appendix C provides a complete list of settings scene-by-scene, whereas Appendix D offers a larger conceptual map of the 'movement' of the drama in time and space.

A second feature involves the style of numbering the verses in the play. In the long manuscript tradition of *Shakuntalā*, each recension assigns numbers to all the verses in the play, with a view to stabilize the contents of the text and their order in it, to prevent errors and changes during scribal reproduction, and to enhance citation, quotation, reference, commentary, and debate as well as textual retrieval, navigation, and memorization. The Bengal recension, for example, has maintained a version of *Shakuntalā* containing about 220 verses (interspersed with prose passages) since at least the fourteenth century, when Vishvanātha cited it in his influential critical work, *Sāhitya-darpaṇa* (1384).[5] In contrast, the Devanagari recension has preserved a text with approximately 190 verses since at least the fifteenth century, when Rāghavabhaṭṭa used it to prepare his full-length Sanskrit commentary on the play—and possibly since the eleventh century, when Bhoja may have used it for his comprehensive theoretical discussion in *Shriṅgāra-prakāsha*.[6]

Different lines of manuscripts and modern editions, however, use different methods of numbering, depending often on their overall organization of the text: some number the verses in each act in a separate series, some number the verses in the introductory parts and the Interludes independently of the main action of each act, and so on. Monier-Williams's 1853 edition of the Devanagari recension, for instance, uses a single series of numbers to identify all the poetic passages in the play; whereas the 1958 Narayan Ram edition of the same recension employs separate series in each textual division. My translation is based on the latter edition, but I have adopted the former's method of consecutive numbering for the whole play. The number assigned to each verse appears at the end of its last line, in medium-face Arabic numerals in brackets, along the right margin of the page. Thus, the marginal symbol [78] represents the seventy-eighth verse in my translation, which appears in scene IV.iv. The concordance of acts and numbered verses is straightforward, as the following tabulation indicates.

ACT	VERSE NUMBERS	NUMBER OF POEMS	SUB-TOTALS
I	1–30	30	
II	31–48	18	Acts I–IV: 94 poems
III	49–72	24	
IV	73–94	22	
V	95–125	31	
VI	126–157	32	Acts V–VII: 97 poems
VII	158–191	34	

The third organizational feature of my translation is an outcome of the second. Given the length and complexity of the play, it is possible to identify the basic building blocks of the whole dramatic action unambiguously, once all its poetic passages have been numbered consecutively. For brevity and precision in my discussion, I refer frequently to numbered segments in the text: any segment numbered *N* is the entire passage from the end of the preceding numbered verse, up to and including the verse that carries the number *N*. Segment 46 in II.v, for example, begins immediately after Verse 45, with Gautama and Nārada 'drawing closer' to the king in his hunting pavilion; and it ends with the final line of Verse 46. A segment of this kind includes not only the prose of the dialogue but also any stage directions appearing inside it; and this working definition is easily modified for the first and last segments in an act or scene (which may not be preceded or closed by a numbered verse). This mechanical specification of 191 consecutive textual segments in *Shakuntalā* has the advantage that it is unaffected by any variations in the sequential and hierarchical organization of the seven acts, the individual scenes, the Invocation and the Prelude, and the six distinct Interludes. The cross-references in the Notes to the Play in the latter half of the book are organized essentially by numbered segment and verse.

The segments of my translation are defined using a principle that is qualitatively very different from the principle of analysis employed in Sanskrit poetics and dramaturgy, which identify the building blocks of dramatic action by breaking down the finished plot into sixty-four ideal *sandhyāṅga*s, 'sub-stages' or 'jointed parts of the body' of the play (though the number may vary in actuality).[7] In the case of *Shakuntalā*, one such classical sub-stage of the plot corresponds, on an average, to about three textual segments, as I have defined them. The boundaries of my segments do not always match the beginnings and ends of the dramatic units defined by classical and post-classical commentators, but they do coincide in most cases with the points where individual acts and scenes begin and end.

Language and Prose

Shakuntalā is a multilingual play composed in prose and verse in Sanskrit and Prakrit. 'Sanskrit' in this context (and beyond) is a spectrum of styles, genres, and linguistic registers; the variation is sufficient for discourse at two different positions on this gradient to be mutually incomprehensible, for all practical purposes. In Kālidāsa's text, as transmitted to modern times, linguistic registers play an important role in the prose representation of dialogue; a register technically is a linguistic variety related to an occupation, a practice, or a subject area, so that the register of medicine, for example, is very different from that of engineering. Within a given language or verbal spectrum, registers differ not only in their vocabulary but also in their syntax and rhetorical devices. Act III of the play uses a register of eros and emotion, whereas Act V employs the distinct registers of law, logic, and rhetoric; after translating Acts I–IV with increasing ease and rapidity, I found Acts V–VII surprisingly dense and unfamiliar because of shifts in register and consequent changes in imagery, allusion, and tone. Qualitatively, Sanskrit is the principal language of the play—the vehicle of a large part of its dialogue and all its stage directions—and it serves as a unifying medium in the text, but the discourse in it is not homogeneous.

'Prakrit' also is a singular noun, but it explicitly designates a whole range of differentiated speech varieties, many of them mutually incomprehensible and hence on the verge of diverging as separate languages. Sanskrit–Prakrit drama uses four varieties of Prakrit; in *Shakuntalā*, the Prakrit-speaking characters employ Shaurasenī (from the northern region around Mathura), Mahārāshṭrī (from the western-peninsular region), and Māgadhī and Ardha-Māgadhī (both associated with the eastern region around Bihar, but with different social associations).[8] Shakuntalā, Anasūyā, and Priyaṁvadā, for example, converse in Shaurasenī; the songs sung by the Actress (I.ii) and Haṁsapadikā (V.i) are in Mahārāshṭrī, the most poetic of the Prakrits; whereas the Fisherman (VI.i), classified as an 'untouchable' by caste and socially the 'lowest' character on the stage, uses Ardha-Māgadhī in his prose dialogue as well as his verse (Verse 126, a rarity in that medium).

The multilingualism of the play points to a fundamental artifice of classical Indian theatre that cannot be ignored. Most male characters, such as kings, court officials, priests, and learned ascetics, speak Sanskrit onstage; but some men of so-called lower status (such as Māḍhavya) and all children and women (including the divine Aditi and the celestial Sānumatī) use Prakrit—though Priyaṁvadā and the goddesses of the sacred grove are localized exceptions among the female voices, since Verses 76 and 83 are both in Sanskrit. In most scenes in *Shakuntalā*, Sanskrit- and Prakrit-speaking characters are present together on the stage, address each other exclusively in the languages assigned to them, and participate in complicated verbal exchanges across multiple divisions of language, speech variety, register, and style without a shared lingua franca. An outline map of the full terrain of this artificial aesthetics of communication becomes visible in Appendix A.2, which lists all fifty or more speaking parts in the play by gender as well as linguistic medium. The conceptual implication of this multilingualism in classical Indian theatre (which has no formal counterparts anywhere else) is that the reader and listener-spectator is a multilingual connoisseur, who is at home in all the verbal mediums in the play-script and on the stage. In practice, however, Sanskrit functions as the common medium even for knowledgeable audiences: every Prakrit passage in the text of *Shakuntalā* is accompanied by an interlinear Sanskrit *chhāyā* or literal rendering; and I, like many other readers and scholars since classical times, have relied on it for my translation.

On the whole, the play's dialogue is more formal in Sanskrit than in Prakrit. This qualitative inequality is reinforced by the fact that 182 of the text's verses are in Sanskrit, and inevitably have a greater impact because of their quantity as well as their variety of verse-form and figuration, complexity of poetic technique, and range of aestheticized emotion. The prose in both mediums, however, is equally supple, and accommodates rapid changes in topic, register, and style to a much greater extent than modern English. A single piece of dialogue by a character may move swiftly and elastically from colloquial and emotional expression to empirical observation, to philosophical or theological statement, and to moral speculation and back, without striking a note of incongruity. The soliloquies by Māḍhavya (in II.i) and by Anasūyā (in IV.ii) demonstrate this flexibility in Prakrit prose; many of Dushyanta's passages in Sanskrit extend this property beyond the boundaries of prose, since they move from dialogue, introspection, and aside to intricate poetry in verse on one expressive continuum.

My translation represents this complexity of verbal texture by adopting a uniform 'middle diction' in contemporary English across the text, with modulations against it to mimic the movements in style and register in both prose and verse.[9] But my version avoids verbal contractions as well as colloquialisms and poeticisms, and it does not attempt linguistically to reproduce the multilingualism of the original. Nevertheless, it incorporates significant differences in vocabulary, sentence structure, rhythm, and tone to distinguish the speech of the characters who use Prakrit from the discourse of those who employ Sanskrit. The 'voice' of each character is one of my central concerns, and the middle diction has provided me with a background against which to create fine-tuned variations in tone among the characters grouped by language in the original. This method enables me to distinguish Shakuntalā's voice from Dushyanta's, the king's voice from Kaṇva's, Māḍhavya's voice from Vātāyana's, the voices of Anasūyā and Priyaṁvadā from each other and from the voices of other pairs of female characters, and the individual voices of all these from those of the City Superintendent, the two policemen, and the Fisherman, who serve as a dramatic ensemble in VI.i.

A vital point about the dialogue in Sanskrit and Prakrit prose in *Shakuntalā* is that its striking naturalness at many junctures is a deliberate effect. In classical Indian theory and practice, all discourse in literary works is crafted; it is fashioned in order to intensify both the patterning and the signifying power of language; and its literariness or aesthetic intensification therefore is a result of systematic deviation from everyday discourse. In order to represent natural speech in a literary work, a poet has to use the figure called *svabhāvokti*—a trope that actually un-weaves the literariness woven into the discourse, and returns it to a state of ordinary usage without embellishment.[10] To convey the crafted quality of even the simplest Sanskrit and Prakrit prose, my translation uses a layer of unobtrusive alliteration throughout the text, tying the prose passages together at the level of sound, and binding the prose as a whole to the poetry.

Poetry and Figuration

Each verse in *Shakuntalā* is a self-contained poem; more than half the verses in the play can stand as independent poetic pieces on well-defined themes of general significance.[11] Each poetic passage in the play is composed in a specific verse-form, which is always metrical, whether in Sanskrit or Prakrit (see Appendix H). Verse in both languages uses a wide variety of sound patterns, including assonance, consonance, alliteration, and rhyme; but these features are defined as figures of speech, to be used at the poet's discretion, and the definitions of verse-forms do not require the use of internal or external rhyme.

Both Sanskrit and Prakrit define verse-forms rather than metres: the prescribed prosodic patterns are for verses that are grammatically, syntactically, and semantically complete, and not for so-called lines without such closure. Each verse-form in this system represents one complete utterance, and may be analysed into smaller units, but these are 'measured strides' (*charaṇa*s) that are neither like the feet nor like the lines that serve as compositional units in Greek, Latin, or English verse. A *charaṇa*, in fact, contains several units resembling feet in Europhone prosody; and a *charaṇa* may be treated heuristically as an analogue of a metrical line, but is not composed, written, or performed like one.

Shakuntalā uses twenty-seven different verse-forms, of which twenty-three are in Sanskrit and four are in Prakrit. This represents an immense rhythmic and tonal variation in the verbal fabric of the play, which mirrors the diversity of characters, voices, situations, and themes in its multifarious narrative and action. The Sanskrit *āryā* verse-form contains four measured strides, and appears thirty-three times; and each of the other verse-forms in the play also is divisible into four measured strides, and hence has a poetic structure analogous to that of a quatrain in English. The consistency of four-part verse-forms in the text defines one of the powerful mechanisms that binds its diverse subject matter into an organic unity.

My translation renders the 191 poetic passages in *Shakuntalā* as poems with comparable features in contemporary English. Since my goal is to adhere as closely as possible to the original text in design, content, and particular and general effect, and especially to communicate as much as possible of what it conveys—though not always by the same means—I have chosen to translate the poems in rhythmic free verse with a flexible line-length. I have not attempted to reproduce the quatrain-like organization of most of the Sanskrit and Prakrit verse-forms mechanically in four-line poems; my poems usually run longer in English, but their internal structure closely mimics the four-part poetic structure of their counterparts in Kālidāsa's text.

The linguistic properties of Sanskrit and Prakrit enable them to compress verbal expression to an incomparable degree, even while multiplying the amount of meaning, suggestion, and significance conveyed. I have preferred to capture that semantic range without trying to replicate the brevity; in fact, at most points in the text, and especially with the passages in verse, my goal has been to unpack what is implicit and make it explicit (if necessary), and to elaborate what is explicit into its variety of multiple meanings (as needed). As a result, my translation inevitably contains more words than the Sanskrit–Prakrit original, but it is a comprehensive, self-contained, and reliable literary English version of what the Devanagari recension of *Shakuntalā* communicates to its audience.

My rhythmic free verse, however, is not driven solely by content. As attentive readers will notice, its texture is bound tightly almost everywhere by assonance, consonance, alliteration, half-rhyme, and occasional full-rhyme. Moreover, in mimicking the internal organization of Kālidāsa's poetic thought, I also imitate its overall syntactic disposition: since a verse in Sanskrit or Prakrit is a single utterance spanning the length of its verse-form, most of my poems in English unfold as single sentences that reproduce the poetic grammar and syntax of the original without bending the natural flow of English. The single utterance in a given verse may be structured as a compound sentence with two or more main clauses; as a complex sentence with multiple subordinate and sub-subordinate clauses; or even as a compound-complex sentence, with complex sentences embedded inside a compound sentence (or vice versa). Examples of this variety, which can test the syntactic ingenuity of any poet in English, range from Verses 13, 29, 57, and 70–71 to the dense constellation in 162–165 and 168. Perhaps the most complicated but satisfying instance of this kind is Verse 58, in which Kālidāsa constructs a single sentence in a rare and difficult Sanskrit verse-form (the *hariṇī*), with several embedded clauses describing Dushyanta's physical and psychological state, but with the main clause focused topically on the gems in his golden bracelet, and the principal action explaining how and why his tears stain those precious stones.

At the core of the poetry of *Shakuntalā*, however, is its figuration, and my translation is the first to attempt a rendering of the figures in the play on a large scale. Figures of speech produce or enhance specific features or patterns in the sound of a language; in contrast, figures of thought—also called tropes—create new meanings and concepts by twisting, deviating from, or altering common sense, everyday reasoning, or standard logic. Onomatopoeia, alliteration, and rhyme are instances of figures of speech; simile and metaphor are examples of tropes that reconfigure our familiar ways of thinking about things, or make us think about objects, relations, and processes in new ways. Sanskrit and Prakrit invent and use a large number of figures, approximately seventy-five of which constitute the basic repertoire of a poet in the classical period; of these, Kālidāsa's text contains poetic examples of about fifty, among which simile and metaphor (together with their varieties) are only two.[12]

Tropes in Sanskrit

Even for performers and general readers, understanding the grammar and logic of tropes at a basic level is important because they are constitutive components of the poetic and imaginative structure of a play such as *Shakuntalā*. Verse 122, for example, contains three figures of thought that are unfamiliar to most modern audiences, even though their methods and outcomes are not. When the party of ascetics begins to leave after the confrontation with Dushyanta in V.v, and as Shārańgarava turns viciously on Shakuntalā and leaves her cowering in terror, the king clinches a vital point by saying:

> The moon opens water lilies at night, not lotuses by day,
> While the sun opens lotuses by day, not lilies at night;
> So also a man, who controls his passions and senses,
> Couples only with a wife who is his own,
> not another man's.

Dushyanta's main topic in this statement is the moral proposition that a man who has achieved self-control is faithful to his wife, which completes one of his arguments against Shārańgarava and Shakuntalā. If he were speaking in everyday discourse, he would articulate that topic directly and immediately at the beginning of his utterance. But here he deviates from normal practice, and starts with a statement about natural phenomena that contains two undeniable facts: that water lilies open at night and remain closed during the day, and that lotuses follow the contrasting and complementary temporal rhythm, opening by day and closing at night. These botanical processes have no intrinsic connection with the proposition that Dushyanta wishes to lay out, and hence are not a part of his subject, but he nevertheless uses them to say something about his real topic.

This particular variety of deviation from the expected topicalization of an utterance constitutes the trope of *aprastuta-prashaṁsā*, 'an invocation of something that is not part of what is actually presented' in an utterance. Dushyanta exploits two possibilities built into the trope to make his case.[13] On the one hand, his goal is to offer a general proposition as a moral truth in his own defence, and he invokes the water lily and the lotus as its particular instances among natural phenomena, so that his trope or twist of reasoning proves a general claim with the help of irrefutable particulars. On the other hand, he invokes two phenomena in the natural world that are similar in meaning and implication to a phenomenon in the human world, and hence establish his case by the power of similitude (which is why the trope also looks like an extended simile or parallelism). Dushyanta combines the two possibilities of the trope to employ the poetic equivalent (an enthymeme) of the rigorous logical and argumentative procedure (a syllogism) of demonstrating the validity of a general claim with undeniable facts as evidence and proof, while the principle of similitude serves as its underlying warrant.

But the warrant of similitude is not given or self-evident, and Dushyanta's utterance actually establishes it separately by drawing on a second trope, called *tulya-yogitā* in Sanskrit, 'a conjuncture of comparables'.[14] While this trope focuses basically on the 'pairing of two equal objects', its expanded version accommodates a combination of several things that share the same property, and it may be used either to affirm or to refute a specific proposition. Under this configuration, Verse 122 brings together six distinct entities, or three pairs of objects with a common attribute: moon and water lily, sun and lotus, and man and wife. The three pairs are truly comparable because they share the property of faithfulness, since the moon makes only the water lily 'blossom' (and not the lotus), the sun does the same only to the lotus (and not the water lily), and a man with self-control does the same to his own wife (and not the wife of another man). This common attribute of fidelity, raised to the status of a natural phenomenon spanning the human, botanical, and mineral realms, demonstrates the similitude that binds the three paired instances, but Dushyanta—being Dushyanta—pushes their resemblance towards mutual identity and substitutability by metaphorically equating a wife's 'sexual blossoming' in faithful marriage with the diurnal blossoming of the water lily (at night) and the lotus (by day). This erotic metaphor, which alludes to the mythological motifs of moon and water lily and of sun and lotus as natural pairs of 'husband and wife', renders the warrant of his logical argument technically unshakable.[15]

At the same time, however, the validity of inference from particular instances to a general truth also cannot be taken for granted, and Dushyanta 'seals the deal' by placing the *aprastuta-prashaṁsā* and the *tulya-yogitā* inside the separate, encompassing figure of *arthāntara-nyāsa*.[16] This trope, which 'bridges a divide in meaning', juxtaposes one part of a statement with another in order to move from a generalization to a specific example, or from a concrete instance to a generality. Verse 122 employs the latter configuration by placing the paired instances of moon-water lily and sun-lotus in its first half, and the broader proposition about man and wife in the second half (in the original as well as my version), and by bridging the two with a logical connective (*hi* in Sanskrit, rendered as 'So' in English). As a result, the reasoning that is merely implicit in the first two measured strides of the verse becomes explicit as it shifts with valid inference into the last two strides.

Verse 122 defines only one dramatic moment among many in *Shakuntalā*, but its local intricacy is worth elucidating because it is representative of the play's poetic craft on the whole. In comparison, Verses 44–45, 74–75, 117, 162, and 188, for instance, involve more formidable figural and rhetorical organization, and draw us into more multifarious themes and aesthetic effects. Previous English translations have dealt with this dimension of Kālidāsa's text with different results; since Verse 122 is common to the Bengal and Devanagari recensions, it is easy to compare its treatment by different translators. In the case of the Bengal recension, for example, William Jones (1789) renders the passage in prose as follows:

> The moon opens the night flower; and the sun makes the water lily blossom; each is confined to its own object; and thus a virtuous man abstains from any connection with the wife of another.[17]

In contrast, Chandra Rajan (1989) translates it into free verse:

> The moon wakes only night-blooming lilies,
> the sun day-lotuses only:
> the man with mastery over his passions
> turns away from the touch of another's wife.[18]

In the case of the Devanagari recension, Barbara Stoler Miller (1984) uses cadenced verse emphasizing brevity:

> The moon only makes lotuses open,
> the sun's light awakens the lilies—
> a king's discipline forbids him
> to touch another man's wife.[19]

In comparison, W.J. Johnson (2003) tries to render the verse in metre and half-rhyme, with the following result:

> Nightflowers open for the moon alone,
> Sunflowers for the sun:
> No one self-restrained would touch
> A woman contracted to another man.[20]

All four versions mix up the species of flowers and their properties in relation to sun, moon, day, and night, and hence destroy the basis of the 'conjuncture of comparables' and of the 'invocation of what is not explicitly in the subject', as well as the logic of the 'bridging of divided meanings'. Only one part of the confusion originates in the fact that, even though William Jones was also a first-rate botanist, problems with the formal botanical identification, differentiation, and classification of the Indian water lily (*kumuda*) and lotus (*paṅkaja*) were not resolved until the second half of the twentieth century.[21] Despite his early date, however, Jones is actually the only one to capture the thrust of the inference in the encompassing trope precisely, when he uses the connective 'thus' in the latter half of Dushyanta's statement. The more recent translators employ the colon or the dash to reduce the inferential structure of the enthymeme to a mere juxtaposition.

A vital function of the figuration in *Shakuntalā* is its combined contribution to the visualization of the action (its ekphrastic function) and to the characterization of the individual figures in the drama (its ethical function).[22] Dushyanta delivers more than half the play's dialogue, and hence has more lines than all the other characters together; he also delivers 108 of the text's 191 verses. A high proportion of what we take to be his character therefore emerges on the page and in the theatre through the figuration of his words, and much of what we attribute to his ethos is figurative and figural. As my translation seeks to show consistently, the density of tropes in a single poetic passage such as Verse 122 points to the extraordinary precision with which Kālidāsa configures his characters as agents of thought, emotion, and action.

The Recognition of Shakuntalā

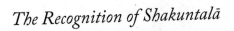

Dramatis Personae

Characters are identified here in the order of their appearance, with brief descriptions, and with their gender indicated in parentheses. All the characters onstage and offstage have speaking parts, which add up at least to fifty.

Extended lists of Dramatis Personae appear in Appendix A, which provides more detailed descriptions and information on entrances by acts and scenes; and also separates characters by gender and original stage language. Appendix B offers notes on the names of the characters, the meanings of the names, and their relation to characterization. Appendix C specifies settings in greater detail by act and scene, whereas Appendix D outlines a larger conceptual map of time and space in the play.

CHARACTERS ON THE STAGE

STAGE MANAGER (m), who represents the director of the present production

ACTRESS (f), who represents a member of the present company of performers

DUSHYANTA (m), the hero; a youthful king of the Puru dynasty at Hastināpura

CHARIOTEER (m), who drives Dushyanta's hunting chariot

VAIKHĀNASA (m), an old celibate ascetic at sage Kaṇva's ashram

TWO DISCIPLES (m), adolescent novice ascetics

SHAKUNTALĀ (f), the young heroine, half-celestial by birth; the adoptive daughter of sage Kaṇva, and also an ascetic at his ashram

ANASŪYĀ and PRIYAṀVADĀ (both f), Shakuntalā's close friends

MĀḌHAVYA (m), Dushyanta's court jester and confidant

KING'S BODYGUARD (all f), a troop of Greek warrior women, with a leader

RAIVATAKA (m), a guard and usher at Dushyanta's hunting camp

BHADRASENA (m), the chief of Dushyanta's army

GAUTAMA and NĀRADA (both m), adolescent novice ascetics

KARABHAKA (m), the queen-mother's messenger

APPRENTICE PRIEST (m), a young adult ascetic

GAUTAMĪ (f), an older female ascetic, the maternal figure at Kaṇva's ashram

DISCIPLE (m), an adolescent novice ascetic

ASCETICS' WIVES (all f), a group of women of various ages

KAṆVA (m), a famous celibate sage, the spiritual leader of a community of ascetics at his ashram; the adoptive father of Shakuntalā

SHĀRAṄGARAVA and SHĀRADVATA (both m), adult ascetics who serve Kaṇva

ASCETICS (all m), who provide the escort for Shakuntalā to Hastināpura

VĀTĀYANA (m), Dushyanta's aged chamberlain at the palace

VETRAVATĪ (f), Dushyanta's principal aide and all-purpose female assistant

TWO BARDS (both m), on the royal staff

SOMARĀTA (m), Dushyanta's personal priest and priest to the royal family

CITY SUPERINTENDENT (m) of Dushyanta's capital, Hastināpura

JĀNUKA and SŪCHAKA (both m), two policemen

FISHERMAN (m), who finds the lost ring that Dushyanta had given to Shakuntalā

SĀNUMATĪ (f), a celestial female who serves Menakā, Shakuntalā's mother

PARABHRITIKĀ and MADHUKARIKĀ (both f), young female palace attendants

CHATURIKĀ (f), Dushyanta's assistant for painting and art

MĀTALI (m), Indra's celestial charioteer

SUVRATĀ and SECOND ASCETIC WOMAN (both f), at Kashyapa's celestial ashram

SARVADAMANA (m), the son of Dushyanta and Shakuntalā

KASHYAPA (m), a divine sage whose celestial ashram is located on Mount Meru

ADITI (f), Kashyapa's divine wife

GĀLAVA (m), Kashyapa's assistant

CHARACTERS OFFSTAGE

ASHRAM CRIER (m), who makes a public announcement

PRIEST (m), at Kaṇva's ashram

DURVĀSĀ (m), a powerful and irascible sage, who places a curse on Dushyanta and Shakuntalā that changes the course of the play

GODDESSES OF THE SACRED GROVE (all f), at Kaṇva's ashram

HAṀSAPADIKĀ (f), a minor queen of Dushyanta, a former favourite

CHARACTERS ONLY MENTIONED IN THE DIALOGUE

VISHVĀMITRA (m), a human sage, Shakuntalā's biological father

MENAKĀ (f), an *apsarā* or celestial being, Shakuntalā's biological mother

INDRA (m), the principal god of the Vedic pantheon, Dushyanta's friend

QUEEN-MOTHER (f), Dushyanta's mother

SHACHI (f), Indra's divine wife and mother of their son Jayanta

VASUMATĪ (f), Dushyanta's current chief queen

MITRĀVASU (m), Vasumatī's brother and a royal official

TARALIKĀ (f), Vasumatī's personal attendant

PISHUNA (m), Dushyanta's chief minister

DEATH RING and THE INVINCIBLES (all m), a gang of antigods in the celestial realm

JAYANTA (m), Indra and Shachi's divine son

SHĀKLYA (m), an ancient ascetic at Kashyapa's celestial ashram

SPECIAL DEVICES

Mango Tree and Jasmine Vine; Fawn; Red Goose; Lion Cub.

MUSIC AND DANCE

Invocation: Music, before and after.

Prelude: Actress's song onstage, with musical accompaniment.

Announcement by Ashram Crier: Percussion, before and after.

Haṁsapadikā's song backstage: With musical accompaniment.

Sānumatī's short dance: With music.

Live music: Between acts (by classical convention), and during scene changes.

BASIC SETTINGS

Invocation: Backstage.

Prelude: Stage front or centre.

Act I, main action: An enchanted forest; a sacred grove on the grounds of Kaṇva's ashram. One day in early spring.

Act II: Dushyanta's hunting camp near the enchanted forest, with a royal pavilion and a natural arbour on its grounds. One day or several days at the onset of summer.

Act III: The grounds of Kaṇva's ashram, with an arbour on the banks of the River Mālinī. From midday to nightfall, on one day in summer.

Act IV: Multiple locations on the grounds of Kaṇva's ashram. From daybreak to late morning on one day several months later.

Act V: Dushyanta's royal palace and its grounds at Hastināpura. From early evening to nightfall, several days later.

Act VI: Several locations on the grounds and in the buildings of Dushyanta's palace complex. Delayed spring, the following year or later. Scenes probably on different days, spread over months or years.

Act VII: The 'skyway' from heaven to earth, and Kashyapa's celestial ashram on Mount Meru. Several years after the events in Act V, and perhaps also those in Act VI.

Act I

INVOCATION

[I.i]

That body of water, which is the creator's first creation;
That body of fire, which carries the burnt offerings
of the sacrifice, when performed in the proper way,
as food for the gods;
That body of the priest, who performs the sacrifice;
Those two heavenly bodies, the sun and the moon,
which create and regulate time;
That body of space, which stands at rest and spans the universe,
which carries the quality of sound, the object of hearing;
That body of earth called nature, the source of all seeds;
That body of air, which gives breath to all living things—
These are the eight enumerated bodies, evident to the senses,
with which Shiva is endowed,
And may he, the lord and master, present in all of them,
protect all of you. [1]

End of Invocation

PRELUDE

[I.ii]

Enter STAGE MANAGER.

STAGE MANAGER (*turning his face to look towards the backstage*): My good woman! If your business in the greenroom is finished, please come here now.

Enter ACTRESS.

ACTRESS: Here I am, sir—here I am.

STAGE MANAGER: My dear! Most of the folks in this audience are wise and well-informed. We should definitely present them with a brand-new play today—a composition by Kālidāsa called *The Recognition of Shakuntalā*. So please invest the best effort in each and every part.

ACTRESS: Sir, you have managed and directed us so well that, for the most part, there will be no mistakes, no laughter at our expense!

STAGE MANAGER: Noble woman, let me tell you the truth:

I am not satisfied
With my knowledge of theatre-craft
Until its connoisseurs
Acknowledge my skill—
Even the most powerful mind,
The most disciplined consciousness,
Lacks self-confidence. [2]

ACTRESS: Dear sir—that is how it is! Please issue your instructions on what is to be done next.

STAGE MANAGER: What else but to give the present audience the pleasure of listening? So sing about this summertime, which started not so long ago. This, indeed, is the time

Of joyful plunges into water;
Of forest winds fragrant from the touch
 of trumpet-flowers;
Of siestas in deep shade, where sleep comes easily;
Of days that end in enchanted evenings. [3]

ACTRESS: Exactly so. (*She sings.*)

To express their equal fondness
 For the flowers of the mimosa tree,
Bees buzz and gently kiss
 The tips of their tender pistils,
And lovely young women
 Pluck the blossoms
To deck their ears with dangling earrings. [4]

STAGE MANAGER: A perfect song, my dear! Amazing—the audience all around us is spellbound by your harmony, as though it were at a standstill in a painted picture. So, which play in our repertory should we revive, to entertain these folks?

ACTRESS: Oh, great sir! But you have already instructed us to put on a performance of a brand-new play, *The Recognition of Shakuntalā*.

STAGE MANAGER: My dear woman, you have reminded me most aptly—indeed, for a moment I had totally forgotten. Because:

I was blown away
And carried off
By the momentum of your melody—
Just as King Dushyanta

Is captivated and carried off
Very swiftly
By the momentum of this antelope. [5]

Exit STAGE MANAGER *and* ACTRESS.

End of Prelude

[I.iii]

Enter DUSHYANTA, *with bow and arrow in hand, riding on a hunting chariot with his* CHARIOTEER, *in pursuit of an antelope.*

CHARIOTEER (*looking at both Dushyanta and deer*): My abiding king!

As I watch you with your bow and arrow,
Pursuing this black antelope, you give my eyes
 a glimpse
Of Shiva in his form as Pinākī the hunter—
As though he were present right here and now. [6]

DUSHYANTA: Charioteer, this deer has lured us along, and made us go a long way. Even at this moment, it is still in motion.

Look! It twists its graceful neck to cast a glance
Again and again at the chariot chasing it;
Terrified of the arrow aimed at it,
It compresses its haunches into its chest;
Its mouth hangs open from exertion,
And strews its path with half-chewed blades
 of sacred grass;
Leaping high, bounding fearfully,
It seems to flee much more
Through the air than along the ground. [7]

I have pursued it relentlessly, so how has it speeded up and started disappearing from sight?

CHARIOTEER: Since the ground was uneven, I tightened the reins to reduce our chariot's speed. The buck in full flight therefore put some distance between himself and us. But now that we are on even ground, it will not stay out of range for long.

DUSHYANTA: Then slacken the reins, slacken them!

CHARIOTEER: As you command. (*He mimes the chariot's acceleration.*) Look, look, your majesty!

As soon as I slacken the reins,
Our horses gallop with their bodies at full stretch,
Their plumes and tails unwavering in the wind,
Their ears perked up, their hooves
Outpacing even the clouds of dust they raise—
As though they cannot tolerate
The antelope's manoeuvres ahead of them. [8]

DUSHYANTA: True. These horses outrun the stallions of Indra and the stallions of the sun. For, as things speed past,

What is small is suddenly magnified,
What is fragmentary becomes whole,
Shapes that are warped straighten out
    before my eyes—
In the chariot's state of motion,
Nothing near or far stays fixed, even for a moment. [9]

Watch me as I bring down the antelope! (*He mimes stringing an arrow on his bow.*)

VOICE BACKSTAGE [VAIKHĀNASA]: Wait, wait, O king! This deer belongs to sage Kaṇva's ashram. Do not kill it—do not kill it!

CHARIOTEER (*listening and looking*): Sir, some ascetics have positioned themselves between you and the black buck, which is now within your arrow's range.

DUSHYANTA (*thrown into confusion*): Stop the horses immediately!

CHARIOTEER: As you say. (*He mimes bringing the chariot to a halt.*)

Enter VAIKHĀNASA *and his* TWO DISCIPLES.

VAIKHĀNASA (*raising his hand*): King, do not kill—do not kill—this deer. It belongs to the ashram.

So withdraw the arrow
You have strung so well on your bow.
Your weapon is meant
To serve and protect those in distress—
Not to assault the innocent. [10]

DUSHYANTA: Here, I withdraw it. (*He does as he says.*)

VAIKHĀNASA (*with joyous satisfaction*): A fitting act for a king who is the shining light of Puru's dynasty.

Your birth is worthy of the Puru clan.
May you, in turn, have a son
Who also turns the wheel of the law as king,
And has the same qualities as you. [11]

TWO DISCIPLES (*raising their hands*): Indeed, may you have a son who turns the wheel of the law as king.

DUSHYANTA (*bowing to all three*): I accept your blessing.

VAIKHĀNASA: Your majesty, we have set out to gather fuel for our sacred fire. The ashram of Kaṇva, the father of our community, is visible from here, on the near bank of the River Mālinī. If a visit does not disrupt your business, then please enter the ashram, and accept the hospitality with which we honour guests. And, also—

When you see for yourself
How the pleasant activities of ascetics
Proceed without interruption,
You will appreciate how well your arm,
'Decorated with the scars of battle',
Serves and protects us. [12]

DUSHYANTA: Is sage Kaṇva present at the ashram?

VAIKHĀNASA: He has appointed his daughter Shakuntalā to welcome and honour guests, while he is away at Somatīrtha, the sacred shrine of the moon, to alleviate some misfortune that troubles her destiny.

DUSHYANTA: All right—I will meet her. I am sure that, once she knows my devotion, she will tell the great sage about it.

VAIKHĀNASA: We take our leave of you.

Exit VAIKHĀNASA *and his* TWO DISCIPLES.

DUSHYANTA: Urge the horses on once more, charioteer! Let us purify ourselves with the holy sight of the ashram.

CHARIOTEER: As you command. (*He mimes driving the chariot at a brisk speed.*)

DUSHYANTA (*looking all around*): One knows without being told—that these are the outskirts of an ashram set in what is called an ascetics' grove.

CHARIOTEER: How so?

DUSHYANTA: You see this, do you not?

Grains of wild rice that have dropped from the beaks
Of parrots nesting in hollow trunks, here and there,
Have sprouted into plants at the feet of the trees;
Yellow stones, the colour of opal, are visible
here and there,
Slick with the oil of the *iṅgudī* nuts that have been
crushed with them;
Trusting deer wander here and there, their movements
unperturbed
Even by our noise, which they have to bear;
And paths that lead from ponds, here and there,
Are streaked with water that has dripped
From garments made of sheets of bark,
wet from bathing. [13]

CHARIOTEER: So true.

DUSHYANTA (*after they have travelled some distance*): Please stop the chariot here, at the edge of the ashram, so that we do not disturb the residents of this sacred grove, and I can get off.

CHARIOTEER: I have pulled the reins, your majesty—please alight!

DUSHYANTA (*after disembarking*): It is said that one should visit a forest hermitage in humble garb. So keep these for me. (*He takes off and hands over his weapons and royal ornaments.*) Please rub down the horses while I visit the ashram's residents.

CHARIOTEER: As you say.

Exit CHARIOTEER.

DUSHYANTA (*miming a transition by walking about and looking around*): This is the entrance to the ashram. I will go in. (*As he enters, he indicates that he perceives an omen.*)

The space of this ashram is a space of peace,
And yet my right arm twitches palpably.
How can such an omen of love and desire
Find fulfilment in a place of this kind?
What else could it be—if not an omen?
Whenever something is driven by necessity,
The doors of possibility open in every direction. [14]

[I.iv]

VOICE BACKSTAGE [SHAKUNTALĀ]: Come here, friends—come here!

DUSHYANTA (*listening intently*): Ah! I hear conversation to the right of the grove. So let me go there. (*He mimes a short transition by walking about and looking around.*) Oh! These ascetic girls are coming here to water saplings, each with a watering pot of a size that she can carry comfortably. (*He observes the girls closely.*) Oh—they are a sweet sight to behold!

If the bodies of these folks who live in ashrams
Have a pristine quality that is impossible to find
In the women's chambers in a palace—then, indeed,
The qualities of vines that grow wild in a forest
Outdo the qualities of vines cultivated in a garden. [15]

I shall seek cover in the shadow of this tree, and watch and wait. (*He positions himself thus and observes.*)

Enter SHAKUNTALĀ, *accompanied by her two friends,* ANASŪYĀ *and* PRIYAṀVADĀ, *busy watering plants.*

SHAKUNTALĀ: This way, my friends, this way.

ANASŪYĀ: Dear Shakuntalā! My logical conclusion is that the ashram's trees are much dearer to father Kaṇva than you are. That is why he has appointed you to water the roots of these plants—even though you are as delicate as a flower on a vine of nine-petalled jasmine.

SHAKUNTALĀ: I do not do this just because father has ordered it. I feel a sister's love for these saplings. (*She mimes watering the plants.*)

DUSHYANTA (*to himself*): Is she sage Kaṇva's daughter? Even though he is a descendant of the divine sage Kashyapa, he truly lacks sagacity if he compels her to live by the customs of an ashram.

A holy sage who wishes to inflict
The rigours of asceticism
On a body as naturally beautiful as hers
Is exactly like a man who tries to cut
A branch on a hardwood tree
For sacred kindling—with the tender edge
Of a petal plucked from a blue water lily. [16]

So let me not hesitate to hide behind this tree, and wait and watch for a while. (*He does as he says.*)

SHAKUNTALĀ: Anasūyā, my dear—Priyaṁvadā tied my bark dress so tightly that it has made me uncomfortable. So please loosen it.

ANASŪYĀ: As you say. (*She loosens the dress.*)

PRIYAṀVADĀ (*laughing*): Do not blame me for your discomfort! Blame your own youth, which is making your breasts grow—and hence is making your dress feel tight!

DUSHYANTA: It is not as though this highly inadequate dress does not adequately enhance the beauty of Shakuntalā's youth, or her young body's beauty. For:

A lotus is rendered even more beautiful
By the tangle of roots and rhizomes around it
in a pond;
The moon is rendered more beautiful
By the stain on it, even though the stain is dark;
So this girl is rendered more beautiful
By her sorry, shapeless dress, which is her ornament—
For what is not an ornament for those
who are shapely? [17]

SHAKUNTALĀ (*looking into the middle distance straight ahead of her*): That mimosa tree is beckoning me, with fresh twigs waving in the breeze like fingers. Let me water it immediately. (*She mimes walking up to the tree.*)

PRIYAMVADĀ: My dear Shakuntalā! Pause there for a moment—with you so close, that mimosa tree looks as though it is joined in marriage to a vine that is wrapped around it.

SHAKUNTALĀ: That is why you are called Priyaṁvadā, 'the sweet talker'.

DUSHYANTA: Priyaṁvadā does make sweet talk—but she also states the facts about Shakuntalā. For sure,

Her lips are red, like fresh buds;
Her arms resemble tendrils on a vine:
Enchanting youth is packed into her limbs,
Ready to burst into blossom. [18]

ANASŪYĀ: Shakuntalā, dear! There is the vine of nine-petalled jasmine, over there, which is like a bride who chooses for herself—and has chosen the mango tree for her groom. You named her the Forest's Radiance. Maybe you have forgotten.

SHAKUNTALĀ: If I were to forget her, I would be forgetting myself! (*She walks up to the vine and examines it.*) My friend, the jasmine vine has wrapped herself around the mango tree—they have consummated their union in a period of great happiness. With her fresh flowers, the Forest's Radiance has blossomed into her youth, and, with his tender shoots, he is ready for pleasure. (*She gazes, transfixed, at tree and vine.*)

PRIYAṀVADĀ: Anasūyā—do you know why Shakuntalā is staring and staring at the Forest's Radiance?

ANASŪYĀ: I certainly do not. Tell me!

PRIYAṀVADĀ: She is wondering: 'Just as the Forest's Radiance has found her soulmate in the mango tree, will I, too, find my soulmate in a husband?'

SHAKUNTALĀ: That is surely your own wishful fantasy! (*She turns her pot over to empty it out.*)

DUSHYANTA: Is it even possible for Shakuntalā to be Kaṇva's child with a wife who belongs to the same class of priests? That just cannot be so!

This girl, no doubt, is fit to be married to a warrior,
 like me,
For my noble heart is full of hope and desire for her.
In matters riddled with uncertainty,
 men of good lineage
Let their inner selves guide them in making
 the right choice. [19]

Nevertheless, I shall determine the truth about Shakuntalā's origins.

[I.v]

SHAKUNTALĀ (*in alarm*): How awful! This bee was disturbed by the water that I poured—it has flown up from the jasmine vine, and is attacking my face! (*She mimes being pursued by a bee.*)

DUSHYANTA (*watching with great longing*):

O bee—again and again, you get to brush against
This girl's fluttering eyelids,
And against her eyes, watering with fright;
You get to buzz around her ears,
Like a secretive lover whispering sweet nothings;
She drives you away with both her hands,
But you get to taste her lips longing for love—
O you are the one who is truly fortunate,
While I am left fretting, unsatisfied! [20]

SHAKUNTALĀ: This cruel bee just will not go away. I am moving to a different spot. (*She steps away, pauses, and looks around.*) How awful—it is following me here, too. Friends! Save this poor girl from a cruel, hateful bee!

ANASŪYĀ *and* PRIYAṀVADĀ (*together, in amusement*): How can we—who are we to save you? Call out to King Dushyanta for help, since the groves of ascetics are under his protection!

DUSHYANTA [*to himself*]: This is the perfect opening for me to reveal myself. (*Also to himself, at the same time, in broken sentences.*) Do not be afraid . . . do not be afraid. . . . —But then they would know that I am the king. Okay—so what I will say is this . . .

SHAKUNTALĀ (*pausing after she has moved away another step, and looking around*): He is chasing me even here!

DUSHYANTA (*stepping out quickly and revealing himself*):

Even though the king of the Puru clan
Rules the land and punishes those who are evil,
Who is this who dares to behave without propriety
With the daughters of holy men, who are gentle
by nature? [21]

All three girls are agitated at the sight of Dushyanta.

ANASŪYĀ: Noble sir! There is no cause for any great alarm. This dear friend of ours was frightened because she was attacked by a bee. (*She points to Shakuntalā.*)

DUSHYANTA (*turning to face Shakuntalā*): Is everything all right? Are your spiritual exercises proceeding well?

Shakuntalā stands speechless, overwhelmed.

ANASŪYĀ: At this moment, the arrival of a distinguished guest is of great advantage to her. Shakuntalā, please go to your hut and bring fruit for a welcome, along with other offerings. The water in this watering pot will do for the washing of feet.

DUSHYANTA: Your sweet and honest words have already performed the ritual of hospitality.

PRIYAṀVADĀ: If you do not wish for the formalities of a welcome, then please rest yourself from your journey's weariness, on this seat set in cool shade under a *saptaparṇa* tree.

DUSHYANTA: Surely, watering the saplings has exhausted you, too.

ANASŪYĀ: It is only appropriate that we join our guest, Shakuntalā . Let us sit down here.

Everyone takes a seat.

SHAKUNTALĀ (*to herself*): When I look at this man, why do I find myself subject to a desire that is directly in conflict with the forest of asceticism?

DUSHYANTA (*surveying the girls*): Parity of age and similarity of appearance make it a pleasure to witness your mutual friendship.

PRIYAṀVADĀ (*leaning over and shielding her mouth with her hand, to speak aside*): Anasūyā! Who is this man with a handsome and serious face, who makes amorous conversation so cleverly, and hence seems to be a man of power?

ANASŪYĀ (*also aside*): I, too, am eager to find out. Let me ask him. (*Aloud.*) The confidence created by your sweet exchanges with us encourages me to speak up. Which clan of royal sages do you embellish? What country have you left lamenting your absence? And why have you subjected your youthful body to the rigours of visiting an ascetics' grove?

SHAKUNTALĀ (*to herself*): O my heart! Do not be perturbed. Anasūyā is asking about the very things that you are thinking about.

DUSHYANTA (*to himself*): How should I present myself now, and how should I hide myself? Okay—let me speak this way. (*Aloud.*) Dear woman! The king of the Puru dynasty has appointed me as his official for religious affairs. So I am touring this sacred forest to find out whether people's spiritual activities are proceeding without hindrance.

ANASŪYĀ: Devout folks, law-abiding citizens, now have a protector!

Shakuntalā mimes erotic modesty. [*Anasūyā and Priyaṁvadā speak to her, aside.*]

ANASŪYĀ *and* PRIYAṀVADĀ (*recognizing the expressions of emotion visible on the faces of both Dushyanta and Shakuntalā*): Dearest Shakuntalā! If father Kaṇva were present here right now . . .

SHAKUNTALĀ (*showing signs of anger*): What then?

ANASŪYĀ *and* PRIYAṀVADĀ: . . . then he would give away what he values most in life to this distinguished guest, and accomplish his life's goal.

SHAKUNTALĀ: Go away, both of you! You are fixated on something in your heads, and you are acting it out. I am not listening.

[*Their conversation aside ends.*]

DUSHYANTA [*to Anasūyā and Priyaṁvadā*]: I, too, wish to ask the two of you something about the friend you have in common.

ANASŪYĀ *and* PRIYAṀVADĀ: Your request is an honour for us.

DUSHYANTA: It is widely known that the great sage Kaṇva has always lived in a condition of celibacy. Then how is it that your friend Shakuntalā is called his daughter?

ANASŪYĀ: Please listen, good sir. There once was a powerful sage, named Vishvāmitra, who belonged to the lineage of the ancient master, Kaushika.

DUSHYANTA: It is so. I am listening.

ANASŪYĀ: Vishvāmitra fathered our friend. When she was abandoned in this forest, father Kaṇva, a descendant of Kashyapa, took care of her physically and in other ways—and hence became her foster-father.

DUSHYANTA: The word 'abandoned' arouses my curiosity. So I wish to hear this story from the beginning.

ANASŪYĀ: Then listen. Once upon a time, long ago, on these banks of the River Mālinī, while Vishvāmitra was practising harsh forms of self-discipline and spiritual control, some of the gods, who had grown suspicious and fearful of him, sent down to earth an *apsarā* named Menakā, a celestial courtesan, who was capable of dislodging his deepest principles.

DUSHYANTA: The gods dread the penances of others, especially the perfect concentration of those who are not divine.

ANASŪYĀ: In the supremely beautiful season of spring, when Vishvāmitra saw the intoxicating form of Menakā before him. . . . (*She falls silent out of modesty, leaving the sentence incomplete.*)

DUSHYANTA: Everybody knows the rest. From all angles, Shakuntalā has to be the daughter of Menakā, the *apsarā*.

ANASŪYĀ : What else?

DUSHYANTA: That had to be so!

How is it even possible
For such beauty to be born
From the women of humankind?
The radiance of lightning,
The radiance of the sun and the moon,

Cannot arise from the muck
On the surface of this earth. [22]

Shakuntalā bows her head in embarrassment.

(*He continues, to himself.*) My heart's desire has now found the opening that can lead to its fulfilment. But, having heard Priyaṁvadā's teasing about the wish to find a husband, my mind has grown anxious and has fallen into a predicament.

PRIYAṀVADĀ (*smiling and looking at Shakuntalā, then turning to face Dushyanta*): Noble sir—you wish to say something more.

Shakuntalā waves a threatening finger at her.

DUSHYANTA: Your inference is correct. In my eagerness to hear her true life-story, I am curious about something else, too.

PRIYAṀVADĀ: You need not hold back. You can ask ascetics anything.

DUSHYANTA: I wish to know this about your friend—

Will she keep her vow of celibacy,
Which hinders the business of the god of love,
Only until her wedding day,
Or will she live for ever in this forest,
Exchanging looks with deer with intoxicated eyes? [23]

PRIYAṀVADĀ: She is under her father's authority even in her religious life. But, as her guru and guardian, he is determined to give her away as a bride to a suitable groom.

DUSHYANTA (*to himself*): The goal I wish to attain—to attain Shakuntalā—is truly not unattainable.

O heart! Revel in your desire,
Which is not without hope—

Your doubts have been resolved.
The one who, in your anxiety,
Seemed to be like fire, and hence untouchable,
Is a jewel worthy of being touched and held. [24]

SHAKUNTALĀ (*angrily*): Anasūyā—I am going to leave.

ANASŪYĀ: What for?

SHAKUNTALĀ: I am going to tell mother Gautamī about this prattling Priyaṃvadā and her nonsense.

ANASŪYĀ: Dear friend! It is inappropriate for you to walk out as you please on our special guest—without honouring him in the proper way, and leaving him to himself.

Shakuntalā begins to leave without speaking.

DUSHYANTA (*to himself*): The mental states of people driven by love and desire are directly contrary to their physical actions. Just this instant—

I wanted to go after the sage's daughter
as she tried to leave,
But propriety promptly pulled me back;
I did not budge from this position, but in my mind
I left with her and then returned
exactly to this spot. [25]

PRIYAṀVADĀ (*stopping Shakuntalā*): It is inappropriate for you to leave.

SHAKUNTALĀ (*furrowing her brow*): Why?

PRIYAṀVADĀ: You are in debt to me for watering two trees for you. So, come—you can leave once you have paid off your debt.

Priyaṁvadā physically persuades Shakuntalā to turn back.

DUSHYANTA [*addressing Priyaṁvadā*]: Gentle woman! I see that she looks tired from the very act of watering plants. Because:

Her shoulders sag from carrying the water pot,
Her palms are rather red, her arms hang down;
For the same reason, her breasts still rise and fall
From the deep breaths she has to take
    to catch her breath;
Beads of perspiration appear in a row along her brow,
And cause the mimosa blossom that decks her ear
    to wilt;
Her wrapped hair is loose, and its straying strands
    remain unkempt,
Even though she tries to tuck them back
    with one hand. [26]

Therefore, I pay off her debt with this. (*He offers Priyaṁvadā his royal ring.*)

Both Priyaṁvadā and Anasūyā read aloud the letters of the king's name [du-shyan-ta] *inscribed on the ring, and look at each other.*

Do not mistake me for who I am not. This is a gift from the king to identify me as a royal official.

PRIYAṀVADĀ: Then it is not right for this ring to be taken off your finger. Your words are enough to leave her debt-free. (*She smiles, laughs a little.*) Dear Shakuntalā! You have been set free by this kind and noble man—or, shall we say, by the king. You can go now.

SHAKUNTALĀ (*to herself*): If I am able to control myself! (*Aloud.*) Who are you to stop me or send me away?

DUSHYANTA (*to himself, as he watches Shakuntalā*): Could she possibly be as passionate about me as I am about her? Then has my desire for her already found its foundation in reciprocity?

She does not speak in dialogue with my words,
And yet she turns her ear to me whenever I speak;
She does not turn her face to me for any length
of time,
Yet other objects, too, do not hold her attention
for long. [27]

[I.vi]

VOICE BACKSTAGE [ASHRAM CRIER]: Inmates of the ashram! Be prepared, get organized to defend and protect all the creatures of our sacred forest. For, it is certain that King Dushyanta has arrived for a deer hunt in the surrounding area.

The particles of dust raised by his horses' hooves
Are as blood-red as the rays of the setting sun,
And both fall, like a swarm of locusts descending,
On the wet bark garments hung out to dry
On the branches of the ashram's trees. [28]

Moreover—

Terrified at the sight of the king's chariots,
An elephant has charged onto the ashram's
sacred grounds:
The impact of his bulk and weight has crushed a tree;

A cluster of branches clings to one of his tusks
like a garland;
He drags along a tangle of vines, which look
like fetters on his legs;
He terrifies and scatters our herd of black antelope,
As if he were the destruction incarnate
of all our spiritual rituals. [29]

Everyone listens and is alarmed.

DUSHYANTA (*to himself*): How terrible! My men are looking for me and are wrecking the ashram! Maybe I should go promptly to where they are and stop them.

ANASŪYĀ *and* PRIYAṀVADĀ: We are deeply distressed by this account of a wild elephant. Please permit us to go back to our hut.

DUSHYANTA (*shaken*): Please go. I, too, will go, to make sure that the ashram is not subjected to distress.

Everybody rises to leave.

ANASŪYĀ *and* PRIYAṀVADĀ: Noble sir—this time we were unable to give you the honour and hospitality due to a guest, so we are ashamed to invite you back for another visit.

DUSHYANTA: No, please do not say that. I have had the honour of seeing you.

Exit ANASŪYĀ *and* PRIYAṀVADĀ *with* SHAKUNTALĀ, *who looks back at Dushyanta, lingering artfully for a moment on some pretext.*

(*After their exit, he continues in soliloquy.*) My enthusiasm to return to my capital has dimmed. First, let me rejoin my men and set up camp, not far from the sacred forest. I am unable to detach myself and keep my composure in the business of Shakuntalā. Indeed, as I leave the ashram,

My body moves forward
But my heart, delinked from it,
Runs back towards her—
Just as a flagpole
Presses forward in the wind,
But its banner of Chinese silk
Streams backwards with the flow of air. [30]

Exit DUSHYANTA.

End of Act I

Act II

INTERLUDE

[II.i]

Enter MĀḌHAVYA, *Dushyanta's court jester, in a state of dejection.*

MĀḌHAVYA (*with a heavy sigh*): I have seen it all! I am totally sick and tired of playing buddies with this king obsessed with hunting. 'There is a deer!' 'There is a boar!' 'There is a tiger!' Even in the intolerable midday heat, in the sparse shade of summer trees, we are forced to scamper wildly on forest paths, hither and thither, jungle to jungle, grove to grove. We drink water from mountain streams, foul and harsh with a mishmash of fallen leaves. We eat at all irregular hours, consuming meals that consist mostly of skewered meat. I cannot get restful sleep in bed even at night because of the ache in my joints from riding horses hard all day in pursuit of game. And then, at the crack of dawn, I am rudely awakened by the clamour of birdcatchers, those whoresons, who surround the groves with nets to ensnare their prey. Even at this moment, my excessively excessive pain shows no signs of receding. And now I have this blister on top of a blister. Yesterday, when it was certain that the rest of us had fallen behind, his great majesty the king went on chasing a buck and trespassed on the grounds of an ashram—and, thanks to my wretched luck, there he beheld an ascetic's daughter named Shakuntalā. He is in no mind to go back to the city at present. He has been thinking only of her since then, and night has now turned into dawn in his eyes. What is the solution? Let me go and meet him after his morning ablutions.

He mimes a transition to the pavilion, by walking about and looking around.

My dear friend is making his way here, surrounded by his bodyguard of Greek women, who wear garlands of forest flowers and hold bows and arrows ready in their hands. All right. Let me stand here as though I were in distress, with injuries to my arms and legs. Maybe that will get me some rest today!

He positions himself thus, leaning on a wooden staff.

End of Interlude

[II.ii]

Enter DUSHYANTA, *with the women of his* BODYGUARD.

DUSHYANTA (*to himself*):

Even though my beloved will not be easy to win,
My heart seeks her own testimony of her feelings;
Even when desire has no hope of satisfaction,
The mutuality of desire keeps passion flowing. [31]

(*He smiles.*) A lover who interprets his beloved's state of mind in terms of his own is in danger of making himself ridiculous. For,

The loving looks she seemed to give me,
Even while she looked at other things;
The seductive movements she seemed to make
with her hips,
While walking slowly because of their weight;
The anger with which she seemed to speak
to her friend,
Who said, 'Do not go', and prevented her
from leaving—
All those actions seemed to be aimed at me!
A person under the spell of desire sees everything
From his or her own partial point of view. [32]

MĀḌHAVYA (*still standing as he was*): Dear friend! My arms and legs cannot move. So I am forced to greet you only with my speech.

DUSHYANTA (*smiling*): How did you injure your limbs?

MĀḌHAVYA: Why ask about the cause of my tears when you yourself have poked me in the eye?

DUSHYANTA: I do not understand what you mean.

MĀḌHAVYA: Dear friend, does an upright reed growing along a river get bent and twisted on its own, or by the water's current?

DUSHYANTA: The swiftness of the river is the cause.

MĀḌHAVYA: So, with me, too, you are the cause.

DUSHYANTA: How so?

MĀḌHAVYA: Is it appropriate for you to give up your duties of governing, and to conduct business like a woodsman in this confounded place? For me, the truth is that chasing wild beasts rattles my joints and drains my muscles until I am powerless to coordinate my limbs. Therefore, have pity on me, and set me free to find rest for just one day!

DUSHYANTA (*to himself*): He says what I feel—recalling Kaṇva's daughter again and again, my mind, too, is alienated from hunting. Because:

I am not capable of bending my bow,
With bowstring drawn and arrow poised,
At those antelopes who live with my beloved
And teach her the art, as it were, of the loving gaze. [33]

MĀḌHAVYA (*looking at Dushyanta's expression*): I am crying in a wilderness—you are lost in your own thoughts!

DUSHYANTA (*smiling*): What else? I am silent because I cannot pass over a plea made by a true companion of my heart.

MĀḌHAVYA: Me, a true companion of your heart—O may you live long!

He starts to leave.

DUSHYANTA: Stay, my friend—I have not finished speaking.

MĀḌHAVYA: Please continue, sir.

DUSHYANTA: After you have caught up with your rest, please help me with a simple task.

MĀḌHAVYA: Is it the job of eating sweets? If so, I totally accept this assignment!

DUSHYANTA: A task that I will specify in a moment. [*Calling out.*] Who stands guard here?

[II.iii]

Enter RAIVATAKA, *the camp's gatekeeper.*

RAIVATAKA: Your command, majesty.

DUSHYANTA: Raivataka, please ask the general to come here.

RAIVATAKA: As you say.

[*He exits and re-enters with* BHADRASENA, *the chief of Dushyanta's army.*]

His majesty's gaze is fixed in this direction, and he is ready to give you his orders. Please approach him, noble sir.

BHADRASENA [*looking at Dushyanta from a distance, and speaking in soliloquy*]: Hunting has many faults, even in the sacred books, but in the king's view it has only good qualities. Because—

Our king is a man
Whose frequent drawing of his bowstring
Has hardened his chest,
Whose body does not sweat
Even when it has to endure
The sun's scorching rays,
Who is so robust
That he does not look weak
Even when he grows lean—
Like an elephant
Who circulates on mountains,
He is full of essential vitality. [34]

(*He approaches Dushyanta.*) Victory to you, master! We have already slaughtered the wild beasts here. Shall we go somewhere else?

DUSHYANTA: Māḍhavya's criticism of hunting has dimmed my enthusiasm.

BHADRASENA (*aside, to Māḍhavya*): Brother, be firm in your resistance. I shall actively promote the disposition that is already in our master's mind. (*Aloud.*) Your majesty, let this whoreson jabber away! On this subject, you are the one to provide the clinching evidence:

In the course of a hunt,
The hunter's body sheds its belly fat,
Grows trim and fit for exertion.
His mind is greatly stimulated
By the sight of the fear and furiousness
Of the forest animals who are his aim.
Bowmen feel special when their arrows
Strike moving targets with success.
Hunting is falsely called a vice—
What other sport matches its delights? [35]

MĀḌHAVYA: The king is squarely in his senses. But you go on and on about hunting—you run from forest to forest—and you will end up in the mouth of some old bear ravenous for a human nose.

DUSHYANTA: My noble general, we are stationed in the vicinity of an ashram. That is why I do not ratify your recommendation. Today,

Let buffaloes bathe in ponds,
Stirring the water with their horns;
Let deer chew their cud in peace,
Gathered in herds in the shade of *kadamba* trees;
Let fat wild boars rummage without fear
through swamps,

Digging for their favourite fragrant grass;
Let my bowstring be slack, let my bow
remain at rest! [36]

BHADRASENA: As it pleases our all-powerful king.

DUSHYANTA: Pull back the men who have already taken over the forest. Forbid my soldiers from disturbing the peace in the ascetics' grove. For, look:

Ascetics who wholly renounce the world,
For whom peace is primary,
Have a deep and fiery radiance—
Like crystals, smooth to the touch,
That reflect the brilliance of the sun. [37]

BHADRASENA: As you command, lord and master.

MĀḌHAVYA: Your arguments, full of fervour for hunting, are finished, my friend!

Exit BHADRASENA.

DUSHYANTA (*looking at the women of his bodyguard*): Please change out of your hunting gear. Raivataka! For your part, be vigilant on your watch at the camp gate.

BODYGUARD [*in unison*]: Whatever your orders, your majesty.

Exit RAIVATAKA *and the* BODYGUARD.

MĀḌHAVYA: Sir, you have swatted away all the pesky flies! Now please take a seat in the arbour with shady trees, complete with a delightful canopy of vines—so that I, too, may sit in peace.

DUSHYANTA: Lead the way.

MĀḌHAVYA: Follow me, sir.

Both mime a transition to the arbour, and sit down.

[II.iv]

DUSHYANTA: Māḍhavya, my friend, you have not yet won the true rewards for your power of sight. You have not yet seen beauty worth seeing.

MĀḌHAVYA: But, sir, you are sitting right before my eyes!

DUSHYANTA: Everybody sees beauty in their own intimates. But I am speaking with reference to Shakuntalā, the jewel of the ashram.

MĀḌHAVYA (*to himself*): All right—I am not going to let him find an opening there! (*Aloud.*) You look as though you are driven by the goal of winning the ascetic's daughter.

DUSHYANTA: My friend, the heart of a Puru king does not seek forbidden fruit.

She was given birth by Menakā, who abandoned her,
And she was found, a young celestial creature,
By Kaṇva, an ascetic sage—
She is truly like a tender jasmine flower
That was torn from its mother vine
And fell on top of a bitter medicinal tree. [38]

MĀḌHAVYA (*laughing*): Like someone who has lost his taste for sweet dates and wants to eat sour tamarind, you have lost your appetite for the women who are the gems of your palace chambers, and wish to savour this rustic girl instead!

DUSHYANTA: You are saying this because you have not seen her.

MĀḌHAVYA: She must be truly delectable, then, if she can amaze someone like you.

DUSHYANTA: What can I say?

The divine creator visualized and composed
Her image in fusion with the quality of light;
He crafted her ideal form,
Not with his hands but with his mind;
His artfulness in fashioning her body
Came from contemplating it again and again:
For me, she has the brilliance
Of a creation without a duplicate
Among women who are gems. [39]

MĀḌHAVYA: If it is as you say, you have rejected all other beautiful women because of her.

DUSHYANTA: She continues to occupy my thoughts.

Her flawless form is like
A flower whose fragrance no one has inhaled,
A new bud that no fingertips have plucked,
A rough precious stone that no one has cut,
Fresh honey whose flavour no one has tasted.
She is like the wholesome fruit of good deeds—
I do not know whom the god of creation
Will design and designate to savour her. [40]

MĀḌHAVYA: Then you should put her under your protection as soon as possible. May she not fall into the hands of some unsavoury ascetic who slicks his hair with *iṅgudī* oil!

DUSHYANTA: She is someone else's dependent, and her guru and guardian is away.

MĀḌHAVYA: What exactly were the emotions she conveyed in her glances?

DUSHYANTA: By their very nature, the daughters of sages are not bold. Hence:

When she was face to face with me, she lowered
her eyes—
But she found other things as pretexts for smiles
and laughter.
Her modesty was unable to control her desire
as it evolved—
Which she could neither hide nor display. [41]

MĀḌHAVYA: Did you think that she would jump right into your lap the moment she saw you?

DUSHYANTA: When she left with her friends, she showed her desire and feelings for me once more, also under the cover of modesty. This is how she did it:

After taking a few steps, this lovely girl paused
And stood there with her face turned to me—
She said, 'A blade of sacred grass has pricked my foot,'
And pretended to free her bark dress from a tree,
Even though it had not got caught in the branches. [42]

MĀḌHAVYA: O prepare to eat bad food on the road for a long time, a long way from home! I can see that you have transformed this grove of asceticism into a garden of pleasure.

DUSHYANTA: Some of the ascetics have already recognized me. So think of an excuse to visit the ashram again—even if it is just one more time.

MĀḌHAVYA: You are the king—why do you need an excuse? Go and demand that the sages pay their tax with one-sixth of their harvest of wild rice.

DUSHYANTA: You fool! When we protect these ascetics, a different kind of contribution from them also falls into our hands, which is worth accepting, even if we have to sacrifice coins and precious stones. Look:

The fruit of the tribute
That kings collect
From the other classes of society
Is fruit that degrades
With the passage of time—
But the sixth part
That sages and forest-dwellers pay,
Indeed, does not decay. [43]

[II.v]

VOICE BACKSTAGE [GAUTAMA]: It is good that our efforts have been successful.

DUSHYANTA (*listening*): These calm voices indicate that there are ascetics outside.

Enter RAIVATAKA.

RAIVATAKA: Victory to you, noble sir! Two young ascetics have presented themselves at the camp gate.

DUSHYANTA: Please bring them here promptly.

RAIVATAKA: I will do so right away.

He exits, and then re-enters with the two novices.

The two of you may come this way.

The young ascetics pause and look at Dushyanta from a distance.

GAUTAMA: Well, the king's shining person inspires trust. In fact, trust of this sort is fitting when a king is not so different from a sage. For—

Sages live in seclusion, in austere ashrams:
But the ashram where the king
Has accepted residence
Is a palace full of pleasures of every kind.
Sages practise penances:
The acts the king performs day by day,
To accumulate a lifetime's goodness,
Also come from rigorous discipline—
For the protection of his people.
Like an ascetic, the king, too,
Is fully in control of his senses:
That is why these verses,
Which touch the very heights of heaven
With their coupled cadences,
Celebrate him with the holy epithet of 'sage'—
But add the prefix 'royal'
To give him the full title of 'royal sage'. [44]

NĀRADA: Gautama, is this Dushyanta, lord Indra's friend?

GAUTAMA: Who but him?

NĀRADA: Then—

It is no great surprise
That he governs the whole earth

Bounded by the blue borders of the sea,
And governs it by himself,
With his arms as strong as the hardwood logs
That serve as bars on a city's gates—
It is no surprise because
Even the young celestial dancers in Indra's palace,
Who sustain their enmity with demons,
Rest their hopes of victory
Not only on Indra's thunderbolt,
But also on this king's well-strung bow. [45]

GAUTAMA *and* NĀRADA (*drawing closer*): Victory to you, king!

DUSHYANTA (*rising from his seat*): I salute both of you.

GAUTAMA *and* NĀRADA: We wish you well. (*They offer a gift of fruit.*)

DUSHYANTA (*bowing to accept the gift*): Please convey the directives you have for me.

GAUTAMA *and* NĀRADA: The ashram's residents have learnt that you are camping here. They send you a petition.

DUSHYANTA: What is their request?

GAUTAMA *and* NĀRADA: In the great sage Kaṇva's absence, demons are disrupting our sacred sacrifices. Please come with your charioteer to watch over our ashram.

DUSHYANTA: I am honoured to do so.

MĀḌHAVYA (*aside, to Dushyanta*): This petition fulfils your wish!

DUSHYANTA (*smiling*): Raivataka! Convey my words to the charioteer: 'Please have my chariot ready to go, along with my bow and arrows.'

RAIVATAKA: As the master commands.

Exit RAIVATAKA.

GAUTAMA *and* NĀRADA (*displaying delight*):

This is most fitting for your form
As one who honours his ancestors—
The kings of the Puru dynasty
Are consecrated to dispel their subjects' fears. [46]

DUSHYANTA (*bowing*): You may proceed, I shall follow.

GAUTAMA *and* NĀRADA: Victory to you!

Exit GAUTAMA *and* NĀRADA.

DUSHYANTA: Māḍhavya, are you not curious to see Shakuntalā?

MĀḌHAVYA: At first, there was a flood of curiosity—but now, with this news of demons, not a drop is left!

DUSHYANTA: Have no fears. Surely you will stay with me.

MĀḌHAVYA: Then I have a defence against demons!

[II.vi]

Enter RAIVATAKA.

RAIVATAKA: Your chariot is ready and awaits your ride to victory. Also, Karabhaka has arrived from the capital, with a message from the queen.

DUSHYANTA (*in a respectful tone*): Did my mother send him?

RAIVATAKA: Who else but her?

DUSHYANTA: Then please bring him in.

RAIVATAKA: As you say.

He exits, and re-enters with KARABHAKA.

Here is the king—please approach him.

KARABHAKA: Be victorious, noble sir. The queen-mother has sent a command: 'Four days from now, I shall conclude my current ritual of fasting. Please honour the occasion with your presence, my long-lived son!'

DUSHYANTA: Here, the dictates of the business of the ascetics—there, the dictates of my elders. I cannot follow both simultaneously. How should I resolve this dilemma?

MĀḌHAVYA: Suspend yourself between the two options, like Trishaṅku suspended between heaven and earth!

DUSHYANTA: I am truly in a predicament.

The demands on me arise in different places,
And hence divide me, keeping me in two minds—
The way a mountain, rising in the middle,
Splits a river into two divergent streams. [47]

(*He reflects for a moment.*) My mother treats you like a son. So please go to the capital, and inform her respectfully that my mind is occupied with the business of the ascetics. Please perform a son's duties on my behalf.

MĀḌHAVYA: Do not think that I am afraid of demons in reality.

DUSHYANTA (*with a smile*): How could you possibly be afraid of them?

MĀḌHAVYA: I will travel in the style of a royal title-holder, a relative of the king!

DUSHYANTA: The ashram ought to be spared any disruption, so I will send my entire entourage with you.

MĀḌHAVYA: Then I have become the crown prince!

DUSHYANTA (*to himself*): This fellow is quite undependable. He may prattle about my new passion to my palace women. So I will say this to him. (*Taking Māḍhavya's hand, he speaks aloud.*) Dear friend, I am going to the ashram out of respect for the ascetics. I do not feel any true desire for Kaṇva's daughter. After all,

What do we city dwellers have in common
With forest folks raised among fawns
And unskilled in the ways of love?
So do not make the mistake, my friend,
Of taking for the truth what I said to you,
Moments ago, merely in jest! [48]

[*Exit* DUSHYANTA, MĀḌHAVYA, KARABHAKA, *and* RAIVATAKA.]

End of Act II

Act III

INTERLUDE

[III.i]

Enter an APPRENTICE PRIEST, *carrying bundles of long-bladed sacred grass.*

APPRENTICE PRIEST: Amazing—Dushyanta, the ruler of the earth, is so powerful! The moment the king makes his entrance at the ashram, our holy rituals proceed without disruption.

But why go so far as to talk about
His stringing of an arrow—
It is evident that he drives away
Profane disruptions from a distance
Simply with the twang of his bowstring,
Which is like his bow's thunderclap. [49]

But, first, let me go to the master priests and deliver this sacred grass meant to be spread on the ground prepared for sacrifices. (*He mimes a short transition by walking about and looking around, and then calls out.*) Priyaṁvadā! Where are you taking that ointment mixed with the fragrant fibres of lotus roots and leaves—who is it for? (*He listens.*) What are you saying? That Shakuntalā is rather ill from heatstroke? That the balm is for 'rubbing on her body'? Then go quickly, my friend—she is father Kaṇva's very life! In the meantime, I will send some holy water to douse her and cool her down, which Gautamī will deliver by hand.

Exit the APPRENTICE PRIEST.

End of Interlude

[III.ii]

Enter DUSHYANTA, *distraught with desire.*

DUSHYANTA (*sighing deeply*):

I know—what power asceticism possesses;
I know, I know—that this girl is fully
    in her father's power.
And, yet, I also know that I am powerless—
To recover that heart of mine,
    which I lost there. [50]

(*He mimes anguish.*) O god of love! You and the moon are both worthy of our trust, and yet you deceive multitudes of lovers. For,

Your floral arrows and the moon's cool rays
Both look fake to lovers in distress, such as me—
The moon transforms his rays into darts of fire,
And you, in turn, turn your tender flowers
Into hard bolts of lightning. [51]

(*He walks about restively.*) Now that the priests have permitted me to leave at the end of their ritual sacrifice, where shall I go to keep myself entertained, since I have lost all interest in any kind of activity? (*He sighs audibly.*) I just want to see my beloved—what else can I resort to? Let me look around until I catch sight of her. (*He looks up at the sun.*) When the heat of the sun is at its harshest for the day, Shakuntalā usually goes with her friends to spend time under the foliage of vines along the bank of the River Mālinī. So let me go there. (*He mimes walking to the riverbank, and feeling a breeze.*) Ah! This spot, with its pleasant breeze, seems wonderful.

This wind,
Fragrant with the pollen of lotuses,
And wet with the spray
It raises from the waves of the Mālinī,
Is fit to embrace with my arms
So hot with desire. [52]

(*He walks about and looks around some more, miming another transition.*) She should be here, somewhere, ensconced in this arbour with an enclosure of reeds and vines. For (*he looks down*)—

A line of fresh footprints
Is visible in the white sand
Leading up to the arbour's entrance,
With impressions that are asymmetrical—
Lighter at the toes and deeper at the heels
Because of the weight of her hips. [53]

For the moment, let me just peer through the gaps between these branches. (*He walks some more, looks as described, and is filled with joy.*) Ah! I have found the ultimate bliss for my eyes. My dearly beloved girl is reclining on a low stone ledge, with a layer of flowers spread like a sheet under her, with her two friends sitting beside her in attendance. All right, let me listen to their conversation. (*He stands still in the enclosure of reeds and vines, and observes.*)

[III.iii]

Enter SHAKUNTALĀ *with* ANASŪYĀ *and* PRIYAṀVADĀ, *all of whom assume the positions just described.*

ANASŪYĀ *and* PRIYAṀVADĀ (*speaking affectionately, and helping her to cool off*): Shakuntalā, are you feeling better with these lotus leaves fanning you?

SHAKUNTALĀ: Dear friends—are you fanning me?

Anasūyā and Priyaṁvadā look quizzically at each other, puzzled by Shakuntalā's disconnected response.

DUSHYANTA [*in soliloquy*]: Shakuntalā looks as though she is physically very ill. (*He reflects.*) Is this the effect of the heat of the sun, or the result of what is now manifest in my own mind? (*He mimes desire.*) But my uncertainties are beside the point—

Even in an ailing state,
Her body looks so beautiful,
With the lotus balm smeared on her breasts,
And one bracelet, crafted with lotus stalks,
Dangling loosely from her wrist:
Desire and the heat of the sun
May have comparable effects on young women,
But hot weather, on its own,
Does not produce such debilitation. [54]

PRIYAṀVADĀ (*aside*): Anasūyā! Shakuntalā has been full of anxious longing ever since our first encounter with that royal sage, the king. Could it possibly be the cause of her feverish state at present?

ANASŪYĀ [*also aside*]: In my heart of hearts, I have the same question. So let me say this to her. (*Aloud, to Shakuntalā.*) I would like to ask you something, my dear—your fever seems to be running rather high.

SHAKUNTALĀ (*half-rising from the stone ledge*): What do you wish to ask me?

ANASŪYĀ: We are unacquainted with the phenomenon of love. But you look as though you are in the same state as lovers we have read about in books from history. Tell us, what is the cause of your illness? If we do not understand your disorder, we cannot start a cure.

DUSHYANTA: Anasūyā is voicing the very line of reasoning I had in mind. Indeed, my view of the situation was not merely self-centred and self-serving.

SHAKUNTALĀ (*to herself*): My infatuation is very powerful—and yet I am unable to convey it to these friends.

PRIYAṀVADĀ: What Anasūyā says is right. Why are you neglecting your sickness? There is no doubt that you are wasting away day by day, limb by limb. Only the glow of your beauty does not fade.

DUSHYANTA: Priyaṁvadā is simply stating the facts about Shakuntalā. For,

Her cheeks are sunken, sunken;
Her breasts have relinquished their firmness;
Her waistline has shrunk, her shoulders sag,
Her complexion is pale.
Distressed by desire, she looks
Like a jasmine vine whose leaves are dying,
Desiccated by contact with the wind.
Her appearance is deplorable—and yet so dear. [55]

SHAKUNTALĀ: To whom can I say this, except you? I will now become the one who inflicts stress and anguish on her friends.

ANASŪYĀ *and* PRIYAṀVADĀ: That, precisely, is why we are urging you to speak. When one shares a source of sorrow with loved ones, it becomes a source of agony that one can endure.

DUSHYANTA:

It is inconceivable that this girl
Will not tell her companions
About the source of her distress
When they ask her about it,
Even as they hold sorrow and happiness
Equally in the balance;
I am impatient to hear her answer now,
Even though she turned and looked at me earlier
With great longing, again and again. [56]

SHAKUNTALĀ: Ever since that royal sage, the protector of our forest of asceticism, entered my field of vision, my love and desire for him have put me in this state of longing.

DUSHYANTA (*joyously*): I have heard what I wished to hear!

Love first brought me the heat of desire,
And now brings me relief from the heat
With peace of mind—
Just as a day in the season of rain,
At the end of summer,
Is half a day of sun and half of shade,
And brings heat and relief in shifting measures
To the world of animals. [57]

SHAKUNTALĀ: That is why, if you agree to do so, I beg the two of you to make arrangements with him to treat me as an object of compassion and mercy. Otherwise, you will need to offer water mixed with sesame seeds to the gods—an oblation at my funeral rites.

DUSHYANTA: These words from her destroy all my doubts.

PRIYAṀVADĀ (*aside, to Anasūyā*): Shakuntalā can no longer cope with this frame of mind, which has advanced far into a fatal state of attraction. The man with whom she is so deeply infatuated is the jewel in the crown of the Puru dynasty. It is therefore only appropriate to celebrate and advocate and cultivate her desire.

ANASŪYĀ [*also aside*]: You are right.

PRIYAṀVADĀ (*aloud, to Shakuntalā*): Fortunately, your desire has fixed itself on a deserving object. Where does a great river descend, except into an ocean? What tree, other than the mango, supports a jasmine vine that is thick with sheaves of leaves, free in its fecundity?

DUSHYANTA: Is it any wonder that these twin friends shine around Shakuntalā, like Venus and Jupiter in a trine with the moon?

ANASŪYĀ [*aside, to Priyaṁvadā*]: What means can we use, swiftly and secretly, to help our friend fulfil her desire?

PRIYAṀVADĀ: 'Secretly'—needs some thought. 'Swiftly'—is easy!

ANASŪYĀ: How so?

PRIYAṀVADĀ: It is certain that, in recent days, the royal sage, whose gaze of infatuation openly announces his desire for her, has grown lean from sleepless nights.

DUSHYANTA [*responding in soliloquy to Priyaṁvadā's remark*]: It is true—that is what I have become. For,

Night after night, I push this bracelet
Further and further up my forearm
To keep it from slipping easily off my wrist
(Which is ridged with scars from my bowstring,
But grows thinner and thinner day by day)—
Even as the tears hot with inner anguish
Flowing from the corner of my eye
(Nestled for comfort in the crook of my arm)
Stain the gemstones set in this golden ornament. [58]

PRIYAṀVADĀ (*after reflection*): Anasūyā, get Shakuntalā to write a love letter. I will hide it in a pile of flowers and put it in the king's hands, pretending to give him the flowers as a gift from an oblation to the gods.

ANASŪYĀ: This is a handsome, youthful ploy—I like it! [*Aloud.*] But what does Shakuntalā have to say about this?

SHAKUNTALĀ: What scheme of yours am I supposed to think about?

PRIYAṀVADĀ: Think, first, about composing beautiful verses containing a statement about yourself as well as a proposal.

SHAKUNTALĀ: Let me think. But my heart falters—I am terrified of rejection.

DUSHYANTA (*joyously, to himself*):

My fearful girl! The man you are terrified will
    reject you
Stands on this spot eager for a union with you.

A man may or may not succeed in winning
a woman who is divine—
But how can a woman so divine fail when she seeks
to win a man? [59]

ANASŪYĀ *and* PRIYAṀVADĀ: O you Shakuntalā—you critic of your own qualities! Does anybody ever use the lowly edge of a garment to keep off cool autumn moonlight, which brings so much pleasure to the body?

SHAKUNTALĀ (*smiling*): You have now committed me to the task. (*She sits up and begins to think.*)

DUSHYANTA: How apt that I have fixed an unblinking gaze on my love. For:

As she composes her verses,
With one eyebrow raised
And cheeks quickened with excitement,
Her face is a vivid portrait
Of her passion for me. [60]

[III.iv]

SHAKUNTALĀ: Friends, I have figured out the content of my poem. But there are no writing implements at hand.

PRIYAṀVADĀ: Inscribe your message with your fingernails on this lotus leaf, which is as tender as a parrot's belly.

SHAKUNTALĀ (*miming the act of inscription as described*): Listen to this, both of you, and tell me whether it says the right thing.

ANASŪYĀ *and* PRIYAṀVADĀ: We are listening.

SHAKUNTALĀ (*reading aloud*):

I do not know
What you have in your heart,
Heartless man:
But, night and day,
Love intensely heats up
Every part of me
Longing for you. [61]

DUSHYANTA (*emerging suddenly from the enclosure of reeds and vines*):

O woman of delicate parts,
Love burns me to cinders and ashes,
But keeps you glowing steadily with heat—
Just as daylight extinguishes the moon
But does not suppress
The brightness of white lilies in a pond. [62]

ANASŪYĀ *and* PRIYAṀVADĀ (*with great delight*): Our welcome to the very object of desire who appears so promptly, exactly on cue!

Shakuntalā wishes to rise in welcome.

DUSHYANTA: Please, please, there is no need to trouble yourself:

Drained rapidly by great heat,
Your limbs are much too weak
For such formalities—
They are like cut, wilting lotus stalks
Pressed against this bed of flowers
And carrying the fragrance of crushed petals. [63]

ANASŪYĀ: Let our dear guest be so gracious as to take a seat on a part of this stone ledge.

Dushyanta sits down, and Shakuntalā shrinks back in modesty.

PRIYAṀVADĀ: The mutual infatuation between the two of you is evident. But my love for Shakuntalā prevents me from speaking my mind.

DUSHYANTA: My good woman, do not hold back. If we wish to say something but leave it unsaid, it becomes a source of regret in our minds.

PRIYAṀVADĀ: A king should absorb the anguish of any inhabitant of his land who is suffering—that is the law of duty you have to obey.

DUSHYANTA: There is no higher duty.

PRIYAṀVADĀ: The god of love has imposed our friend's present condition on her because of you. It is thus your duty to sustain her very life.

DUSHYANTA: The attraction is equal on both sides. I am completely obliged to you for speaking your mind.

SHAKUNTALĀ (*looking at Priyaṁvadā*): Why are you detaining the royal sage, who is eager to get back to his palace women, for whom he is suffering pangs of separation?

DUSHYANTA:

O woman who dwells in my heart—
My heart is not infatuated
With any other woman,

But if you believe
That it is devoted to someone else,
Then you, with your maddeningly intoxicating eyes,
Have slain me a second time—
Even though I was already slain
By the arrows of love! [64]

ANASŪYĀ: Dear sir, we hear that kings have many loves. So please conduct yourself in such a way that our beloved friend does not become a source of grief for her loved ones.

DUSHYANTA: What more can I say?

Even though I have many wives,
What is truly family for me
Has only two mainstays:
One, the earth, draped in its garment of the sea,
And the other—this friend of yours. [65]

ANASŪYĀ *and* PRIYAṀVADĀ: We are both relieved of anxiety.

PRIYAṀVADĀ (*turning to gaze in a different direction*): Anasūyā, a fawn has raised its head and is looking anxiously at us, in search of its mother—so, come, let us reunite them.

Both girls turn to leave.

SHAKUNTALĀ: Friends! I have no support at all! Please—one of you stay here with me.

ANASŪYĀ *and* PRIYAṀVADĀ: The man who is the support of the whole earth is right next to you.

Exit ANASŪYĀ *and* PRIYAṀVADĀ.

[III.v]

SHAKUNTALĀ: Where have they both gone?

DUSHYANTA: Why are you panicking? The man who is here to serve you is, indeed, very close to you.

O woman with thighs
As strong and supple as an elephant's trunk,
Shall I drive away your body-heat
By fanning cool, moist air over you
With bouquets of lotus leaves?
Or shall I let your feet,
Red as lotus petals, rest in my lap,
And massage them to bring you relief? [66]

SHAKUNTALĀ: I shall not bring blame upon myself by demeaning an honourable man like you by having you massage my feet. (*She wishes to rise and leave.*)

DUSHYANTA: My lovely! The day is not yet done. You are in no physical condition to continue:

How will you weather the heat
Once you leave this bed of flowers
And walk on legs and feet
Sensitive with the tenderness
Inflicted by desire,
With only a bunch of lotuses
Covering your breasts, to keep off the sun? [67]

He persuades her physically to come back.

SHAKUNTALĀ: King Puru's descendant, please be vigilant against violations of propriety. In the heat of desire, I have no control even over myself.

DUSHYANTA: Shy and timid girl, do not be afraid of your elders. When the venerable father of your clan, who understands the essence of law and morality, looks at the whole picture, he will find no flaw in it. Moreover:

One hears that fathers commend and celebrate
Numerous daughters who choose
To become the wives of royal sages
By wedding them in secret, by mutual consent—
In the style of the celestials who sing for the gods. [68]

SHAKUNTALĀ: Please let me go. I shall ask my two friends, too, for advice.

DUSHYANTA: All right. I shall set you free.

SHAKUNTALĀ: When?

DUSHYANTA:

My beautiful woman, I shall let you go
As soon as I have savoured—most gently—
The nectar of this lower lip of yours,
The way a bee, parched with thirst,
Sucks nectar from a tender, newborn blossom
That no one has savoured before. [69]

He wishes to raise Shakuntalā's face for a kiss. She mimes turning away from him.

VOICE BACKSTAGE [ANASŪYĀ]: O red goose, bid goodbye to the gander, your mate! Night has fallen.

SHAKUNTALĀ (*frightened*): King Puru's descendant, it is certain that mother Gautamī is coming here to check on my physical condition. Please conceal yourself in that enclosure of reeds and vines.

DUSHYANTA: As you say. (*He positions himself accordingly.*)

Enter GAUTAMĪ, *carrying a jar of water, accompanied by* ANASŪYĀ *and* PRIYAMVADĀ.

ANASŪYĀ *and* PRIYAMVADĀ: This way, mother Gautamī, this way.

GAUTAMĪ (*drawing close to Shakuntalā*): Dear child, has the fever in your limbs abated?

SHAKUNTALĀ: I can feel some difference in my condition.

GAUTAMĪ: This water infused with sprouts of sacred grass will free your body of all illnesses. (*She mimes sprinkling water on Shakuntalā's head.*) The day has ended. Come, let us go back to our huts.

Exit GAUTAMĪ, ANASŪYĀ, *and* PRIYAMVADĀ, *with* SHAKUNTALĀ *lagging behind.*

SHAKUNTALĀ (*to herself*): My heart, ever since your first accidental meeting with your love, you have not relinquished your cowardice and timidity. Now that you are filled with regret, why are you distressed? (*At the very next step, she turns back, pauses, and speaks aloud.*) O my love, wrapped in vines and foliage, who drives away my fever! I invite you to return for our union.

Exit SHAKUNTALĀ, *deeply saddened, after the others.*

DUSHYANTA (*emerging and moving to stage front, with a heavy sigh*): The process of attaining the objects of desire is riddled with obstacles. For:

I managed, somehow, to raise her face—
Turned towards her shoulder,
With its lovely eyes and long eyelashes,

With its lower lip, pressed again and again
Between her nervous fingers, and made more adorable
By its meaningless mumble of sounds
Trying to enunciate her protestations—
I managed to raise her face, but could not kiss her. [70]

Shall I go somewhere else right now? Alternatively, shall I sit for a while in this arbour, first occupied and then deserted by my love? (*He looks all around.*)

Here is the bed of flowers on the stone ledge,
On which her body has left only an impression;
Here is the love letter, which she inscribed
With her fingernails on a lotus leaf, wilted now;
Here is a bracelet, crafted with lotus stalks,
That slipped off her wrist, and lies ruined:
I stare at these objects with fixed concentration
And find that, suddenly, I cannot exit
From this enclosure of reeds and vines,
Even though it is empty—a zero, a void. [71]

VOICE BACKSTAGE [PRIEST]: O king!

Hosts of terrifying images
Of carnivorous demons,
Lit up like amber clouds at dusk,
Are leaping and leaping at us
From the blaze of our sacred fire
As we begin to perform our evening rituals. [72]

DUSHYANTA: I am coming.

Exit DUSHYANTA.

End of Act III

Act IV

MIXED INTERLUDE

Part 1

[IV.i]

Enter ANASŪYĀ *and* PRIYAṀVADĀ, *as they mime picking flowers and gathering them in a basket.*

ANASŪYĀ: Priyaṁvadā! It is true that Shakuntalā has found a suitable husband, that she has married him auspiciously but in secret, by mutual consent, in the celestial style, and that, at heart, I am happy for her—but all this is very worrisome.

PRIYAṀVADĀ: How so?

ANASŪYĀ: The king completed the rituals of departure and took leave of the priests at our ashram, then returned to the city and made his ceremonial entrance there, and then reunited with the women in his palace chambers—after all that, will he really remember what happened here?

PRIYAṀVADĀ: Have faith in him! A man as handsome as him cannot be devoid of moral qualities. What is more worrisome is the prospect of father Kaṇva's response, when he hears about the events in his absence.

ANASŪYĀ: From what I can see, father Kaṇva will find the developments acceptable.

PRIYAṀVADĀ: How so?

ANASŪYĀ: Parents are determined, first and foremost, to give a daughter in marriage to a worthy husband—and if fate and fortune accomplish that, then they are done with their duty without exertion.

PRIYAṀVADĀ (*looking at the basket of flowers*): My dear, we have already gathered all the flowers needed for our daily prayers.

ANASŪYĀ: But we also have to offer a special prayer of thanks to the goddess of good fortune who protects Shakuntalā.

PRIYAṀVADĀ: Of course!

They resume picking and gathering flowers.

VOICE BACKSTAGE (DURVĀSĀ): Is anyone here? It is I, Durvāsā.

ANASŪYĀ (*listening intently*): It appears that an important visitor has arrived.

PRIYAṀVADĀ [*to Anasūyā*]: Shakuntalā is in the hut. (*To herself.*) But her heart is not there today.

ANASŪYĀ: Yes, she is there. Enough picking of flowers, though!

VOICE BACKSTAGE (DURVĀSĀ):

You brazen girl—
You greet a guest with disrespect!

Absorbed in thought, lost in reverie
About a man who is somewhere else,
You fail to acknowledge me—
A sage of great spiritual power,
Standing right here before you.

I curse you!

The man you are remembering
Will fail to remember you
Even when reminded of who you are—
Like an amnesiac who cannot recall
Anything that has happened before
his loss of memory. [73]

PRIYAṀVADĀ: How terrible! What an unfortunate incident! Distracted, unawares, Shakuntalā has offended a venerable visitor. (*She looks intently towards the backstage.*) Not just anybody—it is the great sage Durvāsā, who dwells in the harshest of places and flies into instant rages. He has delivered his curse and has stormed off, eyes blazing wide, gesticulating madly, deeply dissatisfied. What, except fire, can scorch like this?

ANASŪYĀ: Go, Priyaṁvadā! Prostrate yourself before him and beg him to come back—in the meantime, I shall prepare the water to wash his feet as an honourable guest.

PRIYAṀVADĀ: As you say!

Exit PRIYAṀVADĀ.

ANASŪYĀ (*shaken, walking a few steps with the basket of flowers, and stumbling*): How awful! In my panic, I have let the basket tumble to the ground. (*She mimes gathering up the scattered blossoms.*)

Re-enter PRIYAṀVADĀ.

PRIYAṀVADĀ: What a fiery temperament sage Durvāsā has! Whose pleading does he ever accept? But I managed to arouse some pity in his heart.

ANASŪYĀ (*smiling*): Enough said about him.

PRIYAṀVADĀ: When he refused to return, I pleaded with him: 'Your holiness, this is Shakuntalā 's first offence—she does not understand the power of your spirituality—she is like a daughter—please forgive her this once.'

ANASŪYĀ: What was his response?

PRIYAṀVADĀ: He said, 'My curse cannot be reversed. But its effect can be ended by displaying an ornament that signifies recognition.' He uttered these words and vanished.

ANASŪYĀ: But that is so reassuring! We can breathe again. Just before he left for the city, the king placed his royal ring on Shakuntalā's finger with his own hands—it is inscribed with his name, and it is his token of remembrance and recognition. She possesses the means to end Durvāsā's curse!

PRIYAṀVADĀ: Let us go and offer our prayers to the gods.

They walk about, miming a transition through the grounds of the ashram. PRIYAṀVADĀ *looks around, then continues speaking.*

Look, Anasūyā, there is our Shakuntalā—sitting still, with her face resting on her right hand, as if in a painted picture. Absorbed in her thoughts about her husband, she is unaware even of herself. How could she, then, be conscious of an unexpected visitor who turned up suddenly?

ANASŪYĀ: Let us seal our lips and keep these events secret between us, Priyaṁvadā. We should protect Shakuntalā —she is so vulnerable by nature.

PRIYAṀVADĀ: Who ever uses scalding water to water a young jasmine vine?

Exit ANASŪYĀ *and* PRIYAṀVADĀ.

Part 2

[IV.ii]

Enter a young ascetic DISCIPLE, *awoken before dawn.*

DISCIPLE: Father Kaṇva, our respected guru, has just returned from his pilgrimage, and has asked me to estimate the hour. Let me step out into the open and see what is left of the night. (*He walks about and mimes looking up at the sky.*) Oh—day is already breaking. For:

On one side, the moon, lord of vegetation,
Is sinking beyond the mountain in the west;
On the other side, the sun is becoming visible
Behind the deep red dawn, its forerunner—
As though the simultaneous rising
And setting of these two bodies of light
Governs all creation and destruction
In the world's vicissitudes, its varied conditions. [74]

And also—

When the moon has set in a distant place,
The beauty of the water lily blossoming at night
Becomes a mere memory,
And deprives the eye of present pleasure;

When a lover leaves to live in a distant place,
The grief of separation, just as certainly,
Becomes impossible to bear,
And deprives a frail girl of any chance of happiness. [75]

Enter ANASŪYĀ, *parting the curtain backstage.*

ANASŪYĀ: Folks like us do not understand the ways of love because, as ascetics, we have averted our faces from it, but it is clear that the king has behaved like an ignoble man towards Shakuntalā.

DISCIPLE: Day is breaking, so let me tell guru Kaṇva that it is time for the ritual of departure at dawn.

Exit DISCIPLE.

ANASŪYĀ: What would I accomplish even if I were fully awake and in control of my consciousness? My arms and legs fail to function properly at this time, even in their most intimate tasks. May the god of love find some way to fulfil love and desire. For he has made our friend Shakuntalā fall in love with a man of zero heart—a man of false promises. Alternatively, all this could be the result of Durvāsā's rage. Why else would the sagacious king sweet-talk Shakuntalā, and then fail to send her even a letter for so long? If this is the effect of Durvāsā's curse, then maybe we should send the king his ring of remembrance as a reminder from here. But which of the ashram's mournful ascetics would we ask to carry the ring to the king? There is no doubt that everybody will say, 'It is all Shakuntalā's fault'—I have resolved to tell father Kaṇva, just back from his travels, that she is married to the king, and is pregnant with his child, but so far I have been unable to speak to him. What—what—should one do in such a situation?

Enter PRIYAṀVADĀ.

PRIYAṀVADĀ (*joyously*): Hurry up, so that we can finish the rituals to ensure the auspiciousness of Shakuntalā's departure from her father's home!

ANASŪYĀ: How come?

PRIYAṀVADĀ: Listen—a short while ago I went to ask Shakuntalā, 'Did you sleep peacefully through the night?' I found father Kaṇva there, holding her in his arms as she bowed her head in shame, and commending her by saying: 'The patron of a sacrifice is temporarily blinded by the smoke of good fortune rising from the sacred fire, but the oblation he throws into the flames still reaches its destination. Dear daughter, like knowledge given to a deserving pupil, you are a gift to be celebrated, not mourned. I will send you to your husband straight away, under the protection of holy men.'

ANASŪYĀ: Who gave father Kaṇva an account of the events in his absence?

PRIYAṀVADĀ: When he entered the shelter where sacrifices are performed, a disembodied voice, speaking in metrical verse, said to him (*quoting the words in Sanskrit*):

O priest,
Think of your daughter as a vine
Of the supernatural *shamī* tree,
Which, for the good of the earth,
Carries fire in its trunk, its womb—
A womb now bearing the hot seed
That Dushyanta has planted in it. [76]

ANASŪYĀ (*embracing Priyaṁvadā*): I am so happy! But the joy that I am experiencing is mixed with sadness, since Shakuntalā is being sent away today.

PRIYAṀVADĀ: The two of us will manage to dispel our unhappiness one way or another. May she, poor thing, somehow find happiness.

ANASŪYĀ: For precisely that reason and in anticipation of such a situation, I have stored a garland of enchanted, long-lasting *bakula* blossoms in a bowl, which is fashioned from a coconut shell and hangs from a branch on that mango tree. Please reach up and take it down into your hands. In the meantime, I will also prepare a balm for Shakuntalā, with deer musk, river-clay from pilgrimage sites, sprouts of sacred grass, and other auspicious things.

PRIYAṀVADĀ: That is the right thing to do.

Exit ANASŪYĀ. *Then* PRIYAṀVADĀ *mimes taking down the bowl from a branch within reach, and finding the flowers in it.*

VOICE BACKSTAGE [KAṆVA]: Gautamī! Please ask Shāraṅgarava and others to serve as an escort for Shakuntalā.

PRIYAṀVADĀ (*as she mimes listening*): Anasūyā ! Hurry up! The ascetics who are going to the king's capital, Hastināpura, are being summoned.

Re-enter ANASŪYĀ, *with a platter carrying various cosmetics and ornaments.*

ANASŪYĀ: Let us go.

They walk about, miming a transition.

PRIYAṀVADĀ (*looking around*): There is Shakuntalā, sitting with her hair freshly washed in a ritual bath at sunrise, clutching handfuls of wild-rice grain, surrounded by the wives of sages offering her words of farewell. Come, let us approach her together.

End of Mixed Interlude

[IV.iii]

Enter SHAKUNTALĀ, *with* GAUTAMĪ *and other* ASCETICS' WIVES, *who take up the positions just described.*

FIRST WOMAN: Daughter—win the title of 'chief queen', which signifies your husband's highest esteem!

SECOND WOMAN: Daughter—be mother to a brave son!

THIRD WOMAN: Daughter—be your husband's greatest love!

Exit the ASCETICS' WIVES, *all except* GAUTAMĪ.

ANASŪYĀ *and* PRIYAṀVADĀ (*drawing close to Shakuntalā*): May your ritual bath at sunrise bring you happiness.

SHAKUNTALĀ: Welcome to both of you. Please sit here with me.

ANASŪYĀ *and* PRIYAṀVADĀ (*sitting down, with the platter in their hands*): Dear friend, you have to prepare for departure. We will help you get ready with auspicious cosmetics and ornaments.

SHAKUNTALĀ: I should be very grateful for this. After today, there will be no friends to help me dress and get ready. (*She begins to weep silently.*)

ANASŪYĀ *and* PRIYAṀVADĀ: This is a blessed time—it is not right to weep.

They mime wiping away Shakuntalā's tears, then applying cosmetics and ornamenting her.

PRIYAṀVADĀ (*in soliloquy*): Shakuntalā's face and form are worthy of gold ornaments, but we have to make do with whatever the forest of asceticism offers us.

Enter GAUTAMA and NĀRADA, *carrying silk garments, containers for cosmetics, and jewellery.*

GAUTAMA *and* NĀRADA: Here are some more ornaments and things. Please use them to embellish her.

The women onstage are astonished to see the materials they present.

GAUTAMĪ: Nārada, son, where did you find all this?

NĀRADA: Father Kaṇva's power made it possible.

GAUTAMĪ: Did he conjure up these things with the magical power of his mind?

GAUTAMA: No, certainly not! Father Kaṇva said, 'Go pluck flowers from the trees in the grove for Shakuntalā.' And, when we did that:

One tree gave us these silk sheaths, white
    as the moon;
Another tree poured out the lac to decorate
    her feet with bridal red;
Other trees put out hands, with palms raised
    from the wrists,
As if the god of the forest had their branches
    for his arms,
And offered us these jewels, as fine
    as newly sprouted leaves. [77]

PRIYAṀVADĀ (*looking at Shakuntalā*): My dear, these gifts from the enchanted trees are signs that you shall have the pleasures of a goddess in your husband's home.

Shakuntalā mimes embarrassment.

NĀRADA: Let us go, Gautama. Let us tell father Kaṇva, who has just finished his bath, about the gifts from the trees.

GAUTAMA: Okay.

Exit GAUTAMA *and* NĀRADA.

ANASŪYĀ *and* PRIYAṀVADĀ: Hey, Shakuntalā—we ourselves have never used cosmetics or ornaments! So we are going by what is familiar to us from paintings.

SHAKUNTALĀ: I know how skilful you are.

Both friends continue to mime preparing Shakuntalā for departure.

[IV.iv]

Enter KAṆVA, *fresh from his bath in the river.*

KAṆVA [*in soliloquy*]:

My heart is grieving, because Shakuntalā
 will leave today,
My throat is dry, because I have been
 choking back my tears,
My vision is clouded, because of anxiety.
When love causes a man like me,
Who has renounced the world and lives at peace
 in a forest,
To experience so much suffering,
Then how much greater must a householder's
 suffering be

When he has to part with a daughter
for the first time? [78]

He walks about, lost in thought.

ANASŪYĀ *and* PRIYAṀVADĀ: Shakuntalā, you are ready now. Please put on these two silk sheaths.

Shakuntalā rises and mimes putting on the garments, with help.

GAUTAMĪ (*to Shakuntalā*): Here is your father—tears of joy are flowing from his eyes, and he is looking at you as though he were embracing you with his gaze. Please greet him appropriately.

SHAKUNTALĀ (*humbly*): Father, my obeisance to you.

KAṆVA: Dear daughter!

As Sharmishṭhā did with Yayāti,
May you become your husband's greatest love;
As Sharmishṭhā begot Puru, may you beget a son
Who will become a magnificent king. [79]

GAUTAMĪ: Sir, this is truly a benediction for the gift of a daughter to a bridegroom, and not just a common blessing.

KAṆVA: Come, circumambulate the holy fire.

May this fire—
Fed with sacred kindling
From the four sides of the altar,
Surrounded on every side
By the sacred grass spread on the ground—
May this holy fire purify you
With its flames that destroy
Moral flaws and evil deeds

With the incense of the oblations
Consigned to them. [80]

Everybody walks in a circle about the fire.

We can now depart. (*He looks around.*) Where are Shāraṅgarava and the others who will accompany Shakuntalā?

Enter SHĀRAṄGARAVA, SHĀRADVATA, *and other* ASCETICS.

ASCETICS [*in unison*]: Here we are, sir.

KAṆVA: Lead the way for your sister.

SHĀRAṄGARAVA: This way, please, come this way.

Everybody mimes a transition.

[IV.v]

KAṆVA: You trees of the ashram's grove!

This Shakuntalā, this girl—
Who never took a drink of water
Without watering you first,
Who was fond of wearing flowers in her hair
But never plucked a single leaf from you,
Who celebrated the birth
Of every blossom on your branches—
Give her permission to leave,
For today she departs for her husband's home. [81]

He mimes listening to a koel's birdsong.

The trees, who have been Shakuntalā's
close companions
All through her life of dwelling in the forest,
Have conveyed their answer through the koel's song—
They have given her permission to depart. [82]

VOICES BACKSTAGE [*the* GODDESSES *of the enchanted grove, in unison*]:

May the path of Shakuntalā's journey
Be a path of peace, wafted by a pleasant breeze,
May its dust be as soft and fine as the pollen of lotuses,
May it be cooled all the way by trees
That shade it from the heat of the sun,
May it have a lovely midway sanctuary
Of lakes with lotuses in bloom. [83]

Everybody listens in astonishment.

GAUTAMĪ (*to Shakuntalā*): Child, thank the goddesses of the forest, who love you like your companions in the ashram, and have permitted you to leave.

SHAKUNTALĀ (*bowing in thanks as she walks about slowly, then speaking aside*): Priyaṁvadā, I long to see my noble husband—but now that it is time to depart, my feet find it difficult to move.

PRIYAṀVADĀ: You are not the only one in anguish, because of your separation from the sacred forest—the forest, too, seems to be in the same condition, because of its separation from you. For:

The doe has thrown up its morsel of sacred grass,
The peacock has stopped dancing,
The vine is shedding its yellow leaves
As though it were shedding tears. [84]

SHAKUNTALĀ (*miming a sudden recollection*): Father, let me say goodbye to my sister-vine, the Forest's Radiance.

KAṆVA: I know that you love her with a sibling's love. Here she is, on our left.

SHAKUNTALĀ (*walking up to the vine and gathering it in her arms*): O Forest's Radiance, you have wrapped yourself around your mango tree, but please hold me tightly in your tendril-arms that spread out. Starting today, I will be transformed into a city dweller living far away.

KAṆVA (*to Shakuntalā*):

With your own good deeds, you accomplished
What I had determined for you in advance—
You have united with your husband,
A mate whose nature is the same as yours.
This jasmine vine with nine petals on her flowers
Has united in the same way with her mango tree—
I am now free of all anxiety about her and you. [85]

Let your feet start your journey from this place.

SHAKUNTALĀ (*to Anasūyā and Priyaṁvadā*): This vine will now be in your hands, where it will have assured protection.

ANASŪYĀ *and* PRIYAṀVADĀ: In whose hands will we be—who will protect us?

They begin to weep silently.

KAṆVA: Anasūyā, do not cry! Indeed, both of you need to give strength to Shakuntalā.

Everybody mimes a short transition.

SHAKUNTALĀ: Father, when the doe, who grazes around my hut, and whose movements have slowed down recently because of her pregnancy—when she has delivered her fawn successfully, please make sure that you send a messenger to give me the good news.

KAṆVA: I will not forget to do so.

SHAKUNTALĀ (*miming a sudden pause in her movements*): Who is this behind me, tugging at my garments? (*She turns around to look.*)

KAṆVA:

It is the fawn who has been like a son to you.
When a blade of sacred grass cut his young mouth,
You healed the gash by rubbing it with *iṅgudī* oil,
And let him nibble on handfuls of corn—
He refuses to let you go. [86]

SHAKUNTALĀ [*to the fawn*]: My child! Why are you clinging to the woman who has been your companion, but has to abandon you today? I have taken care of you ever since you were orphaned at your mother's sudden death. Please stay back—you are still attached to me, but father will be the one to worry about you now.

She breaks into fresh tears and resumes walking.

KAṆVA:

Be strong, dear daughter,
And stop the flow of tears
That clouds the vision of your eyes—
Your eyes with their long lashes—
For, if your vision is clouded,
Your feet will stumble
On the uneven ground along your path. [87]

[IV.vi]

SHĀRAṄGARAVA: Sir, it is said that one should accompany a dear one, who is departing, only up to the edge of a body of water. Here is the shore of the lake. It would be appropriate for you to give us your message for the king at this point, and return to the ashram.

KAṆVA: Then let us pause in the shade of this banyan tree.

Everybody comes to a halt.

(*He speaks to himself.*) What message should I send to the honourable king Dushyanta? (*He ponders.*)

SHAKUNTALĀ (*aside, to Anasūyā*): Look, on the water! The red goose is crying out in longing because she cannot see her mate, even though he is nearby but is hidden by lotus leaves. My reason tells me that what I am suffering is much worse.

ANASŪYĀ (*also aside*): Please do not talk like that.

Even this goose
Somehow gets through the night
That lengthens out with anguish
Without her mate—
The bond of hope
That unites the two
Enables them to endure
The grave pain of separation. [88]

KAṆVA: Shārańgarava, here are the words from me that you should say to the king, after you have presented Shakuntalā first.

SHĀRAŃGARAVA: Your instructions, sir.

KAṆVA:

Your majesty,
After you have reflected on the facts—
That we are people
Whose wealth is discipline and moderation,

That your own lineage is a lofty one,
That Shakuntalā's transaction with you
Was loving and natural,
That her kinsmen were unable to mediate—
When you have considered all this
With a disposition of goodness and goodwill,
Please regard her
As one of equal dignity among your wives.
Anything beyond this
Lies in the power of fate and destiny,
And is not for the bride's family
To ask for or say. [89]

SHĀRAṄGARAVA: I have fully absorbed your message.

KAṆVA [*to Shakuntalā*]: I have to give you instructions, too. We may be forest-dwellers, but we know something about worldly matters.

SHĀRAṄGARAVA: Indeed, nothing is alien to wise men.

KAṆVA: Once you have found your place in your husband's family:

Always serve your elders;
Be friends with your fellow-wives;
If, sometimes, your husband is disaffected with you,
Do not let anger sway you to act against him;
Be generous to the class of servants;
Do not be arrogant about your fortunate condition—
Women who conduct themselves in this way
Are worshipped as the mistresses of their homes,
But girls whose behaviour is contrary
Become a source of unhappiness for their families. [90]

What does Gautamī think?

GAUTAMĪ: These are the best instructions for women. [*She addresses Shakuntalā*]. Be sure to bear them in mind.

KAṆVA [*to Shakuntalā*]: Come, embrace me with your friends.

SHAKUNTALĀ: Will Anasūyā and Priyaṁvadā turn back from here?

KAṆVA: We have to find good husbands for both of them, too. It is not appropriate for them to go with you to Hastināpura. Gautamī will accompany you.

SHAKUNTALĀ (*embracing Kaṇva*): Uprooted from my father's lap, like a sandalwood vine uprooted from the base of Mount Malaya, how will I transplant myself in another land?

KAṆVA: Why are you so frightened, child?

Your husband belongs to a family of high descent;
Once you have the position of his wife of honour,
You will be occupied constantly with royal duties;
Like the east that gives rise to the sun,
You will soon give birth to a radiant son;
Absorbed in nurturing him, you will forget
The sorrow of your separation from me! [91]

Shakuntalā falls at his feet.

May you attain everything I wish for you.

SHAKUNTALĀ (*rising and approaching Anasūyā and Priyaṁvadā*): Embrace me together, both of you.

ANASŪYĀ *and* PRIYAṀVADĀ (*doing so*): If, for any reason, the king does not recognize you, show him the ring inscribed with his name.

SHAKUNTALĀ: Coming from both of you, this uncertainty makes me tremble.

ANASŪYĀ *and* PRIYAṀVADĀ: Do not be afraid. Love is simply wary of events taking an undesirable turn.

SHĀRAṄGARAVA: The sun has climbed four hand-widths into the sky—a quarter of daylight time is gone. With all due respect, let Shakuntalā please hurry up.

SHAKUNTALĀ (*facing in the direction of the ashram*): Father, when will I see the sacred grove again?

KAṆVA: Listen—

After you have spent a long life as the wife
of Dushyanta,
During his reign as the king of the earth to the ends
of the four oceans,
After he has placed on the throne the incomparable
son you bear him,
After he has passed on his burden of responsibility
for the whole clan,
You will come back with him to live in the peace
of this enchanted grove. [92]

GAUTAMĪ: Child, the auspicious time of departure has passed. Let your father return. Brother Kaṇva, you should turn back now—otherwise, this Shakuntalā will keep chattering away for a very long time.

KAṆVA [*to Shakuntalā*]: My sacred obligations have been interrupted.

SHAKUNTALĀ (*embracing Kaṇva again*): My father's body is already harrowed by rigorous discipline. So please do not grieve for me too much.

KAṆVA (*sighing deeply*):

How will my sorrow be soothed away, my child,
When, coming and going, I will see
The shoots of wild rice flourishing
Where you planted and watered them
Near the threshold of your hut? [93]

Go. May your path be auspicious.

Exit SHAKUNTALĀ *and her* ESCORT, *towards the far line of trees.*

ANASŪYĀ *and* PRIYAṀVADĀ (*watching them into the distance*): O—O—O—Shakuntalā has disappeared from view behind the trees.

KAṆVA (*sighing again*): Anasūyā, she who always walks with the right steps is gone. Stop grieving, both of you, and follow in my footsteps back to the ashram.

ANASŪYĀ *and* PRIYAṀVADĀ: Father, how are we going to enter this grove, which is so desolate now without Shakuntalā?

KAṆVA: The force of your love makes it seem so.

He walks about, lost in thought.

Ah! Sending Shakuntalā off to her husband's home has brought me some peace of mind. Because,

A daughter, indeed, is only borrowed wealth:
Now that I have given her away to her husband,
My deepest self is free of anxiety—
The way it is free when it discharges a debt. [94]

Exit KAṆVA, ANASŪYĀ, *and* PRIYAṀVADĀ.

End of Act IV

Act V

[V.i]

Enter DUSHYANTA *and* MĀḌHAVYA, *seated in a room in the palace at Hastināpura.*

MĀḌHAVYA (*as he mimes listening*): My friend, do pay attention to the sounds coming from the music room in the women's chambers. One can hear the melodious notes of a flawless song. I think queen Haṁsapadikā is learning and rehearsing a new composition.

DUSHYANTA: Be quiet! Then I can listen, too.

VOICE BACKSTAGE (HAṀSAPADIKĀ *sings*):

O black, black bee,
    Always eager to suck
Nectar from the freshest flowers,
    Why have you now forgotten
That blossom on a vine
    Whose juices you savoured
So intimately, greedily,
    And whom you left to languish,
Living among lotuses,
    Once you had your satisfaction? [95]

DUSHYANTA: Oh—what a song! It releases a whole flood of emotions.

MĀḌHAVYA: Do you find a deeper meaning in the lyrics?

DUSHYANTA: I was once in love with this singer. That is why I can understand her reprimand, which refers to my subsequent relationship with queen Vasumatī. Māḍhavya, my friend, please go as my messenger, and say to queen Haṁsapadikā: 'You have rebuked me soundly and skilfully!'

MĀḌHAVYA: As you say, my friend. But when queen Haṁsapadikā's maids grab me by my hair and beat me up, nothing can save me—the way nothing can save an errant sage when one of lord Indra's *apsarās* grabs him by his dreadlocks and beats him up.

DUSHYANTA: Go, deliver my message urbanely, with all civility.

MĀḌHAVYA: What choice do I have?

Exit MĀḌHAVYA.

DUSHYANTA (*in soliloquy*): Why has this song disturbed me so deeply, even though I am not aware of being separated from anyone I love? Perhaps:

When even a man
Who is happy and at peace
Is suddenly agitated
At the sight of beautiful things
And the sound of sweet words,
It must be that his mind
Is stirring up memories
Of his loves from past lives—

Memories and residues that sit still,
Without his knowledge,
Deep inside his heart and being. [96]

DUSHYANTA *remains seated in his disoriented state for a few moments, then exits.*

[V.ii]

Enter VĀTĀYANA, *the king's chamberlain, on the palace grounds.*

VĀTĀYANA (*in soliloquy*): Ha! There is no ambiguity about my present state.

This bamboo staff that I hold in my hands today
Was the big stick of authority and punishment
That I inherited, by custom, when I started to serve
As the king's chamberlain, supervising
 his women's rooms—
Now that so much time has passed since
 my youthful days,
It serves me as a crutch in the infirmities of old age. [97]

Oh! It is true that my master's duties under the law cannot be pushed to one side. But it is also true that he has just concluded the day's business in the hall of justice. I therefore have no appetite to inform him that sage Kaṇva's followers have arrived. The responsibilities of governance are truly devoid of leisure.

Harnessed once and for all,
The sun's stallions are always galloping;
The wind flows non-stop, night and day;
Shesha, the cosmic serpent,
Bears the earth's weight on his head

Through every moment in time—
The king's duties, too, under the law,
With their six divisions, are never done. [98]

So let me perform my own duty first.

He walks about and looks around, miming a short transition [to the secluded canopy where DUSHYANTA *is seated, with* VETRAVATĪ *in attendance nearby. Vātāyana observes the king from a distance, and continues his soliloquy].*

Here is my lord and master—

With his mind under stress
From taking care of his subjects
Like a father caring for his children,
He has resorted to a little solitude
To relax at the end of the day,
The way a bull elephant
Resorts to a cool place
After leading and guarding his herd
With great care all day
In the torrid heat of the sun. [99]

He approaches and addresses Dushyanta.

Victory to you, lord and master! Some ascetics, accompanied by two women, have arrived at the palace gate—they live in the forest along the foothills of the snow mountains, and have brought a message from sage Kaṇva. Please weigh this information, and decide what is to be done.

DUSHYANTA (*respectfully*): These ascetics are carrying a message from sage Kaṇva?

VĀTĀYANA: Yes, sir.

DUSHYANTA: Then deliver this instruction directly to Somarāta, our royal-family priest: 'Please welcome the members of sage Kaṇva's community with the proper rites, and usher them in personally.' I shall wait to see them in a setting that is suitable for a visit by holy men.

VĀTĀYANA: As you wish, lord and master.

Exit VĀTĀYANA.

[V.iii]

DUSHYANTA (*rising from his seat*): Vetravatī, lead me to the pavilion of the fire sacrifice.

VETRAVATĪ: This way, master, this way.

They both walk, miming a transition.

DUSHYANTA (*in soliloquy, voicing his dejection and weariness*): Creatures of every kind find happiness when they attain their desired objects. But it is certain that the goal-driven labours of kings end in disappointment.

The fame that comes with kingship
Brings satisfaction
Only to its seeker's enthusiasm,
But the protection that he must provide
For what he has gained
Produces pain and distress;
Like the royal parasol,
Whose shaft he has to hold up with his hands,
Kingship brings him relief
From sweat and labour—
But also demands more labour and sweat. [100]

VOICES BACKSTAGE [TWO BARDS]: Victory to you, lord and master!

[*Enter* TWO BARDS *of the royal court.*]

FIRST BARD:

You strive strenuously every day
For your subjects' benefit
Without fretting about your own desires,
For that is how the business of your office goes—
Just as a tree bears the brunt
Of the heat of the sun on its head,
And keeps the summer blaze from those
Who seek shelter in its shade. [101]

SECOND BARD:

You wield the big stick of punishment
And, with the rule of law, you tame
Those who travel on the road of evil;
You settle disputes, resolve conflicts,
Bring peace to warring factions,
And give your subjects security—
Prosperity makes it possible
For people to live in harmony,
But you are the one and only instrument
That enables them to achieve unanimity. [102]

DUSHYANTA: My mind has been depressed, but listening to these royal bards has raised my spirits again.

[*Exit the* TWO BARDS.] *Dushyanta resumes his transition, walking about with fresh energy, led by Vetravatī.*

VETRAVATĪ: Here is the forecourt of the pavilion, freshly washed and embellished with the presence of the cow whose milk provides the ghee for the fire sacrifices in the sanctuary. Please mount the platform, your majesty.

DUSHYANTA (*climbing by supporting himself on Vetravatī's shoulder, and standing up on the platform surrounding the main firepit*): Vetravatī, why would sage Kaṇva send his disciples to me?

Has something interrupted the spiritual activities
Of these ascetics who practise harsh self-discipline?
Or has anybody done anything inappropriate
To the creatures who inhabit the sacred forest?
Or have my own wrongdoings, somehow,
Prevented flowers from blossoming on vines?
I have grown anxious because I cannot answer
The questions of this sort perplexing my mind. [103]

VETRAVATĪ: The way I reason it, these ascetics are pleased with your good actions, and have come to felicitate you.

[V.iv]

Enter VĀTĀYANA *and* SOMARĀTA, *followed by the party of* ASCETICS, *with* SHAKUNTALĀ *and* GAUTAMĪ *walking ahead of* SHĀRAṄGARAVA, SHĀRADVATA, *and the others.*

VĀTĀYANA: This way, good people, this way.

SHĀRAṄGARAVA [*while still at the edge of the forecourt*]: Shāradvata!

It is amazing that this king
Is so effective in his unwavering stance
With the maintenance of law and morality,
And that nobody here, from any caste or class,
Has fallen into evil ways—and yet my mind,
Acquainted only with constant isolation,
Thinks that this palace full of people
Is really a house engulfed in flames. [104]

SHĀRADVATA: Sir, I think you grew anxious and alarmed when you entered the teeming city.

I look at the crowds of city people
With their worldly satisfactions
The way a man, fresh from a bath,
Looks at an unwashed man still grubby with oil,
The way a pure person looks at an impure one,
The way a man whose mind has been wakened
Looks at a man still sleeping the sleep of ignorance,
The way a person who is free and independent
Looks at someone still restrained by bonds. [105]

SHAKUNTALĀ (*aside to Gautamī, with foreboding*): Why is my left eye twitching uncontrollably, as though in a bad omen?

GAUTAMĪ [*also aside*]: My child, may anything that is inauspicious perish! May the gods of your husband's family grant you happiness! (*She performs a quick circumambulation to ward off evil.*)

SOMARĀTA (*gesturing towards Dushyanta*): Ascetics, here is the king. He has already arisen from his throne, but he is waiting for you. He is the venerated protector of people of all classes and castes, at all stages of life.

SHĀRAṄGARAVA: Great priest, this aspect of the king is worthy of high praise, but we are humble folk. In our view:

Trees laden with fruit bow to the ground;
Freshly formed rainclouds hang low over the earth;
True men maintain humility, despite
  their lofty fame—
That is the nature of those who strive for
  the good of others. [106]

VETRAVATĪ [*aside, to Dushyanta*]: Master, the faces of these sages seem to be coloured with pleasantness—I think that they have come with a polite petition that should be no cause for anxiety.

DUSHYANTA (*looking at Shakuntalā*): And this honourable woman—

Who can she be,
With her physical beauty
Obscured by silken sheaths like veils,
Standing among these ascetics
Like a fresh sprig
Sprouting in the midst of yellow leaves? [107]

VETRAVATĪ: Master, I am overcome by curiosity, and my reason fails me. Her appearance certainly makes her extremely desirable.

DUSHYANTA: That may be so, but let it pass. It is not appropriate to look at someone else's woman.

SHAKUNTALĀ (*placing her hand on her breast, and speaking to herself*): My heart, why are you quaking like this? Take courage, while I try to grasp my noble husband's feelings.

SOMARĀTA (*advancing and addressing Dushyanta*): These are the ascetics, sir, welcomed with due honour. They have a message from their master that is worth hearing.

DUSHYANTA: I am listening.

ASCETICS [*in unison*]: Victory to you, your majesty!

DUSHYANTA: I bow to all of you.

ASCETICS: May you attain what you desire.

DUSHYANTA: The spiritual practices of sages proceed without hindrance?

ASCETICS:

While you are their guardian,
How can hindrances disrupt their discipline?
While the sun is shining,
How can darkness overwhelm the light? [108]

DUSHYANTA: That makes my title of 'king' truly meaningful. And sage Kaṇva prospers for the good of the world?

ASCETICS: Men who have perfected their self-discipline control their own well-being. He asks after your welfare, and sends you this message.

DUSHYANTA: What are sage Kaṇva's instructions for me?

SHĀRAṄGARAVA: He says, 'I have accepted with affection and happiness your wedding to my daughter, which the two of you carried out with mutual passion and mutual consent, making your vows in private in the style of the celestials. For:

You are counted as the foremost of honourable men,
And Shakuntalā is the embodiment of goodness
and virtue;
So even the creator would not be able to find fault,
after the longest time,
In the marriage of a bride and a groom whose qualities
are equal. [109]

Acting in accordance with the law, please therefore accept this bride who now carries your child.'

GAUTAMĪ: Noble sir! I, too, wish to say something, even though there is no occasion for me to speak. Because:

She did not think it necessary to ask her elders
for permission,
And you, too, did not consult your family, or hers;
Since the deed was done in secret,
with mutual consent,
What could I say to find fault or deter
either of you? [110]

SHAKUNTALĀ (*to herself*): What will my noble husband say now?

DUSHYANTA: What is this preposterous fable?

SHAKUNTALĀ (*to herself*): The disposition of his words is inflammatory.

SHĀRANGARAVA: Why do you call it a fable, sir? You yourself are extremely skilled in the ways of the world, viewed from every angle. So you know that:

When a married woman
Continues to live at her father's house,
People start to cast doubts on her,
Even if she is true and chaste—
That is why a bride's family
Wishes her to live with her husband,
Whether he desires her or not. [111]

DUSHYANTA: Did I marry this lady at any time in the past?

SHAKUNTALĀ (*in despair, to herself*): My heart, your fears have come true!

SHĀRANGARAVA:

Is this revulsion towards your vows?
Or is it disdain for law and duty?

Or is this just a disavowal
Of your actions and their consequences?

DUSHYANTA: How did such a fanciful lie become a question at all?

SHĀRAṄGARAVA:

Moral flaws of this kind
Reach their maximum
In people who are intoxicated
With power and wealth. [112]

DUSHYANTA: I am deeply insulted.

GAUTAMĪ [*to Shakuntalā*]: My daughter—stop being modest for a few moments. Let me remove the veil from your face. Surely your husband will recognize you then. (*She mimes removing the upper sheath.*)

DUSHYANTA (*to himself, as he inspects Shakuntalā*):

Like a black bee circling a jasmine flower
Covered with frost at dawn,
I hover around this woman,
The flawless beauty of whose form
Is presented to me voluntarily—
Unable to decide whether or not
I took her in marriage earlier,
I am unable to take her now,
And also unable to let her go. [113]

He stands transfixed, lost in thought.

VETRAVATĪ [*in soliloquy*]: Our master is a man of exceptional morality. Who else would stop to think when shown and offered such a beautiful form unasked?

SHĀRAṄGARAVA: Your majesty, why are you standing so still, without a word?

DUSHYANTA: Ascetics, even after sustained reflection, I am certain that I have no memory of taking this honourable woman as my bride. Then how can I accept her now, and how can I acknowledge that I am the father of the child that physical signs clearly indicate she is carrying in her womb?

SHAKUNTALĀ (*to herself, turning her face away*): The noble king doubts the very fact of our marriage. How can my long-term dreams ever be fulfilled?

SHĀRAṄGARAVA: King, do not say such things!

Does sage Kaṇva deserve to be dishonoured by you—
He who has gladly blessed the daughter
Whom you took at your will in a secret union—
He who has given you, as a gift,
The very wealth that you stole from him—
He who has accepted you as a worthy man,
Even though you resemble a thief? [114]

SHĀRADVATA: Shārangarava! Stop speaking now. Shakuntalā! We have said what we were asked to say. The king has responded with suspicion. Offer a counter-response to convince him.

SHAKUNTALĀ (*aside, turning away*): When the condition of passion has been totally transformed, what is the use of a reminder? It is certain that I, too, am culpable now. (*Aloud.*) My noble husband—. (*Breaking off, to speak in soliloquy.*) Since doubt and mistrust have taken over, this personal address is improper. (*Aloud again.*) Descendant of King Puru, it is inappropriate of you to use such heart-rending words to reject a person like me, who is simple-hearted by nature, after deceiving me with your promises in the sacred grove.

DUSHYANTA (*covering his ears*): Silence this evil!

Do you wish to stain
The reputations
Of your clan and mine
And bring me down,
The way a river
Wrecking its banks
Muddies clean waters
And topples trees? [115]

SHAKUNTALĀ: All right! If you are saying these things because you really think I am someone else's wife, then I will show you your ring—your own token of remembrance and recognition—and dispel your doubts.

DUSHYANTA: That is a good idea.

SHAKUNTALĀ (*touching the place of the ring on her hand*): Oh—oh! The ring is not on my finger! (*Shocked and in despair, she looks at Gautamī.*)

GAUTAMĪ: It must have slipped off when you took a ritual bath at Indra's Ford, the midway sanctuary of lakes, in the waters at the shrine of Shachi.

DUSHYANTA (*smiling*): This is proof of the common saying, 'Women's minds are spun with cunning.'

SHAKUNTALĀ: The gods have displayed their indomitable power. Let me say something else to you.

DUSHYANTA: Listening is all that is left for me to do.

SHAKUNTALĀ: You will recall that, one day, in an arbour with jasmine vines in the sacred grove, you were holding a bowl made of lotus leaves, filled with water.

DUSHYANTA: I am listening.

SHAKUNTALĀ: Just then the fawn named Baby Long Eyes, whom I had raised like a son, came into the arbour. You called to him tenderly, saying, 'Drink this water first.' But he refused to nuzzle up to your hands because he did not know you. When I took the bowl, he drank the same water lovingly from my hands. Observing the incident, you remarked, 'All creatures trust only their own companions, and the two of you live together in this forest.'

DUSHYANTA: Only lustful men are seduced by the honey of such words, which self-serving women conceive in their wombs of lies.

GAUTAMĪ: Great sir, it is improper of you to say such things. This girl, raised and nurtured in the forest of asceticism, is completely unacquainted with deception and guile.

DUSHYANTA: O ascetic crone!

The female of the species develops her cunning
Without instruction—this is observable
Even in species other than the human.
What, then, can be said about people
Who also possess knowledge, such as sages?
With her inborn cunning, the mother koel
Gets birds of other species to raise her young
Before the baby koels learn to fly—and fly away. [116]

SHAKUNTALĀ (*furiously*): You ignoble man! Do you think that everybody else is the same at heart as you? You dress yourself in the garb of law and morality, but you are as treacherous as a pit camouflaged with straw to trap the innocent. Who would want to emulate you, or follow in your footsteps?

DUSHYANTA (*to himself*): This fury that Shakuntalā displays seems to be completely genuine, and makes me doubt myself. Because:

It seems that when she found
My lack of memory hardening my heart,
And hence leading me to reject her claim
About the consummation of love's bond
In the forest's privacy, a towering rage
Turned her bloodshot eyes a fiery red,
And made her arch her eyebrows so much
That even the bow belonging to the god of love
Snapped under the strain of their curvature! [117]

(*Aloud.*) My good woman, Dushyanta's character is renowned everywhere. Nonetheless, you have accused me of cheating and deceit. But when I examine myself, I cannot see the fraudulence.

SHAKUNTALĀ: Then I have been proved and pronounced to be a wanton woman—just because I put my trust in the Puru dynasty, and let myself fall into the hands of a man who had honey on his lips but poison in his heart.

She hides her face and weeps.

SHĀRAṄGARAVA: When your own impulsive actions hit back at you, the outcome is agony and pain.

That is why one should examine
The elements of a relationship
Before consenting to a secret union;

When one does not really know
A person's heart or character,
Love is easily transformed
Into hatred and enmity. [118]

DUSHYANTA: But, sir, why these words of blame and dire warning for me—when nothing warrants them, except your trust in this woman?

SHĀRAṄGARAVA (*turning to his fellow ascetics, but addressing Dushyanta obliquely, with scorn*): Do you hear the logic of this topsy-turvy response?

The utterances of a person
Who, since birth, has never learnt
The artifice of deception
Are unwarranted—
But the utterances of people
Who make fraudulence
Their special subject of study
Provide a warrant for the truth! [119]

DUSHYANTA: O truth-teller! Let me assume for a moment that I am as dishonest as you say, but what would I gain by swindling this woman?

SHĀRAṄGARAVA: Personal destruction, character assassination—ruin.

DUSHYANTA: The thought that the kings of the Puru dynasty wish for such ruin is not a thought to be treated with reverence.

SHĀRADVATA: Shārañgarava! What is the point of this exchange? We have delivered our guru's message. Let us go back. (*Then he addresses Dushyanta.*)

This woman is married to you—
Accept her or abandon her, as you please.
A husband's power over his wife is absolute. [120]

Gautamī! Walk ahead of us.

The ASCETICS *start to leave.*

SHAKUNTALĀ: What! I have been deceived by this liar—and now you are abandoning me here?

She starts to follow the others.

GAUTAMĪ (*pausing*): Shāraṅgarava, my son, Shakuntalā is following us, weeping pitifully. Abandoned heartlessly by her husband, what will my poor child do?

SHĀRAṄGARAVA (*turning angrily to Shakuntalā*): Where to, pushy woman? Are you trying to walk out to a path of independence?

Shakuntalā cowers in fear.

Shakuntalā!

If you are what the king says you are,
Then what place do you have in sage Kaṇva's family?
But if you know that your marriage vows are pure,
Then even slavery in your husband's home
will be acceptable. [121]

DUSHYANTA: O ascetic, why are you deceiving this good woman with crooked reasoning? The whole point is that:

The moon opens water lilies at night, not lotuses
by day,
While the sun opens lotuses by day, not lilies at night;

So also a man, who controls his passions and senses,
Couples only with a wife who is his own,
and not another man's. [122]

SHĀRANGARAVA: Your devotion to recent affairs of state and to recent affairs of the heart has made you forget your earlier devotion to Shakuntalā. You have already broken the moral law by breaking your bond with her—so why are you afraid of doing something immoral now?

[V.v]

DUSHYANTA (*turning to Somarāta, the royal-family priest*): On precisely this subject, I want to ask you, sir—what is wrong and what is right?

I do not know whether I am stupefied,
Or whether Shakuntalā is telling a lie—
Should I risk the mistake
Of abandoning my own legitimate bride,
Or should I risk the mistake
Of illegitimately taking another man's wife? [123]

SOMARĀTA (*reflecting*): If that is the situation, then here is what you ought to do.

DUSHYANTA: Please give me your instructions.

SOMARĀTA: Let this gentle woman reside in my home until she delivers her child. If you wish to know why I am recommending this, then please listen. Spiritual masters have already predicted that you will have a son who will turn the wheel of kingdom and law. If sage Kaṇva's grandson carries the birthmarks of a great king, then welcome Shakuntalā into your palace chambers with all the honours of a queen. If the outcome is the opposite, then send her back to her father, as predetermined for such a situation.

DUSHYANTA: As you wish, my guide!

SOMARĀTA (*to Shakuntalā*): My child, please follow me.

SHAKUNTALĀ: O mother earth—open up—open up and swallow me!

Exit the ASCETICS, *followed by* SOMARĀTA, *with* SHAKUNTALĀ *behind him. Dushyanta, unable to remember under the curse, stands reflecting on Shakuntalā for a few moments, with Vetravatī in attendance.*

VOICE BACKSTAGE [SOMARĀTA]: Amazing! Amazing!

DUSHYANTA (*listening intently*): What could have happened?

Enter SOMARĀTA, *in a flurry.*

SOMARĀTA (*wonderstruck*): Your majesty! A great marvel has occurred!

DUSHYANTA: What is it?

SOMARĀTA: Lord and master, as soon as sage Kaṇva's disciples left,

Shakuntalā began to lament her misfortune—
She raised her hands and wept.

DUSHYANTA: And then?

SOMARĀTA:

Near the shrine of Menakā, the celestial *apsarā*,
A body of light shaped like a woman
Swooped down on her, and whisked her away. [124]

Everybody onstage mimes astonishment.

DUSHYANTA: I have already closed discussion on the topic of Shakuntalā. Why are you reopening it now, with fruitless arguments and counter-arguments? Please go and rest.

SOMARĀTA (*examining Dushyanta closely*): May you be victorious.

Exit SOMARĀTA.

DUSHYANTA: I am uneasy and apprehensive, Vetravatī. Please lead me to my bedchamber.

VETRAVATĪ: This way, your majesty, come this way.

DUSHYANTA:

I am unable to recall
The sage's abandoned daughter
In the guise of a bride,
And yet I find myself
Anxious and confused,
Grieving and longing—as though
My heart were trying to convince me
That she, indeed, is my wife. [125]

Exit VETRAVATĪ *and* DUSHYANTA.

End of Act V

Act VI

MIXED INTERLUDE

Part 1

[VI.i]

Enter the CITY SUPERINTENDENT, *Dushyanta's brother-in-law, followed by two policemen,* SŪCHAKA *and* JĀNUKA, *escorting a* FISHERMAN *as their prisoner in restraints, near the marketplace.*

SŪCHAKA *and* JĀNUKA (*beating the fisherman*): Tell us, you thief, where did you steal this ring belonging to the king, studded with gems and inscribed with his name?

FISHERMAN (*cowering, as he mimes fear*): Masters, have mercy! I do not do that sort of thing.

SŪCHAKA: So, did the king give it to you as a gift, thinking that you were a great, pious brahmin?

FISHERMAN: Please listen, my lords! I am just a lowly fisherman who lives at Indra's Ford.

JĀNUKA: You scoundrel, did we ask you for your caste?

SUPERINTENDENT: Sūchaka, let him tell the whole story in sequence—do not put obstacles in his way.

SŪCHAKA *and* JĀNUKA (*to the Superintendent*): Exactly as you say, chief. (*To the fisherman.*) Talk, you scum!

FISHERMAN: I make a living for my family as a fisherman, with nets and hooks as the tools of my trade.

SUPERINTENDENT (*laughing sarcastically*): That is a clean occupation!

FISHERMAN:

One should never sacrifice
Whatever occupation
One inherits naturally by caste,
No matter how much
It might be criticized—
Even the gentle priest
Who keeps a compassionate heart
Is forced to slaughter animals
For his holy sacrifice. [126]

SUPERINTENDENT: Okay, okay—what happened with the ring?

FISHERMAN: The other day, I caught a *rohu*, a red carp, at the ford. When I cut it open, I saw this ring in its stomach, gleaming with gems. I came to the market today and showed it to a jeweller. That is when you caught me trying to sell it. Now you can beat me up or let me go. This is the story of how I got the ring.

SUPERINTENDENT: Jānuka, this slimy lizard stinks of raw fish, so he must be a fisherman, no doubt. But the fact that he tried to hawk the ring is highly suspicious—he should be questioned further. So let us take him to the palace.

SŪCHAKA *and* JĀNUKA (*to the Superintendent*): Exactly as you say, chief. (*To the fisherman.*) Walk, you plunderer.

[*All of them mime a transition to the palace gate.*]

SUPERINTENDENT: Sūchaka, you and Jānuka guard this fisherman carefully outside the palace gate, while I go in and tell the king about the ring and how we recovered it, and get his orders and come back.

SŪCHAKA *and* JĀNUKA: Go in, chief. Make his majesty happy and get his thanks.

Exit the SUPERINTENDENT.

SŪCHAKA: Jānuka, the boss has been gone a long time.

JĀNUKA: It is possible to meet kings only at appointed times.

SŪCHAKA (*pointing to the fisherman*): My hands are itching to put the garland of death around this man's throat.

FISHERMAN: Good sir, it is not right of you to think of killing for no reason.

JĀNUKA (*looking towards the palace gate*): I see the chief with a document in his hand, returning with the king's orders. Now you will be sacrificed to the vultures—or fed to the dogs.

Re-enter the SUPERINTENDENT.

SUPERINTENDENT: Sūchaka! Release the fisherman. His story about finding the ring has been verified.

SŪCHAKA: Exactly as you say, chief.

JĀNUKA: This fellow made his way through the front door of the house of death and came back! (*He unties the ropes restraining the fisherman.*)

FISHERMAN (*bowing to the Superintendent*): Please, sir, what do you think of my occupation now?

SUPERINTENDENT: The king has also sent you a reward in coins, equal to the value of his ring. [*He gives the bundle, tied in a piece of cloth, to the fisherman.*]

FISHERMAN (*bowing again, as he takes the reward*): My lord and master, I am deeply honoured and obliged.

SŪCHAKA: This is called mercy—to be taken off the execution block, only to be put on an elephant's back for a victory parade.

JĀNUKA: Chief, call it an award, not a reward. By the looks of it, the ring must be very dear to the king.

SUPERINTENDENT: I do not think that the king sets too high a value on the gemstones set in the ring, even though they are valuable. But the moment he set his eyes on it, he remembered someone very dear to him. He is unsentimental by nature but, for a moment, his eyes brimmed with tears.

SŪCHAKA: You have been of royal service to his majesty.

JĀNUKA: You can say that we have been of royal service to this fisherman—for his profit. (*He looks at the latter with envy.*)

FISHERMAN: Masters, half the coins in this bundle are yours to share—a donation to cover the cost of flowers for your daily prayers.

JĀNUKA: That is good enough!

SUPERINTENDENT: Mister Fisherman, you have now become a great and dear friend of ours! Good wine, with a bouquet of *kadamba* flowers, should be a witness to the beginning of a beautiful friendship. Let us make our way to the winemaker's shop.

Exit the SUPERINTENDENT, SŪCHAKA *and* JĀNUKA, *and the* FISHERMAN.

Part 2

[VI.ii]

Enter SĀNUMATĪ, *an* apsarā, *on a small craft descending by the skyway.*

SĀNUMATĪ: It turned out well for me—before I left the celestial realm, I was able to complete my repetitive duties as an attendant at the bathing pool for my fellow-*apsarās*, while my male counterparts were performing their morning ablutions there. Here on earth, I shall now observe the situation of the royal sage, Dushyanta, at first hand. Because of my intimate friendship with Menakā, I am as attached to her daughter Shakuntalā as I am to any limb of my own body—and I have already done what Menakā directed me to do earlier, for Shakuntalā's cause. (*She looks all around.*) It is definitely time for the spring festival, so why are there no visible preparations for it at the royal palace? I have the capacity to see and know everything with my yogic powers, but I should restrain my curiosity in order to honour Menakā's command. So let me use my knowledge of invisibility to turn invisible, and closely follow these two young women patrolling the palace garden, and gather essential information. (*She mimes disembarking from her skycraft and positioning herself as described.*)

Enter the two female attendants, PARABHRITIKĀ *and* MADHUKARIKĀ, *the former holding and examining a sprig of mango buds as she appears onstage, and the latter following close behind.*

PARABHRITIKĀ:

O sprig of mango buds,
I have seen you, at last!
Tinged with a little red,
A little green, a little yellow,
You are the very life
Of this season sweet as honey—
The gracious gift
Of spring's auspiciousness.
I bow to please you! [127]

MADHUKARIKĀ: Parabhritikā, what are you muttering to yourself?

PARABHRITIKĀ: Madhukarikā, the koel, my namesake, goes mad with joy at the sight of a fresh mango sprout, just like me.

MADHUKARIKĀ (*drawing close, with delight*): Is the season of spring finally here?

PARABHRITIKĀ: This is the time for you to sing, intoxicated with the spirit of the season, with its sheer sensuous pleasures.

MADHUKARIKĀ: Give me a hand up, my dear, so that I can stand on my toes and pluck a sprig of mango buds for myself, and offer it in supplication to the god of love.

PARABHRITIKĀ: Only if I get half the fruit of your prayer!

MADHUKARIKĀ: That is what you would get, even if you did not ask for it. We share the same spirit, even though our bodies are two. (*She reaches up, with support, and breaks off a sprig from a mango tree.*) Amazing—even though this sprig has buds that have not opened, just breaking it off has emitted so much fragrance. (*She cups her hands together in reverence.*)

O sprig of mango buds!
I consecrate you to the god of love,
Who carries a bow—
May you make the hearts
Of men on the open road
Easy targets for young women,
And may you become
The first of the five arrows
That the god of love aims at them! [128]

As a ritual gesture, she tosses away the consecrated sprig.

Enter VĀTĀYANA, *the chamberlain, throwing aside the curtain backstage angrily in response to Madhukarikā.*

VĀTĀYANA: Stop, you fool! Why are you plucking mango sprigs, when the king has banned the spring festival?

PARABHRITIKĀ *and* MADHUKARIKĀ (*frightened*): Noble sir—kindly forgive us! We did not know about the ban.

VĀTĀYANA: Have you not heard that the trees that blossom in the spring and the birds who live in them have already followed the king's prohibition? For:

Even the mango flower that sprouted a while ago
Has not opened and produced its pollen yet.
The *kurvaka* flower, ready to blossom,
Is still enfolded in the form of a bud.
The cycle of cold weather is over,

But the songs of the male koels have stopped
in their throats.
It seems that even the god of love is quivering in fear,
And has returned his half-drawn arrow
to his quiver. [129]

PARABHRITIKĀ *and* MADHUKARIKĀ: There is no doubt about it. Dushyanta, the royal sage, is very powerful.

PARABHRITIKĀ: Noble sir, it has been just a few days since Mitrāvasu, the kingdom's administrator, left us at the feet of the chief queen, Vasumatī, placing us in her protective custody. That is how we came to be assigned to the task of patrolling the garden of the women's chambers. Since we are new arrivals, we did not hear the earlier report about the ban on the spring festival.

VĀTĀYANA: Fine. Do not do it again.

PARABHRITIKĀ *and* MADHUKARIKĀ: Noble sir, we are very curious. If you think that we are worthy enough to know, please tell us—why has the king banned the spring festival?

SĀNUMATĪ: Human beings are very fond of festivities. There must be some grave reason for the ban.

VĀTĀYANA [*to himself*]: Why should I not mention it, since everybody already knows? [*Aloud.*] Have you two not followed the trajectory of the public outcry over the rejection of Shakuntalā ?

PARABHRITIKĀ *and* MADHUKARIKĀ: We heard about it from the administrator's lips, but only up to the part where the ring was recovered.

VĀTĀYANA (*to himself*): Then there is very little to tell. (*Aloud.*) It is certain that, ever since the king saw his ring and remembered that Shakuntalā really was his wife, whom he married in secrecy and abandoned in ignorance, he has been sunk in deep remorse and regret. For:

The king has begun to find everything pleasant
    intolerable;
He does not meet his ministers every day, as before;
He spends the night in sleeplessness,
Tossing and turning on the edge of his bed;
And when, compelled by courtesy, he responds
Politely to the queens in his inner chambers,
But addresses each of them as 'Shakuntalā',
He is overcome with shame for the longest time. [130]

SĀNUMATĪ: I love this!

VĀTĀYANA: In his overwhelming despondency, the king banned the spring festival and its celebration of love.

PARABHRITIKĀ *and* MADHUKARIKĀ: It is very apt.

VOICE BACKSTAGE [VETRAVATĪ]: Please, your majesty, this way.

VĀTĀYANA (*listening attentively*): Oh—the king is coming here. Go about your business!

PARABHRITIKĀ *and* MADHUKARIKĀ: As you command, sir.

Exit PARABHRITIKĀ *and* MADHUKARIKĀ. [VĀTĀYANA *and* SĀNUMATĪ *remain on the stage.*]

End of Mixed Interlude

[VI.iii]

Enter DUSHYANTA, *dressed to reflect his grief and remorse, led by* VETRAVATĪ *and accompanied by* MĀḌHAVYA, *carrying a stick.*

VĀTĀYANA (*looking at Dushyanta*): Ah! The beauty of those who are beautiful is evident under all conditions. The king looks handsome even in his suffering. For:

He has stopped donning distinctive royal ornaments;
He is wearing only one gold bracelet, on his left wrist;
His lips are pale from sighs; his eyes have dark circles
From sleeplessness at night, caused by anxiety—
And yet, like a great gem tested on a touchstone,
He remains untarnished, because of his inner
radiance. [131]

SĀNUMATĪ (*looking at Dushyanta*): Indeed, even though he abandoned and thus dishonoured her, it is only right that Shakuntalā is still miserable for this man.

DUSHYANTA (*walking about slowly, lost in thought*):

Earlier, when my dear love—
The one with the eyes of a doe—
Tried to awaken
This cruel heart of mine
With happy memories,
It remained asleep:
But now, when there is only
The grief of guilt and remorse,
It is wide awake. [132]

SĀNUMATĪ: The poor woman—this is truly her fate!

MĀḌHAVYA (*aside, to the audience*): The king is infected with the Shakuntalā disease again! Who knows how he will be cured?

VĀTĀYANA (*approaching Dushyanta*): Victory, lord and master! The grounds of this pleasure garden have been inspected thoroughly. You can now enjoy yourself wherever you wish.

DUSHYANTA: Vetravatī, I authorize you to inform the noble chief minister Pishuna that, because I awoke late, it will not be possible for me to take the seat of justice now. The honourable minister should submit a written report on all the cases of our citizens that he has examined today.

VETRAVATĪ: As you command, master.

Exit VETRAVATĪ.

DUSHYANTA: Vātāyana, you, too, should go about your business.

VĀTĀYANA: As you command, master.

Exit VĀTĀYANA.

MĀḌHAVYA: You have driven away the pesky flies! Now you should engage your heart and mind with the pleasures of this garden, which is neither too warm nor too cool at this time of day, and hence beautiful.

DUSHYANTA: My dear friend! It is so true, what is said about misfortune—'The moment they find an opening, calamities stick together and come rushing in.' So:

On one side, my mind is free
Of the delusion that damaged
My love for the daughter of the sage—
But, on the other side, my friend,
The god of love, so keen to strike,
Has strung an arrow
Of spring's mango blossoms on his bow. [133]

MĀḌHAVYA: Hold it right there! No worries—I will use my stick to whack this sickness of love out of existence! (*He raises his stick, intending to hit the budding twigs on the nearest mango tree.*)

DUSHYANTA (*smiling*): Oh, let it be. I have witnessed your feats of strength, your divine brilliance. My dear friend, shall we sit down here, so that I can keep my eyes engaged with these images of vines and tendrils which, in part, make up a simulacrum of Shakuntalā?

MĀḌHAVYA: A short while ago, in your instruction to Chaturikā, the attendant at hand, you said: 'I am going to spend this time in the canopy of fragrant flowering vines. Bring my drawing board there, with the picture of the noble Shakuntalā that I painted with my own hands.'

DUSHYANTA: The canopy is the kind of place that keeps my heart engaged. So please lead me there.

MĀḌHAVYA: This way, sir, come this way.

Māḍhavya and Dushyanta mime a short transition, with Sānumatī following.

This canopy of fragrant flowering vines, with seats of carved stone inlaid with gems, is decorated with bouquets of blossoms. It is a very welcoming place, so please enter and sit down. (*They both do so.*)

SĀNUMATĪ: I shall stand behind the vines and look at the painting of Shakuntalā, and then I shall go back and tell her about the many forms of her husband's love for her. (*She positions herself to observe.*)

DUSHYANTA: Dear friend, I can now recall the whole sequence of earlier events involving Shakuntalā. I related the events to you when they occurred. But you were not with me when I abandoned her. Between then and now, you have not referred to her at all. Like me, did you, too, forget her?

MĀḌHAVYA: I did not forget. But when you narrated everything at the hunting camp, you said at the end that it was all untrue, just a joke. Dim-witted that I am, I accepted your statement. Or else fate, indeed, is powerful.

SĀNUMATĪ: So that is what it is.

DUSHYANTA (*in sudden, intense recollection*): Save me, my friend!

MĀḌHAVYA: Hey—what is this? You should not do this—it is most inappropriate. Real men do not give in to grief. A mountain does not move even in a tempest.

DUSHYANTA: My friend, I am completely devastated whenever I remember my love's condition when I abandoned her for no reason.

When I rejected her at the pavilion of the fire sacrifice,
She wanted to follow her companions and walk out,
But she came to a halt when Shāraṅgarava,
Her father's disciple and surrogate,
Shouted at the top of his voice, 'Stop right there!'
With eyes soiled, streaming with tears,
She shot another look at me—cruel me—
Which still burns through, like a poisoned
arrow. [134]

SĀNUMATĪ: Ah—this is his full acknowledgement of responsibility for his actions. I am very pleased with his remorse.

MĀḌHAVYA: In my considered opinion, some minion of the heavens carried away noble Shakuntalā.

DUSHYANTA: Who but a celestial would dare to touch her—she who thinks of her husband as her god? I have heard that Menakā, the *apsarā*, is certainly the one who gave life to dear Shakuntalā. In my heart of hearts, I feel that Menakā's assistants carried her away.

SĀNUMATĪ: What is truly surprising is not the king's memory but his amnesia.

MĀḌHAVYA: If it is as you say, then Menakā will make sure that you reunite with your wife at the right moment.

DUSHYANTA: How so?

MĀḌHAVYA: It is certain that no parent wishes to see a daughter suffering in separation from her husband.

DUSHYANTA: My friend!

Was that first union with her a dream,
Or was it a grand illusion,
Or was it just a delusion of my mind,
Or was it the diminished fruit
Of my meagre good deeds?
All of it is gone, never to return—
The hope and desire in my mind
Are like riverbanks levelled by floods. [135]

MĀḌHAVYA: Do not say that. This ring is proof positive that unions driven by necessity occur unexpectedly.

DUSHYANTA (*looking at the ring*): Oh, even this ring that fell from Shakuntalā 's hand, unattainable now, has become an object of mourning.

O virtuous ring,
From the outcome of your actions,

It seems that your moral merit
Is as low as mine,
For you won a place on her hand,
Beautiful with its red fingernails—
And yet fell off. [136]

SĀNUMATĪ: If the ring had fallen into someone else's hands, then it would have truly become an object of mourning.

MĀḌHAVYA: Tell me, my friend, what was your intention in putting this ring, inscribed with your name, on her finger?

SĀNUMATĪ: He is driven by the same curiosity as I am.

DUSHYANTA: Listen, as I was leaving for the capital, my love asked me with tearful eyes: 'When will my noble husband send a message from the city?'

MĀḌHAVYA: What happened then?

DUSHYANTA: Placing my ring on her finger, I said,

'My love, count one letter of my name
Inscribed on this ring
For each day that I am gone—
By the time you have counted
The letters and the days,
The messenger I send to welcome you
To the inner chambers of my palace
Will be at your side.' [137]

And that was one task that my cruel heart, in its delusional state, never finished.

SĀNUMATĪ: Fate, for sure, ruined this lovely sequence!

MĀḌHAVYA: How did this ring find its way into the stomach of the red carp cut open by that fisherman?

DUSHYANTA: While Shakuntalā was bathing at goddess Shachi's shrine, in the sanctuary of lakes at Indra's Ford, the ring slipped from her finger and fell into the holy waters.

MĀḌHAVYA: That is it!

SĀNUMATĪ: So that is why this royal sage was afraid of breaking the law, when he could not ascertain his marriage to Shakuntalā. Is this not the reason why this kind of secretive love requires a token of recognition?

DUSHYANTA: All right—then let me reproach this ring.

MĀḌHAVYA (*to himself*): He has taken the road travelled by lunatics!

DUSHYANTA (*gazing at the ring in his hand*): You ring!

What made you fall
From her hand
And sink in the water,
When her hand has such soft
And lovely fingers?

Alternatively—

Things that are insentient
Are unaware of goodness,
And cannot tell right from wrong.
But how could I, a sentient being,
Reject my love? [138]

MĀḌHAVYA (*to himself*): I am starving—will my own pangs of hunger devour me?

DUSHYANTA: My love, please show yourself to this man, whose heart is hot with remorse for rejecting you for no reason at all.

[VI.iv]

Enter CHATURIKĀ, *an attendant, parting the curtain backstage, and positioning herself to display a drawing board in her hands, with a painting mounted on it.*

CHATURIKĀ: Here is the painted queen.

MĀḌHAVYA: Excellent, my friend! What makes the representation of emotions in this picture so beautiful is the arrangement of the body and its parts. My gaze cannot stand still—it is slipping and sliding from one well-developed part to another, from breast and hip and torso to navel and below.

SĀNUMATĪ: Oh, my! This is the king's superb skill in painting. I feel as though my friend Shakuntalā were standing right here before me.

DUSHYANTA:

I correct and improve
What is flawed in the painting,
But the lines can capture
Only some of Shakuntalā's beauty. [139]

SĀNUMATĪ: The king's words are shaped by his modesty and his love, which now has the gravity of remorse.

MĀḌHAVYA: My friend, three women have become visible to me in the painting! All of them are beautiful and worthy of display. Which of them is Shakuntalā?

SĀNUMATĪ: It is evident that this artless, short-sighted buffoon is unacquainted with beauty of this kind.

DUSHYANTA: Which one is she, in your inference?

MĀḌHAVYA: To my mind, Shakuntalā is the one portrayed with her hair tied in a bun, the flower in her hair drooping as her hair comes loose, her face beaded finely with fresh perspiration, one arm held in the pose of watering a plant—the one who looks a little tired from her exertion, and stands in the rear of a mango tree sprouting tender new leaves nurtured by the irrigation. The other two girls are her friends.

DUSHYANTA: You are very skilful in your observation. This picture also carries the physical marks of my feelings:

The stains left behind
By my sweating fingertips
Wherever they rested
On the edges of the painting
Are perceptible to the eye—
And that blot in the paint
Shows where my teardrop fell
Straight on the cheek
Of the painted Shakuntalā. [140]

Chaturikā, this product of my pastime, which keeps my mind amused, is only half done. Go, bring me my brushes and paints.

CHATURIKĀ: Noble Māḍhavya, please hold the drawing board while I fetch the painting materials.

DUSHYANTA: I will hold it myself. (*He does so.*)

Exit CHATURIKĀ.

(*He then resumes, with a sigh*):

Earlier, I gave up the Shakuntalā who stood
before my eyes,

And now I give credence to her simulacrum
    in a painting—
I have become a man, my friend, who walks away
From the abundant waters of a river in his path,
In order to chase the waters of a mirage. [141]

MĀḌHAVYA (*to himself*): His highness has fled from a river and jumped into an illusion! (*Aloud.*) My friend, what remains to be represented in this painting?

SĀNUMATĪ: He probably wants to depict Shakuntalā's favourite haunts.

DUSHYANTA: Listen—

I have to paint the bank of the River Mālinī,
Where pairs of happy swans sit in the sand;
Across the river, I have to paint
The foothills of the sacred snow mountains,
Where herds of deer are settled, content and unafraid;
I have to paint the tree, and the branches of the tree,
Where bark garments are hung out to dry,
And under which a doe, lovingly,
Rubs her left eyelid on a black buck's horn. [142]

MĀḌHAVYA (*to himself*): I suspect that the king is going to fill this picture with a gaggle of ascetics with long beards and longer dreadlocks.

DUSHYANTA: And another thing, my friend—I still have to paint Shakuntalā's embellishments.

MĀḌHAVYA: What exactly are those?

SĀNUMATĪ: They will be in accordance with her life in the forest, her youthfulness, and her boldness.

DUSHYANTA:

I have not yet painted her earrings—
The winter flowers, threaded with lotus filaments,
Dangling from her earlobes to her cheeks.
I have not yet portrayed the necklace
That rests between her breasts—
Fashioned with lotus stalks that glow
As mildly as the rays of the full winter moon. [143]

MĀḌHAVYA: But why is she standing behind the tree as though she were frightened, half covering her face with the out-turned palm of one hand, her fingers fanned like lovely blood-red lotus petals? (*He scrutinizes the painting at close range.*) Oh—this lowlife—this black bee—this thief of nectar—is attacking her face!

DUSHYANTA: Then stop this insolent rogue—drive him away!

MĀḌHAVYA: You have the power over rogues and scoundrels, so only you can do so.

DUSHYANTA: All right, I will do it. O favourite guest of flowering vines! Why are you giving yourself so much trouble by buzzing around Shakuntalā's face?

Perched on a flower here,
This queen bee is full of thirst;
But she is so enamoured of you
That she does not sip its nectar—
For she is waiting for you to join her first. [144]

SĀNUMATĪ: This bee has been restrained in a very polite and law-abiding fashion.

MĀḌHAVYA: Even when restrained, this species of black bee remains antisocial in its ways.

DUSHYANTA: You buzzing bee, why are you not obeying my orders? Then hear me now!

You should know that her lip is fresh, untouched,
Like a delicious bud on a young tree
That has never been distressed;
You should know that I have tasted it, savoured it,
With great tenderness, in a festival of love—
If you so much as touch my love's red lip,
Then I will put you away in a prison
    of lotus stalks. [145]

MĀḌHAVYA: How will the bee not be terrified by the prospect of such harsh punishment? (*Then laughing, to himself.*) He has gone crazy. And, in his company, I have gone crazy, too. (*Aloud.*) My friend, this is just a picture!

DUSHYANTA: What—just a picture?

SĀNUMATĪ: Thanks to the jester, I have now been able to understand what really happened, what it means. Then what can I say about the king, who is actually experiencing things exactly as he has painted them?

DUSHYANTA: My friend, why have you done such a terrible thing?

Here I was, experiencing the happiness
Of seeing my love standing before me,
A witness whose heart was fully lost in her—
And then you, with your reminder,
Changed her back into a picture. [146]

He weeps silently.

SĀNUMATĪ: This trajectory of separation, which creates a conflict between the king's earlier state and his current condition, is truly extraordinary.

DUSHYANTA: Dear friend, why am I experiencing such agony without respite?

My sleeplessness at night
Prevents me from dreaming
Of my union with her—
And my tears by day
Prevent me from seeing
Even my painted Shakuntalā. [147]

SĀNUMATĪ: You have now completely dispelled the suffering you caused with your rejection.

Enter CHATURIKĀ, *excited and out of breath.*

CHATURIKĀ: Victory, victory, master! I was returning with your box of paints, when—

DUSHYANTA: When what?

CHATURIKĀ: —when chief queen Vasumatī, who was with her maid Taralikā, snatched it from my hands, saying, 'I will give it personally to his majesty.'

MĀḌHAVYA: You escaped—how fortunate!

CHATURIKĀ: One end of the queen's wrap got caught in the low branch of a tree and, while Taralikā was busy freeing it, I ran for my life.

DUSHYANTA: My friend, queen Vasumatī is on her way here, and she is a very proud and haughty woman. Please hide this picture of Shakuntalā—and protect it.

MĀḌHAVYA: You should really say, 'And protect yourself!' (*He takes the drawing board and rises.*) If you manage to survive the deadly poison of the women's chambers, then please look for me in the Palace of the Clouds.

Exit MĀḌHAVYA *with the painting, in haste.*

SĀNUMATĪ: The king now has a strong attachment of the heart to Shakuntalā, and his bond of love with queen Vasumatī has grown weak, but he still treats his old relationship with honour and respect.

[VI.v]

[*A room in the palace.*] *Enter* VETRAVATĪ, *document in hand.*

VETRAVATĪ: Victory to you, lord and master.

DUSHYANTA: Vetravatī, you did not see the chief queen on the way here, did you?

VETRAVATĪ: What else? But she saw the document in my hand, and turned back.

DUSHYANTA: The queen understands the priority of the kingdom's business, and refrains from interfering in my official work.

VETRAVATĪ: Lord, the honourable minister Pishuna has sent a request: 'May his majesty please personally review my written report on the important matter of just one citizen, concerning the full assessment of his estate, which took an inordinate amount of time and which I have audited thoroughly.'

DUSHYANTA: Give me the report, let me look at it.

VETRAVATĪ *hands him the document.*

(*He mimes reading the report.*) What is at issue here? Dhanamitra, a sea-merchant who plied a fleet of trading vessels, has perished in a shipwreck. He seems to have been celibate and childless, without a son to inherit his wealth. The honourable minister notes, 'His entire fortune from maritime trade should therefore be annexed to the royal treasury.' Childlessness is truly painful and harrowing. A man in possession of great wealth will surely have many wives. An inquiry should be conducted—it is possible that one of his wives is pregnant.

VETRAVATĪ: Your majesty, people have heard that the daughter of an eminent merchant of Ayodhya was his legitimate wife. She must have recently conceived a child, because she has just publicly performed the canonical ritual to ensure the birth of a son.

DUSHYANTA: Then the unborn son in her womb is the rightful heir to his father's fortune. Please go and communicate this decision to the honourable minister.

VETRAVATĪ: As you command, sir. (*She starts to leave.*)

DUSHYANTA: Wait—come here.

VETRAVATĪ: Here I am.

DUSHYANTA: But how do we know whether it is the dead man's child or not?

So here is a royal proclamation:
If any subjects of the kingdom
Lose a near and dear one
Without a lawful inheritor,
Then Dushyanta will serve as a surrogate,
To help preserve their inheritance—
Except for those in illicit relationships. [148]

VETRAVATĪ: This is what will be proclaimed. [*She exits briefly and re-enters, but mimes a longer passage of time.*] Like timely rain, the king's proclamation has been greeted with cheers.

DUSHYANTA (*with a long and mournful sigh*): The sea-merchant's story shows how a family without a son is unhoused, and loses its wealth to a stranger on the death of its last male. Like earth planted with untimely seed, this will be the condition of the Puru dynasty, too, after me.

VETRAVATĪ: May such evil perish!

DUSHYANTA: Curses on a man like me who disdained and dishonoured good fortune when it came to him unasked.

SĀNUMATĪ: I am sure that he has cursed himself while keeping my friend Shakuntalā in mind.

DUSHYANTA:

I abandoned Shakuntalā—my wife by law,
And the fame and honour of my dynasty—
Even though she carried my seed in her,
Like earth planted with timely seed
That yields an abundant harvest of fruit. [149]

SĀNUMATĪ: But your dynasty's line of succession will not be disrupted now.

CHATURIKĀ (*aside, to Vetravatī*): Hey, this sea-merchant's story has doubled his majesty's grief. Go and get noble Māḍhavya from the Palace of the Clouds to comfort him.

VETRAVATĪ: You are right.

Exit VETRAVATĪ.

DUSHYANTA [*in deeper despair*]: Oh, it is grievous—the forefathers of the dynasty are intent on the uncertainty of my legacy. Why?

It is grievous because the ancients drink
The ritual water that I offer them,
Even though their tears contaminate it
As they ponder anxiously
On who in this clan, after me,
Will sacrifice the food they need for sustenance—
Because I do not have a son. [150]

He faints and becomes comatose.

CHATURIKĀ (*staring at him in fright*): Be strong, master, be strong!

SĀNUMATĪ: Terrible—terrible! Even though he has a son, the light of his life, he is experiencing the blight of darkness, because he does not know. I will tell him the truth right now and bring him happiness! But, no—the gods will arrange something of the kind very soon, as I heard lord Indra's mother, Aditi, say while comforting Shakuntalā. The gods are eager for their portions of sacrificial offerings, and they will enable the husband to welcome his lawful wife with honour. It is therefore not fit for me to delay my departure from here any longer. Let me use the time to comfort my dear friend in the celestial realm with news of these events.

Exit SĀNUMATĪ *by the skyway, turning briefly in dance-like movements before she boards the skycraft.*

[VI.vi]

VOICE BACKSTAGE [MĀḌHAVYA, *in the distance*]: O save this brahmin!

DUSHYANTA (*recovering consciousness and listening alertly*): Oh! That sounds like Māḍhavya's voice in a pitiful condition. Hey, is anybody here?

Enter VETRAVATĪ, *agitated, rushing in.*

VETRAVATĪ (*fearfully*): Save him, master, save your friend, who is in great danger.

DUSHYANTA: Who has overpowered the poor man?

VETRAVATĪ: Some invisible creature seems to have attacked him and hauled him up to the roof of the Palace of the Clouds.

DUSHYANTA (*rising*): This should not be happening. Do demons attack even my palace buildings? Or maybe it can happen.

When it is impossible for a man
To understand his own mistakes
In his daily round of frenzy and negligence,
Then how can it be possible for him
To understand the separate path of action
Each and every creature of the realm
Chooses to follow independently? [151]

VOICE BACKSTAGE [MĀḌHAVYA]: Save me, my friend, save me!

DUSHYANTA (*shouting with urgency, as he mimes breaking into a run*): Do not be afraid, my friend, do not be afraid!

VOICE BACKSTAGE [MĀḌHAVYA]: Save me, my friend! How can I not be terrified? Someone I cannot see is twisting my neck, and is bent on breaking me into three pieces, like a stalk of sugarcane.

[*Dushyanta mimes sprinting to the Palace of the Clouds, with Vetravatī and Chaturikā running behind him.*]

DUSHYANTA (*shouting as he arrives at the building, looking all around him*): Bring me my bow!

Enter the Greek women of the king's BODYGUARD, *sprinting to catch up with him. The leader carries Dushyanta's bow, with an arrow strung on it.*

LEADER *of the* BODYGUARD: Here is your bow, master, ready with its leather guard to protect your hand.

Dushyanta takes the bow and arrow. [*Then a new voice speaks from the roof of the palace building.*]

VOICE BACKSTAGE [MĀTALI, *addressing Māḍhavya*]:

I am like a tiger eager to drink
Fresh blood from your neck,
And I am beating you up
As you thrash about like an animal.
Dushyanta, who takes up his bow
To drive away the fears of folks in terror—
If he can save you now, then let him save you! [152]

DUSHYANTA (*outraged and furious*): Is he targeting me with his words? You demon! You wait—you will not survive this. (*He readies his bow.*) Vetravatī, lead the way to the stairs!

VETRAVATĪ: This way, lord, come this way.

Everybody mimes rushing up the stairs.

DUSHYANTA (*arriving on the roof and looking all around*): There is no one here—no one at all.

VOICE BACKSTAGE [MĀḌHAVYA]:

Help! Help! I am looking at you. Can you not see me? Like a mouse caught by a cat, I have given up all hope!

DUSHYANTA: O you, whoever you are, so proud of your knowledge of invisibility, my arrow will detect you. Strung on my bow,

This arrow will kill you,
Because you deserve to die,
But, in the same move,
It will save this brahmin's life—
The way a swan, given
A mixture of water and milk,
Will ingest the milk but not the water. [153]

(*He raises his bow, ready to shoot.*)

Enter MĀTALI *suddenly, letting go of* MĀḌHAVYA *and shedding the invisibility that has concealed both of them.*

MĀTALI: Your majesty!

Lord Indra has made the anti-gods
The targets of your arrows—
Train your bow on them.
Good men do not aim
Harsh arrows at the class of friends—
They use their eyes to send
Looks of love and grace. [154]

DUSHYANTA (*shaking in bewilderment, fumbling to withdraw his arrow*): Oh, Mātali—it is you, lord Indra's charioteer! Welcome!

Enter MĀḌHAVYA, *still recovering from his ordeal.*

MĀḌHAVYA: His majesty is happily welcoming the very man who tortured me like an animal to be sacrificed.

MĀTALI (*smiling*): Abiding king, Indra has a task for you—listen to why he has sent me.

DUSHYANTA: I am attentive.

MĀTALI: You are. There is a gang of anti-gods in the celestial realm, who call themselves the Invincibles—they are the sons of the demon named Death Ring, a monster with a hundred hands.

DUSHYANTA: Yes. I have heard of them earlier from sage Nārada.

MĀTALI:

It is certain that it is impossible
For your friend Indra to defeat this gang.
It is the opinion of the gods
That you are the only one
Who can slaughter them on the battlefield.
The moon is able to dispel
The darkness of the night,
Which the sun, with his seven stallions,
Does not succeed in driving away. [155]

Since you have already taken up your arms, please board Indra's chariot, and ride to victory.

[*He gestures towards the skycraft, now a celestial chariot drawn by Indra's stallions, which has reappeared on the skyway and descends to the stage.*]

DUSHYANTA: I am deeply gratified by the honour of Indra's invitation. All right—but why did you conduct yourself like this with Māḍhavya?

MĀTALI: Let me tell you about that, too. I saw you, abiding king, disabled by the torment in your mind from an unknown cause. I did what I did in order to arouse your anger in response to your condition. For—

When its kindling is stirred,
A fire flares and burns more brightly.
When it is prodded and provoked,
A cobra hisses and rears its hood.
When he is truly shaken up, a man often finds
The strength he needs within himself. [156]

DUSHYANTA (*aside, to Māḍhavya*): My friend, the orders of Indra, the highest of the gods, cannot be disobeyed. Please convey the facts of the situation to the honourable chief minister Pishuna, and say on my behalf:

'Until I return, your intellect
Has to serve and protect
My subjects on its own.
My bow, strung for battle,
Is now fully engaged
In a different kind of action.' [157]

MĀḌHAVYA: As you command, sir.

MĀTALI: Abiding king, please board Indra's chariot.

Exit DUSHYANTA, *who mimes climbing into the craft, which departs by the skyway, with* MĀTALI *at the reins. Exit* MĀḌHAVYA, VETRAVATĪ, CHATURIKĀ, *and the* BODYGUARD *separately.*

End of Act VI

Act VII

[VII.i]

Enter MĀTALI *and* DUSHYANTA *by the skyway, riding on Indra's chariot.*

DUSHYANTA: Mātali, even though I carried out Indra's orders successfully, I feel that I did not deserve the honour that he conferred on me.

MĀTALI (*smiling*): Abiding king, I believe that both of you were left dissatisfied.

For your part, you think that your deeds
    were lightweight
Compared to the weighty honour that Indra
    conferred on you;
For his part, Indra was astounded by your deeds,
And thinks that the honour is incommensurate. [158]

DUSHYANTA: Please do not say that. The honour that I received at my departure was far beyond anything I could have wished for, because he made me share his divine throne in the presence of the other gods, and—

He took the garland of celestial coral flowers
    on his chest,

Smeared with yellow sandalwood paste,
    and placed it round my neck;
He smiled as he watched his son, Jayanta,
    watching enviously,
Longing for the garland in his heart of hearts,
    standing next to us. [159]

MĀTALI: Is there anything that you cannot claim from the king of the gods? Look—

Indra's heaven is a paradise of pleasure,
And two things, only, have ever liberated it
From the demons who are the thorns in its flesh:
Long ago, the smooth claws of Vishṇu's avatar,
Half-lion, half-man—and now your arrows,
Just as smooth at the knots of their joints. [160]

DUSHYANTA: On this very subject, Indra's power deserves to be praised.

Think even of the success
Of servants who succeed
With the tasks assigned to them
As a gift of their masters' glory—
Could the dawn, the sun's charioteer,
Have become the destroyer of darkness
If the sun had never placed him
At the chariot's helm? [161]

MĀTALI: These words suit you well. (*After they have travelled some distance.*) Abiding king, observe how good the fate of your fame has been—your renown has reached the realm of the heavens here.

Groups of celestial scribes
Have reflected on your deeds,

And are writing them down
In verses packed with meaning
And worthy of being sung,
On clouds like sheets of bark
From the wish-granting tree,
Inscribing the letters and words
In the brilliant cosmetic colours
Left over when their women
Have finished adorning themselves. [162]

DUSHYANTA: While we were ascending to the celestial realm earlier, I was looking forward eagerly to my battle with the demons, and did not pay attention to the highway to heaven. Tell me, on which air-current are we travelling?

MĀTALI:

This is the path of the wind
That is called the Abundant Flow.
It carries the great river of the sky
Located in the blue,
It drives the constellations,
It absorbs the congregation of sunrays—
It remains devoid of darkness
Because of Vishṇu's second stride
In his incarnation as a dwarf,
Who measured out its span
From earth to heaven. [163]

DUSHYANTA: That is why my inner self, like my outer limbs, is full of joy. (*He looks over various parts of the chariot.*) We have descended along the path of the clouds.

MĀTALI: How did you arrive at this inference?

DUSHYANTA:

> With pied cuckoos in flight
> Passing between the spokes of its wheels
> And with its stallions illuminated
> By flashes of lightning,
> Your chariot tells me
> That we are travelling
> Just above the level of the clouds
> Saturated with moisture,
> Which keeps the rims of its wheels
> Wet with drops of condensation. [164]

MĀTALI: Abiding king, in a few moments we will arrive in the land of your sovereign rule.

DUSHYANTA (*looking down*): In our descent at high speed, the world of human beings is a truly amazing sight. For—

> The flat ground remains farther away
> As the peaks of mountains zoom towards us;
> Trees cease to be indistinguishable in a mass of green
> As their branches become distinct to our sight;
> Fine lines in the distance, without a trace of water,
> Now acquire breadth and visibility, and become rivers.
> Look, the earth seems to move closer and closer,
> As though someone were heaving it up
> towards me. [165]

MĀTALI: Your observation is exact. (*He gazes in awe and wonder.*) Oh, the earth's beauty is sublime!

DUSHYANTA: Mātali, what is this enormous mountain that I see stretching from the eastern to the western seas, with molten gold streaming down its sides, towering like a wall of clouds at sunset?

MĀTALI: Abiding king, this is Mount Meru, the home of the demigods who are half-human, half-horse, who serve the god of wealth but practise austerities to perfection. [It is the axis of the world, the axis of the continents, the peak around which all the planets revolve.] Look—

Sage Kashyapa, father and lord
Of gods and demons, progenitor of species,
A son of the sage Marīchi, himself the son
Of the creator who created himself,
Sits on Mount Meru with his wife, Aditi,
Practising his spiritual discipline. [166]

DUSHYANTA: Then it would not be right to forego this auspicious opportunity to pay homage to sage Kashyapa and his wife Aditi. I wish to express my reverence for the noble sage with a ritual circumambulation, before proceeding further.

MĀTALI: That is an excellent idea!

They mime descending to Mount Meru.

DUSHYANTA (*in astonishment*):

We did not touch earth as we touched down,
And so the rims of the chariot wheels
Did not squeal and grind, and raised no clouds
of dust to see.
Since you did not have to pull the reins
To slow the chariot, there were no jolts—
It landed on the ground, but did not seem
to land. [167]

MĀTALI: This is the only difference between Indra's chariot and yours.

DUSHYANTA: Where is the ashram of sage Kashyapa?

MĀTALI (*gesturing with his hand*):

The ashram stands just beyond that place
Where an extreme ascetic is buried
Up to his waist in an anthill's anterior,
Rooted to the spot like the stump of a tree—
Whose dreadlocks are piled high on his head
And infested with the nests of birds,
Whose neck and throat are pricked painfully
By the cluster of thorns on a garland of vines,
Who wears a sloughed snakeskin on his chest
And stands staring straight at the sun. [168]

DUSHYANTA: As we pass, I shall pay my respects to this ascetic who mortifies himself.

MĀTALI (*reining in the stallions*): We have now entered sage Kashyapa's ashram, with its celestial coral trees that his wife Aditi cultivates.

DUSHYANTA: This is a place of greater peace and detachment than Indra's heaven. It is as though I have entered a lake filled with the waters of immortality.

MĀTALI (*bringing the chariot to a halt*): Abiding king, please alight.

DUSHYANTA (*stepping off the chariot*): What will you do now?

MĀTALI: I have secured the chariot. I, too, am getting off. (*He does so.*) You may come this way. (*He turns around.*) You may view the sacred groves of various sages.

DUSHYANTA: Actually, I am observing them with great wonder.

Even in a forest full of celestial trees
Ready to fulfil every wish they have,
These ascetics live only on the air they breathe,
And perform the rituals essential for life;
They take their holy baths in water that has turned
A lustrous yellow with the pollen of golden lotuses;
They meditate while sitting on carved stone slabs
Studded with gems; they live in the proximity
Of celestial women, but choose to deny their senses.
They live among the objects of spiritual discipline
That crowds of other ascetics wish to win,
And yet they practise the strictest forms
of austerity. [169]

MĀTALI: The desires of great souls are always aimed at heaven. (*He walks about, then calls out.*) O ancient Shāklya! What is sage Kashyapa doing at the moment? What did you say? That he is speaking to a group of great sages' women, in response to a question raised by Aditi about the duties of devoted wives?

DUSHYANTA (*listening intently*): His theme is such that we should wait for a more suitable time to meet him.

MĀTALI (*looking at Dushyanta*): Please sit and rest under this *ashoka* tree—in the meantime, I shall look for an opportune moment to inform sage Kashyapa, Indra's father, that you have arrived.

DUSHYANTA: Whatever you think is appropriate. (*He sits down.*)

MĀTALI: Abiding king, let me go and get this done.

Exit MĀTALI.

DUSHYANTA (*perceiving an omen*):

> O my arm, why do you twitch, as a good omen,
> When I have no hope of fulfilling
> my heart's desire here?
> For, good fortune, once shunned, can only
> be found again
> With great hardship or in great pain. [170]

[VII.ii]

VOICE BACKSTAGE [SUVRATĀ]: Control yourself—do not be so unruly! Why is he back to his usual self?

DUSHYANTA (*listening intently*): This is not a place for unruliness. Who needs to be restrained? (*He looks in the direction of the voice and reacts with surprise.*) Oh—who is this child with an extraordinary physique, being led by two ascetic women?

> Who is this boy, who is dragging along
> A reluctant lion cub, forcing it to play with him—
> A cub that he has interrupted
> While feeding at its mother's teats,
> Which are left half-full in the middle of the feed—
> The fur at whose neck is askew
> With all the push and pull of rough play? [171]

Enter the boy SARVADAMANA, *engaged as described, accompanied by* SUVRATĀ *and a* SECOND ASCETIC WOMAN.

SARVADAMANA: Open your mouth, lion! I am going to count your teeth.

SUVRATĀ: You little bully! Why do you keep tormenting these animals, who are like our children? The sages are right to call you Sarvadamana—'He Tames Everybody'.

DUSHYANTA: Why is my heart drawn to this boy, as though he were my own child? It is clear that childlessness makes me feel a father's tenderness.

SECOND WOMAN: The lioness will pounce on you if you do not let go of her baby.

SARVADAMANA (*grinning*): Ooooh—I am terrified! (*He thrusts out his lower lip impudently.*)

DUSHYANTA:

This boy carries the seed
Of great future glory—
He seems to me like a spark
Just waiting for a mass of firewood
To start a blaze. [172]

SUVRATĀ: Dear child, please let this cub go! I will give you another toy.

SARVADAMANA: Where is it? Give it to me! (*He thrusts out his hand.*)

DUSHYANTA (*looking at the boy's hand*): Why does he also bear the marks of a king who will turn the wheel of law and power? For—

His hand, stretched out with the hope
Of seizing the object of his greed,
Has fingers interlinked by a natal web—
It looks as lovely as a lotus, single and unique,
The gaps between whose petals are invisible
As it opens in the soft red flush
    of a fresh new dawn. [173]

SECOND WOMAN: Suvratā, he cannot be stopped with just the promise of a toy. You go. There is a clay peacock in my hut, painted in bright colours, belonging to sage Mārkaṇḍeya's son. Bring it here and give it to him.

SUVRATĀ: Fine.

Exit SUVRATĀ.

SARVADAMANA: I will play with the cub until then. (*He looks at the second woman and laughs.*)

DUSHYANTA: I find this mischievous boy truly heart-warming.

Only fortunate fathers are muddied by
The mud on the limbs of their sons—
Who show the new buds of their teeth
When they burst into laughter without reason,
Who make themselves adorable
With their babble of baby talk, who assert
Their right to climb into their fathers' laps. [174]

SECOND WOMAN: He just does not take me into account. (*She looks around.*) Are any of the sages' sons here? (*She notices Dushyanta.*) Noble sir! Please come here. Set the cub free from the torment of being forced to play with this boy.

DUSHYANTA (*approaching, with a smile*): Hey, you son of a sage!

Why are you going against the ashram's ways
With your behaviour,
Harassing this cub in so many ways?
Why are you putting a blemish on your self-control,
And even on the security and happiness
Of every kind of creature,
To which you have been bound since birth—
Like a black baby snake
That sits like a blot on a sandalwood tree? [175]

SECOND WOMAN: Noble sir, he is not a sage's son.

DUSHYANTA: Like his physique, his conduct indicates that he is not. I made that assumption because of the nature of this place. (*As asked, he separates the boy from the cub. Then, finding the boy's hand, he continues, to himself.*)

If every part of me
Finds so much happiness
In contact with this seedling
Of someone else's clan,
Then how much peace and satisfaction
He must bring
To the mind of the fortunate man
From whose body he sprang! [176]

SECOND WOMAN (*looking at Dushyanta and boy together*): Astonishing—it is astonishing!

DUSHYANTA: What, noble woman?

SECOND WOMAN: I am amazed at how much the boy resembles you. I am astonished because he does not know you—and, yet, he does not resist you, and seems to fit with you naturally.

DUSHYANTA (*touching the boy fondly*): If he is not a sage's son, then what clan does he come from?

SECOND WOMAN: The Puru clan.

DUSHYANTA (*to himself*): What? He belongs to my clan! That is why this honourable woman thinks that he resembles me. [*Aloud.*] Puru's descendants maintain a distinctive commitment to family—

In their prime, when they are intent
    on the earth's protection,

They desire to live in palaces with every kind
of pleasure;
But, in their later years, they build homes
in sanctuaries with trees,
With one lawful wife to share a life of austerity. [177]

[Is he the child of one of my ancestors who is here?] But human beings cannot reach this celestial region by their own natural powers.

SECOND WOMAN: That is so, sir. This boy's mother was able to give birth to him in sage Kashyapa's ashram because of her connection with an *apsarā*.

DUSHYANTA (*aside*): Ha! This is the second indicator of hope for me. (*Aloud.*) So who is the famous king whose wife she is?

SECOND WOMAN: Who can even think of pronouncing the name of that man who rejected and abandoned his lawful wife?

DUSHYANTA (*to himself*): This story surely points to me. If only I could ask for the name of the boy's mother! But it is ignoble to ask about someone else's wife.

Enter SUVRATĀ, *with clay peacock in hand.*

SECOND WOMAN: Sarvadamana! Look at how beautiful this *shakunta* is.

SARVADAMANA: *Shakunta*? Where is my mother?

SUVRATĀ *and the* SECOND WOMAN: Because of the similarity between his mother's name and the word *shakunta* for a bird, this mother's darling has confused the two.

SECOND WOMAN: Dear child, I asked you to admire this peacock's beauty.

DUSHYANTA (*to himself*): So is his mother's name 'Shakuntalā'? But two people may have the same name. Is it possible that a mirage with an identical name has turned up now—to derange my mind with false hope?

SARVADAMANA: I love this lovely bird! (*He takes it.*)

SUVRATĀ (*frightened suddenly, as she looks at the boy*): Oh—I do not see the protective amulet on his arm!

DUSHYANTA: No, no, do not panic. While he was wrestling with the cub, the amulet fell off here. (*He bends, intending to pick it up.*)

SUVRATĀ *and the* SECOND WOMAN: Do not pick it up! What—oh—he has picked it up! (*They hold their hands to their breasts and look at each other, wonderstruck.*)

DUSHYANTA: Why did you forbid me?

SUVRATĀ: Listen, O king. This amulet is fashioned from a sacred plant called the Peerless Herb, and it was sage Kashyapa's gift to the boy at his birth ceremony. If it ever falls off, only he or his parents can pick it up—and no one else.

DUSHYANTA: And what if someone else does?

SUVRATĀ: Then it turns into a serpent that bites.

DUSHYANTA: Have you both witnessed its transformation into a serpent?

SUVRATĀ *and the* SECOND WOMAN: Many times.

DUSHYANTA (*to himself, with great joy*): Why should I not celebrate the fulfilment of my heart's desire? (*He embraces the boy.*)

SECOND WOMAN: Suvratā, let us go. Let us deliver this news to Shakuntalā, who is still preoccupied with penances.

Exit SUVRATĀ *and the* SECOND ASCETIC WOMAN.

SARVADAMANA: Let me go. I shall go to my mother.

DUSHYANTA: My son! You can welcome your mother with me.

SARVADAMANA: My father is Dushyanta. Not you.

DUSHYANTA: Your hotheaded dissent is quickly convincing me.

[VII.iii]

Enter SHAKUNTALĀ, *with her hair in a single braid signifying mourning.*

SHAKUNTALĀ: Even when I heard that Sarvadamana's amulet remained untransformed as a stranger picked it up, I did not entertain any hope of my fate being transformed. Nor did I dream, as Sānumatī had said, that such a turn of events would be possible.

DUSHYANTA (*on seeing her*): It is honourable Shakuntalā!

Dressed in threadbare grey garments,
With her face worn out by austerity
And her hair done in a single, mournful braid—
A woman who endures the long separation
That I have inflicted on her severely, without pity,
But whose ways still remain the ways of purity. [178]

SHAKUNTALĀ (*seeing Dushyanta wasted with remorse*): He does not look like my noble husband. Then who is this man who defiles my son with his touch at this moment, even though the boy is protected by a magical amulet?

SARVADAMANA (*drawing close to Shakuntalā*): Mother, I do not know this man—he embraced me and called me his son.

DUSHYANTA: Beloved woman, even my cruelty towards you has connected itself to a favourable outcome, for I see that you have recognized me today.

SHAKUNTALĀ (*to herself*): Be calm, my heart—be calm! This is the end of hatred, and fate is finally kind to me. He really is my noble husband.

DUSHYANTA: My love!

Beloved woman with a beautiful face,
The good fortune that restored
My memory of earlier events
And dispelled the darkness of my delusion
Has now brought you face to face with me,
The way that bright star, Rohiṇī,
Is united with her mate, the moon,
After an occultation. [179]

SHAKUNTALĀ: Victory—to my noble—vic—. (*She chokes with tears before she can finish, and falls silent.*)

DUSHYANTA: Noble Shakuntalā!

Even though your tears
Broke up the word 'victory',
I have really won, because
The twin petals of your lips
May be pale and unadorned,
But I have seen the flower of your face. [180]

SARVADAMANA: Who is he, mother?

SHAKUNTALĀ : Ask your fate, my son!

DUSHYANTA (*falling at Shakuntalā's feet*):

> O woman whose body is beautiful,
> May the agony that my abandonment
> Engendered in your heart be dispelled—
> That was a time when an incomprehensible
> Yet powerful delusion overcame my mind.
> When a person's nature is plunged
> Deep into darkness, that is how it responds
> To objects that may bring great good fortune—
> A blind man will even throw away
> A garland of flowers placed round his neck
> Because he thinks, mistakenly, that it is a snake. [181]

SHAKUNTALĀ: Please rise, noble sir. I am sure that, during those days, some awful deed from my past began to bear fruit and hindered the fruition of good actions, which alienated my noble husband from me, and made him cruel, even though he is kind.

Dushyanta rises to his feet.

So how did he remember this grieving wife?

DUSHYANTA: I will tell you everything after the arrowhead of pain has been extracted from the wound.

> O woman whose body is beautiful,
> Today my first wish is to wipe away
> These teardrops
> Enmeshed in your eyelashes—
> These teardrops
> That I scorned

In my deluded state of mind,
These teardrops
That vexed your lower lip—
I wish to wipe them away
And wipe out
The remorse and regret. [182]

He wipes Shakuntalā's eyes.

SHAKUNTALĀ (*observing the ring, inscribed with Dushyanta's name, on his finger*): Noble sir, this is the ring!

DUSHYANTA: Indeed, the recovery of this ring brought back my memory of earlier events.

SHAKUNTALĀ: This ring did great damage when it was nowhere to be found—just when it was needed to persuade my noble husband.

DUSHYANTA: Please put it on—let the vine wear this flower as an emblem of its union with the season of spring.

SHAKUNTALĀ: I do not believe in this ring. Let my noble husband wear it.

[VII.iv]

Enter MĀTALI.

MĀTALI: Congratulations, abiding king, on your auspicious union with your lawful wife, and on your first view of your son's face!

DUSHYANTA: My heart's deepest desire has tasted its exquisite fruit, Mātali. Indeed, Indra would not know about these events, would he?

MĀTALI (*smiling*): Is there anything that the gods do not know? Please come—sage Kashyapa is ready, you can see him now.

DUSHYANTA: Shakuntalā, please take charge of our son. I wish to present you with me when I see the sage.

SHAKUNTALĀ: I am hesitant because it would be immodest of me to appear before my elders in my noble husband's company.

DUSHYANTA: It is appropriate to do so at fresh beginnings and on festive occasions. Come, come!

They all walk about, miming a transition. Enter sage KASHYAPA *with his wife* ADITI *at his side, both seated formally.*

KASHYAPA (*looking at Dushyanta*): Aditi—

This is the man
Who is the ruler of the earth.
Famous by the name of Dushyanta,
He leads the armies
On the battlefields of Indra's wars.
Your son's sharp-edged thunderbolt,
Reduced to a mere ornament,
Depends on his bow
To accomplish its tasks. [183]

ADITI: One can gauge his power just from his appearance.

MĀTALI: Abiding king, here are the father and the mother of the gods, looking upon you with the love and affection of parents. Please approach them.

DUSHYANTA: Mātali!

This is the divine couple
Whom the ancient poets described
As the source and embodiment

Of twelve kinds of radiance—
This is the divine couple
Who generated Indra,
The lord and master of the three worlds—
This is the divine couple
Whom Vishṇu, the supreme being
Who generated himself,
Chose as the repository
Of his incarnation as a dwarf—
This is that divine couple
Which pairs the son of Marīchi
With the daughter of Daksha,
Each of whom is separated
From Brahmā, the creator,
By a single generation! [184]

MĀTALI: What else?

DUSHYANTA (*approaching Kashyapa and Aditi*): Dushyanta, the humble servant of your son Indra, bows to both of you.

KASHYAPA: My son! Live long. Protect the earth.

ADITI: Son! May you be a warrior without equal.

SHAKUNTALĀ: I worship at your feet, along with my son.

KASHYAPA: Dear daughter!

Your husband is like Indra,
Your son is like Jayanta, Indra's son.
May you become like Shachi, Indra's wife—
No lesser blessing is worthy of you. [185]

ADITI: My child, may you have your husband's fullest love. May your son live long and bring happiness to the families of both his parents. Please seat yourselves.

Everybody sits down, with their faces turned towards Kashyapa.

KASHYAPA (*gesturing towards each, in turn*):

This faithful wife, Shakuntalā,
This son with the best of qualities,
And you yourself, Dushyanta—
By great good fortune,
The three of you are gathered here
Like devotion, wealth, and law. [186]

DUSHYANTA: Great sir, my heart's desire was fulfilled earlier. My blessed opportunity to see you has come afterwards. Your grace, truly, has no harbinger. For—

The flower blossoms first,
The fruit emerges later;
Clouds are formed earlier,
The rain arrives afterwards:
This is the natural order
Of cause and effect.
But your grace acts so swiftly
That it reverses the sequence—
Your rewards reach us
Before your actual blessing. [187]

MĀTALI: This is how the gods confer their grace.

DUSHYANTA: Great sir, I married Shakuntalā, who obeys your commands, in the secret style of the celestials, and after some time had passed, her kinsmen brought her to me, but in my amnesia I rejected and abandoned her, and hence committed a transgression against sage Kaṇva, your direct descendant. Later, when I saw my ring, I recovered my memory, and knew that I had married his daughter earlier. All this seems very strange to me.

The disorder of my mind
Was the kind of disorder one finds
When a man perceives an elephant
Present before him in actuality
But denies that it exists—
And then, once it is gone,
Begins to doubt himself,
And is convinced of its existence
Only when he sees its footprints. [188]

KASHYAPA: My son, do not feel guilty about your transgression. Your mind did not create its delusions on its own. Listen.

DUSHYANTA: I am attentive, sir.

KASHYAPA: As soon as Menakā came to Aditi, accompanied by Shakuntalā, who was evidently distressed by the loss of the ring in the waters at Shachi's shrine, I understood through my power of concentration that you had abandoned this self-disciplined and faithful wife under the influence of Durvāsā's curse, and nothing else. And that the curse would last only until you set your eyes again on the ring.

DUSHYANTA (*with a deep breath*): I am now free of blame.

SHAKUNTALĀ (*to herself*): I am fortunate that my noble husband is not the kind of man to abandon me without reason. I really have no memory of being put under a curse. Or my heart was so empty in the void of separation that I did not know I had been cursed. That is why my friends, Anasūyā and Priyaṁvadā, left me with the message, 'Show your husband the ring.'

KASHYAPA: My dear daughter, your heart's desire has been fulfilled. Do not bear anger or ill-will towards your husband, who walks with you as a companion in morality.

Your husband abandoned you when Durvāsā's curse
Curtailed his memory and turned him into
    a cruel man—
Now that the darkness of his ignorance
    has been dispelled,
You are the only one who will possess power over him.
One cannot see one's true image in a mirror
    that is soiled—
But once the mirror is clean, that image
    is clearly visible. [189]

DUSHYANTA: Honourable sir, what you say is true.

KASHYAPA: Son, have you celebrated this son or not, who is your child by Shakuntalā, whose legitimacy we have affirmed by scripture and ritual?

DUSHYANTA: Indeed, sir, the glory and existence of my dynasty rest on him.

KASHYAPA: Moreover, you should consider him to be the one who is destined to turn the wheel of law and kingdom. Look:

He will be a warrior without equal,
With no surviving enemies,
And he will cross the oceans on a chariot
That moves smoothly and silently,
To conquer the seven continents on earth.
In this forest of asceticism, today,
He is known as Sarvadamana, 'He Tames Everybody',

Because he overpowers every creature with his strength.
In future times, his name will be Bharata—
'The bearer of the earth, the one who sustains
the world'. [190]

DUSHYANTA: Great sir, since you have performed his rites of passage, these are the hopes we have of him.

ADITI: Noble husband, this happy news about the fulfilment of a daughter's deepest desires should be broadcast immediately to her father, sage Kaṇva. Her loving mother, Menakā, is in my service, right here at the ashram.

SHAKUNTALĀ (*to herself*): Honourable Aditi has expressed my wish exactly.

KASHYAPA: Because of his mental powers and spiritual discipline, Kaṇva is already aware of everything.

DUSHYANTA: That explains why the great sage was not enraged with me.

KASHYAPA: Still, we must formally announce this heart-warming news to him.

Enter GĀLAVA, *a disciple of Kashyapa.*

GĀLAVA: Here I am, sir, at your service.

KASHYAPA: Gālava, please go immediately by the skyway and inform the honourable sage Kaṇva on my behalf: 'With the ending of the curse, Dushyanta has recovered his memory and has accepted dear Shakuntalā as a part of himself.'

GĀLAVA: As you command, master.

Exit GĀLAVA.

KASHYAPA: Dear king, you, too, should ride on Indra's chariot with your wife and son, and proceed to your capital.

DUSHYANTA: As you command, sir.

KASHYAPA: My son, what other favour of love can I offer you?

DUSHYANTA: What can be a greater gift of love? If you wish to add something, then let it be this final benediction:

May those who rule the earth
    Strive for the good of the earth.
May those with powerful minds
    Achieve empowerment of mind.
And may that self-created god,
    That dazzling dark-blue god,
Whose power fills the worlds from end to end,
    Bring my rebirths to an end. [191]

Exit KASHYAPA, ADITI, DUSHYANTA, SHAKUNTALĀ, SARVADAMANA, *and* MĀTALI.

End of Act VII

***Here ends the play called* The Recognition of Shakuntalā**

Afterword

PLOT, CHARACTER, AND THE RING IN *SHAKUNTALĀ*

Story and Plotted Action

Classical and post-classical Sanskrit poetics places the kind of work that modern audiences also recognize as a 'play' in two categories at once. On the one hand, it is a verbal composition that is distinguished by its literary qualities, and is to be judged by the norms of imaginative literature as an autonomous art. On the other hand, it is also a performance vehicle, and has to fulfil the practical criteria that determine theatrical success, independent of its literariness. A play is able to maintain its dual identity—as self-sufficient artefact and functional play-script—because it is composed specially as a 'verbal-and-visual poem', which employs the dramatic mode of representation, and vividly visualizes the action latent in its subject matter for enactment on the stage.[1]

In such a perspective, however, a work of verbal-visual poetry can meet the demands of both literariness and performance only if it fuses dramatic and narrative art. A Sanskrit–Prakrit play therefore frames its action with a story that has the capacity to captivate the imaginations of its audience; and its dramatized narrative provides the playwright as well as the performer with the materials, means, and contexts to craft the necessary aesthetic effects in language and in the theatre. It is specifically the kind of story that contains a well-defined primary action centred on a dominant character or protagonist, whose thoughts, feelings, choices, acts, and qualities can be presented effectively in the dramatic mode.[2] In practical terms, this is the mode in which the protagonist interacts with other characters, delivers dialogue and other discourse, acts in ways that can be enacted mimetically and non-mimetically, and participates in situations and events that can be depicted in a moving spectacle.

Sanskrit poetics and dramaturgy give this fusion of drama and narrative a distinctive aesthetic dimension by aligning it with two principles of representation. One is that the story of a play, as fashioned or refashioned in its dramatic structure, should focus on the protagonist's overall 'state of being' or 'encompassing emotional state', and on the more transitory feelings and emotions of its various characters.[3] The other is the principle that the story of a play should represent its protagonist's quest for a particular object or objective, that the quest should be a successful one, and that its inception, evolution, and conclusion should define the play's beginning, middle, and end, and hence serve as its 'thread' of coherence and continuity.[4] These principles together provide a Sanskrit–Prakrit play with its unique foundation: the dramatic action it represents is anchored in a quest-narrative, and its representation itself is anchored in emotion, which reaches its audience in the highly aestheticized and concentrated form of a rasa (Appendix G).

The plot of a play—its specific selection and arrangement of situations and events in a fixed, hierarchical, overarching sequence in poem as well as performance—emerges from this integration of dramatized story and embedded action, quest-narrative and concentrated emotion. The dependence of the plot on these elements is particularly significant in the case of the *nāṭaka*, the most comprehensive of the classical Indian dramatic genres and the closest in theatrical experience to a modern play. Due to its length and thematic scope, a *nāṭaka* has to be based on a story that can sustain dramatic interest on several fronts, can display both emotional depth and emotional range, and unfolds as a whole that is complex and multilayered (Appendix E). In practice, the use of a manifold narrative means that the overall dramatic action has to be plotted on several levels simultaneously, with three kinds of plot or plot elements organized in a hierarchy by structure and function: a principal plot, one or more secondary plots, and several incidents or smaller units plotted at a tertiary level.

The principal plot of a *nāṭaka* is centred on its protagonists, who drive the main part of the action in the text and on the stage with their respective quests for specific objects or objectives. When a play has more than one protagonist—such as a hero and a heroine who are qualitatively on par with each other, and therefore have comparable, if not commensurate, agency—the principal plot has to interrelate their quests and objectives. This kind of plot, which is the most inclusive one constructed for a Sanskrit–Prakrit play, establishes a composite trajectory for the dramatic action as a whole, and hence has internal divisions and movements apart from those introduced by plotting at other levels.[5] In the case of *Shakuntalā*, the principal plot is a composite of Dushyanta and Shakuntalā's respective 'quest-streams'.

As my translation of Vishvanātha's fourteenth-century summary of the basic features of a *nāṭaka* indicates in Appendix E, each protagonist may be surrounded by several secondary characters who are preoccupied with his or her quest and its successful completion. The activities of each such group of characters define a secondary plot, and a play of this kind will have as many secondary plots as it has protagonists. A romantic-heroic *nāṭaka* with a hero and a heroine tracing their own trajectories towards a common goal, for example, will contain at least two distinct secondary plots that continually feed into the composite principal plot.[6] In *Shakuntalā*, the secondary plot that flows into Dushyanta's quest-stream centres on Māḍhavya, with Vetravatī as a key supporting figure; whereas the secondary plot that flows into Shakuntalā's quest-stream centres on Kaṇva, with Anasūyā and Priyaṁvadā as vital supporting characters.

Apart from its principal and secondary plots, a *nāṭaka* also draws on a series of separate, tertiary incidents. Usually smaller in scope and shorter in duration than the discernible episodes that make up the bulk of the main action and its secondary components, these incidents often fill in gaps in the overarching story, introduce unexpected turns of events, add obstacles to or remove them from the protagonists' quests, or maintain the momentum and continuity of the drama locally. Tertiary incidents may involve a protagonist and one or more secondary or tertiary characters, or only a set of characters other than a protagonist; and they may be inserted directly into the principal plot or a secondary plot, or they may serve in an interlude at the beginning of an act.[7]

In *Shakuntalā*, as translated here, Scenes I.iii and V.i, for example, are both tertiary incidents featuring Dushyanta, in the former instance with his Charioteer and Vaikhānasa and the two Disciples (all tertiary characters), and in the latter with Māḍhavya (an onstage secondary character) and Haṁsapadikā (an offstage tertiary character); both these incidents are placed directly in Dushyanta's quest-stream in the principal plot.

Scene VI.i, situated as Part 1 of the Mixed Interlude at the start of Act VI, is a self-enclosed tertiary incident with only tertiary characters, but it dramatizes a singular turning point in the composite main action: the recovery of Dushyanta's ring, and the termination of Durvāsā's curse on the lovers. In contrast, the Mixed Interlude at the beginning of Act IV contains two separate tertiary incidents (IV.i–ii), which feature an offstage protagonist (Shakuntalā), secondary onstage and offstage characters (Anasūyā, Priyaṁvadā, and Durvāsā), and a tertiary character on the stage (the Disciple in IV.ii). Both incidents technically are inserted into Kaṇva's secondary plot, but through it they feed into Shakuntalā's quest-stream in the principal plot, and from there into the composite trajectory of the main action. The most significant tertiary incident in the play is defined by Kashyapa, whose intervention in the main action brings both Dushyanta and Shakuntalā's quests to coordinated and satisfactory conclusions.

Sanskrit poetics and dramaturgy distinguish further between the plotting of the action and its mode of presentation in the verbal text and the theatrical performance. A dramatic work as a whole actually contains more than the story and its dramatization that comprise the play as such, and the playwright and the performer therefore have to distinguish among three categories of material and three modes of presentation. The first of these is the main body of the work—the play itself—which is designed to be acted before an audience; the enactment presents its action directly, in a mode that may be mimetic, stylized (non-mimetic), or a combination of the two; and its overall mode of presentation thus consists of theatrical enactment and spectacle.[8]

However, a dramatic work may also contain some parts that are incorporated into the dramatization, but cannot be presented directly on the stage by means of either acting or visual representation. These parts are usually presented as diegetic components—narration, report, summary, explanation, or exposition—embedded inside the mimetic and stylized enactment of the whole. Thus, an onstage character, or even a voice offstage, for instance, may recount or describe an event that is essential to the story but is kept out of the audience's sight. The mode of presentation of these portions of the play is (indirect) diegesis or diegetic discourse, as distinct from the mode of mimesis and especially (direct) mimetic enactment.[9]

Besides the main mimetic action and its diegetic components, a Sanskrit–Prakrit dramatic work also contains portions that perform a meta-theatrical function outside the play. These portions contain material and discourse that do not belong to the plot, and they may be presented to the audience independently in a mimetic or non-mimetic mode. In the play-script as well as in performance, the meta-theatrical portions frame the play or dramatic body of the work as a whole, in ways that are analogous to the framing of narratives in the dialogic epic poetry of the Rāmāyaṇa (600 BCE–200 CE) and the Mahābhārata (400 BCE–400 CE).[10] The aesthetic function of the meta-theatrical material and discourse surrounding a play is to isolate and identify the main body of the work as an artefact or fiction, to be distinguished from ordinary, non-artefactual reality.

In this sense, the outer, meta-theatrical frame of a Sanskrit–Prakrit play directly addresses a live audience in a physical theatre; establishes the conditions of authorship, genre, production and performance, and reception of the play on the specific occasion of its delivery; and, most important, sets up that performance as a concrete event in the theatre, and the action of the play—as presented on that particular occasion by means of enactment and spectacle in the auditory and visual channels—as an event that occurs only on the stage, and is fully circumscribed by its (artificial) conventions.

The meta-theatrical frame of *Shakuntalā* is constituted by the Invocation and the Prelude placed at the very beginning (I.i–ii), and the final passage delivered on the stage (Verse 191, spoken by Dushyanta). The two opening pieces together comprise the *pūrva-raṅga* or the 'preliminaries to the play', the equivalent roughly of a composite Prologue in modern Euro-American theatre, or, more precisely, of an Induction to a Ben Jonson play in English. The Invocation is delivered in a disembodied voice (conventionally, by the Stage Manager), whereas the Prelude is presented in the mode of mimetic enactment, with an actor and an actress in the present production company playing a fictionalized Stage Manager and an Actress (taken by some interpreters to be the lead actor and actress in the production). The concluding verse of the play (called the *bharata-vākya*) structurally and functionally mirrors the opening Invocation, is delivered by the male protagonist, and closes the meta-theatrical frame, so that the entire dramatic action is contained within the theatre where it is performed, and is not to be confused with everyday life.[11]

Against this analytical backdrop, we can trace the trajectory of the composite principal plot of *Shakuntalā* quite precisely, using a combination of classical Sanskrit concepts and modern theatrical terms. In my own view—as distinct from the common view summarized at the end of Appendix E—the 'seed' of Kālidāsa's play lies in I.iii, in Dushyanta's brief interaction with Vaikhānasa, between the old celibate's entrance in Segment 10 and his exit in Segment 13. This portion of the mimetically presented action defines the initial dramatic situation out of which all the possibilities of the hero's actions—as well as the heroine's—germinate, and it constitutes the play's 'initial thesis'.[12]

Dushyanta's effort to assess the possibilities for himself, to discover and choose an appropriate object that he desires, and to define his quest for it begins in the very next line of Segment 13, and culminates in Verse 19 (I.iv). His sustained effort after that to set his quest on its proper course, to overcome early uncertainties, doubts, and obstacles, and to devise circumspect strategies to attain his goal stretches from Segment 20 (I.v) to Verse 57 (III.iii), the latter defining the point at which he finds his first affirmation of Shakuntalā's reciprocal passion for him. Shakuntalā's mirror quest for Dushyanta and his love as a soulmate emerges in the action's foreground in Segment 54 (III.iii), and culminates in her candid statement in her letter to him, inscribed with her fingernails on a lotus leaf (Verse 61). The movement from Segment 13 onwards constitutes the play's 'first antithesis'.[13]

Once the lovers are face-to-face, with both explicitly acknowledging their mutual infatuation (starting with Verse 62), their interactive efforts move them directly towards a union, which is foreshadowed in Verse 69 and is dramatically confirmed in Shakuntalā's soliloquy in prose at the moment of her exit in Segment 70. In my interpretation, the 'womb' of the principal plot—where the objective or end of the whole dramatic action appears for the first time in an 'embryonic' form—becomes visible in Verse 69 (in the hero's trajectory) and in Segment 70 (in the heroine's intertwined trajectory). The first antithesis ends with Segment 68, and Segments 69 and 70 together mark the location of the work's 'first synthesis'.[14]

But this is followed immediately by our first glimpse of the long 'second antithesis' of the dramatic action as a whole. The voice backstage that I attribute to Anasūyā—but which may also be interpreted plausibly as a 'voice in the sky' that intervenes almost mystically—prefigures the lovers' descent into the 'darkness' of separation, discord, and derangement with its chilling sentence, 'Night has fallen' (Segment 70). The second antithesis then formally begins at the top of Act IV—which is how Vishvanātha construes the composite principal plot of *Shakuntalā* in his *Sāhitya-darpaṇa* in 1384. This exceptionally long antithesis responds to the first synthesis in the play's 'womb', and extends all the way to the end of Act VI, or, in my preferred reading, to the end of VII.i. The second or final synthesis, which fully resolves the action as a whole, commences with Segment 171 (VII.ii), and runs to the last lines of the play (Verse 191), completing the five-stage progression of the integrated plot.[15]

Character and Characterization

The definition of the protagonist as the dominant figure in a play's story, whose quest drives the main action, ensures that the plot, character, and characterization are thoroughly intermeshed in its verbal and visual composition. While characters are unique to a play in the concrete forms that they take (Dushyanta is Dushyanta, and not just any king, and Anasūyā is Anasūyā, and not merely a stereotypical 'heroine's girlfriend'), the process of characterization that produces them is heavily inflected by the formal features of the play, which in turn are regulated by its genre. The various properties of the *nāṭaka* that Vishvanātha summarizes in the passage quoted in Appendix E, for example, affect the kinds of characters that Shakuntalā, Māḍhavya, Kaṇva, and Priyaṁvadā are, and how we perceive them in the unfolding situations and events in the plotted action of *Shakuntalā*. One kind of map of the play's overall integration of its three-dimensional characters with its many-layered plotting—and their divergent functions in it—may be sketched out as follows.

Dushyanta

The protagonist of a *nāṭaka* is driven either by love and desire or by heroic energy, and his quest therefore is either romantic or heroic. But the two emotional states are also complementary in the genre, so when one of them is primary, the other is secondary: a *nāṭaka* that focuses on dramatizing a love story, for example, also contains significant heroic elements. In a romantic-heroic play of this kind, the hero is 'consistently noble' by definition, and the heroine who is the object of his desire is his equal in character (as indicated in Verse 85 and Segment 189), so the dramatic action as a whole is driven by their reciprocal quests for each other.[16]

In this generic context, the text of *Shakuntalā* exercises great care to establish Dushyanta's character from the moment he appears before us, and to articulate his qualities as they emerge from his decisions and acts in each successive situation in which he is on the stage (in all the acts, except IV). For example, the dialogue in the play's opening scene (I.iii) explicitly represents him as strong and powerful, highly skilled at hunting, acute in his observation and verbal expression, swift in his physical responses, alert to his duties and moral responsibilities even in the heat of physical exertion, and circumspect in his judgement and decision-making. Once he has selected Shakuntalā as his desired object and defined his nascent quest (Verse 19), Scenes I.iv and I.v display his exemplary social skills as he begins his effort and charts the principal trajectory of his quest: with the three young women in the sacred grove, he is consistently modest, self-effacing, and gracious, adroit with his 'amorous conversation' and considerate at every turn, yet firm in his pursuit of specific information that will streamline his quest (especially Segments 22–24).

In Act II, the five episodes belonging to Māḍhavya's secondary plot (II.i–iv and vi) and the one episode from Kaṇva's secondary plot (II.v) then build on Dushyanta's chief character traits: Bhadrasena dramatizes his physical prowess, heroism, and passion for hunting (II.iii); Māḍhavya's exchanges with him highlight his sensitivity, his romantic and idealistic tendencies (rather than his sexual appetite), and his poetic and artistic imagination (especially II.iv); the two young ascetics, Gautama and Nārada, memorialize his power, majesty, and spiritual self-discipline (II.v); and Karabhaka's visit to deliver a message from his mother foregrounds his qualities as a son and a family man (II.vi).

By the beginning of Act III, when Dushyanta appears in a state of impatient infatuation, lovesickness, and desire, we have a well-rounded portrait of the noble human hero of a multilayered love story. As the intertwined strands of his and Shakuntalā's respective trajectories of action unroll before us, along with the strands of the corresponding secondary plots, Dushyanta becomes more and more three-dimensional. In this part of the main action, we observe him as a lover characterized by high seriousness and romantic idealism, by emotional depth and self-understanding, by self-surrender to the object of his desire, and by an unclouded consciousness of the complexities of love, desire, and their impediments (III.ii–v).

In Act V, we then witness an expansion of his personality as a conscientious and hard-working ruler, as a fair and impartial administrator of justice, as a mindful and courteous host, and especially as a superb debater—equally adept in deliberative, forensic, and epideictic rhetoric—who has to apply his skills rationally under the most trying personal and official circumstances, in order to prevent the destruction of his character and reputation. In Act VI, Dushyanta displays his innermost world at close quarters as he faces up to his guilt and moral culpability with respect to his rejection and abandonment of Shakuntalā. He expresses his regret and remorse without self-regard, even as he slides into intense repentance and displays his vulnerability to despondency and despair in the presence of his palace staff. His doubts and self-doubts put him in a delusional state in which he can no longer distinguish between fact and fiction, leading to a virtual psychological breakdown onstage, in which we watch him weep, faint, and fall into a coma. And yet, as this act is at pains to show, he recovers his 'specialized personas' periodically in the midst of the emotional crisis—as a just and generous king (VI.v), as the most devoted of masters and friends, and as the most skilled and courageous of warriors (VI.vi). Act VII then depicts Dushyanta as the noble hero in his most comprehensive and elevated form. We see him as the military leader par excellence, as the meticulous observer of his environment (VII.i), as dynastic inheritor and doting father, as faithful husband and complete soulmate (VII.ii–iii), and as a sagacious human citizen of the cosmos in conversation with the gods (especially VII.iv).

Viewed through a classical lens (rather than a modern one), the dynamics of Dushyanta's characterization in the play, on the inside as well as the outside, appears to be a unique, manifold evolution of character in which the hero grows and changes in our perspective from scene to scene, and yet retains his core characteristics. These character traits deepen in meaning and widen in scope as he is steadily transformed by his shifting circumstances, his responses to them, his assessments and decisions, his specific acts, and his ability to adjust and respond afresh to the incremental and cumulative outcomes of his actions. His most heroic facet is his consistency in remaining focused on his quest and its singular goal through all his changes of emotional fortune, whether his objective recedes from his grasp, eludes his understanding, or seems to draw closer and fall within his reach. Although he is circumscribed by the horizon of expectations set up by the genre of the *nāṭaka*, Dushyanta is hardly a stereotypical or predictable king. As the seed of the dramatic action germinates in Scenes I.iii–v into multiple possibilities—each with a bundle of potential developments—he begins to move holographically across the stage, until his character has evolved structurally and temporally in every direction—on the planes of emotion, action, reason, and morality—by the culmination of Scene VII.iv.

If we step outside the classical and post-classical framework of Sanskrit poetics, then it is useful to note that Dushyanta is the kind of hero who is fully human and cannot exceed the limits of nature or of natural causality on his own (for example, Segment 178), so his qualities are projected at the limits of plausibility solely within the human realm. He therefore exceeds the human beings around him in his capacities—he is superior to them in degree but not in kind, and he is not superior to the environment that contains all of them. He can exceed his natural environment only with the help of divine or celestial agency at special moments in his fictive biography.[17] He cannot find Shakuntalā on his own once she has been whisked away by Sānumatī after the confrontation at the fire sanctuary; he cannot break out of his subsequent psychological breakdown on his own, and Indra has to send down his celestial charioteer, Mātali, to achieve a breakthrough; and, like other human beings, he cannot reach Mount Meru on his own, where Shakuntalā and their son Sarvadamana (to be renamed later as Bharata) are living in the safety and security of Kashyapa's celestial ashram. Within his human environment, Dushyanta has to live, think, feel, and act within the constitutive constraints of dharma: dharma as cosmo-moral law, given by the gods (divine law); as *rāja*-dharma (law relating to kings and kingship); as *jāti*-dharma (law relating to a caste-group or caste); as *sādhāraṇa*-dharma (law common to all classes of human beings, including natural law and positive law); and as *sva*-dharma (law pertaining to oneself, or deliberative ethics and morality).[18]

In a cross-cultural perspective, this composite circumscription of what Dushyanta is and can be inside his fictive world explains exactly why he must have the extraordinary specific qualities as well as the whole range of qualities that Dhanañjaya enumerates in the tenth century for a 'noble hero'. In order to be what he is—at a minimum, a king, a father, and a lover—and in order to do what he needs to do—as a dynast, to produce and nurture a son who can inherit his kingdom and, as a lover, to recover Shakuntalā, who has already given him a son—he has to be a 'hyper' human subject, a man who can fully integrate within himself all the faculties and skills that are necessary to accomplish such goals. Thus, he must embody the development of cognition, logic and reason, rhetoric, poetry and the arts, emotional sensitivity and range, desire and passion, physical strength and agility, mental and physical endurance, and spiritual discipline and self-discipline, among other factors, to their maximum. He has to be a fearless and vigorous *chakravartin*, a wise and self-controlled *rājarshi*, and a youthful and handsome *rasika* rolled into one, who must be able to overcome all the obstacles in his way and succeed in his quest. He thus occupies the space of an idealized hyper-human subject, who represents the full range of human experience and arouses all the major and minor emotions in his audience, on the borders of romance and myth and at the outer limits of the high mimetic mode—he is not, and cannot be, the fallen leader of Aristotelian tragedy, who is brought down by a fatal flaw, whose destruction arouses mainly pity and fear, and who inhabits a much smaller, more provincial world.[19]

Shakuntalā

Like Dushyanta, Shakuntalā acquires her character by a cumulative process in the play, beginning with a set of basic qualities that are established when she first appears on the stage, and ending with the massive transformation that the intervening events bring out in the course of the main action. She is featured in Acts I, III, IV, V, and VII, and her character develops discontinuously across this sequence, fragmented textually not only by the division into acts but also by the separation of diegetic discourse from mimetic enactment in the body of the play. The polarity of diegesis and mimesis is significant because several decisive moments in her fictive biography—such as the first union or consummation of *sambhoga shriṅgāra* with Dushyanta, the drama of Durvāsā's curse, the discovery of her pregnancy, her transportation to the celestial realm, and the birth of Sarvadamana (or Bharata)—occur offstage but are reported on the stage (see III.vi, IV.i–ii, V.v, and VII.ii). If, however, we examine the fragments in sequence, we notice that, in Act I, Shakuntalā appears before us as a spirited, spontaneous, and strong-willed adolescent; as her interactions with Anasūyā and Priyaṁvadā as well as Dushyanta indicate unambiguously, she is both irrepressible and rebellious. Her lack of docility and conformity, her refusal to bend easily to someone else's will, remain with her all the way to Act VII, where she unerringly puts Dushyanta in his place when he tries to return the recovered ring to her. These traits, in fact, are central to what she shares as a 'soulmate' with Dushyanta, who is just as wilful and independent, and the combination of their temperamental qualities is what they transmit biologically to their son, Sarvadamana, as his exceptional indomitability (VII.ii and iv).[20]

As spring in Act I turns to mid-summer in Act III, we see Shakuntalā matured rapidly by her first experience of infatuation and love, and practically sick with desire—as Anasūyā suggests, she is in 'a fatal state of attraction', and as Shakuntalā herself puts it, she 'is not in control of herself' (Segments 58 and 68). But, even at this stage, her independence persists as a shaping force in her decisions and conduct: when Dushyanta seeks to kiss her, she turns away because it is not her choice, but once she has reassessed her situation and her own desire (a few moments later, in stage time), she boldly invites Dushyanta back for their 'union', which is now her decision (Segment 70). By the end of Act III, the audience knows that Shakuntalā is a three-dimensional woman, who was raised in a secluded, alternative society in a forest and who identifies herself as an ascetic, but who is nevertheless amazingly 'street smart' in dealing directly with a famous king, who is intellectually mature and morally and ethically circumspect beyond her years, who is neither submissive nor cowed down by her situation, and who, despite the pressures on her, learns to be sexually bold and emotionally unafraid.

This evolving courage undergirds Shakuntalā's choices and actions in Act IV. At the start of this phase, she basks in the afterglow of her union with Dushyanta, is driven to distraction by her separation from him and his inexplicable silence, and is burdened with a pregnancy that needs public explanation (IV.i–ii). Between these developments, she has offended the irascible sage Durvāsā unintentionally, and remains unaware (until VII.iv) that he has placed Dushyanta and her under a curse (that is amendable but irrevocable) for her violation of etiquette. But once she has father Kaṇva's approval and blessing, she prepares to travel to reunite with Dushyanta at his palace at Hastināpura (IV.ii–iii). In the protracted course of the departure from the ashram, she displays the depth of understanding of the institution of family (whether by filiation or by affiliation), of her participation in community, of her friendship with Anasūyā and Priyaṁvadā, and of her immersion in nature (IV.iv–v). If Act IV thus depicts Shakuntalā at her most sensitive and receptive, Act V demonstrates her fieriness of temperament, her unapologetic willingness to stand up for herself and for what is right, and her eloquence in addressing Dushyanta as an equal, and even as his moral superior (V.iv–v).[21]

Shakuntalā's three-dimensionality in the play reveals an important feature of Kālidāsa's approach to characterization. Each of his characters, like a person in everyday life, has a multiplex *svabhāva* or 'nature'—a set of qualities that have accumulated from past actions, and that do not fit together in one flat paradigm. His characters respond to their fictive circumstances with thought and circumspection, and hence have what M.M. Bakhtin calls an 'interiority' that is not developed in comparable ways or to a comparable extent in earlier epic literature.[22] They are adaptable, and adjust their conduct to suit the situations in which they find themselves, so that different character traits become visible in different circumstances, which makes them so lifelike. Shakuntalā is not the same in the successive acts in which she appears, and yet she does not cease to be what she has been earlier: like Dushyanta, she evolves without losing her consistency or integrity. As a result, her character is a continually evolving 'whole' that exists only in time, and no one part, isolated at a given moment, can represent its temporal entirety and unity.

Māḍhavya and the King's Entourage

In Vishvanātha's perspective in *Sāhitya-darpaṇa*, Māḍhavya is the lead character in a well-defined secondary plot that provides multichannel support to Dushyanta in his quest for Shakuntalā, and hence contributes directly to the king's strand of the principal plot.[23] Māḍhavya is Dushyanta's official court jester and confidant, and his premier personal adviser, emotional healer, and comical as well as serious 'cheerleader-in-chief'. The secondary plot that coheres around Māḍhavya includes all the secondary and tertiary characters who are part of the king's royal staff (at the palace) and entourage (at the hunting camp), the most important among them being Bhadrasena, the chief of the army (II.iii); Vātāyana, the aged chamberlain (V.ii and VI.ii–iii); Somarāta, the priest who serves the king, his family, and his clan (V.iii–v); and Vetravatī, the king's aide or all-purpose assistant (Acts V and VI). The staff also includes Chaturikā, the king's skilled assistant in painting and art (VI.iv–vi); the Charioteer, a classical equivalent of an articulate royal chauffeur (I.iii); Raivataka, the 'man mountain' who serves as guard and usher at the hunting camp (Act II); minor figures such as the messenger Karabhaka (II.vi) and the two royal bards (V.iii); as well as the all-female bodyguard of Greek warrior women, with a designated leader who carries the king's powerful bow and arrows (Acts II and VI).

This extensive secondary plot, which runs through parts of Act I and most of Acts II, V, and VI, also contains tertiary incidents that can be separated analytically from its sequence of interwoven events. Among the minor incidents linked to the Māḍhavya plotline, and reported diegetically onstage or depicted without elaboration, are those centred on the message from the queen mother delivered by Karabhaka (II.

vi); the offstage song sung by Haṁsapadikā, the king's former favourite among his queens (V.i); Vetravatī and Chaturikā's separate offstage encounters with Dushyanta's chief queen, Vasumatī, and her maid Taralikā (VI.iv–v); and the activities of the kingdom's chief minister, Pishuna, who deals with revenue and justice but also steps in as the representative of the king when the latter is absent (VI.v–vi). The incident involving Parabhritikā and Madhukarikā in the palace garden is a larger incident subordinated to Māḍhavya's plotline through Vātāyana, and it is further integrated with the running story through Mitrāvasu, queen Vasumatī's brother and hence a brother-in-law of Dushyanta, who is the kingdom's administrative manager and also the patron of the two girls patrolling the garden (VI.ii). Moreover, on its periphery, Māḍhavya's secondary plot is loosely connected by theme to the first part of the Mixed Interlude in Act VI, which is a separate tertiary incident tied directly to Dushyanta's quest-stream in the play's composite principal plot.

The Sanskrit critical tradition conceives of Māḍhavya as Dushyanta's closest childhood friend, which explains the extraordinary bond of trust, reliance, intimacy, and friendship between the two men.[24] When Dushyanta finds Māḍhavya's life threatened in VI.vi, for instance, he brings his full strength, skill, and power into play to save his companion, regardless of the risks to his own life. The mysterious or inexplicable feature of Māḍhavya's character is that he is a poor, practically uneducated brahmin: he is a vegetarian (II.i), has cravings for sweets and food (II.ii and VI.iii), is myopic (VI.iv), is quite thoughtless (II.vi and V.i) and underinformed (VI.iv), is tactless and undependable (II.vi), and speaks Prakrit, not Sanskrit (throughout). Nevertheless, he is the only one who can help the king understand his own emotions (II.iv) and, under the greatest psychological stress, to hold himself together (VI.iii–iv); and he is authorized exclusively to represent the king in personal matters (II.vi) as well as official business (VI.vi). Māḍhavya feels sufficiently secure to criticize Dushyanta behind the latter's back and to his face, and has the meta-discursive insouciance to manage the king's image in the eyes of the audience (Acts II and VI).

Māḍhavya is a jester and not a trickster—a distinction that is vital to an understanding of his character and of such literary figures in general.[25] As a secondary structural device, he performs two vital functions in relation to the principal plot and to Dushyanta's quest. For one, he is the voice and locus of common sense and reason in the play's discourse as well as action, and repeatedly anchors the mythic, romantic, epic, and fabulated events around him to reality on the ground in the ordinary human world. As Dushyanta waxes eloquent in the natural arbour at the hunting camp about Shakuntalā's sensuous beauty, her celestial origins, and his own infatuation, Māḍhavya intervenes strategically to bring him down to earth with his blunt question, 'Did you think that she would jump into your lap the moment she saw you?' (II.iv). For a second function, Māḍhavya actively uses laughter to subvert the seriousness, idealism, and aesthetics of the erotic mood (in its *sambhoga shriṅgāra* phase, as explained in Appendix G), and his laughter is coupled to but distinct from his common sense. Early in the palace garden scene, for example, as Dushyanta reiterates his remorse, Māḍhavya raises his stick to 'banish this sickness of love' (VI.iii). As the leading figure in his secondary plot, Māḍhavya's own contribution to the principal action thus unfolds as a combination of comic relief and doses of realism and forthrightness, satire and irony, laughter and subversion.

But Māḍhavya's role in the play as a whole is more momentous than the comic and realistic modes might suggest. His disappearance from the whole action during Acts

III and IV, and especially from the scenes of confrontation in Act V, is doubly crucial. In the first stretch, his absence allows order to be restored to Dushyanta's pursuit of his desires—and to Shakuntalā's pursuit of hers—so that the eros or *shriṅgāra* generated in the play (Act I) proceeds to its proper consummation or *sambhoga* (Act III). In the latter stretch, Māḍhavya's absence allows Dushyanta's memory to fail plausibly—under the supernatural agency of Durvāsā's curse—as the king deals with Shakuntalā and her escort of ascetics (Act V); and it enables the untranscendable karmic consequences of that failure to transform the erotics of conjunction (*sambhoga shriṅgāra*) into the anti-erotics of disjunction (*vipralambha shriṅgāra*; see Appendix G).

When Māḍhavya reappears in Act VI, his laughter and common sense concertedly counteract the effects of the *vipralambha* condition on an expanded scale, enabling Dushyanta to gradually work his way through guilt and remorse, repentance and dejection, delusion and melancholy, as well as abjection and worsening psychosomatic symptoms (weeping, fainting, coma). Māḍhavya's banter and banality, his farcical realism and literal myopia, combine to bring Dushyanta out of his darkest moments: the jester cheers up the king in the pleasure pavilion, deflates his self-pity and maudlin self-recrimination, and then destroys his delusions about his painting (VI.iii–iv).

In his final incident onstage, Māḍhavya becomes part of Mātali's celestial intervention (under invisibility on the rooftop of the Palace of the Clouds), and serves as the instrument to lift Dushyanta out of what English poetry calls 'the slough of despondency' (VI.vi). This culmination of Act VI marks the apex of Māḍhavya's role in the play: among all the devices available to restore the hero to his nobility—his strength, courage, wisdom, rationality, practicality, and self-control—it is the jester alone who can cure him of his ills. What this moment demonstrates in epic-classical space-time is that laughter and realism are not only transgressive, subversive, or oppositional, but also rise above the reactive mode to become actively and independently curative. Māḍhavya's plotline may be subsidiary to the main action, but Kālidāsa integrates it so thoroughly into the main plot that Dushyanta's quest cannot be streamlined or completed without it.

Kaṇva, Anasūyā, and Priyaṁvadā

Kaṇva, in many respects, represents the conservative core of the play, specifically in relation to the social and temporal orders embedded in the *varṇāshrama* system, which represents the division of society into four caste-groups and the division of life into four stages marked by rites of passage. Conservative interpretations have long identified four of the Sanskrit verses assigned to Kaṇva as the 'greatest' in the play, but they are didactic rather than imaginative, and define a moral rather than an aesthetic centre of the action (Verses 78, 81, 89, and 90).[26]

Nevertheless, Kaṇva is essential for the play precisely because he pins down the poetry to what Sheldon Pollock, following Bhoja's *Shriṅgāra-prakāsha* (eleventh century), views as the underlying 'social aesthetic' of Sanskrit *kāvya* (highly aestheticized imaginative literature).[27] Kaṇva stabilizes love and desire in *Shakuntalā* with a surrounding frame of marriage, family, ancestors, and descendants, and he counterbalances emotion, impulsive action, and freedom of choice with moral responsibility, ethical obligation, duty, discipline, and law. Without him as a firm and visionary moral agent to channel desire and emotion, the *sambhoga shriṅgāra* of Shakuntalā and Dushyanta in Kālidāsa's play would be reduced merely to the ancient counterpart of a modern 'consensual one-night stand' or its shorter, spontaneous equivalent—which is exactly what it is for the more cynical and manipulative Dushyanta depicted in the earlier version of the story in the Mahābhārata.[28] In the absence of Kaṇva (as he is dramatized in the play), there would be no gravity to Shakuntalā's pregnancy or to her journey to Hastināpura, no moral ballast to her fierce fight with Dushyanta at the fire sanctuary, no quest for fairness and restorative justice on her part, and especially no tragedy of the pregnant woman and single mother rejected and abandoned without just cause (Acts IV and V).

In practice, however, the greatest impact of Kaṇva and his concentrated presence in Act IV—which is central to the secondary plot built around him—is emotional, not ideological. The surprising fact is that, of all the parts of the play, this is the act that comes alive the most for many Indian readers and viewers today: its verbal representation and mimetic enactment of a bride's departure for her husband's home is so vivid and emotionally precise that very little of the phenomenon seems to have changed qualitatively in 1600 years. Thus, perhaps paradoxically, the secondary plot in which Kaṇva is the lead character carries more ideological baggage than any other element in *Shakuntalā*, and yet performs the most affecting dramatic function on the page and in the theatre.

But Kaṇva is not the only point of gravity for the play, even though he appears soon after the first synthesis, and Act IV stands at the beginning of the extended second antithesis: Kashyapa in Act VII, together with the final resolution of which he is the main agent, provides a second anchor for the action.[29] Kashyapa is a character of divine descent—he is a son of Marīchi, one of the sons of the creator-god Brahmā, and hence is Brahmā's direct grandson, along patrilineal as well as matrilineal axes populated entirely by males and females descended from the god who generates his offspring solely from himself. Kashyapa's wife, Aditi, is a daughter of Daksha, Marīchi's brother; and, as Verse 184 tells us, Kashyapa and Aditi are the divine parents, not only of Indra, the chief god of the Vedic pantheon (corresponding very closely to Zeus in the Greek pantheon), but also of the god Vishṇu's incarnation, in the early history of the present universe, as a divine dwarf (his *vāmana* avatar).[30] Kashyapa's mythology, in fact, is vast: over thousands of human years, he fathers numerous gods, anti-gods, and celestial beings, together with entire orders and species of beings and creatures in other realms, including some portions of the human race. He therefore is one of the Prajāpatis, the ten original 'procreators of the multitudes of living things of all kinds' that crowd the (Hindu) universe.[31] Kashyapa is a stabilizer of the action because, in the final scene, he sets the whole sequence of events involving Dushyanta and Shakuntalā—and all the other characters—in order, chronologically and structurally, causally and morally.

The complication in the story as dramatized in *Shakuntalā* is that Kaṇva himself is a direct patrilineal descendant of Kashyapa, but he appears as a human *rishi*, a seer or visionary who belongs to a special class of agents who connect the divine and human worlds in various ways, and who transmit and preserve divine cosmo-moral law in the human realm. In both the Mahābhārata's version of the story and Kālidāsa's play, Kaṇva is identified not only as Kashyapa's descendant but also as the visionary sage who, along with his family of poets, originally received and transmitted a large number of the hymns preserved in the eighth mandala or book of the *Rig-veda samhita*. Kaṇva's spiritual authority in *Shakuntalā* thus arises, in part, from his status as one of the visionary poets of the *Rig-veda*, a principal scriptural text of Hinduism, and Kālidāsa memorializes this with the Vedic mantra that

Kaṇva chants in IV.iv, to bless Shakuntalā's imminent journey to Hastināpura (Verse 80).

In a classical framework, Anasūyā and Priyaṁvadā are female characters situated in Kaṇva's secondary plot. With Shakuntalā, they form a triumvirate tightly knit together by female friendship—Dushyanta compares them to 'Venus and Jupiter in trine with the moon' (Segment 58)—but the functional hierarchy of the three young women clearly separates Shakuntalā as the *nāyikā* or heroine.[32] If we apply the patterns of everyday human life to Shakuntalā, then she may be as young as fourteen years in Act I, and certainly no more than fifteen or sixteen; Priyaṁvadā and Anasūyā are a little older, and may be seventeen and eighteen, respectively, with Anasūyā projected as the oldest of the three. Considered more qualitatively, Anasūyā and Priyaṁvadā make a pair because they are closer to each other in age and experience than they are to Shakuntalā, who is distinctly younger and looks up to them for emotional security and guidance (as in Segment 69).[33]

At the mechanical level of plot, it is surprising to discover that the play-script assigns almost exactly the same amount of verbal discourse and hence equal stage time to Anasūyā and Priyaṁvadā in Acts I, III, and IV together, which indicates how skilfully Anasūyā is represented in the action to create the impression that she is in the foreground in relation to her friend. A further measure of the sophistication of the play's verbal craft is that, even though Shakuntalā is the female protagonist, the amount of discourse—the number of words to deliver onstage—assigned to her in these three acts is only about two-thirds of the discourse assigned to either Anasūyā or Priyaṁvadā.

In the formulaic version of Sanskrit criticism, Anasūyā and Priyaṁvadā are classified as the heroine's *sakhī*s or intimate friends, and hence are assumed frequently to be stock characters without depth or roundness. But Kālidāsa characterizes them as distinctive individuals in their words and actions, and gives both of them an interior dimension that exceeds their functions in the plot, just as he portrays even tertiary characters in the play—such as the Disciple who appears in IV.ii—as vivid representations of people with thoughts, feelings, and powers of expression.

As a round rather than flat character, Anasūyā is practically an adult woman: she is consistently thoughtful about others, judicious about issues and opinions, and generally in control of her emotions and responses, even as she cares deeply about Shakuntalā, Priyaṁvadā, Kaṇva, and the ashram community (see note on Anasūyā's name in Appendix B). But as her transformative longer soliloquy in IV.ii shows, she exercises a great deal of rationality as she faces up to her own emotions and works through them, in relation to intricate social situations (such as Shakuntalā's pregnancy, before knowledge of her marriage has become public). As Anasūyā's adroit management of the first encounter with Dushyanta—of his status and personality, of a formal four-way conversation that quickly borders on the intimate—demonstrates more dramatically in I.iv–v, she thinks with circumspection as well as moral clarity, and is a skilful negotiator of social etiquette with imposing male presences, even when the man may be a complete stranger (who tries to misrepresent himself as a so-called royal official).

Anasūyā, in fact, is the one who helps Shakuntalā understand her own attraction to Dushyanta, who encourages the emerging relationship and contributes to its consolidation, and who manages many of its practical aspects. In I.iv, for instance, she initiates the substantive conversation with Dushyanta, answers his questions, and narrates the story of

Shakuntalā's origins; and, in III.v, she joins Priyaṁvadā to leave the lovers alone with each other for the first time, and warns them from a distance of Gautamī's arrival at the riverbank. She is the one who has to inform Kaṇva about Shakuntalā's pregnancy, even though he already knows about it mystically (IV.ii); and, most important, she is the one who makes the decision not to inform Shakuntalā about Durvāsā's curse, which the heroine is too distracted to hear and understand (IV.ii and v). In effect, as an evolving three-dimensional agent, Anasūyā is second only to Kaṇva in moving this secondary plot forward in its facilitation of the protagonists' respective quests for a shared objective.

Priyaṁvadā may sometimes appear to blend into Anasūyā, especially when both young women speak in unison on the stage, or when they work conspiratorially to aid Shakuntalā's relationship with Dushyanta. But Priyaṁvadā's character is differentiated at several levels: she is more impulsive, less circumspect, more likely to be thrown into turmoil, and less likely to offer mature advice. Anasūyā waits and reflects before speaking or deciding, but Priyaṁvadā rushes off to do things (such as chasing after Durvāsā in IV.i) and is decidedly a chatterbox ('this prattling Priyaṁvadā and her nonsense', as Shakuntalā puts it in I.v). Nevertheless, Priyaṁvadā is the sole hinge in the secondary plot on which several transformations turn. In Acts III and IV, she is the one who pushes Shakuntalā towards greater openness with Dushyanta; who concocts the device of a love letter inscribed on a lotus leaf; and, most important, who persuades Durvāsā to amend the conditions of his curse, and hence brings the 'ring of recognition' into play—without which Dushyanta's recovery of his memory would be impossible. With these manifold similarities and differences binding them, Anasūyā and Priyaṁvadā emerge as each other's well-defined complements—young women, inseparable friends and Shakuntalā's intimates, who enclose key events in Kaṇva's secondary plot like a pair of inverted commas or quotation marks.

The Dramatic Ensemble

Kālidāsa's methods of characterization in *Shakuntalā* reveal a new level of intricacy when we turn to Act VI. The first five acts of the play display two main kinds of characterization: (a) the representation of characters who are individuals, whether round or flat, ranging from the protagonists down to Vaikhānasa (I.iii), Raivataka (Act II), and the unidentified Disciple (IV.ii); and (b) the representation of groups of anonymous or stock characters who function collectively onstage roughly like a chorus, such as Vaikhānasa's two accompanying disciples (I.iii), the three unnamed ascetics' wives (IV.iii), and the larger party of ascetics escorting Shakuntalā (V.iv–vi).[34] In the *praveshaka* of VI.i, a different kind of Interlude that introduces the montage of the whole act, Kālidāsa employs a third kind of characterization: instead of assigning the task of recovering and restoring the lost ring to a notable individual or to a chorus-like group (which would be the preferred device in a Greek tragedy), he assigns it to a dramatic ensemble, which he then orchestrates without resorting to the functions of a chorus. A dramatic ensemble, in this sense, is distinct from an acting ensemble (in which actors practise enactment in a collective mode), because the dramatic device conceives of its limited action as being collective in its composition and effect in the plot, even though its members are individuals.

The dramatic ensemble of VI.i contains four characters with distinct stage personalities, who function in tandem as a collective agent to metamorphose the situation surrounding the protagonists. The group brings together the City Superintendent, a brother of one of Dushyanta's minor wives and hence the king's brother-in-law (Sanskrit *shyālah*, antecedent of the modern Indian *sālā*), but nevertheless supposedly a low character; two lowly policemen who serve the Superintendent, caricatured with the epithets Sūchaka and Jānuka (the 'informer' and the 'informed', respectively); and a Fisherman, born into a so-called untouchable occupational caste, and hence the lowliest of the play's low characters (Appendix A). The ensemble nature of this group—which is very different from the chorus-like groups in this play, and especially from the choruses played onstage by twelve to fifteen actors in Greek tragedies—becomes evident in the structural interdependence of its four agents. None of them can perform the task of recovering and restoring Dushyanta's ring independent of the others, and each of them carries out only one designated part of the task, so that the task as a whole requires all of them to complete their contributions for its accomplishment. The four characters enter as an ensemble in one configuration (in the marketplace), and exit in ensemble at the end of the Interlude in a changed configuration (headed for the wine shop).

Kālidāsa is the inventor of the successful dramatic ensemble on the world stage in the ancient period, but Shakespeare reinvents the device for modern times in plays such as *A Midsummer Night's Dream*, where the bumbling troupe of actors staging the play-within-the-play comprises a comical ensemble, and *Romeo and Juliet*, where the Capulets and the Montagues constitute paired ensembles warring in the streets of Venice in a blood-soaked tragedy. As a playwright's device, a dramatic ensemble carries out a plot function that is inherently complex because it has several, interdependent parts; and such a device is successful when the plot function is well-defined, and the characters of the ensemble's individual members are tailored to the specific parts of that function, so that the necessity, internal cohesion, and overall dramatic efficacy of the collective are structurally integrated into the mechanics of the plot. In *Shakuntalā*, the *praveshaka* in VI.i is an autonomous tertiary incident that is fastened directly to Dushyanta's trajectory in the principal plot, where it performs the coordinated ensemble functions of finding the lost ring (done by the Fisherman), unearthing the story of its discovery (the City Superintendent and the two policemen together), delivering the ring and the narrative to the king in person (the Superintendent, using his family connection), and hence breaking his spell of amnesia under Durvāsā's amended curse (accomplished by the ring as such).

The Drama of the Ring

The ring, which appears as a centrepiece, develops a curious history in the course of the dramatic action: the play's title seems to refer to it, but does not name it explicitly. As Barbara Stoler Miller observed in 1984, 'the exact [grammatical] form and meaning' of 'the Sanskrit compound *abhijñānashākuntalam* are controversial even among Sanskrit critics and commentators'.

> The word *abhijñāna* means 'recognition', or 'recollection'; it is used in the play to refer to the ring Dushyanta gives as a token to Shakuntala. . . . A more exact translation of the title might be '[The drama of] Shakuntala [remembered] through the ring of recollection', where the entire compound refers to the implied word *nāṭaka* (drama), and a word like *smrita* (remembered) may be supplied according to a rule of Sanskrit grammar governing elision in compound words.[35]

Miller's suggested rendering of the title adds further, unnecessary ambiguity because its syntax obscures the direct object of the act of remembering, and may be expanded to say, 'The play about Shakuntalā, who is remembered through the ring of recollection.' But, even with this clarification, Miller's interpretation remains limited by the fact that it reduces *abhijñāna* to the unitary process of recollection or remembrance, when the original Sanskrit word is polysemous at its root and actually seeks to represent a complex mental activity with multiple components. As V.S. Apte, among others, glosses the neuter noun in question, the process of '*abhijñāna* is a combination of *anubhāva* or direct perception and *smriti* or recollection; as when we say "This is the same man I saw yesterday" [with] *anubhāva* or direct perception leading to the identification . . . and the memory leading to the reference to past action . . .'[36]

In this rather precise conceptualization, *abhijñāna* has three distinct referential meanings, approximately in the following order of decreasing frequency of usage: '1. Recognition; 2. Remembrance, recollection; knowledge, ascertainment; 3. A sign or token of recognition ([whether] person or thing)'. Ideally, all these denotations would be incorporated into any interpretation of the play's title, because they are semantically interconnected and inseparable, even though, as Apte puts it, 'the reading [*abhijñāna*]*shākuntalam* is grammatically indefensible'. Wendy Doniger's account of 'Rings of Rejection and Recognition in Ancient India' in 1998 broadens the semantic field that Apte demarcates, but it does so without the acuteness necessary to produce an epistemological breakthrough. What Apte indexes using a late-nineteenth-century English vocabulary needs to be unpacked with the advantages of a twenty-first-century perspective: etymologically, *abhijñāna* points not only to a coordination of the faculties of cognition (in the present) and memory (from the past), but to the distinct processes of re-membering and re-cognizing (both occurring here and now) as well as knowing and identifying and representing and interpreting—all of which lie along a continuous causal gradient, a particular step-by-step sequential order of cause and consequence.[37]

Within and against the grammatical illegibility or undecidability of the multivalent term *abhijñāna* in its title—a curious flaw, given the meticulous aesthetics of the main text—the play itself does something delightfully playful and imaginative with the eight elements in the causal sequence specified above. In Act I, when Dushyanta offers his royal signet ring, inscribed with his name, to Priyaṁvadā and Anasūyā as payment of Shakuntalā's debt to the former, he uses it first as a token that misidentifies him (as a royal official rather than as the king himself). But Anasūyā and Priyaṁvadā immediately expose his disingenuousness—to his face, but as gently as possible—and construe the ring as a token that, by definition, identifies its wearer correctly and unambiguously. As the two young women return the disproportionately valuable ring to its owner in this playful exchange at its earliest appearance in the plot, they establish it as a device that already couples the contrary functions of representation and misrepresentation, identification and misidentification (I.v).

In the first part of the Mixed Interlude of Act IV, after Durvāsā has cursed Shakuntalā and Priyaṁvadā has persuaded the sage to amend his curse, Anasūyā observes that

> Just before he left for the city, the king placed his royal ring on Shakuntalā's finger with his own hands—it is inscribed with his name, and it is his token of

> remembrance and recognition. She possesses the means to end Durvāsā's curse! (Segment 74)

In this diegetic moment, Anasūyā represents the ring as an object with a fourfold function: (a) it serves as a gift that its owner gives voluntarily to its recipient, who becomes its new legitimate user; (b) it serves as a transitive emblem of ownership, because the owner's name inscribed on it—a publicly displayed signifier—now includes the new user in its signification; (c) it serves as a trigger of remembrance, because it reminds the recipient of the giver and of his commitment to her; and (d) it serves as a potential trigger of recognition, because it can enable him to recognize her in the future, as the recipient of his gift and as the object of his commitment. In its short last sentence, this remarkably condensed and suggestive passage coalesces all four functions of the ring into its power to terminate Durvāsā's curse.

This conjuncture on the verbal surface represents a deeper articulation of cognition and memory as faculties that make various interconnected processes possible in the first place. When Durvāsā curses Shakuntalā offstage, she is so distracted by her reverie of Dushyanta and their union that her cognition fails to function in relation to the sage who has appeared suddenly and unexpectedly before her in the ashram. In Apte's terms, in her state of distraction, her cognitive faculty fails to initiate '*anubhāva* or direct perception' of the person standing before her. This failure of Shakuntalā's cognition to perform its most basic task in the present—which is one of the foundations of sociality and social etiquette—becomes the pretext for Durvāsā's enragement and his disproportionately vindictive curse.

In Act VII, as part of the resolution of 'the whole business' of the play (as Vishvanātha defines it for the *nāṭaka* genre,

Appendix E), Shakuntalā says in her penultimate soliloquy on the stage:

> I really have no memory of being put under a curse. Or my heart was so empty in the void of separation that I did not know I had been cursed. (Segment 189)

Like Anasūyā's remark in IV.i, Shakuntalā's private observation is also very precise and far-reaching. If there is no cognition of an object that is present within the field of one's sensory perception or phenomenological consciousness at a given moment, then no memory of that object or its experience is formed and stored in the mind, and it therefore is not possible to remember that object at a later time. In other words, *Shakuntalā* gives us a closely formulated analysis of how the faculties of cognition and memory operate, and how present experience as well as remembered experience are formed and retrieved.

The play's last two acts complicate this picture by providing Dushyanta's and Shakuntalā's own accounts of and responses to the ring, independent of each other. In Act VI, when Dushyanta shares his remorseful confidences with Māḍhavya, he reports that, 'as I was leaving for the capital, my love asked me with tearful eyes: "When will my noble husband send a message from the city?"' In response to Shakuntalā at that moment,

> Placing my ring on her finger, I said,
>
> 'My love, count one letter of my name
> Inscribed on this ring
> For each day that I am gone—
> By the time you have counted
> The letters and the days,

> The messenger I send to welcome you
> To the inner chambers of my palace
> Will be at your side.' (Segment 137)

So Dushyanta actually gives his signet to Shakuntalā as a clever, practical timing device: the letters of his name inscribed in the metal are to serve as a means of counting, like beads on an abacus, and when the counting is coordinated with the natural periodicity of the earth's diurnal round, the improvised abacus functions like a ticking clock, long before the invention of oscillating pendulums and numbered dials. Thus, first and foremost, Dushyanta conceives of his gift to Shakuntalā as an elementary mechanism for tracking time, and as an equivalent of an alarm on a clock or calendar—and not as a token to trigger either recollection or recognition. Even when he decides impulsively, moments later in the same scene, to 'reproach this ring' for not being on her finger at the fire sanctuary, he still does not spell out its role as an aid to memory or cognition, focusing instead on its erotics as an ornament (Segment 138).

In contrast, as Dushyanta and Shakuntalā come face-to-face for the first time in about seven years in Act VII, her first response to his image 'wasted with remorse' is non-recognition:

> He does not look like my noble husband. Then who is this man who defiles my son with his touch at this moment . . ? (Segment 179)

But once she has recognized him—only because of what he says to her—and he has fully expressed his 'remorse and regret' by falling at her feet, she sees the ring on his finger as he wipes away her tears, and it becomes an object of recognition in itself, and does not function as a means: 'Noble sir,' she says, 'this is the ring!' Only in response to this moment does Dushyanta, for the first time, acknowledge its function as a token of remembrance with the statement that, 'Indeed, the recovery of this ring brought back my memory of earlier events'—which, in terms of dramatic structure, completes the process of her recognition of him (immediately after Verse 182).

In the act of acknowledging the ring's identity, Dushyanta confirms his own identity to Shakuntalā, so that the ring, in fact, does not serve to identify her to him; he then tries to give her the ring again, but now as an emblem of their reunion and of the completion of the full cycle of love. Shakuntalā, however, rejects the fresh gift for three clear reasons: (a) because the ring 'did great damage when it was nowhere to be found', and hence for the effects it has had through its absence rather than its presence; (b) because it failed to be present 'just when it was needed to persuade my noble husband', and hence, again, for its effects in absence; and (c) because 'I do not believe in this ring', and hence for its undependability as a token of trust or commitment, and for its incapacity to perform the functions intended for it.

When Shakuntalā voices the play's final reference to the ring, her suggestion that 'Let my noble husband wear it' is neither a condemnation of the object itself nor an insult to Dushyanta, but a matter-of-fact assertion that, so far as she is concerned, the ring does not work in any of the extra roles imposed on it—as a gift, as a device to activate memory or cognition, as an instrument of recollection or recognition, as a proxy abacus or a crypto-clock, as a publicly visible emblem of union or reunion, as a means of persuasion, as a token of love and commitment, and so on. The only function that the ring can and does perform is its straightforward original function, of identifying its owner and confirming his identity, which is inscribed on its body of metal with the letters of his name. Thus, as its dramatic exposition comes full circle, *Shakuntalā* seems to shrink the ring back to its own small circumference, without an aura of symbolic, emblematic, and figurative representation. The *abhijñāna* in the title of the play, therefore, is not so much ambiguous as it is ungrammatically, self-deconstructively ironic.

Underneath its circuitry, however, Kālidāsa's *nāṭaka* provides us with a 1600-year-old model of cognition and memory that has the kind of clarity that we routinely associate with the clinical precision of modern times. On one side, when Shakuntalā fails to produce the ring on cue during the confrontation at the fire sanctuary in Act V, its absence does not affect Dushyanta's cognitive faculty. In fact, throughout his encounter with the ascetics' party and with Shakuntalā, he demonstrates repeatedly and at several levels that his cognition is in full working order, not only in his forensics but also in his asides and interior monologues. What the absence of the ring in those scenes amounts to is a failure to jog his memory, which implies that an act of remembering 'causes' an act of recognition, and when the former does not occur the latter also cannot. On the other side, Shakuntalā's recapitulation of the fact that she cannot remember being cursed, and that she never knew that she had been placed under a curse, implies that, phenomenologically, a particular act of cognition 'causes' a particular memory to come into existence, to be stored, and potentially to be retrievable.

Taken together, these two insights add up to the incisive position that the faculties of cognition and memory are connected to each other by a two-way channel of causality, in which a definite cognitive act has to precede the creation of a specific memory, and that a process of remembering then has to precede a process of re-cognition. This is something we have understood independently, with equal certainty, in the modern period only after the long, arduous development from Immanuel Kant to William James, and to contemporary clinical psychology and the scientific study of memory and cognitive development.[38]

But where does the ring come from, in the first place? One possible source that Orientalists cite is a short Buddhist tale, known as 'Katthahari Jātaka', in the Pali canon. In this narrative, Brahmadatta, king of Banaras, meets a forest girl while wandering in a forest and seduces her; she conceives the Bodhisattva. The king gives her his signet ring and says, 'If it is a girl, use the ring to provide for her support, but if it is a boy, bring child and ring to me.' When the woman brings her son and the ring to the palace, Brahmadatta rejects them out of shame. She performs an 'act of truth', saying, 'If this son is yours, may he stay suspended in mid-air, but if he is not, may he fall to the ground and die.' She then tosses the child up into the air. The Bodhisattva, seated cross-legged in mid-air, declares that he is the king's son, and thus compels Brahmadatta to accept his mother and himself.[39]

But a narrative that is much closer in language and culture, and hence a likelier source for Kālidāsa, is an episode late in the Rāmāyaṇa. After realizing that Rāvaṇa has abducted Sītā to Laṅkā, and may be holding her prisoner in a citadel on the island, Rāma arranges for his new ally Hanumāna, a *vānara* with supernatural powers (later deified as 'the monkey god'), to reconnoitre the location. Hanumāna sets out with two aids, in case he is able to make contact with Sītā: an oral ekphrastic description in verse, which would enable him to recognize the place (since he does not know her by sight); and a royal signet ring, which would enable her to recognize him as Rama's representative (since she does not know him by sight). After some exploration, Hanumāna locates Sītā in a garden at Rāvaṇa's palace, with female demons guarding her; he hides in a tree and watches and listens to the women (who are near *ashoka* trees—as Dushyanta is in Segment 170) until he is certain of Sītā's identity and situation; and when the guards leave for a while and Sītā is alone, he emerges from the tree (much to her surprise and alarm) and gives her the ring to identify himself.[40]

Dushyanta's encounter with Shakuntalā in Act I has more elements in common with the Rāmāyaṇa episode than with the Jātaka: he does not know her by sight; he observes her for a while with her companions in a cultivated grove (while he hides behind a tree); he emerges suddenly from the surrounding foliage, much to the girls' alarm (who do not know him by sight); and he identifies himself as a representative of the king when he gives them his ring (which, in his case, unlike Hanumāna's, is a misidentification). The homology of the two scenes ripples with comic ironies when the ring enters the picture for the first time, and these ironies are magnified when, in her last intimate words to Dushyanta in the play (in Act VII), Shakuntalā says: 'I do not believe in this ring. Let my noble husband wear it.'

Appendices

The following appendices synthesize information from a number of sources listed in the Select Bibliography at the end of this book. My references to the sources are general rather than specific, and hence are incorporated here by the author's last name, rather than in separate endnotes.

The tradition of Sanskrit poetics, dramaturgy, and literary criticism that I invoke begins with Bharata's *Nāṭyashāstra* (third century). Two of its influential summaries and interpretations appear in Dhanañjaya's late-classical *Dasha-rūpaka* (tenth century) and Vishvanātha's post-classical *Sāhitya-darpaṇa* (1384). All my references here to the Mahābhārata are to van Buitenen's English translation. Comparisons with other English translations of *Shakuntalā* are based on Miller; Rajan; and Johnson. My discussion of Sanskrit and Prakrit terms draws on Apte; and of Sanskrit and Prakrit versification, on Apte's Appendix A, 'Sanskrit Prosody' (following page 1758 of the dictionary).

Most contemporary theatre practitioners, however, are unlikely to find these specialized sources helpful on their own. Directors, dramaturges, actors, and stage personnel should consult the following items in the Select Bibliography for reliable and useful accounts of the Indian performance tradition and its relation to *Shakuntalā*: Baumer and Brandon; Bose; Gandhi; Gitomer; Miller; Raghavan; Richmond; Sengupta and Tandon; and Vatsyayan. For new perspectives on Indian theatre, they also should see various articles in Liu's *Handbook* by Aparna Dharwadker; Foley; Madhavan; Mason; Richmond; and Singh.

Appendix A

EXTENDED DRAMATIS PERSONAE

1. In Order of Appearance

Characters are described here in greater detail than in the Dramatis Personae accompanying the translation of the play. Each character's first appearance on the stage or offstage, or first mention in the dialogue, is specified by act and scene; and his or her gender is mentioned in parenthesis after the name. For information about characters' names and their meanings, see Appendix B.

CHARACTERS ON THE STAGE

Act I

I.ii

STAGE MANAGER (m): A composite figure representing the master of the players' company and the director and stage manager of the present production, as played by an actor onstage; the conventional *sūtra-dhāra* of a classical

Sanskrit play, who 'holds the thread' of continuity and coherence running through the work.

ACTRESS (f): An actress in the present production, as played by an actress on the stage; the conventional *naṭī* of a classical play.

I.iii

DUSHYANTA (m): A king of the Puru dynasty, who rules at Hastināpura; the *nāyaka* or male protagonist.

CHARIOTEER (m): Dushyanta's royal charioteer.

VAIKHĀNASA (m): An old celibate ascetic at Kaṇva's ashram. (For layout of ashram, see Illustration 3.)

TWO DISCIPLES (m): Novice ascetics at Kaṇva's ashram.

I.iv

SHAKUNTALĀ (f): The daughter of Menakā (a celestial being or *apsarā*) and Vishvāmitra (a human sage); adopted and raised by Kaṇva; the *nāyikā* or female protagonist.

ANASŪYĀ *and* PRIYAṀVADĀ (both f): Shakuntalā's intimate friends at Kaṇva's ashram.

Act II

II.i

MĀḌHAVYA (m): Dushyanta's court jester and confidant, a poor brahmin.

II.ii

KING'S BODYGUARD (all f): A troop of Greek warrior women, with a designated leader.

II.iii

RAIVATAKA (m): A gatekeeper and guard at Dushyanta's hunting camp. (For layout of camp, see Illustration 3.)

BHADRASENA (m): A general, the chief of Dushyanta's army, who accompanies the king on his hunting expedition.

II.v

GAUTAMA *and* NĀRADA (both m): Adolescent novice ascetics at Kaṇva's ashram.

II.vi

KARABHAKA (m): The queen-mother's messenger.

Act III

III.i

APPRENTICE PRIEST (m): A young man at Kaṇva's ashram, in training as a specialist in Vedic sacrifice.

III.v

GAUTAMĪ (m): An older female ascetic, the maternal figure at Kaṇva's ashram.

Act IV

IV.ii

DISCIPLE (m): A novice ascetic at Kaṇva's ashram.

IV.iii

ASCETICS' WIVES (all f): A group of women of various ages at Kaṇva's ashram.

IV.iv

KAṆVA (m): A celibate sage with supernatural powers; the spiritual guide and master of the community of ascetics at his ashram, located in an enchanted forest at the foothills of the Himalayas, north-east of Dushyanta's capital, Hastināpura. (For locations, see map in Illustration 2.)

SHĀRAṄGARAVA (m): An adult ascetic, who serves as Kaṇva's envoy to Dushyanta, and leads Shakuntalā's escort to Hastināpura.

SHĀRADVATA (m): Another adult ascetic, second to Shāraṅgarava in Shakuntalā's escort.

ASCETICS (all m): Several male ascetics of various ages at Kaṇva's ashram who, together with Gautamī, escort Shakuntalā to Hastināpura.

Act V

V.ii

VĀTĀYANA (m): Dushyanta's aged chamberlain at the palace. (For layout of palace, see Illustration 4.)

VETRAVATĪ (f): Dushyanta's principal aide at his palace, a woman who serves as an all-purpose assistant.

V.iii

TWO BARDS (both m): Poets and performers patronized by the royal court.

V.iv

SOMARĀTA (m): Dushyanta's *purohita*, the priest of the royal family.

Act VI

VI.i

CITY SUPERINTENDENT (m): Responsible for law and order in Hastināpura; the brother of one of Dushyanta's lesser queens, and hence the king's brother-in-law or *shyālah*.

SŪCHAKA *and* JĀNUKA (both m): Two policemen who serve the superintendent.

FISHERMAN (m): A poor resident of Indra's Ford, born into a caste classified as 'untouchable' in classical society. (For location, see Illustration 2.)

VI.ii

SĀNUMATĪ (f): An *apsarā*, a celestial female with supernatural powers; Menakā's friend and assistant, and hence a friend to Shakuntalā.

PARABHRITIKĀ *and* MADHUKARIKĀ (both f): Novice palace attendants, recent additions to the retinue of Dushyanta's chief queen, Vasumatī.

VI.iv

CHATURIKĀ (f): One of Dushyanta's palace attendants, trained in the arts, who also assists him with painting.

VI.vi

MĀTALI (m): The god Indra's celestial charioteer, who escorts Dushyanta from earth to heaven and back.

Act VII

VII.ii

TWO ASCETIC WOMEN (both f): Female ascetics at Kashyapa's celestial ashram, who serve Shakuntalā; the first is called SUVRATĀ, the second is unnamed. (For layout of celestial ashram, see Illustration 4.)

SARVADAMANA (m): The son of Dushyanta and Shakuntalā, born and raised at Kashyapa's ashram; destined to be renamed as Bharata, and to be the founder of the future nation (Bhārata or India) named after him.

VII.iv

KASHYAPA (m): A sage of divine origin (grandson of Brahmā, the god of creation), who lives in his celestial ashram on Mount Meru.

ADITI (f): Kashyapa's wife, also of divine origin.

GĀLAVA (m): Kashyapa's celestial disciple and assistant.

VOICES BACKSTAGE

Thirteen of the onstage characters also deliver dialogue offstage. The other five backstage voices belong to characters who do not appear on the stage; they are identified here with asterisks, and are described further under the next heading.

Act I

I.i, Verse 1: Stage Manager (Invocation)
I.iii, Segment 10: Vaikhānasa
I.iv, Segment 15: Shakuntalā
I.vi, Verses 28–29: Ashram Crier*

Act II

II.v, Segment 44: Gautama

Act III

III.v, Segment 70: Anasūyā
III.v, Segment 72: Priest (at ashram)*

Act IV

IV.i, Segment 73: Durvāsā (twice)*
IV.ii, after Verse 76: Kaṇva
IV.v, Verse 83: Goddesses of the enchanted grove (in unison)*

Act V

V.i, Verse 95: Haṁsapadikā (song)*

V.iii, Segment 101: Two bards of the royal court (in unison)
V.v, Segment 124: Somarāta

Act VI
VI.ii, after Verse 130: Vetravatī
VI.vi: Māḍhavya (four times) and Mātali (once)

Act VII
VII.ii, Segment 171: Suvratā

CHARACTERS NOT ON THE STAGE

Five characters or groups who participate directly in the dramatic action actually do not appear on the stage. Besides the Ashram Crier (I.vi), the Priest (III.v), and the goddesses of the enchanted grove (IV.v) listed above, the two offstage participants who are important in the plot are Durvāsā and Haṁsapadikā.

IV.i

DURVĀSĀ (m): An irascible sage, an unexpected visitor at Kaṇva's ashram, who remains out of the audience's sight, but places a curse on Shakuntalā and Dushyanta that changes the course of the action on the stage.

V.i

HAṀSAPADIKĀ (f): A lesser queen at the palace, a former favourite of Dushyanta, whose song shows that Durvāsā's curse has taken effect on the king.

CHARACTERS ONLY MENTIONED IN THE DIALOGUE

Act I

MENAKĀ (f): An *apsarā* or celestial female. In events preceding the action of the play, the god Indra sends her down to earth to seduce Vishvāmitra, a powerful human sage. Menakā conceives Shakuntalā in this union, but abandons her in infancy; Kaṇva finds the child being protected by birds, and raises her in his ashram. In the play, when Dushyanta abandons the pregnant Shakuntalā, Menakā arranges for her rescue, and helps her deliver and raise her son, Sarvadamana, in the celestial ashram of Kashyapa and Aditi, Indra's parents.

VISHVĀMITRA (m): A sage who practises severe austerities, whom Indra dreads for his spiritual power, and who is Shakuntalā's biological father. The fact that he is of human origin and a kshatriya or warrior by birth legitimizes Dushyanta's quest for Shakuntalā in a marriage by mutual consent.

INDRA (m): The chief god of the Vedic pantheon, who lives in his own heaven called *svarga*. In the play, he is a close friend of Dushyanta, who leads his divine armies to victory in a war against the antigods.

Act II

QUEEN-MOTHER (f): Dushyanta's mother, who lives at the palace in Hastināpura.

Act IV

SHACHI (f): A goddess, Indra's wife. In the play, a shrine for pilgrims is dedicated to her at Indra's Ford (midway between Kaṇva's ashram and Dushyanta's capital), and the ring is lost and recovered in the waters at the shrine. (See Illustration 2.)

Act V

VASUMATĪ (f): Dushyanta's current chief queen.

Act VI

MITRĀVASU (m): The manager of administrative affairs for the kingdom, who recommends Parabhritrikā and Madhukarikā to his sister, queen Vasumatī; like the City Superintendent, a brother-in-law of Dushyanta.

TARALIKĀ (f): Queen Vasumatī's personal attendant.

PISHUNA (m): The chief minister of the kingdom, who works closely with Dushyanta on matters of the treasury, justice, and public welfare.

DEATH RING *and* THE INVINCIBLES: The anti-god Kālanemi (literally, 'Death Ring') and his sons, who form a violent gang called 'the Invincibles' in the realm of the gods and antigods, and go to war with Indra.

Act VII

JAYANTA (m): Indra's son (by Shachi), who also lives in *svarga*, and is envious of Dushyanta.

SHĀKLYA (m): An ancient ascetic, who serves sage Kashyapa at the latter's celestial ashram.

2. By Gender and Language

This list groups the characters with speaking parts and onstage appearances by gender, in the order of appearance. Eight male characters—Māḍhavya, Raivataka, Karabhaka, City Superintendent, Sūchaka, Jānuka, Fisherman, and Sarvadamana—speak Prakrit in the original, and their names are marked with asterisks in the following table. All the other male characters and voices use Sanskrit. Among the female characters, Priyaṁvadā speaks Prakrit, but quotes Verse 76 in Sanskrit, whereas the goddesses of the sacred grove speak only in Sanskrit (Verse 83). All the other female characters and voices use Prakrit.

MALE	FEMALE
On the stage	*On the stage*
Stage Manager	Actress
Dushyanta	Shakuntalā
Charioteer	Anasūyā
Vaikhānasa	Priyaṁvadā
Two Disciples	King's Bodyguard
Māḍhavya*	Gautamī
Raivataka*	Ascetics' Wives
Bhadrasena	Vetravatī
Gautama	Sānumatī
Nārada	Parabhritikā
Karabhaka*	Madhukarikā
Apprentice Priest	Chaturikā
Disciple	Suvratā
Kaṇva	Second Ascetic Woman
Shārangarava	Aditi
Shāradvata	

MALE	FEMALE
Ascetics	*Backstage voices only*
Vātāyana	Goddesses of the enchanted grove
Two Bards	Haṁsapadikā
Somarāta	
City Superintendent*	
Sūchaka*	
Jānuka*	
Fisherman*	
Mātali	
Sarvadamana*	
Kashyapa	
Gālava	
Backstage voices only	
Ashram Crier	
Priest	
Durvāsā	

Among the male characters, the Disciple in IV.ii may be one of the Two Disciples accompanying Vaikhānasa in I.iii, and the Ascetics in the group escorting Shakuntalā in Acts IV–V would include recognizable members of the ashram community (for example, Vaikhānasa, the Two Disciples, and Gautama and Nārada). Among the female characters, for plausibility the King's Bodyguard would have at least four women warriors (including one troop leader), and there would be at least three Ascetics' Wives in IV.iii. Excluding the backstage voices, the Dramatis Personae then represents twenty-eight male and twenty-two female characters, for a total of fifty distinct speaking parts on the stage. With the inclusion of characters who appear only as backstage voices, the number of speaking parts is at least fifty-four.

Appendix B

CHARACTERS AND NAMES

Many of the characters in *Shakuntalā* carry different names and epithets (and variations in spelling) in different manuscripts, recensions, and modern printed editions. Aside from changes arising from error and confusion in transmission, the variations are not entirely systematic: some may be due to the particular choices of scribes, editors, or patrons; some, due to script systems (Bangla in Bengal, Sharada in Kashmir, Devanagari elsewhere); and others, due to regional stylistic and aesthetic predilections. Some texts—and translations—adopt distinctive personal names for some characters (for example, Shakuntalā, Anasūyā, and Priyaṁvadā) but generic epithets for others, taken from the inventories of character-types in Sanskrit poetics (for example, the equivalent of 'king' for Dushyanta, 'buffoon' for Māḍhavya, 'chamberlain' for Vātāyana, and 'doorkeeper' for Vetravatī).

The primary and secondary as well as tertiary characters in *Shakuntalā* are highly individuated, even when their functions in the plot conform closely to the prescriptions of Sanskrit dramaturgy. In a modern English dramatic environment, the use of descriptive terms rather than personal names goes against the grain of the play, as it creates the misimpression that well-rounded characters are flat, impersonal stereotypes. My translation therefore employs personal names wherever they are available in the textual tradition, replacing some of the epithets used in the Devanagari recension and the Narayan Ram edition. There are several exceptions—such as Stage Manager, Actress, Charioteer, Ashram Crier, Two Bards, City Superintendent, and Fisherman—which are explained below and in the Extended Dramatis Personae in Appendix A.

In many instances, the personal names are important because their specific meanings and contexts illuminate the representation as well as the interpretation of character and action, as much in words as on the stage. The following list is selective, and follows the general order in which characters appear in the play. Among them, Dushyanta, Shakuntalā, Māḍhavya, Kaṇva, Kashyapa, Anasūyā, and Priyaṁvadā are discussed in greater detail in the Afterword.

DUSHYANTA (m): Duhshanta in the Mahābhārata and in Pischel's edition of the Bengal recension; Dushmanta in Jones's text and translation; Dussanta in Shauraseni (Prakrit); and Dushyanta in Rāghavabhaṭṭa's fifteenth-century Sanskrit commentary. In J.A.B. van Buitenen's interpretation, the term 'Duhshanta' describes 'a man who is ill-tamed'. The Mahābhārata portrays the king as 'ignoble'; Kālidāsa rewrites the character as 'consistently noble', and hence is able to recast Dushyanta and Shakuntalā as soulmates in a romantic-heroic love story and Bharata as the son of ideal lovers and parents.

CHARIOTEER (m): Called *sūta* in the play-script. This word has two divergent applications in Sanskrit, for sons born of proscribed couplings between lower-caste men and higher-caste women among the *dvija* or three upper-caste groups (brahmins or priests, kshatriyas or warriors, and vaishyas or merchants). (a) A son of a kshatriya father and a brahmin mother is called a *sūta*, and his enforced occupation is that of charioteer. (b) A son of a vaishya father and a kshatriya mother is also called a *sūta*, but his enforced occupation is that of bard. Dushyanta's Charioteer in Act I belongs to the former category, and hence speaks Sanskrit. See note on Two Bards below.

VAIKHĀNASA (m): Literally, 'old celibate ascetic', which scholars and translators interpret variously as an epithet or a personal name. The word is applied to an aged ascetic who has grown emaciated with sexual abstinence and self-mortification.

SHAKUNTALĀ (f): Literally, 'the girl [under the protection] of the birds'; a descriptive term that becomes a proper noun, and hence a personal name. According to the story within the story of the Mahābhārata and of Kālidāsa's play, Shakuntalā is the daughter born of Menakā's liaison with Vishvāmitra, on the banks of the River Mālinī, in the epic age. Menakā, an *apsarā* or celestial being, abandons the infant near the river and returns to her life in Indra's heaven. A family of birds (called *shakunta* in Sanskrit, a word also used for peacocks, as in VII.ii) feeds and protects the child until, one day, Kaṇva goes to wash at the river—in the environs of his ashram—and discovers her near the bank. He calls her Shakuntalā to memorialize her state as a foundling protected by birds, and adopts and raises her as his own daughter at the ashram. The play alludes to this background in VII.ii, when Suvratā refers to a painted-clay toy peacock as a *shakunta*, and the young Sarvadamaṇa mistakes the word for his mother's name.

ANASŪYĀ (f): In the play, Anasūyā embodies the literal meaning of her name, 'a woman who is free of spite, envy, and ill-will'. In Sanskrit myth outside the play, Anasūyā is the name of the wife of the divine sage Atri, who is one of seven original sons of the god Brahmā; Atri is therefore a brother of Marīchi (Kashyapa's father) and of Daksha (Aditi's father), and is a 'paternal uncle' to both Kashyapa and Aditi, who appear in Act VII. Atri and his wife Anasūyā are the biological parents of the sage Durvāsā, who places the curse on Shakuntalā and Dushyanta in Act IV. Kālidāsa's fictional Anasūyā reflects some of the famous qualities of her mythical counterpart: chastity, loyalty to friends, generosity of spirit, and rigorous spiritual self-discipline.

PRIYAṀVADĀ (f): 'A sweet-spoken woman, one who is skilled at sweet talk', a description that serves as a personal name. Both Shakuntalā and Dushyanta allude to this literal meaning in Segment 18. Kālidāsa also uses this epithet for Pārvatī (Shiva's consort), the heroine of his poem *Kumārasaṁbhava*.

ASHRAM CRIER (m): Epithet devised for my translation, by analogy to 'town crier'. It labels the unidentified voice backstage that delivers the public announcement (called a *chulika* in Sanskrit dramaturgy) heard across the ashram grounds in Verses 28–29, at the beginning of I.vi.

MĀḌHAVYA (m): Prakrit variant of Sanskrit Māḍhavya, derived from Mādhava, one of Vishṇu's names (in his incarnation as Krishna), and hence a name for a Vaishnava brahmin. His Prakrit name and discourse indicate that he comes from a line of impoverished brahmins who cannot afford an education in Sanskrit, and hence cannot pursue their hereditary occupation as priests and scholars. As a Vaishnava brahmin in north India, Māḍhavya would fastidiously maintain a vegetarian diet and observe the rules of pollution, despite his lapsed occupational status—hence his distaste for meat at the hunting camp and for 'unclean' water in the forest (II.i).The fact that Dushyanta nevertheless treats him as a confidant and intimate friend (for example, in II.iv and VI.iii–iv), entrusts him with important personal and official tasks (II.vi and Segment 157), and responds intuitively to his cry for help and spares no effort to save him (VI.vi)—together with the fact that Māḍhavya reciprocally 'saves' Dushyanta from a psychological breakdown in Act VI—indicates that the two men share a deep childhood bond that bridges their differences of birth and social position.

RAIVATAKA (m): Literally, 'the mountain named Raivataka'; hence, 'a man mountain'. His name suggests that he is a gatekeeper with a large physique—the classical antecedent of a modern-day 'bouncer', but comically a 'gentle giant'.

BHADRASENA (m): 'Noble warrior'; also addressed as *senapati*, 'chief of the army', a label for a stock character in a *nāṭaka* with a king as its hero.

GAUTAMA and NĀRADA (both m): The play-script in the Narayana Rama edition identifies them only as 'disciples', but the dialogue gives them these personal names (IV.iii). Several sages who are prominent in Indian myth, religion, and philosophy carry 'Gautama' as a primary or alternative name: for example, Bharadvāja; Shatānanda, son of Gotama and Ahalyā; the Buddha; and the founder of the Nyaya philosophical system. 'Nārada' is the name of one of Brahmā's sons, a wily divine sage who constantly mediates between gods and humans, interferes in their affairs, and creates confusion between them. Kālidāsa's choice of these names for bright, adolescent disciples at Kaṇva's ashram is a humorous swipe at Indian religion and intellectual history, a literary joke for fellow poets and connoisseurs.

DURVĀSĀ (m): 'The man who lives in a foul place'; an 'irascible sage' famous for his unreasonable conduct. In V.S. Apte's words, he is 'very hard to please' and curses many creatures 'to suffer misery and degradation'. He is the son of the divine sage Atri and his wife Anasūyā; since Atri is a son of Brahmā, the god of creation, and hence a brother of Marīchi (father of Kashyapa) and of Daksha (father of Aditi), Durvāsā is a 'paternal cousin' of both Kashyapa and Aditi in the play. Kaṇva, Shakuntalā's adoptive father, is descended from Kashyapa (Segments 16 and 188), so Durvāsā also belongs to a distant 'paternal branch' of Kaṇva's lineage. In the Mahābhārata, Durvāsā is the sage who—in one of his rare happy gestures—gives a potent mantra to Kuntī, the mother of some of the epic's heroes. Kuntī uses that magical formula to invoke the gods Sun, Dharma, Wind, and Indra to father sons on her, and hence conceives and gives birth to Karṇa, Yudhishṭhira, Bhīma, and Arjuna, respectively.

KAṆVA (m): Name of a *rishi* (in this case, a human sage, a brahmin by birth) traditionally named as the *kavi* or poet who, along with his 'family of poets', recorded and transmitted the hymns that were collected in the eighth mandala or cycle of the *Rig-veda saṁhitā* around 1000 BCE. He is the progenitor of the lineage (*gotra*) of Kāṇva brahmins. Act IV clearly identifies its fictive character with the Vedic sage of the same name. Also see Appendix D.

The play situates Kaṇva in a large group of *rishi*s or sages. The group includes Kashyapa (his direct patrilineal ancestor, of divine origin), Durvāsā (who belongs to a branch of his paternal genealogy), and Vishvāmitra (a human sage who is Shakuntalā's biological father), all of whom are featured on the stage or offstage. At a remove, the group also includes Atri (Durvāsā's father), Marīchi (Kashyapa's father), and Daksha (Aditi's father), all three of whom are Brahmā's sons and hence of divine origin; and, through literary allusion, Gotama and Bharadvāja (linked to Gautama's name) as well as Nārada (linked to the eponymous disciple in the play). Four of the sages in this group are identified as 'authors' of hymns and verses in the *Rig-veda saṃhitā*: Kaṇva and his 'family of poets' contribute 1315 verses, the second largest such contribution to the scriptural collection (mostly in Mandala 8); Vishvāmitra and his family compose 983 verses (Mandala 3), the fourth largest contribution; Atri and his family author 885 verses (Mandala 5); and Kashyapa and his family contribute 415 verses (especially Mandala 9). Hymns attributed to the Kaṇva, Kashyapa, and Vishvāmitra families appear together among the 108 hymns in Mandala 8. Kālidāsa's recasting of the Shakuntalā–Dushyanta story thus builds on an older pattern in Indian texts.

SHĀRAṄGARAVA (m): Literally, 'the sound of a bow', which refers both to the loud release of an arrow and to the twang or 'thunderclap' of a bowstring. Shāraṅgarava's name characterizes him as a powerful and deadly weapon, a metaphor that resonates with his performance in Act V, where he attacks and counter-attacks Dushyanta in a battle of words, wits, and moral arguments, and leaves Shakuntalā cowering in terror.

HAṀSAPADIKĀ (f): 'The woman who walks with the gait of a swan'. The allusion to lotuses in her backstage song (Verse 95) suggests that, in her youth, she may have had the grace of a swan gliding on water.

VĀTĀYANA (m): The play-script refers to him as *kañchuki*, the label in Sanskrit dramaturgy for the stock character of a king's chamberlain, who plays a key role when the action focuses on sexual intrigues in a palace. Dushyanta, however, addresses him by the name Vātāyana, literally 'horse', which may point to his figurative resemblance to an aged work-horse who continues to serve his master with complete devotion.

VETRAVATĪ (f): Literally, 'female doorkeeper'; the play-script refers to her by the synonymous epithet *pratihārī*; other versions of the play also use another common synonym, *dvārapālikā*, for this stock character in the *nāṭaka* genre. Her distinctive characterization here indicates a strong, energetic, probably athletic, and resourceful young woman who serves Dushyanta as his all-purpose aide or assistant at the palace. She is close to the king, but not as close as Māḍhavya.

TWO BARDS (both m): In epic and classical Sanskrit, a bard is usually called a *sūta*, and is a son born of a proscribed coupling of a vaishya father (merchant caste group) and a kshatriya mother (warrior caste group), or a descendant in such a lineage. In the opening verse of the Mahābhārata, for instance, the 'singer of ancient tales' named Ugrashravas (literally, the sound of whose powerful and passionate words is 'terrifying to the ear'), who performs the epic as it has come down to us, is a *sūta* in this sense—like his famous father, Lomaharshaṇa (literally, the bard whose recitations are 'hair-raising'), before him. But the word *sūta* has a double meaning in the pre-classical and classical caste system; see note on Charioteer above. To avoid confusion, the Devanagari recension of *Shakuntalā* calls each of the Two Bards a *vaitālika*, a poet-performer who specializes in narration using a large class of complex metrical verse-forms called *vaitālīya*. Verses 101–102 are both in Sanskrit, in the *mālinī* verse-form, with fifteen syllables per quarter; see Appendix H. My differentiation of the two senses of *sūta* follows Apte, and diverges significantly from van Buitenen's.

SĀNUMATĪ (f): The name associates her with a 'mountain peak' (*sānu*), which may refer to her current residence with Menakā and Shakuntalā on Mount Meru. She is also known in the Bengal recension by the epithet Mishrakeshī, an *apsarā* or celestial creature 'with mixed hair', which may refer to supernaturally multicoloured hair, or hair of different qualities and textures. It seems likely that the play conceives of her as a celestial attendant with an exotic head of hair.

PARABHRITIKĀ and MADHUKARIKĀ (both f): The first name means 'the girl with the voice of a koel', and Barbara Stoler Miller renders it as 'Little Cuckoo'; the second refers to 'the girl who makes honey [like a bee]', and Miller translates it as 'Little Bee'. Both girls are adolescents in their first employment, and, like several other female and male characters in the play, they make a gendered pair with a shared plot function, mutual resemblance, and complementary qualities.

Among other such female and male pairs in the play are Anasūyā and Priyaṁvadā; Gautamī and Aditi; Vetravatī and Chaturikā; Suvratā and the Second Ascetic Woman; Kaṇva and Kashyapa; Gautama and Nārada; Shāraṅgarava and Shāradvata; Bhadrasena and Vātāyana; Sūchaka and Jānuka; and the Charioteer and Mātali.

CHATURIKĀ (f): Literally, 'the clever and skilful young woman'; in other versions of the play, also labelled as *cheṭi*, a female servant or attendant, a stock figure in Sanskrit–Prakrit drama. She primarily is Dushyanta's skilled assistant for painting and art, but also is involved in other aspects of his palace life, and works with Vetravatī to serve his interests and ensure his well-being in general.

SUVRATĀ (f): A celestial ascetic, 'the woman whose vows and observances are good'. Along with the second, unnamed female ascetic, she serves Shakuntalā at Kashyapa's celestial ashram on Mount Meru, and looks after Sarvadamana in his childhood, as a classical equivalent of a modern nanny or baby-sitter.

SARVADAMANA (m): An epithet meaning 'the [boy or man] who dominates everybody'. Sarvadamana, Shakuntalā and Dushyanta's son, is probably about eight years old when he appears on the stage in Act VII. In the Mahābhārata version of the story, Shakuntalā's pregnancy lasts for three years; she delivers the boy and raises him at Kaṇva's ashram, and travels with him to Hastināpura when he is six years old; and she thus attempts to reunite and reconcile with Dushyanta about nine years after their first union.

KASHYAPA (m): Personal name of a divine *rishi* or sage. He is the son of Marīchi, and hence also is designated in the play's recensions and manuscripts with the patronymic Mārīchi. Brahmā, the god of creation in Hinduism, engenders his progeny 'out of himself'; among his sons are Marīchi and

Daksha; Kashyapa is a son of Marīchi, and hence a grandson of Brahmā. Kashyapa, in turn, becomes the divine originator of many orders and species of beings in the universe, and hence is a *prajāpati*, 'lọrd and father of creatures' (see the Afterword).

ADITI (m): Personal name of Kashyapa's wife or consort. She is the divine daughter of Daksha, who is one of Brahmā's sons and a brother of Marīchi. Genealogically, Kashyapa and Aditi are divine 'first cousins', and they are the progenitors or parents of Indra, the principal god of the Vedic pantheon (and a close counterpart of Zeus in the Greek, and of Jove in the Roman, pantheon). When the god Vishṇu decides to incarnate himself as a dwarf, he chooses to be 'born' from Aditi's womb.

Appendix C

SETTINGS BY ACT AND SCENE

The settings of the play are not specified in the Sanskrit stage directions, and have to be inferred from a close reading of the text. An understanding of the 'when' and 'where' of the action is necessary for its interpretation, but the text compresses and dilates both time and space, and its structure creates a dynamic correlation between events and their representation. The original is divided into seven acts, but not into scenes; as the action evolves in each act and across the acts together, time and location change fluidly, as in a modern cinematic montage. In this context, the following chart offers readers, theatre personnel, and potential spectators a preliminary orientation to the time and location of each event and situation in the play. The settings are identified by the scene divisions marked in boldface along the left margin of my translation, with capital Roman numerals designating acts, and lower case numerals specifying the distinct scenes in each act.

The *Nāṭyashāstra* tradition theoretically requires an act in a play to represent events that occur on a 'single day', so that it possesses the unity of time, and each act in *Shakuntalā* seems to follow this prescription. But plausibility requires that some of its acts (especially Acts II and VI) represent events that take place at different times or in significantly different situations, even when they appear to display a unity of place. In the following notes, I leave open the possibility that, underneath its tightly integrated surface, the play actually exploits a 'double time-scheme', of the kind that Shakespeare invents independently for his *Othello*.

Act I

I.i
Invocation: Backstage, chanted or recited by Stage Manager, with strings and percussion before and after.

I.ii
Prelude: Stage front or centre, with the set ready around the Stage Manager and the Actress for the act to follow.
Main action: One day in early spring, without perceptible breaks in the onstage representation.

I.iii
Open ground in an enchanted forest, with Kaṇva's ashram and its sacred grove visible on the banks of the River Mālinī in the distance. Early morning.

I.iv–v
The sacred grove. Later that morning, with the action proceeding without a break.

I.vi
The sacred grove continued, but stage time has progressed faster than clock time, so that it is plausibly near sundown at the Ashram Crier's announcement and twilight at Dushyanta's exit.

Act II

Main action: Dushyanta's temporary hunting camp near the enchanted forest, with a royal pavilion and an arbour on its grounds. From morning to midday or later, on one day or on different days, around the onset of summer.

II.i
Open space at the hunting camp, with a transition to the entrance of the royal pavilion. Morning.

II.ii
The royal pavilion at the hunting camp. A little later in the morning.

II.iii
The royal pavilion continued, with a transition at the end to a natural arbour nearby. Late morning.

II.iv
The arbour at the hunting camp, with natural seating or portable campsite furniture. Late morning or midday.

II.v
Unmarked transition back to the royal pavilion. Daytime.

II.vi
The royal pavilion continued, without a perceptible break.

Act III

Main action: The grounds of Kaṇva's ashram, with a transition to a natural arbour on the banks of the River Mālinī, with a low stone ledge shaded by trees and a small enclosure of reeds and vines nearby. From midday to nightfall, apparently on one day in the summer.

III.i
Open space on the grounds of Kaṇva's ashram. Midday.

III.ii
The grounds of the ashram, with a transition to the sandy riverbank and its arbour. Midday.

III.iii–iv
The arbour on the riverbank continued, with stage time progressing steadily to late afternoon.

III.v
The arbour continued without a break, but with stage time shifting to the red glow of sundown and to nightfall by the end of the scene.

Act IV

Main action: The grounds of Kaṇva's ashram, with multiple locations outdoors, including the sacred grove, a space for Vedic rituals, and a clearing with a banyan tree and a view of a lake. The events represented in IV.iii–vi take place from daybreak to late morning on a single day in late autumn, several months after the events in Act III. The scenes in the two parts of the Mixed Interlude (IV.i–ii) occur on different days during that interval, and are designed to indicate the longer passage of time in words as well as performance.

IV.i

Mixed Interlude, Part 1: The sacred grove, with a transition near the end towards the buildings on the grounds of the ashram. Early morning.

IV.ii

Mixed Interlude, Part 2: Open spaces on the ashram grounds. The Disciple and Anasūyā appear simultaneously on the stage in this part of the Interlude, but are unaware of each other, and hence may be at different locations, but both their soliloquies occur around daybreak, immediately after waking from sleep. The Anasūyā–Priyaṁvadā dialogue and the transition at the end of the scene proceed without a break shortly after sunrise. Kaṇva's return from his pilgrimage and Shakuntalā's departure for Hastināpura possibly take place on successive days, or are separated by several hours on one night.

IV.iii

Open space on the ashram grounds, with natural seating. Near it, an area reserved for fire rituals. The latter has a Vedic firepit, and the demarcated ground surrounding it is padded with long sacred grass harvested from the enchanted forest. Shortly after sunrise.

IV.iv

The space with natural seating in the previous scene continued, with one transition midway to the sacred ground around the firepit, and a second transition at the end of the scene to the sacred grove on the ashram grounds. Steady progression in time.

IV.v

The sacred grove continued, with short transitions to different locations in the grove. Morning.

IV.vi

Unmarked transition to the end of the ashram grounds, on the edge of a small lake, with a banyan tree nearby, and with the sacred grove and ashram buildings in one direction and a thick line of trees visible in the distance in the other. Stage time progresses steadily to late morning.

Act V

Main action: Dushyanta's royal palace and its grounds at his capital of Hastināpura, with a secluded canopy in one area and the forecourt of a pavilion for rituals around a sacred fire in another. From early evening to nightfall continuously in late autumn, several days after Shakuntalā's departure from Kaṇva's ashram.

V.i

One of the king's rooms in the palace at Hastināpura. Daytime, soon after Durvāsā's curse has come into effect and well before Shakuntalā's arrival in the city.

V.ii

The grounds at the rear of the palace, with a canopy at one end for the king's private use, and a pavilion for fire rituals (or a 'fire sanctuary'), with a forecourt, at the other. Near sundown, shortly before Shakuntalā's arrival.

V.iii

Extended transition from the canopy to the pavilion, with action along the way ending at its forecourt. No perceptible break in time.

V.iv–v

The forecourt of the pavilion, with Dushyanta standing on the raised platform around the firepit throughout. Stage time and clock time coincide in these two scenes, with evening turning steadily into nightfall by the end of the act.

Act VI

Main action: Multiple locations in the city of Hastināpura and on the palace grounds, with marked and unmarked transitions between them. Daytime in each scene, but the scenes most likely are discontinuous and spread over months, perhaps even years. The events in this act occur in the interval between the end of Act V (when Shakuntalā is visibly pregnant) and the beginning of Act VII (when her son Sarvadamana may be about eight years old). However, these events need not span the whole interval, since Dushyanta leads a war for Indra's army in heaven between the end of Act VI and the beginning of Act VII, which may consume a few years of human time.

VI.i

Mixed Interlude, Part 1: A city market in Hastināpura, with a transition to an area outside the entrance to Dushyanta's palace. Most plausibly, several weeks after Shakuntalā's disappearance in late autumn at the end of Act V.

VI.ii

Mixed Interlude, Part 2: Dushyanta's pleasure garden, with mango trees, outside the women's chambers at his palace. At one end, a canopy covered with flowering vines, with carved stone seats under it. At the other end, a 'skyway' on which the *apsarā* Sānumatī descends from the celestial realm, to observe events on earth on behalf of Shakuntalā's mother, Menakā. The action of Part 2 of the Interlude takes place in an open space under the mango trees. Delayed spring in the garden, the year following Shakuntalā's disappearance (late autumn) and the recovery of the ring (early winter), or later.

VI.iii
The pleasure garden continued, with a transition to the canopy.

VI.iv
The canopy in the pleasure garden continued.

VI.v
At one end, one of the king's rooms (an administrative workspace) in the palace. At another end, the Palace of the Clouds, with stairs going up to its roof. The skyway in between, for Sānumatī to ascend to the celestial realm at the end of this scene. Possible break in time after the preceding scene.

VI.vi
The room in the palace continued, with a transition midway to the roof of the Palace of the Clouds. The skyway still in place, for Mātali and Dushyanta to ascend to Indra's heaven at the end of the act.

Act VII

Main action: In the celestial realm and at Kashyapa's ashram on Mount Meru, between Indra's heaven and earth. 'Celestial daytime' throughout the act in one continuous interval, several years after the events of Act V, and some months or years after those of Act VI—assuming a passage of eight to nine years in human time between Acts IV and VII.

VII.i
The skyway from Indra's heaven to earth. The action begins during a descent on the skyway, and continues through a transition to Mount Meru in an intermediate celestial realm.

VII.ii–iii
An open space, with one or more *ashoka* trees, on the grounds of Kashyapa's celestial ashram on the mountain peak.

VII.iv
The open space on the ashram grounds continued, with a short transition midway to a separate location for the audience with Kashyapa and Aditi.

Appendix D

TIME AND SPACE IN THE DRAMATIC ACTION

Kālidāsa's text identifies Kaṇva as the *rishi* or visionary poet and sage whom the oldest Indian scriptural tradition names as the human recorder and transmitter of the hymns assembled mostly in the eighth mandala (cycle) of the *Rig-veda saṃhitā*. This collection was compiled in historical time by about 1000 BCE, but probably drew on material composed and accumulated over the preceding two or three centuries. This general date fits well with the independent modern historicization of the events represented in the Mahābhārata, which suggests that the epic's interlocutor Janmejaya may correspond to a king who lived around 900 BCE and is mentioned in more than one Vedic source. In the Mahābhārata's narrative, Dushyanta and Shakuntalā are early ancestors of Janmejaya, and may precede him in clock time by as much as 300 years, or roughly fifteen generations, which would also locate Kaṇva around 1200 BCE. This is the most plausible historical date we can assign to the approximate beginning of what emerges as the 'epic time' represented imaginatively in the story of Dushyanta and Shakuntalā in both the Mahābhārata and Kālidāsa's classical play.

Shakuntalā, however, is not a historical play about real-life personages and events. It is an imaginative work that takes a well-known story (from the earlier Mahābhārata) and dramatizes it for aesthetic effectiveness in words and on the stage, fictionalizing its subject matter extensively. In the process, Kālidāsa's text resets the story of Dushyanta and Shakuntalā in three distinct, comprehensively imagined 'worlds' that depend on and interact with each other on many levels, and that readers and spectators have to negotiate alongside the fictive characters. Each of these worlds, and the three together, can be characterized in multiple ways, but their features in the play may be summarized at a basic level as follows. (For the graphic representations of some aspects of these 'worlds', see Illustrations 1–4.)

One is the world of Dushyanta as king, which is centred on his palace and his capital—the city Hastināpura, a major site of urban life and culture in ancient north India. It is a domain of rational thought and action in a kingdom populated by a diverse, 'normal' human society; it is tied to the practicalities of governance and administration, finance and revenue, law and justice, peace and security, and people's quests for fairness, happiness, pleasure, and prosperity. This is the world we encounter especially in Acts II, V, and VI.

The second is the world of Kaṇva and the community of ascetics at his ashram, isolated in a large, dense forest along the foothills of the Himalayas. It is a domain of rigorous spiritual practice in a natural environment—which also contains supernatural elements—where human beings, animals, and plants coexist in ideal harmony. In contrast to the palace, the city, and 'normal' society composed of castes and classes with divergent goals, the ashram embodies an 'alternative' conception of life, social organization, and sustenance, engendering a homogenous community with a single objective—the acquisition of *tapas* or 'hot spiritual energy' through extraordinary austerity, mortification, and self-discipline. This is the world we encounter mainly in Acts I, III, and IV. (On ascetics and *tapas*, see the explanation of Segment 10 in the Notes to the Play.)

The third is the world of gods and celestial beings, which exists in 'heaven' (Indra's *svarga*) and in intermediate realms (such as Mount Meru), and is populated by different kinds of beings of supernatural origin: *sura*s (gods), *asura*s (anti-gods), *rākshasa*s (demons), *gandharva*s and *apsarā*s (celestial musicians and dancers or entertainers), *kinnara*s (the Indian counterparts of centaurs), and so on.

While the king's world is governed by familiar laws of physical existence and cause-and-effect, the ascetic's world contains enchanted landscapes, magical powers, and supernatural forces and presences that overcome human limitations. In contrast to both, the divine world transcends the human and natural realms completely—celestial beings traverse the skies and control their visibility (for example, Sānumatī and Mātali), thoughts travel without material means of communication (for example, between Kashyapa and Gālava), effects precede causes (for example, in Kashyapa's 'grace'), and the future is known (for example, to Indra). This is the world we encounter in bits and pieces throughout the play, but principally in Act VII.

The three worlds of *Shakuntalā* may be described as the human, the natural, and the divine, or as the worlds of kings, ascetics, and gods, or as the worlds of palace, ashram, and heaven. Whichever configuration we choose, Kālidāsa's play emerges as an instance of cosmic drama: it is the kind of drama that cannot be contained by categories such as tragedy and comedy; that depicts a fully human hero like Dushyanta seeking a soulmate in a half-celestial female like Shakuntalā; and that shows humans in conversation with the gods, demigods walking on earth, and the whole earth itself in an astonishing aerial perspective—together with the common ground of everyday life in extraordinary detail.

In this framework, the time of the city is 'classical time', in which the king speaks in the poetic cadences of classical Sanskrit, and his palace has the features of an imperial residence around the turn of the fifth century CE. The time of the ashram, however, is 'epic time'—some 1500 years earlier in history—in which the supernatural pervades the natural environment, and which implies that when Dushyanta enters the enchanted forest and the sacred grove (I.iii) and meets Shakuntalā on the riverbank (III.iii), he travels back to a different time zone. And the time of Indra's heaven and Kashyapa and Aditi's Mount Meru is 'celestial time'—a timelessness in cosmological space that transcends time and space.

Appendix E

GENRE AND CLASSIFICATION

Performer, Performance, and Play

In classical Indian theatre, a *naṭa* (masculine) or *naṭī* (feminine) is a performer who imitates and creates a visual representation of a person, an object, an event, or a state of affairs. Both words derive from the Prakrit verb *naṭ*, which means not only 'to move about, gesticulate, play, dance, act', but also, in a linguistically more complicated sense, 'to cause the body to move, make gestures, dance, or perform an enactment'. The causative form of the verb emphasizes the voluntary and controlled nature of the performer's imitative action, his or her freedom to choose the mode, means, and style of representation, and the distinction of the representation from what it represents.

Sanskrit dramatic and performance theory describes a performer's representation as an *āropa*, a 'superposition of the form' of one entity on another, a process in which he or she voluntarily 'assumes the form' of someone else, and hence trans-forms himself or herself into another personage. The underlying master term is *rūpa* or form, which designates not only an outward appearance, a figure that others see, an image, a resemblance, or a simulacrum, but also the corporeal shape and physical manifestation of the 'state, nature, or property' of the entity being represented. The performer's voluntary self-transformation into the shape or figure of someone or something else, using movement, dance, or enactment, is thus a well-rounded personation of another identity.

Over the past millennium, this classical definition has been consolidated in the modern Indian languages (from Hindi and Punjabi to Bengali and Marathi) in the gender-neutral words *bahurūpī* and *bahurūpiyā* and their variants, which characterize the performer or actor as a man or a woman 'with many forms', who can assume any form at will and whose core identity is many identities.

The principal Sanskrit word for performance, *nāṭya*, derives its meaning from *naṭa*, and designates the entire field of the practices of actors, dancers, musicians, and playwrights, which necessarily are shaped by training, discipline, skill, and aesthetics, and are put into action in the performance space of a theatre. This is the sense in which the term gives the *Nāṭyashāstra* its name, as the first and most comprehensive disciplinary work on the theory and practice of performance in the performing and poetic (or 'visual and verbal') arts together.

The term for a dramatic work is also derived from the basic meaning of *naṭa*. It is called a *rūpaka*, a 'vehicle for the assumption of forms', because it is conceived of as a verbal composition, produced in advance by a skilled poet, which provides the performer with a narrative and discursive framework for his or her self-transformation or personation of a character in an imagined situation or action. A *rūpaka*, by definition, has two facets: it is a composition in words with intensified literary qualities, and hence can be evaluated as a 'poem', without reference to performance; and, at the same time, it is a 'play-script', which has to be judged by the criteria of theatrical production apart from its literariness. While *nāṭya* or aestheticized performance opens out the entire field of the actor's disciplined practice, the *rūpaka* as a work of dramatic literature serves expressly as an indispensable means to meaningful enactment.

Sanskrit poetics and criticism define ten major kinds and eighteen minor kinds of *rūpaka*s. Among these twenty-eight dramatic genres of short and long works, the *nāṭaka* is historically the most comprehensive, artistically demanding, and aesthetically pleasing kind of play, in words as well as performance. *Shakuntalā* is a *nāṭaka*, and, in the canonical judgement of the Kashmiri philosopher and critic Abhinavagupta (around 1000 CE), drama represents the best of classical Sanskrit literature, the *nāṭaka* represents the best kind of drama, and *Shakuntalā* represents the best of that genre. The staging of this play therefore involves dealing with a work that is equally exceptional as a poem or literary text and as a play-script or performance vehicle.

The two facets of the *rūpaka*—as poem and as play-script—essentially place the playwright and the performer on par with each other, as collaborative yet autonomous sources or agents of creativity. In this idealized conception, the poet composes or assembles a well-crafted, imaginative text that verbally accomplishes its aesthetic goals, even while ensuring its theatricality. The performer then uses his or her special skills to 'translate' the play-script into a moving spectacle onstage that meets the criteria of successful performance without sacrificing the poetry of the verbal composition. In the Sanskrit–Prakrit tradition, the playwright ought to visualize the dramatic action of his text with the same degree of precision with which the performer seeks to render the words into a dynamic representation in the theatre.

The Genre of the *Nāṭaka*

The classical Sanskrit *nāṭaka* resembles a modern full-length play in some of its features (such as its division into acts and its treatment of scenes), but it differs significantly in others (such as its construction of plot and its conception of character). To assess these similarities and differences, and especially to evaluate the dramatic qualities of *Shakuntalā* as a *nāṭaka*, it is useful to review Vishvanātha's fourteenth-century definition of the genre, which summarizes much of the critical debate of the preceding 500 years in the Sanskrit–Prakrit world.

> The *nāṭaka*, the best and fullest kind of play,
> Has a plot that uses a famous story, and lays it out
> In five main stages in their proper sequence.

It depicts the pleasures of love and desire, etcetera,
The range of good deeds, good qualities,
Various sorts of splendour and prosperity,
And the sources of happiness, of sorrow and grief—
Along with a steady stream of emotions
    in all their variety.

It is organized into acts—at least five, and up to ten.
Its hero comes from a well-known lineage,
And may be a king with spiritual discipline, a 'royal sage',
Who is consistently noble—or he may be
A god or a celestial being with the same good qualities.

A *nāṭaka*'s main body of emotion
Is made up either of love and desire or of heroic energy,
And its parts provide a taste of all the emotions.
Its ending offers a full resolution of its business,
And arouses great wonder and astonishment.

It has four or five important characters
Completely occupied with the object of the hero's quest.

[*Parichchheda* 6, Verses 7–11]

The five main stages that this passage mentions are the *sandhi*s of the overall plot, which are 'junctures' in the dramatic action that may not coincide with the boundaries of the acts into which the play is divided. In modern terms, the five stages of the plot may be conceptualized as the following kind of division and succession: (a) an opening dramatic situation or 'initial thesis' in which a protagonist is placed and in which he or she determines the nature and object of his or her quest; (b) a 'first antithesis' to that situation, and the complications it produces in the chosen quest; (c) a 'first synthesis' that brings the initial thesis and antithesis to a temporary or transitory culmination, in which the objective of the quest becomes visible for the first time in an embryonic form; (d) a 'second antithesis' that responds dialectically to the first synthesis (which, in the process, becomes another thesis that triggers fresh developments in the action), and expands into a new set of complications that postpone the protagonist's certainty of success in his or her quest; and (e) a 'final synthesis' that brings the quest and the dramatic action to a successful and aesthetically satisfying close.

In the analysis of Yadunandan Mishra, for example—which sums up a consensus among many modern Indian scholars of Sanskrit—the initial thesis of the action runs from the beginning of I.iii (the entrance of Dushyanta and the Charioteer in pursuit of the antelope) to the end of II.iii (after Bhadrasena's exit at the hunting camp); the first antithesis to the dramatic situation stretches from the beginning of II.iv (the start of Dushyanta's first conversation with Māḍhavya about Shakuntalā) to the end of Act III; the first synthesis encompasses Act IV and the action in Act V up to the moment when Gautamī removes Shakuntalā's upper sheath (just after Verse 112); the second antithesis moves from Dushyanta's soliloquy in Verse 113 to the end of Act VI; and the final synthesis spans all of Act VII. (For an alternative account of the five constituent stages of *Shakuntalā*, see my Afterword.)

Appendix F

ACTING, STAGING, AND PERFORMANCE

This Appendix provides basic information about and critical orientations towards various aspects and contexts of acting, staging, and performance in the classical Indian tradition, with a specific focus on *Shakuntalā* as a performance vehicle. It seeks to introduce and review select terms, concepts, and practices very briefly, but in a way that is accessible to theatre practitioners around the world today.

Classical Theatre and Stage

There is no archaeological record of a theatre building from classical times in India, and there is only one surviving description of an actual performance of a Sanskrit–Prakrit play (of the opening act of Harsha's *Ratnāvalī*, staged by an all-female troupe with gender-neutral casting, in Banaras in the eighth century; see Raghavan, 'Sanskrit Drama', p. 16). But it is possible to construct a simplified and speculative picture of theatrical practice in the period, based on prescriptions in the *Nāṭyashāstra*, references in other sources, and evidence from premodern theatrical spaces preserved in temples.

A common playhouse most likely was a brick-and-wood building with a thatched roof; in the case of a rectangular floor plan, its dimensions would be 96 feet by 48 feet. One half of the space would be taken up by the auditorium, which would seat about 200 listeners and spectators on floor-mats and on a few benches along the walls. The other half, comprising the performance space, would be divided into three areas: a greenroom, behind a wall facing the audience; a stage rear along the wall, probably at a raised level; and a stage front, with the playing area as a whole measuring up to 24 feet by 12 feet. Two doorways in the back wall served for the cast and crew's entrances from and exits to the greenroom; they may have been covered with curtains that could be thrown aside for dramatic entrances, such as Anasūyā's in IV.ii and Vātāyana's in VI.ii. Any 'voices backstage'—such as the Stage Manager's voice reciting the Invocation in I.i, or Durvāsā's voice issuing the curse in IV.i—would be projected from the greenroom. An ensemble of musicians would be seated along the wall at stage rear, between the two doorways, and would provide music with vocals, strings, and percussion. Performances would take place in the daytime, using natural lighting; however, in regional styles such as the *kuṭiyaṭṭam* in Kerala, illumination may be provided by large, stationary oil lamps as well as smaller, portable ones.

Acting Companies and Modes of Performance

Actors' companies and troupes in the classical period were patronized by kings, courtiers, and wealthy merchants; for example, the tenth-century Sanskrit poet and playwright Rājashekhara, a royal official, sponsored performances at his home, along with his wife, Avantisundarī. Some companies may have been the equivalent of resident or repertory companies, with a designated performance space in a palace or temple complex, or with a playhouse for the general public in an urban location. Others were travelling troupes that also served smaller towns and the countryside, pilgrimage centres, and popular festivals and fairs, and often performed in temporary, improvised, or open-air spaces.

In general, these troupes and companies were trained in two modes of performance: the 'natural' or mimetic mode, especially for popular entertainment and socially mixed audiences; and the 'stylized' or artificial mode, reserved mostly for literary drama and audiences of connoisseurs. The text of *Shakuntalā* requires the application of both modes. The bulk of the scenes featuring Anasūyā and Priyaṁvadā, for example, or with Māḍhavya on the stage, have commonplace action and conversational dialogue that are driven by the logic of *svabhāvokti*, 'discourse about things as they are'; whereas some portions require stylized enactment and delivery, such as Dushyanta and his Charioteer miming their pursuit of an antelope in I.iii, and Mātali and Dushyanta descending on the skyway in VII.i.

Acting and Enactment

In a classical performance, a Sanskrit–Prakrit play is enacted on a bare stage, without scenery (painted or otherwise) and with only a minimum of props (such as furniture). In this context, the actors' skills, together with the visualization conveyed precisely and comprehensively by the dialogue, engage the spectator's imagination actively, so that he or she 'sees' the dramatic action as a moving spectacle in his or her 'mind's eye', without its literal or material manifestation on the stage. The actors let the words of the play-script do the performative talking or visual performing; but they do reinforce the imaginative impact of their acting and delivery with make-up and costume, and with special techniques for more elusive effects. In I.iii, for instance, the actors playing Dushyanta and the Charioteer would mime all the aspects of the hunt, without a physical chariot or a forest background on the stage, using the dialogue and poetry to accomplish the necessary 'word-painting' of the scene for the spectator's imagination. Contrary to some misinterpretations of tempo in classical Indian *abhinaya* (acting and enactment), most of *Shakuntalā* would be played in a 'natural style' at a natural or 'medium' pace, with only the action in select small portions either slowed down or speeded up exceptionally for dramatic intensity (for example, Sānumatī's dance at her exit in VI.v, or the ensemble mime of sprinting in VI.vi, respectively).

In this general context, Sanskrit dramaturgy defines four areas of training and self-discipline for actors and stage performers: (a) movement, of the body as a whole and of particular parts—such as the eyes, eyebrows, cheeks, lips, head, arms, fingers, and feet—and including the full discipline of mime; (b) voice and sound, for the effective delivery of dialogue and the verbal component of the play-script; (c) the skilful use of make-up, costume, and stage props, including devices such as masks and puppets; and (d) specialized methods for the voluntary representation of involuntary physical states that signify otherwise unobservable mental conditions, specifically tears and sweat, horripilation and trembling, change of voice and change of colour, and fainting and complete immobility. An actor playing Dushyanta, for example, has to draw on all four skill sets in rapid succession, and even simultaneously, in the course of Act VI.

As a play-script, *Shakuntalā* also incorporates several structural and rhetorical devices that are part of the actor's classical repertoire. The various kinds of Interludes in Acts II, III, IV, and VI use diegesis—narration, report, and description, as distinct from mimesis or imitative enactment—to inform the audience about events in the overall dramatic action that occur offstage, that cannot be represented directly on the stage, or that the playwright chooses to place in the background. Māḍhavya's interlude in II.i is an extended soliloquy, whereas the Apprentice Priest's interlude in III.i is a conversation with an unseen and unheard interlocutor offstage. In contrast, the two parts of the Mixed Interlude in IV.i–ii together involve dialogue, vivid report, quick exits and entrances, two simultaneous scenes onstage, and vital narrative transitions; whereas the rather different kind of Interlude in VI.i brings in a new ensemble of figures in a new setting and a new dynamic at an extraordinary juncture in the story. The Interludes, by definition, do not include the protagonists, so the actors who play the secondary and tertiary characters in them have to draw on skills that are comparable in quality to those of the actors in the leading roles.

The rhetorical devices in the play-script are more special to Sanskrit dramaturgy. The *Nāṭyashāstra* distinguishes between three kinds of verbal components in performance, all of which are heard or overheard by the audience, but under different conditions: (a) discourse at any given moment on the stage that is heard by all the characters present, as is the case with most of the dialogue in a play-script; (b) discourse that is not heard by any characters other than the speaker, as in a 'soliloquy' and an 'interior monologue'; and (c) discourse that is specifically directed by a speaker at some characters but not others on the stage, such an 'aside' shared by two or more characters. All three kinds of delivery, of course, are always 'overheard' by the spectators in the audience.

The asides in the third kind of situation can be differentiated further in themselves. (i) At some moments, two or more characters may speak 'privately' to each other, while the other characters on the stage are aware that they are doing so; this happens, for instance, in the middle of Segment 22 in I.iv, when Anasūyā and Priyaṁvadā first speak privately to Shakuntalā, while Dushyanta waits out of earshot; and Dushyanta then asks to speak privately to the two friends, while Shakuntalā waits. In a classical performance, a speaker raises his or her hand in the stylized *tripatākā* gesture (the 'three-finger flag') to indicate an explicit aside.

(ii) Alternatively, one character may utter an aside to another without the others on the stage being aware of their secretive communication; this happens, for example, in the asides between Shakuntalā and Anasūyā in Segment 88 in IV.vi, when they exchange quick observations about the red goose visible on the lakefront on the edge of the ashram grounds. Or (iii) a character may speak aloud in an aside directed at no one onstage, but expressive of his or her response to a situation and informative for the audience. In a classical performance, such an aside is classified as *ākāsha-bhāshitam*, 'an utterance in the air or in [empty] space', and a character delivers it by raising his or her face noticeably and speaking aloud; this happens with the final piece of dialogue in Act III, when Dushyanta responds to the priest's 'voice backstage' in Verse 72 with his own words 'in the air', even though he does not possess the priest's supernatural power of communication at a distance. The play-script of *Shakuntalā* thus requires actors to cultivate their skills in voice and verbal delivery to a high degree of refinement.

A vital goal of the art of *abhinaya* is to convey the emotions of the protagonists and other characters to the spectator in an aestheticized form (rasa). The basic conception of rasa and its aesthesis (reception), and the rasas represented in *Shakuntalā*, are annotated in Appendix G. An essential component of acting in this context is stylized gesture and movement, which provide performers with general devices that can be incorporated into even the so-called natural style. A standard device of this sort is *parikramah*, literally 'walking about', which is stylized as a formulaic, non-mimetic movement on the stage to represent a shift in the action. Performers mime changes of scene and setting, transitions between episodes or incidents, and movement between locations by walking in a distinctive manner around the stage, along its perimeter, or in a closed loop, while looking around themselves. The stage directions in the *Shakuntalā* play-script consistently use the verbal phrase *parikramya-avalokya cha*, 'walking around and looking about', to designate what I have translated most often as 'miming a transition'. Contemporary performers may innovate stylized gesture and movement to represent such transitions in the action, which usually mark the boundaries of scenes and scenes-within-scenes.

Select Productions of *Shakuntalā*

Since the end of the eighteenth century, audiences have attended live performances of *Shakuntalā* in a variety of forms in several hundred stage productions in theatres across the world. These include productions in Sanskrit–Prakrit, in India and abroad, and in translation, in modern Indian as well as Asian and Europhone languages. They also include adaptations of various kinds (from the original Sanskrit–Prakrit play, from the Mahābhārata narrative in Sanskrit, and from Europhone translations of these); and versions of the play in forms such as classical European opera, modern rock opera, innovative ballet, and long and short musical compositions and songs. Many of these productions have involved well-known modern writers, stage directors, actors, theatre personnel, and theatre companies around the globe. Besides print and live theatre, *Shakuntalā* has reached modern listeners and spectators also in media such as film, television, video, and audio recordings. The selective list below is a small sample to indicate the range of productions, genres, and media that have featured *Shakuntalā*.

Theophile Gautier, author, Paris Opera, 1858 (ballet-pantomime, with music by Ernest Reyer; French).

Karl Goldmark, composer, Overture, opus 13, Hungary, 1865 (musical composition).

Anandodbhava Natyagriha, Pune, 1880. Production of Annasaheb Kirloskar's *Saṅgīta Shakuntalā*, paradigmatic work in the *saṅgīta nāṭaka* genre (Indian musical theatre or 'opera'; Marathi).

Luge-Poe, dir., Theatre de l'OEuvre, Paris, 1896 (French).

Alexander Tairov, dir., Kamerny Theatre, Moscow, 1914 (Russian).

V. Shantaram, dir., *Shakuntalā*, 1943; script by Dewan Sharar, an adaptation of Kālidāsa (film; Hindi).

Prithvi Theatres, Bombay; Prithviraj Kapoor, founder; inaugural production, 1944 (Hindi).

Franco Alfano, author, opera (Italian). First version, 1921; script and score thought to be destroyed in an air raid in World War II; reconstituted afresh in a second version, 1952; first version recovered, 2005; second version performed by Teatro Grattacielo, New York, 2013.

Chinese Youth Theatre, Peking, China, 1957 (Chinese, trans. by Ji Xianlin).

Hindustani Theatre, Delhi, India; Habib Tanvir, founder and manager. Production in 1957–58: dir. by Moneeka Misra, script by Qudsia Zaidi, costumes by Shama Zaidi; ten performances. Production in 1959: dir. by Narendra Sharma, script by Qudsia Zaidi and Niaz Haider, costumes and décor by M.S. Sathyu; thirty-six performances (Hindustani translations).

Sanskrit College, Calcutta, at the Kālidāsa Jayanti (anniversary festival), Ujjain, 1958 (Sanskrit).

Jerzy Grotowski, dir., Theatre of the Thirteen Rows, Poland, 1960 (Polish).

V. Shantaram, dir., *Stri*, 1961; a second version of the Shakuntalā story in the Mahābhārata and Kālidāsa (film; Hindi).

Joy Zinoman, dir., Studio Theatre, Washington DC, USA, 1982 (English).

Shashin Desai, dir., International City Theatre, Long Beach, California, USA, 1991 (English).

Gate Theatre, Notting Hill, London; adaptation by Peter Oswald, 1997 (English).

Celeste Innocenti, dir., Chronos Theatre Group, San Diego, USA, 2009 (English).

Tarek Iskander, dir., Union Theatre, London, UK, 2009 (English).

Charles Roy, Pleiades Theatre and York University, Toronto, Canada, 2009 (English adaptation).

George Drance, dir., La MaMa E.T.C., Magis Theatre Company, New York, USA, 2010 (English).

Patrick McCartney and Annie McCarthy, authors, stop-animation version (online), Australian National University, 2010 (English).

Rae Robinson, dir., Humboldt State University, California, USA, 2012 (English adaptation by Margaret Kelso).

Hemant Panwar and Vaishali Panwar, dir., various cities, Canada, 2014 (fusion dance drama).

K.N. Panikkar, dir., National School of Drama Repertory Company, New Delhi, India 2014; text by Udayan Vajpeyi; production in the *kuṭiyaṭṭam* style of Kerala; featured at the sixteenth Bharat Rang Mahotsav (annual national theatre festival; Hindi).

Snehal Desai, dir., James Madison University, Virginia, USA, 2015 (English).

Gems Modern Academy (high school), Dubai, 2015; rock opera, also featured at the Edinburgh Fringe Festival (English).

Appendix G

RASA IN THEORY AND PRACTICE

Emotion and Rasa

As literary work and as performance vehicle, a play conveys not only the specific actions of its characters, but also the states of being and major and minor emotions from which their intentions, decisions, and actions spring.

Employing a combination of mimetic enactment (the spectacle onstage) and diegetic representation (narration, report, summary, and so on), the classical Sanskrit–Prakrit performer focuses especially on a character's feelings and moods in relation to the action in progress, capturing them in the totality of his or her *abhinaya*, and conveying them to a theatrical audience as effectively as possible, so that the spectator can experience those emotions live, and savour them with pleasure in a concentrated aesthetic form. In a *nāṭaka* such as *Shakuntalā*, aimed at telling (or retelling) and depicting a love story, the poet's goal is to communicate verbally the whole range of emotions through which the well-known hero and heroine pass, and the actors' goal is to capture and communicate the couple's experience of love, desire, consummation, separation, and reunion in all its scope and depth in a moving enactment.

The poet and the performer work in different mediums with different resources—language and verbal-visual enactment—but their narrative materials, conceptual means, and affective objectives are the same. In their respective representations of a hero and a heroine involved in a quest for love, the poet and the performer draw on a common theory of emotion (*bhāva*) and aesthetic outcomes and effects (rasa). In this theory, a protagonist in a particular narrative framework experiences five kinds of emotional states, conditions, or processes that are interlinked by cause and consequence and general concomitance.

First, a protagonist is in a stable, encompassing 'state of being' or 'emotional state' (*sthāyī bhāva*) which persists over time and across situations, and defines the basic emotional zone that he or she occupies during a series or sequence of events. There are eight such general and enduring states of being or emotion in which a given protagonist may find himself or herself for the duration of a particular dramatic action (see table below).

These *sthāyī bhāva*s, however, are too large and amorphous in their external aspect, and too variable at the level of concrete particulars in their internal aspect, to be directly representable as emotions that an audience can grasp or relish dynamically. What provides the actual content of a *sthāyī bhāva* is a set of concrete elements belonging to four separate categories: (a) *vibhāva*s, which serve as the stimulants, or the triggers and intensifiers, that launch a particular *sthāyī bhāva* in a character or protagonist; (b) *anubhāva*s, which emerge as the character's immediate, initial feelings, sensations, physical conditions, and so on, as responses to or outcomes of the triggering and the intensifying of an emotional state in the first step; (c) *vyabhichārī bhāva*s, which appear then in the character's overall subjective state as relatively short-lived, rapidly evolving, secondary or subsidiary emotions and feelings that are associated with the kind of emotional zone he or she has come to occupy; and (d) *sāttvika bhāva*s, psychosomatic states into which a character may fall involuntarily, depending on the particular small-scale, transitory feelings that he or she is experiencing at a given moment.

The *Nāṭyashāstra*'s famous rasa-sutra or 'formula of rasa' (formula for the production of concentrated, aestheticized emotion) says that a poet or a performer should represent a protagonist's stable emotional state—the frame that contains all his or her actual feelings—by combining the appropriate *vibhāva*s, *anubhāva*s, *vyabhichārī bhāva*s, and *sāttvika bhāva*s in a text or a performance, which will then stimulate a concentrated and aesthetic version of that state in a theatrical spectator. In this fourfold combination, the poet and the performer seek to convey the rasa or 'concentrate, taste, or flavour' of the particular *sthāyī bhāva* to be represented in their respective mediums of language and enactment. The emotional states and their aesthetic representations may be translated as follows.

STHĀYĪ BHĀVA OR STABLE EXISTENTIAL EMOTIONAL STATE	RASA OR EMOTIONAL CONCENTRATE IN AESTHETIC REPRESENTATION
Rati (sexual love, desire)	*Shriṅgāra* (eros)
Hāsa (laughter and merriment)	*Hāsya* (mirth)
Shoka (sorrow and grief, suffering)	*Karuṇa* (compassion)
Krodha (anger and rage)	*Raudra* (fury)
Utsāha (enthusiasm and courage)	*Vīra* (heroism)
Bhaya (fear and terror)	*Bhayānaka* (terror)
Jugupsā (disgust, horror, and hatred)	*Bībhatsa* (revulsion)
Vismaya (astonishment and wonder)	*Adbhuta* (wonder)

The crucial feature of this system is that the representation of a protagonist's evolving emotional state that reaches the spectator is a scaled representation of the corresponding existential emotion with which we are familiar in everyday life. That is, the poet and the performer who seek to capture and convey a fictional hero's or heroine's emotional state do so by extracting the most important constituents of the same state as people experience it in everyday life, and by communicating that essence to an audience.

The *Nāṭyashāstra* makes it explicit that such an essence is gustatory and not philosophical, so it is like the extract, flavour, or physical concentrate of a food that can be relished or savoured. A concentrate of this sort is necessarily a small-scale representation of a real-life *sthāyī bhāva*, which extends over long periods of time and manifests itself in many places, and which contains a great deal of inconsequential raw material. The rasa that a listener-viewer savours while attending a performance of a play is thus like a small amount of extract that gives him or her the best possible taste of a fruit, without the peel or rind, the seeds or stone, or the excess of roughage and pulp.

The Rasas in *Shakuntalā*

In theory, at the most basic level, a *nāṭaka* may foreground either the element of love or the heroic element in the story it retells. *Shakuntalā* chooses to highlight the *rati bhāva* (love and sexual desire) as its primary stable emotion, and subordinates its hero's *utsāha bhāva* (heroic energy); its predominant aesthetic effect therefore is the *shriṅgāra* rasa (eros) and not the *vīra* rasa (heroism). This has immediate consequences for the interpretation and theatrical representation of its protagonists and dramatic action: among its various narrative threads, the love story of Dushyanta and Shakuntalā has to define the principal plot, the qualities that make them the subjects and objects of desire have to gain precedence, and Dushyanta's characteristics as lover, husband, soulmate, and fellow-parent have to subordinate his roles as warrior and king.

Moreover, as a full-length play focused on love and desire, *Shakuntalā* has to represent the Dushyanta–Shakuntalā relationship in all its aspects. It thus has to depict the entire phenomenon of falling in love, from chance meeting to passionate consummation (*sambhoga shriṅgāra*); and it also has to display the whole process of encountering obstacles, breaking vows, dissolving commitments, experiencing guilt and remorse, and reconstituting love at a deeper level (*vipralambha shriṅgāra*). Kālidāsa's play proceeds symmetrically through these two phases of love: the first three acts dramatize the constructive phase of Dushyanta and Shakuntalā's relationship, whereas the next three acts portray its destructive phase, and the final act then synthesizes the two into a state of renovated love and companionship 'in morality'.

The emotional state of eros, however, is complicated by its organization. Contrary to Rabindranath Tagore's famous observation that the play contains two unions—as opposed to the single union at the end of a Europhone romantic comedy—the symmetrical structure of *Shakuntalā* actually contains three unions. The first is the consummation at the end of Act III, an 'initial union' based on sexual desire and mutual infatuation that embodies the idea of *sambhoga shriṅgāra*; the second is the 'failed union' of Act V, when Shakuntalā attempts to reunite with Dushyanta but is rebuffed comprehensively, which stands for the core of *vipralambha shriṅgāra*; and the third is the 'final union' of Act VII, which unifies them in a child and represents the structural principle of *nirvahaṇa*, 'the cessation of the flow' of action. These three moments of eros in the aesthetic and affective dynamics of the play are inflected by the three instances of Shakuntalā's abandonment by three kinds of 'family' in the encompassing narrative:

her first abandonment, in infancy, by her biological mother Menakā, as part of an obscure celestial design (mentioned in Act I); her second abandonment, after the initial union, by her legitimate husband, Dushyanta, under a curse (Acts IV–V); and her third abandonment, immediately after the second one, by the ashram community—her adoptive family—on moral grounds (Act V).

As concentrated poetic expressions of the characters' general emotional states, particular emotions, and more transitory feelings, perceptions, and sensations, the 191 verses in the play (181 of which are in classical Sanskrit) serve as the principal vehicles of rasa, and hence are vital components of any performance on the stage. Since the primary rasa is *shriṅgāra*, the majority of the verses convey the various emotional nuances of *sambhoga shriṅgāra*, erotic conjunction, and *vipralambha shriṅgāra*, erotic disjunction. Since the heroic mood is the secondary rasa in the play, verses distributed in the text's background focus on Dushyanta's characteristics as warrior and king, as indicated by the examples tabulated below.

But the play also uses this manifold context to dramatize all the other major and minor emotions, which play supporting roles. All six of the other *sthāyī bhāva*s and their corresponding rasas thus appear alongside eros and heroism, and may be found in the following selective examples.

RASAS IN *SHAKUNTALĀ*	LOCATION AND EXAMPLES
Primary Rasa:	
Shriṅgāra (eros)	Acts I–VII
Sambhoga (erotic conjunction)	Verses 15–20, 24–27, 38–42, 50–69, 107, 113, 122, 127, 128, 179–82

Vipralambha (erotic disjunction)	Verses 70, 71, 75, 88, 95, 115, 125, 129–32, 140, 146, 147, 149, 178

Secondary Rasa:

Vīra (heroism)	Acts I–VII Verses 6, 8, 34, 35, 44, 45, 98–102, 148, 153–55, 158–62, 171–73, 183, 190

Tertiary or 'Supporting' *Rasa*s:

Hāsya (mirth)	II.i–ii
Karuṇa (compassion)	IV.iv–vi
Raudra (fury)	Verse 117, Segment 153
Bhayānaka (terror)	Verse 7
Bībhatsa (revulsion)	Verse 152
Adbhuta (wonder)	VII.i

'Mixtures' of Tertiary *Rasa*s:

Shriṅgāra (*sambhoga*) + *Hāsya*	II.iv
Vīra + *Hāsya*	II.iii
Raudra + *Bhayānaka* + *Bībhatsa* + *Adbhuta*	VI.vi

If we expand this selection of examples to a full inventory, then it is possible to demonstrate that *Shakuntalā* fulfils all the criteria for the aesthetic representation of emotions (rasa) that Vishvanātha mentions in his definition of the *nāṭaka* quoted in Appendix E. Readers and actors who familiarize themselves with the translation in detail will be able to establish close correspondences between the verses and prose passages in the play and the emotions listed above in various categories. As poetry, the play may be self-evidently *rasātmaka* ('brimming with aestheticized emotion') in its verbal composition, but its emotional power will not affect a theatrical audience unless performers are able to translate the words, especially the individual verses, into moving enactment and spectacle on the stage.

Appendix H

VERSIFICATION

The text of *Shakuntalā* translated here contains 191 numbered verses. Of these, 181 verses are in classical Sanskrit, and one (Verse 80) is an imitation of a Vedic mantra (in the *trishṭubh* verse-form). The remaining nine verses are in Prakrit, each assigned to a different speaker in the play: Verses 4 (Actress), 61 (Shakuntalā), 84 (Priyaṁvadā), 88 (Anasūyā), 95 (Haṁsapadikā), 110 (Gautamī), 126 (Fisherman), 127 (Parabhritikā), and 128 (Madhukarikā).

Versification in Sanskrit and Prakrit is metrical, but a metrical pattern is defined for an entire verse, which articulates one complete utterance in a simple, compound, complex, or compound-complex sentence, and hence is syntactically as well as semantically closed and self-contained. Unlike prosody in Greek, Latin, and English and other modern Europhone languages, Sanskrit–Prakrit prosody treats a verse-form—

rather than a line—as the proper unit of metrical patterning. The system divides a verse-form internally into different kinds of smaller building blocks, but none of them is independent of the whole, in either the process of composition or that of interpretation. Rhyme is a well-defined figure of speech, but it is not a required structural feature of a verse-form.

In Prakrit, the basic building block or analytical element of a metrical pattern is the vowel; it may or may not be combined with one or more consonants to constitute a 'syllable' phonologically, but it is measured for its own 'duration' (*mātrā*): a short vowel (a, i, u) is a single measure or one *mātrā*, whereas a long vowel or diphthong (ā, ī, ū, e, ai, au) is a double measure or two *mātrā*s (with some single measures counted as double under specific conditions). The distribution of single and double 'vowel durations' in a complete verse-form then defines its metrical pattern. *Shakuntalā* draws on four distinct Prakrit verse-forms from this system of *mātrā-chhanda*s or *mātrā-vritta*s for its nine Prakrit verses, which are listed with their occurrences in Table 2 below.

Sanskrit uses two separate systems of metrical versification. One is equivalent to the system of vowel durations or *mātrā*s in Prakrit. The other, more inclusive system in the language employs the syllable (*akshara* or *varṇa*) as its basic building block; in the simplest case, a syllable is 'light' if the vowel at its core is short, and it is 'heavy' if the vowel is long or is a diphthong. Combining this with more complicated rules and exceptions, the system of syllabic verse-forms (*akshara-chhanda*s or *varṇa-vritta*s) defines a metrical pattern according to the distribution of light and heavy syllables over the length of a single verse.

In Sanskrit as well as Prakrit, the vowel durations or weighted syllables in a given verse-form are organized according to principles of symmetry and asymmetry. The whole verse-form may be divided internally into halves, quarters, and so on; the two halves of a form, for example, may be equal or unequal in length, and they may be symmetrical or asymmetrical in the actual distribution of vowels or syllables. Likewise, the four quarters (*charaṇa*s) may be quantitatively equal or unequal and qualitatively symmetrical or asymmetrical.

Shakuntalā displays all these variations and possibilities in the twenty-two distinct verse-forms it employs in its 181 classical Sanskrit verses: it has seventeen syllabic verse-forms with identical quarters, four syllabic verse-forms with alternate quarters identical, and one verse-form based on vowel duration, with asymmetrical even-numbered quarters. The play does not utilize this range of Sanskrit verse-forms uniformly; its five most preferred forms and groups of forms account for 130 of the Sanskrit verses, as follows:

VERSE-FORM	METRICAL BASIS	FREQUENCY
Āryā	vowel duration; asymmetrical	33
Vasantatilakā	syllable; 18 syllables per quarter	30
Anushṭubh and *Pathyāvaktra* (variant)	syllable; 8 syllables per quarter	29
Shārdūlavikrīḍita	syllable; 18 syllables per quarter	22
Vaṁshasthā and *Drutavilambita*	syllable; 12 syllables per quarter	18

Among these, the relatively short verse-forms (*anushṭubh* and its variant, *pathyāvaktra*) occur twenty-nine times; the medium-length forms (*āryā*, *vaṁshasthā*, *drutavilambita*) together appear fifty-one times; and the long forms (*vasantatilakā* and *shārdūlavikrīḍita*) appear fifty-two times. The text's statistical predilection for medium-sized and large verse-forms explains how it builds up its verbal music and poetic density in Sanskrit, and also why an English rendering of a poetic passage usually runs well over four lines.

The following Tables 1 and 2 provide a basic concordance of verse-forms and verses in the play, with the metrical patterns of some of the more frequently used forms displayed as examples. In the scansions, ᴗ represents a light syllable or a short vowel (single duration), whereas – represents a heavy syllable or long vowel (double duration), according to the category specified. The ∧ represents a caesura (a medial pause, after the first and third quarters, or within a long quarter itself); the | represents a 'half-stop' (roughly equivalent to a semicolon or colon, after the second quarter or first half); and the ‖ represents a 'full stop' (equivalent to a period, after the fourth quarter or at the end of the verse-form).

Verse 80 is excluded from this tabulation, since it is composed in a Vedic *trishṭubh* verse-form, in imitation of a mantra.

1. Sanskrit Verse-forms

Verse-forms Measured by Syllable (Varṇa)

VERSE-FORMS WITH ALL QUARTERS IDENTICAL

Designated variations allowed in particular quarters and particular positions within them.

a. Eight syllables per quarter

i. *Anushṭubh*

Verse 6: – ᴗ – – ᴗ – – – ∧ ᴗ ᴗ – – ᴗ – ᴗ – |

ᴗ – ᴗ – ᴗ – – – ∧ ᴗ – – – ᴗ ᴗ – ᴗ – ‖

I: 5, 6, 10, 11, 22; **II**: 43, 46, 47; **III**: 49, 65, 68; **IV**: 76, 79; **V**: 108, 118, 120, 123; **VI**: 139, 147, 148, 153, 157; **VII**: 166, 170, 171, 172, 180, 185, 186

ii. *Pathyāvaktra*

Special case of *anushṭubh*; included in that count.

b. Eleven syllables per quarter

iii. *Upajāti*

II: 37; **IV**: 99; **V**: 114, 119; **VI**: 135, 149, 151; **VII**: 159, 162, 176, 188

iv. *Shālinī*

V: 124

v. *Indravajrā*

IV: 94; **V**: 98

vi. *Rathoddhatā*

VII: 175

c. Twelve syllables per quarter

vii. *Vaṁshasthā*

Each quarter: ᴗ – ᴗ – – ∧ – ᴗ ᴗ – ᴗ – ᴗ – ∧

I: 16, 19; **III**: 59; **IV**: 73; **V**: 106, 109, 111; **VI**: 138, 143, 154; **VII**: 167, 173, 187

viii. *Drutavilambita*
II: 41; **III**: 64; **V**: 121; **VI**: 133; **VII**: 160

d. Thirteen syllables per quarter

ix. *Praharshiṇī*
VI: 152, 155

x. *Ruchirā*
VII: 191

e. Fourteen syllables per quarter

xi. *Vasantatilakā*
Each quarter: – – ᴗ – ᴗ ᴗ ᴗ – ∧ – ᴗ ᴗ – ᴗ – – ∧
I: 8, 23, 27; **II**: 39, 42; **III**: 56, 66, 72; **IV**: 74, 75, 83, 85, 86, 87, 92; **V**: 96, 97, 100, 116, 117; **VI**: 137, 141, 145, 150; **VII**: 161, 163, 174, 182, 183, 189

f. Fifteen syllables per quarter

xii. *Mālinī*
I: 17; **II**: 34; **III**: 51; **V**: 101, 102, 113; **VII**: 164

g. Seventeen syllables per quarter

xiii. *Shikhariṇī*
I: 9, 20; **II**: 40; **III**: 54; **V**: 104; **VI**: 134; **VII**: 190

xiv. *Hariṇī*
III: 58; **IV**: 91; **VII**: 181

xv. *Mandākrāntā*
I: 29; **II**: 44, 45

h. Nineteen syllables per quarter

xvi. *Shārdūlavikrīḍita*
Verse 36 (each quarter):
– – – ᴗ ᴗ – ᴗ – ᴗ ᴗ ᴗ ᴗ ∧ – – ᴗ – – ᴗ ᴗ ∧
I: 13, 26, 36; **II**: 32, 35, 36; **III**: 55, 71; **IV**: 77, 78, 81, 89, 90; **V**: 103; **VI**: 129, 130, 131, 142; **VII**: 165, 168, 169, 184

i. Twenty-one syllables per quarter

xvii. *Sragdharā*
I: 1, 7

VERSE-FORMS WITH ALTERNATE QUARTERS IDENTICAL

Matching quarters: first and third, and second and fourth, respectively; but designated variations allowed.

j. Twenty-three syllables in each half

xviii. *Mālabhāriṇī*
Odd quarters, 11 syllables; even quarters, 12 syllables.
III: 69, 70; **VII**: 177, 178

k. Twenty-five syllables in each half

xix. *Pushpitāgrā*
Odd quarters, 12 syllables; even quarters, 13 syllables.

I: 28; **II**: 33; **VI**: 136

xx. *Viyoginī*
Odd quarters, 12 syllables; even quarters, 13 syllables.
II: 48

xxi. *Aparavaktra*
Odd quarters, 13 syllables; even quarters, 12 syllables.
IV: 82

Verse-forms Measured by Vowel Length (Mātrā)

xxii. *Āryā*
Verse 2: – ᴗ ᴗ – – – ᴗ ᴗ ^ ᴗᴗ ᴗ – – – – ᴗ – ᴗ – ᴗ | (variant)
ᴗ ᴗ ᴗ ᴗ ᴗ ᴗ – – ^ᴗ – – – – ᴗ – – – ||
Odd quarters, 12 *mātrās*; second quarter, 18; fourth quarter, 15.
I: 2, 3, 12, 14, 15, 18, 21, 24, 25, 30; **II**: 31, 38; **III**: 50, 52, 53, 57, 60, 62, 63, 67; **IV**: 93; **V**: 105, 107, 112, 115, 122, 125; **VI**: 132, 140, 144, 146, 156; **VII**: 179

2. Prakrit Verse-forms

Verse-forms Measured by Vowel Duration

xxiii. *Gāthā*
First half: 30 *mātrās*; second half: 27 *mātrās*.
IV: 84, 88; **V**: 95, 110; **VI**: 127, 128.

xxiv. *Udgāthā*
Each half: 24 *mātrās*.
I: 4.

xxv. *Gīti*
Odd quarters: 12 *mātrā*s; even quarters: 18 *mātrā*s.
III: 61.

xxvi. *Sundarī*
Odd quarters: 12 *mātrā*s; even quarters: 11 *mātrā*s.
VI: 126.

Notes to the Play

These notes are selective rather than comprehensive. They refer to the text of the translation by act, scene, segment, verse, and word or phrase. When a particular word or phrase in a numbered verse or segment is glossed, it is specified here in italics. To minimize repetition, the acts and scenes are identified in bold headings with Roman numerals; the segments are consistently specified using only Arabic numerals in brackets, in the style '[158]'; and individual verses are explicitly labelled in the style 'Verse 25'. For a more detailed explanation of the division and numbering of acts, scenes, segments, and verses, see the first two sections of the Translator's Note.

These notes synthesize reliable information from a large number of print and electronic sources. To avoid adding endnotes to these notes, I have included general cross-references in parentheses only when essential. Interested readers can correlate my statements to the parenthetical citations systematically: all verbal definitions of Sanskrit and Prakrit terms are based on Apte, and follow the alphabetical entries in his dictionary; and references to Miller, Rajan, and Johnson (among others) are linked to the corresponding passages in their translations, and to the notes in a similar format gathered at the end of their respective books. References to other works (for example, *Manusmriti*, *Arthashāstra*, Somadeva Vasudeva) are based on the texts specified in my Select Bibliography and, likewise, can be tracked easily by using their scholarly apparatus.

I.i

[1] *Invocation*: Sanskrit *maṅgalācharaṇam*, 'an auspicious introduction in the form of a prayer (for the attainment of success) at the beginning of any undertaking or . . . composition'. It also is called *nāndī*, 'benedictory verse or verses recited as a . . . prologue at the beginning' of a play, a 'benediction' (Apte). It is recited offstage by the Stage Manager; in the classical style, it is preceded by drums, but in a modern performance it may be delivered with brief music (strings and percussion) preceding and following it. Structurally, the Invocation opens the outermost meta-theatrical frame of a play; this frame becomes the container of the entire dramatic action, and closes with the *bharata-vākya*, the final verse in the text that is recited on the stage by the male protagonist (Verse 191 in *Shakuntalā*, as translated here). The function of the Invocation is to offer a benediction for theatrical art in general; for a specific production and performance of the play at hand; and for the site, environment, and participants (author, performers, spectators) of the performance. At the same time, its aim also is to circumscribe the whole phenomenon of the play as 'auspicious'. The Invocation and the Prelude (see below) together constitute a play's *pūrva-raṅga* or 'set of preliminaries', roughly equivalent to a prologue or induction in the Europhone dramatic and theatrical tradition.

Verse 1, *creator*: literal rendition of Sanskrit *srashṭuḥ*; an epithet for Brahmā, the god of creation in Hinduism. See other references to 'the creator' (for example, Verses 39 and 109). *Sacrifice*: the paradigmatic Vedic ritual, in which a designated agent (the sacrificing subject) gives up something of great value (the sacrificed object), and offers it—through the mediating offices of a qualified priest—as a gift or donation to one or more gods, by consigning it symbolically to a sacred fire, which is said to have the supernatural capacity to convey it to its divine destination. See notes to Verses 7, 80, and 103.

I.ii

[2]–[5] *Prelude*: Sanskrit *prastāvanā*, literally preface, introduction, or exordium. It defines a play's second meta-theatrical frame, set inside the Invocation's outer frame. Its function is to identify the author and the play to be staged; to situate an audience's experience of the dramatic action in a particular production, performance, and theatre; to circumscribe the action as a theatrical fiction and representation; and to foreshadow the play's main themes, overall emotional tone, and general atmosphere. See note to [1].

Verse 2, *connoisseur*: Sanskrit *vidurah*, a wise, clever, knowledgeable man. Later in the classical period, Sanskrit poetics characterizes this kind of listener-spectator as a *rasika* (a person skilled in 'savouring' rasa), which fully anticipates the post-Renaissance Europhone concept of a connoisseur.

[3] *trumpet-flower*: Sanskrit *pāṭala*, the pale red, rosy, or pink trumpet-shaped flower of the tree *Bignonia suaveolens*, common to India and Sri Lanka. The flower is associated frequently in classical Sanskrit poetry with Kāmadeva, the god of love and desire (counterpart of Eros in Greek and Cupid in Latin); with garlands worn by lovers; and with a fragrance that attracts bees. It is related botanically to *Stereospermum colais*, which bears yellow trumpet-flowers; but it should not be confused with the poisonous *Datura* and *Brugmansia* genuses (Indian *dhatura*, 'devil's trumpet' or white thorn-apple, and the American 'angel's trumpet', respectively). On Kāmadeva, see note to [51].

[4] *mimosa*: Sanskrit *shirīshah*, a tree with globular pink flower-heads, most likely of the species now known as *Albizia julibrissin* (Persian or pink silk tree), native to Asia; often generically called 'mimosa' or 'silk tree', both botanically imprecise names. It has been misidentified in recent decades as *Albizia saman* (rain tree, monkeypod) or as *Mimosa pudica* (*chhuī-muī* in Hindi and Urdu), both of which are native to South and Central America and were introduced into India only in the nineteenth century.

[5]: This segment as a whole foreshadows the play's representation of the loss and recovery of memory. *Painted picture*: the first of a long, complex series of ekphrastic tropes (such as similes and metaphors) that visualize character, situation, and dramatic action in terms of pictures and painting.

I.iii

Verse 7: The antelope or black buck here is not a 'natural' animal. It is an enchanted creature in the enchanted forest, and hence is able to outpace Dushyanta's horses and hunting chariot. He pursues it without realizing that he has entered a zone of the supernatural. *Sacred grass*: the first of several interchangeable references to *darbha*, *durva*, or *kusha*, a widespread long-bladed perennial grass, *Desmostachya bipinnata*, native to Asia and Africa. Originally abundant in the foothills of the Himalayas (the location of Kaṇva's ashram), it has been harvested since the time of the *Rig-veda* (about 1000 BCE) for Vedic rituals, in which it is used to cover and pad the sacred ground around the central firepit and the areas that seat the priests and the patrons of sacrifices (in which symbolic offerings to the gods are consigned to the flames in the pit). In III.i, the Apprentice Priest carries bundles of the long-bladed grass on the stage; see note to that scene. On Vedic sacrifice, see notes to Verses 1, 80, and 103.

[9] *Indra* and *sun*: Indra is the principal god of the pantheon in Vedic religion (which precedes classical Hinduism); in the ancient cultures of Indo-European origin, he is a close counterpart of Zeus in the Greek pantheon, and of Jove in the Roman. He is a god of rain, and is associated with the thunderbolt, his terrifying weapon. In Vedic religion, the sun is a god, and his chariot is drawn across the daytime sky by celestial stallions, with dawn as the charioteer (see Verse 161). Indra's chariot, also drawn by celestial stallions and driven by his charioteer Mātali, is featured on the stage in VI.vi and VII.i; see Verse 167 and immediately after for Mātali's comparison of Indra's and Dushyanta's chariots.

[10] *ascetics*: The play includes a large number of characters whom it labels interchangeably as *tapasvin*, *rishi*, and *muni*. A *muni* is a holy man, a spiritual practitioner; the term is applied generically to ancient Hindu as well as Jain and Buddhist figures, including Gautama Buddha (also Nārada; see Appendix B). A *rishi* is specifically a figure first represented in Vedic scripture; he is conceived of as a 'seer or visionary' and as an 'inspired poet' (*kavi*) to whom the Vedic hymns are 'revealed'. See the discussion of *rishi*s in the context of Kaṇva and Kashyapa in the Afterword. In Vedic and epic discourse broadly, most *muni*s and *rishi*s are also characterized as *tapasvin*s, literally 'practitioners of *tapas*'. The word *tapas* signifies 'heat' in its material sense, but metonymically it represents the 'spiritual heat' acquired and accumulated by someone who practises rigorous physical and mental self-discipline and self-mortification. A *tapasvin* thus is a practitioner who has achieved spiritual empowerment through austerity, self-denial, and self-control, and who may have acquired supernatural powers by transcending natural human limitations. Since Vedic times, *tapasvin*s or ascetics often have been *saṁnyāsin*s, 'renouncers' of everyday life in 'normal' human society, who establish their own alternative societies in isolated environments; see note to [78]. In classical and postclassical Hinduism, the yogi often displaces the *tapasvin* of the Vedic and epic periods, using the special techniques of yoga to acquire *tapas* and spiritual power; in *Shakuntalā*, the overt reference to 'yogic powers' occurs in Sānumatī's soliloquy at the beginning of VI.ii. In the Vedic and classical Hindu order, *rishi*s and *muni*s—as distinct from *tapasvin*s and *saṁnyāsin*s still striving to achieve that status—belong to a category of their own, apart from all celestial and non-celestial beings as well as ordinary humans. Some *rishi*s and *muni*s are of divine origin and are called *devarshi*s (Kashyapa, Durvāsā, Nārada). Others are of partially or completely human origin and are classified by caste group: a *brahmarshi* is born a brahmin (for example, Kaṇva, Vasishtha), whereas a *rājarshi* is born a kshatriya (for example, Vishvāmitra in his early career; see note to Verse 68). The play explicitly and radically elevates Dushyanta to the status of a *rājarshi*; see II.v. My

translation generally reserves 'sage' for a *rishi* or a *muni*, such as Kaṇva, Kashyapa, Durvāsā, or Vishvāmitra; and 'ascetic' for any of the other (human) male and female *tapasvin*s at the two ashrams, from Shāraṅgarava and Gautamī to Anasūyā, Priyaṁvadā, and Suvratā. The play-script classifies Shakuntalā, who is half-human and half-celestial by birth, as a *tapasvinī* (female ascetic).

[11] *Puru*: The two Sanskrit epics, the Rāmāyaṇa and the Mahābhārata, celebrate kings from two distinct lineages or clans: the 'solar clan' (*sūrya-vaṁsha*) in the former work, and the 'lunar clan' (*chandra-vaṁsha*) in the latter. According to the *Manusmriti* (an ancient Hindu law-book that acquired its canonical form around 300 CE), the human race is descended from fourteen successive 'primordial humans' or *manu*s; the seventh of these progenitors, Vaivasvata Manu, is the father of Ikshvāku, the first of the solar kings, who rules at Ayodhyā; Rāma, the hero of the *Rāmāyaṇa*, is a descendant of Ikshvāku and is the most famous member of the solar clan; but also see note to [45]. In the genealogies of the *Mahābhārata*, where the Dushyanta–Shakuntalā story is told originally, the lunar clan is descended from Ikshvāku's androgynous sibling Ilā; Puru, the youngest son of Yayāti and Sharmishṭhā, is the sixth king in this line, and a forefather of Dushyanta. Several generations after Dushyanta, Kuru is the lunar king at Hastināpura (the capital city in our text); several generations after Kuru, his descendants—the Kauravas, and their cousins, the Pāṇḍavas—become the warring factions depicted in the epic. The play refers frequently to Puru and the lunar dynasty; when Shakuntalā addresses Dushyanta directly (in Acts III, V, and VII), she calls him *paurava*, 'descendant of Puru'; and the imagery in the dialogue and the verses invokes the moon consistently across the dramatic action, reinforcing Dushyanta's association with the lunar clan (for example, see notes to Verses 16, 75, 122, and 179).

Wheel of the law: in Sanskrit, the chakra (wheel) of dharma (law, duty, lawful governance) that a great king (*chakravartin*) symbolically 'turns', as a sovereign ruler whose dominion extends to the edges of the ocean. In the epic and classical periods, it is represented in the Indian plastic arts as a wheel with twenty-four spokes; in modern times, the image reappears at the centre of independent India's national flag.

Verse 13, *opal*: Sanskrit *upalaḥ*, 'sunstone', the verbal origin of Latin *opalus* and the modern English term for this precious or semi-precious stone. *Iṅgudī*: classified as *Terminalia catappa*, a tree native to Asia and Africa; in modern times, variously called Indian, Bengal, Malabar, tropical, country, or sea 'almond', and known in Pakistan and in Urdu as *lāla bādāma*, and in Hindi and Marathi as *jaṅgalī badāma*. Botanically, the *iṅgudī* tree is unrelated to the almond (*Prunus dulcis*, in the subgenus *Amygdalus*), but its nut is a fruit with a 'stone' or drupe, like almond, peach, mango, and coconut. Traditionally, the *iṅgudī* tree is associated with medicine; the play indicates that the oil extracted from its nut is used in the classical countryside as a nutrient and cleanser for skin, scalp, and hair. See [41] and Verse 105.

I.iv

[16] *nine-petalled jasmine*: Sanskrit *nava-mallikā*, a climbing shrub or vine of the genus *Jasminum*, with a white or yellow flower with nine petals; other species of jasmine have flowers with five to eight petals each. The common jasmine is *Jasminum officinale*, a vine that blossoms in the summer with very fragrant five-petalled white flowers (*chamelī* in modern Urdu and Hindi). The play refers to *Jasminum sambac*, varieties of which have flowers with five to nine petals; it blossoms year-round, but the sweetly fragrant flowers open at night and close by day. In modern languages, this species is known as *motiyā* (Urdu) and *mogarā* (Hindi and Marathi); its flowers are plucked early in the morning, when they are closed like buds. The figuration across the text uses simile, metaphor, metonymy, and other tropes to identify Shakuntalā with both the vine and the nine-petalled flower, which is the variety most highly valued in classical India.

Verse 16, *blue water lily*: See the discussion of water lily and lotus in the Translator's Note, and accompanying endnote 21; also see notes to [11] and Verses 75, 122, and 179.

[17] *bark dress*: The play maintains an imaginative ambiguity about clothing at Kaṇva's ashram: on the one hand, the community may be so isolated in a dense forest along the foothills of the Himalayas that it has no access to cotton fabric (woven on handlooms in India since the third millennium BCE, and after the archaeological interregnum following the Harappan period); on the other, the enchanted forest may be situated in 'early epic time'—many centuries before the classical period that Dushyanta seems to inhabit in his palace and at Hastināpura—and the ascetics therefore live in more 'primordial' conditions, before the spread of cloth. The text explicitly mentions 'Chinese silk' (Verse 30), which arrived in India only around the onset of the Common Era; but it does not refer to any cut and stitched garments or to pouches or bags (the City Superintendent in VI.i, for example, does not carry the Fisherman's 'reward' in a bag or pouch). The skills and implements needed for cutting and stitching materials such as cloth and leather did not reach the subcontinent from Persia until late in the classical period: Sanskrit has no word for 'bag', and all the Indian-language terms for such an object originate independently either in Prakrit (for example, *thailā*) or in Farsi (for example, *bastā*). When Shakuntalā wears anything other than a bark dress, it is a supernatural *kosha*, which appears to be a 'magically' spun-and-woven whole sheath of fine silk or silk-like gauze; see [77] and [113]. All Indian textile garments before the late classical period, such as the male and female dhoti (the latter a forerunner of the modern sari) are wraps; garments such as the *pāyajāmā* or *pājāmā* and the *cholī* are inventions from near the end of the classical period or just after. The interpretation of the play's precise descriptions of natural and supernatural fabrics, garments, ornaments, and cosmetics in their historical contexts adds suggestively as well as restrictively to the possibilities of costume, make-up, and production design on the twenty-first-century stage;

for example, see notes to [28]–[29], transition from III.ii to III.iii, and Verses 30, 70, and 77.

[19] *Forest's Radiance*: a literal rendering of Shakuntalā's epithet for the jasmine vine, *vana-jyotsnā*; Miller translates it as 'Forestlight', which is more approximate but stylistically more felicitous in English. The primary denotation of *jyotsnā* is 'radiance' in general, but Somadeva Vasudeva, 'Inarticulate Nymph', takes it to mean only 'moonlight' and contorts his interpretation of this passage when comparing the Devanagari, Bengal, and Kashmir recensions.

I.v

[20] *bee*: Prakrit *bhama* and *mahuara*, Sanskrit *bhramara* and *madhukara*, respectively; a flying insect in general that 'wanders, whirls, swerves, moves haphazardly', and specifically a 'maker of honey', a bee, a black bee, or a pollinating beetle. These are non-specific terms in the text, and I have rendered all of them as 'bee' in its generic sense in modern English. The image recurs in Acts V–VI, and becomes one of the motifs that binds disparate parts of the play's main action; see especially Verses 95 and 113 and also [144]–[146].

[22] *saptaparṇa*: a common evergreen, *Alstonia scholaris*, native to India, and sometimes called the milkwood pine or the blackboard tree. Traditionally, it is a medicinal plant, but is also prized for its shade (due to its height, circumference, and leathery leaves arranged in whorls).

Verse 23, *intoxicated eyes*: My translation is deliberately ambiguous about whose eyes are 'intoxicated' in this exchange (the deer's or Shakuntalā's); the image foreshadows Dushyanta's more explicitly erotic reference to Shakuntalā's 'maddeningly intoxicating eyes' in Verse 64.

Verse 26: Dushyanta's description of Shakuntalā here provides the ekphrastic basis for his painting of her, presented in VI.iv; also see notes to Verse 60 and [74]. *Mimosa blossom*: see note to [4].

[27] *ring*: this passage introduces Dushyanta's royal signet ring into the main action; the device is analysed in the Afterword, and in note to [74].

I.vi

[28]–[29]: These two connected passages constitute a *chūlikā*, a diegetic piece in drama (consisting of description, narration, report, and so on), delivered as a 'public announcement' (which is context-dependent) by a voice or voices backstage. In performance, it informs the audience about events that have taken, are taking, or shortly will take place offstage, and that will not be represented mimetically on the stage. *Ashram crier*: see entry in Appendix B. *Blood-red*: in classical Indian aesthetics and dramaturgy, red is the colour of eros; its verbal introduction here marks the dominance of *shriṅgāra* rasa in the action, which intensifies with the pervasive red colour in III.v, the scene of *sambhoga*, the culmination of love and desire in the lovers' first union. On rasa, see Appendix G; on plot, see the Afterword.

Verse 30, *Chinese silk*: Sanskrit *chīnāṁshukam*; see note to [17].

II.i

Interlude: I have followed the Tripathi, Dwivedi, and Dwivedi edition in labelling Māḍhavya's extended soliloquy here as a *vishkambhaka*, an 'interlude' between two Acts that is performed on the stage by one or more secondary or tertiary characters, in the absence of the hero and the heroine. The characters in such an interlude mimetically enact a scene, but the plot function of the scene itself is to inform the audience about offstage events and to fill gaps in the represented story-line. The characters therefore use diegetic discourse (whether narration, description, or report, or a combination of these) within the frame of mimetic enactment. This Interlude specifically introduces Māḍhavya and his extended secondary plot—which runs through Acts II, V, and VI—into Dushyanta's quest-stream in the principal plot. See the Translator's Note and the Afterword.

Skewered meat: Māḍhavya most likely is a vegetarian (see the Afterword and Appendix B); his distaste for game is linked to his later objections to hunting (II.ii–iii), and to the play's subsequent devaluation of fishing (VI.i). *Birdcatcher*: literal rendering of Prakrit *sauṇiluddha* and Sanskrit *shakuni-lubdhaka*. This passage has been misrepresented by earlier translators, such as Miller and W.J. Johnson. *Whoreson*: translation of Prakrit *dāsīye-putte* and Sanskrit *dāsyāh-putraih*. This is the first of only two instances of 'earthy language' in the play, the other being Bhadrasena's repetition of this concept, using the Sanskrit term *vaidhaveya* in [35]. *Greek warrior women*: Prakrit *javanī*, Sanskrit *yavanī*. Alexander the Great left behind a colony of Greek soldiers in the Gandhara region (roughly from today's Peshawar to Taxila and Kabul) after his invasion of the subcontinent in 327 BCE. The play suggests that this settler population produced 'warrior women' who were employed as elite royal guards in later Indian kingdoms, and the text adds this as an exotic flair to Dushyanta's colourful entourage.

II.iii

Verse 36, *kadamba*: a tree native to India and Asia, *Neolamarckia cadamba*. Also known as the burr-flower tree, it has fragrant globular orange-yellow flowers that are used in the production of perfume; for its classical use, also see note to [127].

II.iv

Verse 38: This passage, frequently mistranslated, contains three parallelisms, each containing a set of three similes. The first of the parallelisms is relational: Menakā is like a jasmine vine, Shakuntalā originally is like a flower growing on it, and Kaṇva is like a bitter medicinal tree underneath. The second parallelism is spatial:

Shakuntalā falls from the vine onto the top of the tree. The third is processual: Menakā's abandonment of Shakuntalā is like the cutting of the maternal umbilical cord, which is like breaking off the flower by its slender stem; and Kaṇva's adoption of the abandoned infant is like the tree's 'catching' of the falling flower.

Verse 39: This dense passage contains a comprehensive conception of the process of creation in general, and specifically of poeisis, creativity in the human arts. This process involves visualization, composition or organization of material, formation or form, and artful fashioning, which together lead to the emergence of a unique artefact. The unusual thrust of this view of creativity is that, even at the material level, the artist 'crafts' the artefact, 'Not with his hands but with his mind'—by 'contemplating it again and again'.

[43] *pay their tax*: in Sanskrit, the verbal root is *upahri*, 'to fetch, give, offer, present' a gift or a donation (an *upaharah*), especially to a superior and as a compliment; but it also refers to an act of 'taking or seizing'. *One-sixth of their harvest*: according to works such as the *Arthashāstra* (canonical form around 300 CE), this was a standard agricultural tax-rate in the classical period (nearly 17 per cent); about one thousand years later, in Mughal India—as the Marathi bhakti poet Tukaram records it for the 1630s—the standard was one-fourth of a harvest (equivalent to 25 per cent). *Wild rice*: The play notably mentions rice three times (see also Verses 13 and 93), but does not refer to wheat.

II.v

Verse 44: One of the most complex verses in the text, which lays out an extended, multi-point analogy between ascetic and king, or priestly sage (*brahmarshi*) and royal sage (*rājarshi*); it has not been represented adequately in earlier renderings.

Verse 45, *whole earth*: this establishes Dushyanta as a *chakravartin*, a great king who 'turns the wheel of the law'; see note to [11].

Celestial dancers and *Indra's palace*: the female *apsarā*s who provide pleasure and entertainment in Indra's divine palace located in his *svarga*, heaven. *Demons*: in this case, *daitya*s, who are *asura*s or anti-gods and oppose gods such as Indra. *Thunderbolt*: a divine symbol (*vajra*) associated with Indra, who is a god of rain; see Verse 183. *Bow*: Dushyanta's extraordinarily powerful weapon (*dhanusha*); see references in Verses 33, 34, 49, and 183. It is carried for him by the leader of his bodyguard of Greek warrior women, and is featured on the stage in [152]–[153].

II.vi

[47] *ritual of fasting*: Prakrit *uvavāsa*, Sanskrit *upavāsa*, translated literally. *Trishaṅku*: personal name in Sanskrit; Prakrit, *tisaṁkū*. Trishaṅku was a great king of the solar clan who ruled at Ayodhyā (see note to [11]); but his flaw was that he loved his own person to an exceptional degree, and wished to go to heaven in his physical body after death. Trishaṅku tried to fulfil this illegitimate wish by seeking the help of the sage Vishvāmitra (Shakuntalā's biological father in the play), who used his supernatural powers (acquired through *tapas*) to raise the king bodily to heaven. Indra, always in a power struggle with the human sage, then turned Trishaṅku upside down and sent him back earthwards, head-first. But Vishvāmitra stayed the king midway—where he still remains, suspended perpetually between two equal and opposing forces, as a constellation in the southern hemisphere. A Sanskrit version of Kālidāsa's allusion to this myth—cast in Māḍhavya's Prakrit in the play-script, and phrased in my translation as 'like Trishaṅku suspended between heaven and earth'—has been a proverbial expression in India since the late classical period. On Vishvāmitra, see Appendix B; on *tapas*, see note to [10].

III.i

Interlude: classified as a *vishkambhaka* in the Narayan Ram edition; see note to II.i. *Sacred grass* and *sacrifices*: see note to Verse 7.

III.ii

[51] *god of love*: Kāmadeva, invoked here with the epithet *bhagavan-kusumāyudha*, the 'god who attacks with flowers', which refers to the divine 'floral arrows' that he shoots at lovers, his targets and victims. In cultures of Indo-European origin, Kāmadeva (Sanskrit), Eros (Greek), and Cupid (Latin) are exact counterparts, with each of them being named literally for sexual desire and erotic love. See notes to [3] and [128].

Transition from III.ii to III.iii: Dushyanta's final words in III.ii, in prose after Verse 53, together with the first stage direction in III.iii, indicate that the 'low stone ledge' (in the natural arbour on the riverbank), 'with a layer of flowers spread like a sheet over it', is made up like a bed on a wedding night. In the tenth canto of Kālidāsa's *Kumārasaṁbhava*, for instance, Shiva and Pārvatī's marriage bed is covered with petals. Like that long poem, *Shakuntalā* strongly associates the colour red with eros, wedding, and union; so, in a theatrical production, III.iii would commence an intensification of red on the stage, starting with the flowers on the ledge, proceeding to emphasize the colour on Shakuntalā's body (for example, Verses 62, 66, 67, and 69), and culminating in the red glow of sunset around the lovers in III.v. See note to [28]–[29].

III.iii

[58] *fatal state of attraction* and *jewel in the crown*: these phrases render the original Prakrit phrasing and its Sanskrit version as literally as possible. *Trine*: The text describes precisely what modern astronomers classify as a trine, in which a pair of planets appears in close proximity to the moon during a specific interval in lunar time. Dushyanta constructs a trifold parallelism between Shakuntalā, Anasūyā, and Priyaṁvadā and the moon, Venus, and Jupiter, respectively, to celebrate the friendship among the young women as a human analogue of the paradigmatic natural (or supernatural) 'companionship' of three heavenly bodies.

Verse 60: one of the important ekphrastic passages in the play that uses the visual art of painting to configure a verbal image, and that foreshadows the focus on painting and portraiture throughout VI.iv. See notes to Verse 23 and [74].

III.iv

Verse 64, *intoxicating eyes*: see note to Verse 23.

III.v

Verse 66, *elephant's trunk*: this unusual comparison emphasizes the embodiment of Shakuntalā's half-celestial origins in her physical features. I found it difficult to translate and retain poetically, but it is central to Kālidāsa's aesthetics, which pushes against a limit of figuration here; both Miller and Johnson misleadingly omit the image altogether. Vālmīki's Rāmāyaṇa uses exactly the same image to describe Sitā's limbs; for example, 'Her left thigh, as graceful as an elephant's trunk' (*Sundara-kāṇḍa*; Sattar, p. 391).

Verse 68: Dushyanta's declaration in this verse is simultaneously a (sexual) proposition and a (marriage) proposal, and he invokes the paradigm of a union in the *gandharva* style. *Gandharva*s are the male counterparts of *aspsarā*s in Indra's *svarga* or heaven; in this category of being, the males are 'celestial musicians' whereas the females are 'celestial dancers', entertainers, and objects of pleasure for the (male) gods; and *gandharva*s and *apsarā*s go with the flow of desire and pair up freely with each other by mutual consent. In epic and classical Indian law, a '*gāndharva* marriage' is the analogue of a union in the 'celestial style' and is one of the eight legitimate forms of marriage and union in the human realm—but only kshatriyas can practise it, when both the male and the female acting by mutual consent belong to the warrior caste group. Since caste identity is transmitted genealogically (by birth) and is determined patrilineally (by caste of father), Dushyanta makes a special effort in I.iv–v to ascertain Shakuntalā's paternity. Once he knows that Vishvāmitra is her biological father, he is sure that she is genealogically a kshatriya, because Vishvāmitra is famous as a human sage who was born a warrior—though one who sought controversially to attain the status of a *brahmarshi* (a sage of 'brahmin origin') through sheer *tapas*. Dushyanta relies on this certitude to proposition and propose to Shakuntalā at this moment, under the rubric of a 'wedding . . . in secret, by mutual consent— / In the style of the celestials who sing for the gods'. See note to [10].

[70] *red goose*: Prakrit *chakkavāka*, Sanskrit *chakravāka*, called the 'ruddy goose' in English for several centuries. The large-scale zoological reclassification of waterfowl in recent decades now identifies this bird as the ruddy shelduck, in the species *Tadorna ferruginea*. It winters on the Indian subcontinent, arriving in October and departing in April; it inhabits lakes, reservoirs, and ponds, and breeds especially in the Jammu and Kashmir region. It is a central poetic figure in this play because of its colour, and for several concomitant facts: it forms monogamous pairs; it maintains the pairing throughout the year (and not for just the mating season); its pairs are monogamous 'for life'; and the male and the female in a pair care for their young together, until the latter fledge about eight weeks after hatching. In the play-script, the 'voice in the air' that delivers this short prose passage (usually ascribed in interpretation and performance to Anasūyā) uses the Prakrit metaphor *chakkavāka-vahu*, or Sanskrit *chakravāka-vadhu*, literally 'ruddy-shelduck-bride'; I have deliberately changed 'ruddy' to 'red' to indicate the poetic figuration here, and have relied on the explicit colour term to signify the feminine status of bride. Anasūyā's backstage words foreshadow the 'night' that envelopes the lovers in Acts IV–VI, until Dushyanta encounters Sarvadamana on Mount Meru in VII.ii. See notes to [28]–[29] and the transition from III.ii to III.iii.

IV.i

Mixed Interlude: Sanskrit *mishra vishkambhaka*. I have followed the Tripathi, Dwivedi, and Dwivedi edition in identifying IV.i–ii as the two parts of a 'mixed interlude'; these scenes present a mixture of offstage incidents through narration, description, and report by secondary and tertiary characters on the stage, in the absence of the protagonists. The two parts constitute a single, composite representation that conceptually stands between the main action in III.v, which closes temporarily with Dushyanta and the offstage ashram Priest, and its resumption in IV.iii, with the reappearance of Shakuntalā on the stage.

[73] *Durvāsā*: see Appendix B. The conventions of classical Indian dramaturgy require that an 'inauspicious' act, such as a curse, not be enacted mimetically on the stage; Durvāsā's curse on Shakuntalā and Dushyanta therefore is dramatized with a combination of offstage voice and onstage diegesis.

[74] *He has delivered his curse*: the details in Priyaṁvadā's description and narration of Durvāsā's departure from the ashram, immediately after Verse 73, are usually mistranslated; compare the versions in Miller and Johnson. *We can breathe again*: Anasūyā's words here change the role of the ring in the rest of the play's action; see the Afterword and note to [27]. *Look, Anasūyā, there is our Shakuntalā*: Priyaṁvadā's 'verbal painting' of an image of Shakuntalā in prose is the third significant ekphrastic moment in the text, after Verses 23 and 60.

Verses 74–75: This pair of verses is part of a pattern of paired verses assigned to minor characters, which highlights some of the best poetry in the play; for example, see Verses 28–29 (Ashram Crier, I.vi), 34–35 (Bhadrasena, II.iii), 44–45 (Gautama and Nārada, II.v), 101–02 (Two Bards, V.iii), and 127–28 (Parabhritikā and Madhukarikā, VI.ii). In other poetic patterns, compare Verses 74 and 98, and both with Verse 1.

Verse 75, *moon* and *water lily*: these images foreshadow their appearance in Verse 122, discussed in the Translator's Note and in its endnote 21. Also see notes to [11] and Verses 16 and 179.

Verse 76, *shamī*: a tree that, in myth, carries live fire in its trunk. Botanically, it is identified as *Prosposis cineraria* (*khejarī* in

Rajasthani), native to arid and semi-arid environments in Asia; the most famous modern specimen is about 400 years old and is located in Bahrain. In the Mahābhārata, the Pāṇḍavas (the epic's protagonists) hide their weapons safely in a *shamī* tree, when they are required to remain incognito and undetected in the final phase of their exile (before the war). This verse uses a 'mixed metaphor' (the only such instance in the play) in which, as in the logic of the jasmine vine and mango tree in [19], a vine is feminine and a tree is masculine. Shakuntalā therefore can be identified as a 'vine' or sapling of the *shamī* plant (hence a *shamīlatā* in Sanskrit); and, by analogy, Dushyanta's seed in her womb can be equated with the mythical fire in the tree trunk. The parallelism, though tenuous, is vital because it elevates the physical conception of Shakuntalā and Dushyanta's son, the future Bharata, to the level of a 'cosmic' event.

[77] *bakula*: an evergreen tree, *Mimusops elengi*, native to Asia; common modern names included Spanish cherry and medlar (English), *bakula* (Marathi and Bengali), and *maulasarī* (Hindi). It provides excellent shade; produces fragrant, cream-coloured flowers in April and edible, orange-coloured, berry-like fruit in June; and is traditionally prized for excellent red hardwood, ornamental flowers (used in garlands), and multiple medicinal applications in Ayurveda. Anasūyā here refers to 'enchanted, long-lasting *bakula* blossoms' that retain their vital qualities after harvest and storage.

IV.iii

Verse 77: The sacred grove at the ashram is an enchanted place, so its trees are supernatural. *Silk sheath*: Sanskrit *kosha*; see note to [17]. *Lac*: Sanskrit *laksharasah*; a resinous substance deposited by the female of the lac insect (the most commonly cultivated species is *Kerria lacca*) on the branches of specific kinds of trees (for example, *Schleichera oleosa*, commonly *kusum* in Hindi, *kusumba* in Marathi). The collected and processed resin is traditionally a primary source of red pigment and of lacquer, of which India has been a principal supplier internationally since early modern times; in recent decades, the lac industry has been centred on Jharkhand, Chhattisgarh, West Bengal, and Maharashtra. In the classical period, lac production was widespread along the foothills of the Himalayas, the region where Kaṇva's ashram is located in the play; it was used on the subcontinent as a cosmetic for women. *Bridal red*: the colour associated with eros, union, wedding, and marriage. See notes to [28]–[29], the transition from III.ii to III.iii, and Verse 68.

IV.iv

[78]–[81]: This scene as a whole composes the first well-defined stage of the lengthy process of Shakuntalā's departure from the ashram.

[78] *renounced the world*: ascetics often reject normal society and live in alternative communities, usually in isolation from cities, towns, and villages; see note to [10]. *Householder*: in conventional society, a married man who leads and supports a family and its household; in the classical period in India, social organization is normatively patriarchal, and is based on caste groups (*varṇa*s); a man's life is organized concomitantly by normative 'stages' (*āshrama*s), of which the 'household stage' is the second (it is preceded by the stage of education and followed by the stages of retirement and renunciation). The compound *varṇāshrama* refers to an integrated system defined by the structural organization of society and social life by caste and the temporal organization of biography and individual life by stages. This meaning of *āshrama* should not be confused with that of ashram as a physical setting.

Verse 79, *Yayāti*, *Sharmishṭhā*, *Puru*: In the genealogies of the Mahābhārata, Yayāti is the fifth king in the 'lunar clan', and is patrilineally an ancestor of Dushyanta. With his first wife Devayānī, Yayāti fathers Yadu (the progenitor of the Yādavas) and Turvashu (the progenitor of the Yāvanas); with his 'second wife' Sharmishṭhā, he fathers Druhyu (the progenitor of the Bhojas), Anu (the progenitor of all 'non-ritual' *mlechchhas* or outsiders to Hindu society), and Puru, who inherits Yayāti's kingdom. Puru is the progenitor of the 'lunar' line down to Dushyanta and then to Shaṁtanu, who is closer to the epic's central events. Shaṁtanu is the father (with the personified river Gaṅgā) of Bhīshma; and subsequently his wife Satyavatī becomes the great-grandmother (through a different patrilineal line) of the epic's protagonists and antagonists, the Pāṇḍavas and the Kauravas. In Kālidāsa's play, Yayāti and Sharmishṭhā serve as models for Dushyanta and Shakuntalā, and Puru is a model for Bharata. See note to [11].

[80] *gift of a daughter to a bridegroom*: Gautamī compresses this concept into the single word *vara*, bridegroom. It foreshadows Kaṇva's soliloquy in [94], at the end of Act IV, which uses the term *pati*, husband.

Verse 80: a verse in the style of a mantra in Vedic (an antecedent of classical Sanskrit), from the *Rig-veda saṁhitā*, the eighth mandala of which gathers a large number of hymns attributed to the 'historical' Kaṇva and his family of poets. Like many scriptural mantras, this verse meta-discursively participates in the very action it prescribes; more precisely, it is a performative speech-act with illocutionary force and a perlocutionary effect. It invokes and describes a basic Vedic rite of purification very precisely. *Moral flaws and evil deeds*: Sanskrit *duritam*, 'a bad course of action or conduct; evil' (Apte). On Vedic ritual and sacrifice, see notes to Verses 1, 7, and 103.

IV.v

[81]–[87]: This scene as a whole defines the second phase or 'middle' of Shakuntalā's departure. It is set in the enchanted grove on the ashram grounds, and unfolds in three sub-scenes or vignettes. [81]–[83] represent the first vignette, a fabulation in which Kaṇva communicates supernaturally with the trees, and the 'goddesses of the enchanted grove' respond to him; [85]–[86] comprise a second sub-

scene, which focuses on the jasmine vine called the Forest's Radiance; and [86]–[87] constitute the third vignette, which involves the fawn. On the jasmine vine, see notes to [16] and [19]; in the play-script, see Shakuntalā's different, later reference to the fawn in [116].

IV.vi

[88]–[94]: This scene contains the third and final phase of Shakuntalā's departure for Hastināpura; and most of its action is set on the edge of the ashram's grounds, beside a lake (see Illustration 3). Like IV.v, it also unfolds in three well-defined sub-scenes: the vignette of the red goose; that of Kaṇva's message to Dushyanta; and that of messages and blessings from Kaṇva, Anasūyā, and Priyaṁvadā to Shakuntalā herself. Once the departure is complete after Verse 93, the scene closes with a quick transition back to the ashram buildings.

[91] *Mount Malaya* and *sandalwood*: A mountain or range, set in the southernmost portion of the Western Ghats, in modern Kerala; associated strongly in classical Indian texts with the production of sandalwood, of which the species *Santalum album* is indigeneous to southern India. The tree is a source of fragrant wood, oil, and perfume; its wood traditionally is ground by hand, with water on a stone slab, to produce a thick paste, which has cosmetic as well as ritual uses (see Verse 159). Shakuntalā refers to a 'sandalwood vine', the young plant shortly after sprouting.

[92] *four hand-widths*: Shāraṅgarava refers to the practice of using the extended human arm and flat hand (held perpendicular to the arm) to measure the elevation of a heavenly body above the horizon; four hand-widths here corresponds to 45 degrees above the horizontal, and hence to one-quarter of daytime. The principle of this measurement is the same as that of an early modern sextant, first designed in Europe by Isaac Newton in the late seventeenth century, and engineered by other inventors in the early eighteenth.

V.i

[95]: The setting is in one of the king's rooms in his palace at Hastināpura; the women's chambers would be further in the interior, or at the rear of the palace, and the music room would be located there (see Illustration 4). This short scene marks Māḍhavya's last participation in the action before he reappears in VI.ii; see the analysis of his role, in relation to Durvāsā's curse and Dushyanta's amnesia, in the Afterword. *Black bee*: Haṁsapadikā uses it as a metaphor for Dushyanta, who interprets it guiltily as such. See notes to [20], [113], and [144]–[146].

Verse 96, *residues*: of past actions, including actions in previous lifetimes, that karma is said to deposit in the agent. The linguistically complex final quarter of the verse suggests such action-and-consequence, but does not actually employ the technical terms of the theory of karma (for example, *karma-phala*, *saṁskāra*).

V.ii

Verse 98, *sun's stallions*: see the note on [9] above. *Shesha*: chiefly in Vaishṇava mythology, the mythical serpent with multiple heads who holds up the earth, and whose body forms the bed on which Vishṇu lies in the cosmic ocean. *King's duties* and *their six divisions*: Vātāyāna's reference here is generic. For example, the *Manusmriti* (a prescriptive law book) and the *Arthashāstra* (a handbook of politics), both probably given their canonical forms around 300 CE, offer many more divisions of the king's duties overall, and several sets of six divisions in particular areas. In general, however, six broad domains that cover most of a classical king's duties, and on which Dushyanta evidently focuses in the play are: the administration of the kingdom; law and justice; revenue and economy; war, peace, and security; public welfare (of all categories of subjects); and self-discipline and self-cultivation as dynastic monarch and human individual. Acts II, V, and VI especially suggest that the king has to deal with all six areas routinely, on any given day of his life in power.

[99]–[100] *elephant*: Vātāyāna echoes Bhadrasena's imagery in Verse 34. *Snow mountains*: literal rendition of Sanskrit *hima-giri*, an epithet synonymous with 'Himalayas'. *Royal-family priest*: Sanskrit *purohita*, a brahmin who serves a king and members of his family as a personal priest and as a counsellor on matters of morality, ethics, law, and spirituality; one of the stock characters in Sanskrit dramaturgy.

V.iii

[100] *pavilion of the fire sacrifice*: Sanskrit *agni-sharaṇam*, also rendered as 'fire sanctuary'. This is a pavilion on the palace grounds dedicated to the performance of Vedic rituals, with a permanent firepit and ambient platform (which, in the play, face a spacious forecourt). Prescriptions as well as practices in the epic and classical periods indicate that such a pavilion—as distinct from, say, a hall of justice—would be used for rituals related to kingship and state, and for a king's meetings with sages, ascetics, and other spiritual practitioners. Hence Dushyanta's preceding reference in the play-script to 'a setting that is suitable for a visit by holy men'.

[101]–[102] *bards*: Sanskrit *vaitālika*; traditionally also called *sūta*, but the play reserves the latter term for 'charioteer'. See related notes in Appendix B. The two royal bards in this vignette are patronized by the kingdom or state; their official function is heroic rather than spiritual, and they serve as 'living repositories' of the king's heritage as a dynastic monarch. A royal bard thus complements the role of the king's *purohita* (royal-family priest; see note to [99]–[100]), and of the ritual and scholarly priests associated with the royal court, whose official function is to deal with matters of morality, ethics, moral law, and spiritual theory and practice (dharma). Here the bards remind Dushyanta of the principal elements in his role as ruler: as a punisher of evil and unlawful activity, a selfless servant

and protector of his subjects, and an instrument of their unity and unanimity.

[103] *freshly washed* and *cow*: The forecourt has been ritually cleansed, not simply for hygienic and cosmetic reasons, but so that it is free of any 'spiritual pollution' and hence fit to receive the visiting ascetics from Kaṇva's ashram. In Hinduism, the milch cow is a sacred animal (which generates the cross-cultural slang interjection, 'Holy cow!', in English around 1920); cow's milk is churned to produce butter, which is then converted into ghee (a form of vegetable fat that can be preserved without refrigeration for extended periods). Ghee is the commonest cooking medium on the subcontinent until the mid-twentieth century; but it is also a sacred material, since the fire in a Vedic ritual to which sacrificial materials are consigned is fuelled by hardwood and is stoked or fed with ghee. See notes to Verses 1, 7, and 80.

V.iv

Verse 105, *grubby with oil*: before the advent of modern soap, a widespread practice (with origins in ancient India) was to rub the body with a suitable oil as nutrient and cleanser before bathing in a pond, river, or lake, or in water drawn from a well. The reference here most probably is to the *iṅgudī* oil used by the residents of Kaṇva's ashram; see notes to Verse 13 and [41].

[108] *in unison* (added as a stage direction for the Ascetics): early in this scene, the party of ascetics accompanying Shakuntalā functions on the stage like a chorus in Greek theatre.

Verse 109, *embodiment of goodness and virtue*: Sanskrit *mūrtimatī cha satkriyā*, where the last word designates 'good or virtuous action'. Other than this exception, I have avoided using 'virtue' in my translation because of its strong Aristotelian, neo-Aristotelian, and broadly Christian associations in English. But Old English *vertu* comes from Latin *vir*, 'man', appended with the suffix *tut* to form an abstract noun, which is 'manliness' and, by abstraction, 'excellence'.

Latin *vir* is cognate with Sanskrit *vīra*, 'brave, heroic, powerful, excellent man' and *virtut* therefore is cognate with *vīryam*, 'manliness, bravery, courage, heroism, potency, semen' (the last two significations appearing in the Latinate *virility*). In fact, Sanskrit *vīra* and Latin *vir* come from the same reconstructed Proto-Indo-European root **wiro* or **uihro* as the Greek and Latin *heros* and English *hero*; so 'virtue' is the excellence of character that emerges from the good, heroic, or noble deeds or *satkriyā* of a hero—and, by exact correspondence across gender lines, of a heroine. Shāraṅgarava's declaration in my version, that 'Shakuntalā is the embodiment of goodness and virtue', therefore ought to serve as a precise etymological rendering of the abstract phrase in the original. Dushyanta and Shakuntalā's moral equation here is a dramatic flashback to their equation in Kaṇva's Verse 85, and a foreshadowing of Kashyapa's prose statement in [189], that they walk together as 'companions in morality'. *Creator*: Brahmā; see note to Verses 1 and 39.

[110]: Gautamī speaks out of turn here and provokes Dushyanta, who savages her rhetorically when she addresses him again in [116].

[113] *bee*: a recurrent image or motif; see notes to [20] and [144]–[146] and Verse 95.

[116] *Indra's Ford*: a ford located topographically at the juncture where the River Mālinī flows into the River Ganges or Gaṅgā, west of the present-day city of Bijnor in western Uttar Pradesh. Kaṇva's ashram is set on the banks of the Mālinī upstream, near the point where it emerges from the foothills of the Himalayas onto the plains (a thickly forested region in epic and classical times). The ford is approximately halfway between Kaṇva's ashram and Hastināpura, the historical location of which is to the west of the Gaṅgā (towards modern Meerut). The Mālinī, the Gaṅgā, the ford, and the locations of the ashram and the city implied in the play correspond remarkably well to real geographical features observable in India today; see Illustration 2 and also view them on the Internet using Google Earth, if accessible. On *Indra* and *Shachi*, also see Appendix A.

[117] *a pit camouflaged with straw*: This image usually has been misconstrued and mistranslated. *God of love*: see note to [51].

Verse 122: see the analysis in the Translator's Note.

V.v

[124] *the birthmarks of a great king*: in epic and classical culture, a child destined to become a king is born with a number of distinguishing features or 'birthmarks of future greatness', such as webbed hands, long arms, extraordinary physique and bodily strength, and so on. In Buddhist iconography, for example, Gautama Buddha's various physical deformities include some that are 'birthmarks' of kingship (such as his webbed hands) and some of enlightenment (such as the *ushṇīshah* or protuberance at the crown of the skull); in Hindu imagery, the arms of the epic hero, Rāma, extend down to his knees. See Dushyanta's response to Sarvadamana's appearance in Verse 173. *O mother earth*: Shakuntalā's cry as she exits echoes Sītā's words in the final book of the Rāmāyaṇa, when the latter ends her life in the wilderness—after Rāma has abandoned her in a pregnant state (out of concern for his own reputation as a king), and after she has given birth to their twin sons, Lava and Kusha. See notes to Verse 66, and especially to [130]. *Menakā's shrine*: located near the fire sanctuary on the palace grounds, and dedicated to Shakuntalā's mother, an *apsarā* or celestial creature who serves Indra, Dushyanta's divine friend; see Illustration 4 and Appendix A. *Body of light*: the *apsarā* Sānumatī in her celestial form, sweeping down to earth swiftly to save Shakuntalā on behalf of Menakā; see VI.ii–iii in the play-script, especially [127] and [135].

VI.i

Mixed Interlude: Like the *mishra vishkambhaka* or Mixed Interlude to Act IV, this also has two parts, both featuring minor characters, without the hero and the heroine on the stage; see note to IV.i. But, unlike the previous instance, Part 1 here is different from Part 2 in classification as well as function. In Sanskrit, the second part is a *vishkambhaka*, an interlude of the same kind as in Acts II, III, and IV. In contrast, the first part is labelled a *praveshaka*, literally 'entrance, entry point', a scene containing only tertiary or inferior characters (as distinct from secondary or middling characters) which 'introduces or ushers' a new set of offstage factors into the principal and secondary plots, and hence commences fresh developments in the overall dramatic action. The dramaturgical convention is that a *praveshaka* resembles a *vishkambhaka*, but cannot be used at the beginning of either a play's first or last act. When these two kinds are juxtaposed, as here, they constitute a 'mixed' interlude. For the organization, plot function, and innovative thrust of this *praveshaka*, see the Afterword.

[127] *rohu*: Sanskrit *rohita-matsyah*, red carp, zoologically *Labeo rohita*, one of three species of carp original to India; widely known as *rohu* in modern Indian languages. It is an 'oily' freshwater fish common in rivers in what are now India, Pakistan, Nepal, and Bangladesh, and is significantly larger and heavier than the two other kinds of carp native to the subcontinent (*katla* and *mrigal*). It remains a prized food in eastern and northern India today, particularly in the three regions associated with the three main recensions of the play. *The bundle, tied in a piece of cloth* (added stage direction): Not explicit in the play-script; there were no cut-and-stitched bags or pouches in the classical period; see note to [17]. *Kadamba*: reference to a wine infused with the fragrance of *kadamba* flowers; see note to Verse 36. *The beginning of a beautiful friendship*: rendering of Prakrit *padhamasohimadam ichchhīadi*, Sanskrit *prathamasho-abhimatamishyate*; a remarkably exact parallel in word and spirit to the famous line at the end of Michael Curtiz's film *Casablanca* (1942), where Rick says, 'Louis, I think this is the beginning of a beautiful friendship.'

VI.ii

[127] *craft* and *skyway* (opening stage direction): in a classical performance, there would be no physical representation of a skyway

on the stage; this device would be evoked diegetically by Sānumatī's words, and the actress playing the character would use special movements and gestures in mime to indicate her entrance, descent, and arrival on it. See Appendix F, and the discussion of specialized mime in this context in Bose. I have translated *ākāsha-yāna* literally as 'a small craft [on] the skyway' and as 'skycraft' in order to leave open the possibility of other kinds of representation using modern stage machinery. It is important that Sānumatī does not interact or converse with any of the human characters around her, and none of them can see or hear her. All her dialogue in VI.ii–v is delivered as a 'soliloquy' for the benefit of the audience, which is aware of her presence throughout these scenes. *Bathing pool*: In the celestial order, Sānumatī has a secondary status; she serves other *apsarās* (female) and *gandharvas* (males), whose characteristic is that they bathe frequently and fastidiously at pools maintained and serviced for this purpose. *Spring festival*: supposedly a popular annual celebration in Hastināpura, to mark the blossoming of mango trees at the end of the cycle of cold weather, and the beginning of a 'season of love' that fulfils the desires of those who seek love. This may be an ancient or classical precursor of the modern festival of Holi, celebrated on the day of the full moon in the month of Phālguna (February–March), as the sun approaches the Spring equinox (around March 21). In various Hindu solar calendars, the year ends in or just after Phālguna; in the modern Hindi-speaking heartland, for instance—the geographical region where *Shakuntalā* is set—the day of the new moon two weeks after Holi is the end of the year. *Yogic powers*: supernatural powers, such as the power of invisibility and the power of bodily travel between earth and heaven. The play restricts these powers on the stage to characters of celestial or divine origin or ancestry—Kaṇva (Act IV), Sānumatī (Acts V–VI), Mātali (Acts VI–VII), and Kashyapa and Gālava (Act VII)—and none of the fully human characters appears to possess them.

[128] *koel*: Sanskrit *parabhritikā*, 'baby or little koel'; zoologically, *Eudynamys scolopaceus*, native to India and Asia, the songbird that

is a counterpart of the European cuckoo (family *Cuculidae*). Many species of koel and cuckoo are brood parasites: they lay their eggs in the nests of other species, and let the latter hatch them and raise their young. In Verse 116, Dushyanta uses this zoological fact to demolish Gautamī's claim that Shakuntalā is 'unacquainted with deception and guile'. In Verse 164, he refers to the pied cuckoo (*Clamator jacobinus*), native to Asia and Africa, and to the fact that this species is migratory at a specific time of the year: it arrives in India at the end of summer, and hence is believed to be a herald of the annual monsoon. Also in that verse, Dushyanta sees pied cuckoos flying with the celestial chariot at a great height, in a moist wind and amidst rainclouds; he identifies them as the *chātaka* birds of Indian mythology, which proverbially wait for raindrops to quench their thirst—and which, in that vignette, pass close to the chariot-wheels covered with condensation. Here, Parabhritikā is named after the koel for her sweet singing. *We share the same spirit*: Parabhritikā and Madhukarikā mirror Anasūyā and Priyaṁvadā in their embodiment of intimate female friendship. *Five arrows* and *god of love*: see notes to [3] and [51]. On *Madhukarikā*, see Appendix B.

Verse 129, *henna*: Sanskrit *kurvaka*, classified as *Lawsonia inermis*, native to Asia and northern Africa. It appears to have been used since the ancient period to prepare a distinctive dye for skin, nails, and hair as well as cotton, silk, and leather; however, it is mentioned in the play only as a flowering plant, and not as a dye or cosmetic. In Kālidāsa's works, henna is not associated with *mehaṁdī* or *mehndi* (a word of Arabic origin), the practice of using henna paste to inscribe cosmetic patterns on the hands and feet of brides. In its fuller application, *mehndi* is the term for a Muslim wedding rite, which has been incorporated into Hindu custom in the postclassical period. *Enfolded in . . . a bud*: this image has been mistranslated earlier.

[130] *public outcry*: Sanskrit *kaulīnam*. The widespread 'public censure' of Dushyanta for his rejection and abandonment of Shakuntalā, while she is pregnant with their child—and his

subsequent acceptance of her and Sarvadamana in Act VII—is a full inversion of the situation in the final book of the Rāmāyaṇa. In the epic, public criticism is directed at Rāma for his acceptance of Sītā, after her abduction and imprisonment by Rāvaṇa; and it leads Rāma to reject and ostracize Sītā, while she is pregnant with their twin sons. See notes to Verse 66 and to [124].

VI.iv

[139] *Excellent, my friend*: Māḍhavya's first response to the contents of the painting is mistaken and confused due to his myopia.

VI.v

[148] *canonical ritual . . . the birth of a son*: Prakrit *puṁsavaṇā* and Sanskrit *puṁsavanā-saṁskāra*, the earliest 'purificatory' rite of passage prescribed in classical Hinduism, performed ceremonially when a woman perceives the first signs of successful conception, with the objective of ensuring the birth of a son (rather than a daughter). This rite is overtly patriarchal and patrilineal in its disposition.

Verse 150: In this Vedic conception of an 'afterlife', the dynasty's forefathers are 'present' in the celestial realm after death, and are 'nourished' by the food and water that their eldest living male descendant offers them periodically in ritual sacrifices.

VI.vi

Stage directions: In this unpredictable and fast-moving scene, I have inserted some stage directions in brackets, in order to identify the speakers, locations, actions, and temporal sequence left implicit in the play-script.

Verse 153, *swan*: classical Indian poetry follows the convention that a swan (as distinct from other waterfowl) has the characteristic ability to separate milk from a mixture of milk and water, by sucking out the former unerringly with its beak.

[155] *gang of anti-gods*: In the Vedic mythology invoked here, gods (*sura*s or *deva*s) and anti-gods (*asura*s, or *daitya*s and *dānava*s) are the principal agents in the celestial realm, and are at war with each other constantly and perpetually. The anti-gods (distinguished further from the *rākshasa*s or demons) form armies and 'gangs' to fight, defeat, and disempower the gods. The anti-god here is *Kālanemi*, whose name literally means 'the ring of death'; and his one hundred sons have formed a violent gang called *durjaya*, 'the invincibles'. *Sage Nārada*: not the adolescent disciple featured earlier in the play, but the divine sage after whom the fictional disciple is named; Sage Nārada is one of the sons of Brahmā, and he busily intervenes in the affairs of humans and the gods, often causing confusion and setting the two against each other. See note to [10] and entry in Appendix B.

VII.i

Verse 159, *celestial coral flowers*: flowers of the *mandāra* tree, one of the five kinds of plant in Indra's *svarga* or heaven. The species is identified variously as *Erythrina indica* (the tiger-claw tree) and *Erythrina variegata* (the Indian coral); it is indigenous to Asia, Africa, and Pacific Oceania, and produces brilliant scarlet or crimson flowers. It may resemble the tree known in Bengal as *pārijāta*; but it is not related botanically to the *pārijāta* named in Sanskrit, Hindi, and Marathi, which is the night-flowering jasmine, *Nyctanthes arbor-tristis*, and is another of the plants in *svarga*. In Vedic mythology, Indra takes the *mandāra* and the latter *pārijāta* because they were among the plants produced in the primordial 'churning of the ocean' by gods and anti-gods; one narrative associates the *mandāra* with Indra's wife Shachi (or Indrāṇī), who plants it in heaven. Sanskrit commentaries often identify the *mandāra* as the *kalpa-taru* or *kalpa-vriksha*, the celestial tree of plenitude that fulfils all of its worshippers' desires and wishes. These conventional associations underwrite Dushyanta's poetic argument in this verse. *Sandalwood paste*: see note to [91].

Verse 160, *smooth claws*: In Vaishṇava mythology of the classical period, the fourth of Vishṇu's ten principal avatars or incarnations on earth is Narasiṁha, a hybrid of man and lion, who uses his claws to kill the demonic and hubristic king Hiraṇyakashipu.

Verse 161, *the sun's charioteer*: see note to [9].

Verse 162, *the wish-granting tree*: Sanskrit *kalpa-latā*, an epithet for the tree of plenitude in Indra's heaven, often identified with the *mandāra* tree; see note to Verse 159.

[163] *highway to heaven*: Sanskrit *svarga-mārgah*, rendered literally. *Abundant Flow*: Sanskrit *parivaha*, classical name of a major air-current. *Great river of the sky*: Sanskrit *trisrotasam*, glossed as the *ākāsha-gaṅgā* ('the Ganges of the sky') and named Mandākinī. *Vishṇu's second stride*: The fifth of Vishṇu's ten principal avatars is a dwarf brahmin, who descends to earth to punish king Mahābali, a great-grandson of king Hiraṇyakashipu (see note to Verse 160). The dwarf asks the arrogant king for a piece of land measuring three paces; when the king asks him to mark a domain of his choice with three strides, Vishṇu reveals his cosmic form: one stride stretches from netherworld to earth, and the second from earth to heaven. At the end of the third stride, Vishṇu's foot lands on Mahābali's head. Verse 163 suggests that the course of the Abundant Flow is always 'devoid of darkness' because it traces the mythical trajectory of Vishṇu's second stride.

Verse 164, *pied cuckoos*: see note to [128].

[166] *Mount Meru* and *demigods*: In Indian mythology, the celestial Mount Meru rises along the principal cosmic axis; I have inserted one sentence about it that appears in brackets in this passage, in order to make the allusion comprehensible in performance. The

play-script calls it *hemakūṭaḥ*, 'gold mountain', and *Shakuntalā* is the principal reference in Sanskrit literature for this usage. The mountain is the home of Kubera, 'the god of wealth', and hence has 'molten gold streaming down its sides'. Kubera's servants on the mountain are 'half-human, half-horse' creatures called *kinnaras*, a Sanskrit term (literally *kiṁnara*, 'what kind of creature?') cognate with the Greek *centaur*; in the Indian case, a *kinnara* maybe like a centaur (man to the waist, equine quadruped below), or he may be the inverse (horse to the neck, human below). Commentaries on the play-script characterize a *kinnara* as 'a horse-headed man'. *Kashyapa, Marīchi, Aditi*: see Appendix B and the Afterword.

Verse 168, *extreme ascetic*: a classical description of an ascetic in a state of *samādhi*, the final stage of yogic concentration or meditation, under conditions of extreme self-mortification and metabolic stasis.

[169] *celestial coral trees*: Sanskrit *mandāra*; see note to Verse 159.

[170] *ashoka*: an evergreen tree, *Saraca asoka*, with excellent foliage and bright, fragrant orange-yellow flowers, native to the Deccan plateau and western peninsular India. Its name is literally 'the tree without sorrow and grief'; *shoka*, sorrow and grief, is the *bhāva* underlying the *karuṇa* rasa, strongly associated with *vipralambha shriṅgāra*, erotic disjuncture; see Appendix G. The tree's placement at the end of this scene environmentally ushers in the resolution of Dushyanta and Shakuntalā's extended period of suffering. In the Rāmāyaṇa, Sītā is imprisoned in an *ashoka vaṭikā* or garden of *ashoka* trees on Rāvaṇa's palace grounds on the island of Laṅkā; on the likely connection between *Shakuntalā* and that episode, see the Afterword. The *Saraca asoca* species designated in Sanskrit should not be confused with *Polyalthia longifolia*, the 'false *ashoka* tree'.

VII.ii

[173] *the marks of a king* and *natal web*: on Sarvadamana's physical characteristics as a future king, see note to [124]. *Mārkaṇḍeya*:

traditionally, the name of the sage credited with the composition of the *Mārkaṇḍeya Purāṇa*, one of the eighteen principal *Purāṇa*s ('ancient books') compiled before and during the classical period. The play-script may be using this name for a less-than-minor character in the same humorous vein in which it uses the names Gautama and Nārada for two of Kaṇva's disciples; see Appendix B.

[178] *Peerless Herb* and *birth ceremony*: in Sanskrit, the name of the sacred plant is *aparājitā*, 'peerless', classified as an *aushadhi*, a medicinal herb. It is known by the same name in modern Hindi and Bengali, and is often called the blue pea in English; it is identified as *Clitoria ternatea*, where the Latin genus name reflects the flower's structural resemblance to human female genitalia. The birth ceremony to which Suvratā refers is *jātakamma* in Prakrit and *jātakarman* in Sanskrit; it is a child's first rite of passage immediately after birth, which 'welcomes' it into the human world (the *nāma-karaṇa* or naming ceremony is a separate, second rite, performed eleven days later). Compare with note to [148].

VII.iii

[179] *Rohiṇī* and *occultation*: Rohiṇī is the classical Sanskrit name for the star Aldebaran in the constellation Taurus; astronomically an orange giant, it is one of the brightest stars in the night sky. Aldebaran appears in the northern hemisphere as the first bright star past the constellation Orion, as one moves from left to right on the line of the three stars in Orion's belt. As Aldebaran lies close to the plane of the earth's revolution around the sun in the celestial sphere, it is one of the notable stars to be occulted by the moon. Occultation is the general process in which the moon passes between the earth and an astronomical object and therefore hides the latter from view for a brief time; a solar eclipse, in which the moon temporarily obscures the sun, is an example of a particular type of occultation. Aldebaran is occulted or eclipsed by the moon around the autumnal equinox (21 September on the modern calendar); when the star

emerges past the moon's dark edge after an occultation at that time of the year, it usually appears to be 'cradled' by the luminous crescent. Verse 179 invokes this image with astonishing precision: Dushyanta mentions the *yogam* or 'union' of Rohiṇī and the moon at 'the end of the occultation' (*uparagante*), with the latter term signifying the temporary 'eclipse' of the star. Within this astronomically accurate description, the literary allusion is to the Indian myth that Rohiṇī (Aldebaran) is a daughter of Daksha (one of Brahmā's sons) and is given as a bride to the moon. In the play's context, Daksha is the father of Aditi (who therefore is a sister of Rohiṇī), and also is a paternal uncle of Kashyapa (who is the son of Daksha's brother Marīchi, and hence is Rohiṇī's and the moon's brother-in-law). The myth resonates with Dushyanta because he is a king of the lunar clan. See note to [11]; also see Appendix B and the Afterword.

[182] *Awful deed from my past*: Shakuntalā's thinking here invokes the basic theory of karma in a mirror reflection of Dushyanta's reference to it in [96].

VII.iv

Verse 183, Indra's *thunderbolt* and Dushyanta's *bow*: see notes to [9] and Verse 45, and also Appendix B.

[184]–[185]: on the gods and celestial beings mentioned here, see Appendix B; and notes to [9], [45], [47], [160], [163], and [179].

Verse 187: Dushyanta's argument in this verse precisely spells out the limits of causality in the human and natural realms, and its differences from causality in the supernatural or divine realm.

[191]: It is rarely noted that Kashyapa and his celestial assistant Gālava communicate with each other 'telepathically' in this scene: Gālava enters in response to Kashyapa before the latter has asked for him in so many words.

Endnotes

Preface

1. For my discussion in this book, the basic periodization of Indian literary and cultural history is as follows, with all dates approximate: the Vedic period, 1500–600 BCE; the epic period, 600 BCE–400 CE; the classical period, 400–1200 CE; the postclassical period, from 1200 onwards; the modern period, from 1757 onwards; and the postcolonial period, from 1947 onwards. The long interregnum of about 1000 years between Roman theatre and 'Chinese opera' in its first full dramatic and theatrical form in the work of playwrights such as Guan Hanqing under the Yuan dynasty is indicated, for example, in Gainor, Garner, and Puchner, vol. 1; and is mentioned in the epigraph to Raghavan, 'Sanskrit Drama', p. 9.
2. For historical background on the Gupta dynasty and early classical culture in India, see Wolpert, chapter 7; Stein, chapter 2.
3. In the Penguin edition of Kālidāsa in English translation (in progress), see Heifetz; and Reddy. For other recent translations of the plays, see Miller, *Shakuntalā*; Gerow, *Mālavikā*; Gitomer, *Urvashī*; and the translations by Coulson; Johnson; and Rajan. For a broader range of texts and translations, see under Kālidāsa in my Select Bibliography.

4. The play's overall historical and cultural 'life and afterlife' since the classical period is discussed in Thapar, *Shakuntalā*. Its textual transmission, reception, and interpretation is traced in the introduction, individual essays, and notes in Miller, *Theater*; other perspectives are offered in Coulson; Johnson; and Rajan. For richer scholarly details, see Raghavan, 'Sanskrit Drama'; Bose, 'Staging'; and various essays in Sengupta and Tandon. For extensive, specialized coverage of the Sanskrit–Prakrit world, see the works by Pollock.
5. Important editions of the Devanagari recension of the play since the nineteenth century include Monier-Williams, *Shakuntalā*; Kale; and Narayan Ram. On the Bengal recension, see the introduction and notes in Rajan; on the Kashmir recension, see especially Somadeva Vasudeva. Some scholars also discuss separate 'Southern' and 'Maithili' recensions.
6. See Jones. Figueira provides a useful account of Jones's translation and its impact on Europe over a century, but her approach and analysis need to be updated in a twenty-first-century critical perspective. Also see the discussion of modern performances of *Shakuntalā* in Richmond; and of the play in film and various performance genres in Sengupta and Tandon.
7. The contributions of modern Indian scholars can be assessed using Devadhar and Suru; Kale; Mishra; Rajan; Thapar, *Shakuntalā*; Tripathi, Dwivedi, and Dwivedi; and Tripathi.
8. A text's anagogic meaning corresponds approximately to what is called its 'spiritual' meaning in common usage. In Dante Aligheri's fourfold theory of interpretation, a text conveys its meaning at a literal, a metaphorical, an allegorical, and an anagogic level; the last is the most general and comprehensive, and relates the text to the world in its moral-ethical or theological dimension, and hence to the encompassing 'ends' of human life; see the extended discussion of anagogic meaning in Frye, pp. 116–28. The post-Renaissance European tradition of 'cosmic drama', in which gods participate in the action on the stage, is analysed in Brown, especially pp. 115–25.

9. See van Buitenen, general introduction to vol. 1, for an overview of the Mahābhārata.
10. See Rāghavabhaṭṭa in Narayan Ram; and specific works by the other authors as listed in my Bibliography.
11. See Jones; Monier-Williams (both works); and Kale.
12. See Dharwadker and Dharwadker, Preface, on the main features of Rakesh's play; and Afterword, on postcolonial 'disorder'. On *Shakuntalā* as the 'validating creation' of an entire 'civilization', see Gerow, 'Plot Structure', Part I, p. 564; this assessment is based on the philosopher-critic Abhinavagupta's canonization of the play in the late tenth century.

Translator's Note

1. A meta-theatrical element or device in a play takes us 'behind' the main dramatic action, and comments reflexively on it or discloses its meaning. A dedication, prologue, or induction to a play is a meta-theatrical device; so is a 'play-within-a-play', as in Shakespeare's *Midsummer Night's Dream* or *Hamlet*.
2. Dhanañjaya, pp. 90–94. I follow the Sanskrit text, not Haas's English.
3. On spatial form, see Frank. Classical Sanskrit poetics identifies the thematic elements that emerge in the spatial form of a play as its *artha-prakriti*s, which are conceived as points in the 'production of meanings and goals'. The theory juxtaposes the spatial form with the *avasthā*s (states, stages, or conditions) of the hero's (or heroine's) quest, the sequence of which defines the temporal form of the dramatic action.
4. 'Juncture' corresponds to Sanskrit *sandhi*, and 'sub-juncture' to *sandhyāṅga*. These junctures and sub-junctures appear in the overall plot of the play; and each of them 'stitches or sutures' components of its spatial form with stages in its temporal form (see endnote 3).
5. See Vishvanātha; and the discussion of the Bengal recension in Rajan.

6. Rāghavabhaṭṭa is discussed in Miller, *Theater*, especially pp. 333–35; Bhoja is summarized and analysed in Pollock, 'Social Aesthetic' and *Language*.
7. *Sandhyāṅga*s are the smaller units that combine the spatial and temporal elements of a plotted dramatic action. Gerow, 'Plot Structure', Part II, closely analyses the junctures and sub-junctures in *Shakuntalā*, drawing on Rāghavabhaṭṭa's fifteenth-century commentary on the play.
8. The standard range of Prakrit prescribed for a classical play consists of Shaurasenī, Mahārāshṭrī, Māgadhī, and Paishāchī; the first three are the most common 'regional' speech varieties of the period, and the fourth is a 'hypothetical' medium of literary communication for demonic, non-human characters. See the many-sided discussion of Prakrit in various parts of Pollock, *Language*. In *Shakuntalā*, Ardha-Māgadhī replaces Paishāchī.
9. In the Aristotelian tradition, 'diction' (*lexis*) refers to the choice of words (vocabulary) in a given piece of discourse, and also to both choice and order of words (style). In the latter sense, the English literary and critical traditions commonly distinguish among high, middle, and low dictions; high or 'lofty' diction often employs an ornate vocabulary and formal syntax (as in diplomatic discourse and parliamentary speeches), whereas low diction uses 'street language' (as, for example, in many rap lyrics today).
10. In classical Indian poetics as well as modern Europhone theory (especially twentieth-century Russian formalism), the 'literariness' of a text refers to the aesthetic attributes that qualify it as literature, in comparison with texts that are judged to be non-literary. Both traditions define 'embellishment' of discourse as one of the common criteria of literariness, in which crafted verbal devices (such as figures of speech and tropes) set literary language apart from ordinary, everyday usage. Sanskrit criticism employs four main measures of literariness in a text: its figuration (*alaṁkāra*), semantic resonance (*dhvani*), style

(*rīti*), and aestheticized emotion (rasa). Each of these criteria indicates the kind and degree of 'deviation' from 'natural', non-literary discourse (*svabhāvokti*) that a literary text embodies.

11. In Sanskrit–Prakrit literary practice, individual verses or short passages that are exceptionally well-crafted and can be extracted from larger works to stand on their own, are classified as *subhāshita*s, 'beautiful utterances'. Many of the so-called lyric poems in classical Indian anthologies are *subhāshita*s drawn from longer texts.
12. Classical Indian poetics distinguishes between two categories of figures. A figure of speech (*shabda-alaṁkāra*) organizes the pattern of sounds in words in order to intensify the euphony of the verbal medium, without affecting the meaning conveyed (for example, rhyme or *yamaka*; alliteration or *anuprāsa*). In contrast, a figure of thought or a trope (*artha-alaṁkāra*) organizes words in order to create new configurations of meaning that deviate from literal or conventional meanings (for example, simile or *upamā*; metaphor or *rūpaka*). Both categories of figuration involve 'deviation': figures of speech, from sounds in everyday usage; and tropes, from familiar meanings. See Vishvanātha, chapter 10, which defines and analyses seventy-five figures of speech and thought as well as their multiple varieties.
13. Apte defines *aprastuta-prashaṁsā* as a trope that 'by not describing . . . what is not the subject-matter . . . conveys a reference to [what is explicitly the] subject-matter'. Following Vishvanātha, chapter 10, he annotates five varieties of this figure of thought.
14. Apte characterizes *tulya-yogitā* as a trope of 'equal pairing' that appears as 'a combination of several objects having the same attribute, the objects being either all relevant or all irrelevant'.
15. In Europhone logic and rhetoric, the warrant of an argument is a principle or proposition that provides the basis, authority, or sanction to validate the whole line of reasoning. In general and in simplified form: an argument builds on a claim that is

justified by an underlying warrant; that is 'proved' by irrefutable supporting evidence; and that becomes 'true' when it is inferred logically or persuasively from the warrant and the evidence.

16. For Apte, *arthāntara-nyāsa* is a figure of thought in which 'a general proposition is adduced to support a particular instance, or a particular instance, to support a general proposition'.
17. Jones, p. 96.
18. Rajan, p. 241.
19. Miller, *Shakuntalā*, p. 142.
20. Johnson, pp. 67–68.
21. Apte correctly identifies *kumuda* as a 'water lily' of various species (such as *alba* and *odorata*) belonging to the genus *Nymphaea*; and *paṅkaja* as a 'lotus', *Nelumbo nucifera*.
22. *Ekphrasis*, from Greek, is the process (or product) of representing an object as 'a picture in words', or of using techniques borrowed from the plastic art of painting (or sculpture) to create a 'vivid mental image' with language. When a text 'visualizes' a dramatic action in its dialogue and stage directions, it performs an ekphrastic function for its audience. *Ethos*, also from Greek, designates character; disposition; the fundamental values or principles, including moral ones, governing the thought and conduct of a person, or of an imagined or represented personage. Ethics, as principles or values of conduct, is derived from *ethos*; a play therefore exercises an ethical function when it creates and 'fleshes out' a character in its dramatic action, or engages in the broader process of characterization.

Afterword

1. The Afterword is addressed to general readers, and hence avoids using technical Sanskrit terms that are likely to be unfamiliar in the international sphere. My discussion itself, however, tacitly incorporates many of the distinctive concepts, arguments, and analytical procedures of classical Indian poetics and criticism.

This and the following endnotes identify the classical ideas that I have adopted and adapted, and may be particularly useful to readers who wish to trace the sources of my lines of reasoning and explication.

In the opening paragraph, I allude to the notion that drama (a literary mode of representation) is *drishya kāvya*, 'verbal-and-visual poetry', literary composition that has to be heard as well as seen in order to be fully understood and appreciated. Theatre, or aestheticized performance on the stage, is *nāṭya*. This abstract noun is derived from the verb *nat* (to act or perform with bodily movement, to dance), and from the concrete nouns *naṭa* (masculine) and *naṭī* (feminine) for 'actor, performer, dancer, mime'; *nāṭya*, in fact, designates the whole field of an actor or performer's practice. For explanations of these and important related terms, especially *rūpaka* and *nāṭaka*, see Appendix E.

2. The story that provides the narrative frame for a dramatic work or play-script is a *kathānaka*; in its plotted form, as a sequence of events to be enacted and narrated dramatically on the stage, this story is often called the *itivritta* of the play. A dominant character in the story, or a protagonist, is known as the *nāyaka* (masculine) or *nāyikā* (feminine).
3. The narrative and dramatic focus of a play should be its hero's (or heroine's) *sthāyī bhāva*, which I render here as 'state of being' or 'encompassing emotional state'. This norm provides the framework for the play's generation of rasa or aestheticized emotion. See Appendix G for a fuller exposition of *bhāva* and rasa in theory and practice; and see Dharwadker, 'Emotion', for an exposition of the theory of emotion and representation in the *Nāṭyashāstra* (about 300 CE), and for the style of transcribing technical Sanskrit terms used here.
4. The narrative of a protagonist's quest provides a Sanskrit–Prakrit play with a 'teleological' structure, in which his or her pursuit of a specific goal runs like a 'thread' (*sūtra*) through the dramatic action. The director and manager of a theatrical

production therefore is called a *sūtradhāra*, the person who 'holds the thread' that ensures the coherence and continuity of the play in performance.

5. My phrase 'principal plot' corresponds to the Sanskrit term *bindu*, the sequence of events that 'centres' or streamlines the evolving dramatic action.
6. The technical term for 'secondary plot' is *patākā*.
7. My phrase 'tertiary incident' translates the Sanskrit term *prakarī*.
8. In Sanskrit, acting (as activity and as practice) and enactment (as general process) are designated by *abhinaya*. Mimetic enactment is *anukaraṇa*. A 'natural' style of mimetic enactment for general or popular audiences is labelled *loka-dharmī*; whereas stylized, non-mimetic enactment, usually reserved for audiences of connoisseurs, is classified as *nāṭya-dharmī*. For further details, see Appendix F.
9. Diegesis is the mode of representing personages, events, and situations by means of description, report, narrative, summary, commentary, and so on, in the medium of language. In the Greek and Europhone traditions, diegesis is contrasted with mimesis, which 'imitates' the object to be represented in a particular medium of communication; in the context of theatre and performance, 'imitation' comprises mimetic enactment with actors, movement, and spectacle on the stage. See the discussion of diegesis and mimesis in Puchner, pp. 22–28. In the Sanskrit–Prakrit tradition, the bulk of the dramatic action in a play is enacted mimetically; but a significant portion of it is represented diegetically, using special devices. Among the forms used for diegesis are the *vishkambhaka* (Interlude, as in Act III), the *mishra-vishkambhaka* (Mixed Interlude, as in Act IV), the *praveshaka* ('entry or introduction', as in VI.i), and the *chūlikā* ('public announcement', as in I.vi).
10. The technique of narrative framing enables a story-teller to narrate multiple stories coherently within a hierarchical

structure. The basic method is to embed several relatively short secondary narratives (inset stories) inside an encompassing primary narrative (frame story), where the latter provides an immediate context for the former. The Indian epics use dialogue among characters in their main (frame) stories to organize their narration; their numerous secondary (inset) stories are then related by narrators who appear in that circumscribing dialogue. In *Shakuntalā* and many other Sanskrit–Prakrit plays, a meta-theatrical prelude provides an 'outer frame' within which the narrative and dramatic action on the stage unfold.

11. Sanskrit poetics maintains a clear and consistent distinction between existential feeling and emotion (*bhāva*) and its aestheticized counterpart represented in an artwork (rasa). See Dharwadker, 'Emotion', for a critical analysis of this distinction.
12. The initial situation from which the rest of the dramatic action in a play evolves is called the *bīja*, literally 'seed'. In this seminal metaphor, the conception of structure is explicitly organic (rather than mechanical); and a play possesses a natural, organic unity because it 'germinates' from and grows out of a single, original 'seed'. The *bīja* of a play corresponds abstractly to an 'initial thesis' because it delineates an opening situation to which all subsequent developments in the dramatic action 'respond', whether implicitly or explicitly. At the level of the overall plot, this initial thesis is identified as the *mukham* (mouth, face) of the play.
13. 'First antithesis' abstractly translates the term *pratimukham* (literally, the 'opposing face'), which identifies the second portion of the overall plot, in which the protagonist initiates his concentrated effort or striving for his quest and its goal.
14. The 'first synthesis' in the overall plot corresponds to the *garbha* (literally, 'womb'), the moment in the dramatic action when the end of the hero's quest manifests itself in an 'embryonic' form.
15. The 'second antithesis' defines the *vimarsha* (which Apte glosses as a change in the course of the dramatic action due to an

unforeseen reversal or accident); the 'second or final synthesis' is the *nirvahana*, a 'cessation of the flow' of the dramatic action as the protagonist's quest comes to a successful conclusion.

16. 'Consistently noble' renders the qualifier *dhīrodatta*; Dhanañjaya suggests that the *nāyaka* and the *nāyikā* of a *nāṭaka* share this quality.
17. My analysis adopts the terms and categories developed in Frye, chapter 1.
18. The term 'dharma', in general, refers to law, duty, ethics and morality, religion, customary practice, obligation, and responsibility, in a wide range of situations. In the course of its action, the play dramatizes Dushyanta's duties and moral obligations as a king in the specific contexts enumerated here. The intricacy of his responsibilities is in proportion to his role, not only as a 'king' (*rājā*), but as a ruler who is a *rājarshi*, an extraordinary king with the spiritual qualities and accomplishments of a *rishi* or visionary sage.
19. See Aristotle, *Poetics*; and Frye, chapter 1.
20. A detailed analysis along these lines of the play's characterization of Shakuntalā supports Dhanañjaya's suggestion in the tenth century that the 'consistently noble' hero and heroine of a *nāṭaka* are 'equals' in a broader sense.
21. Shakuntalā's expression of her moral superiority to Dushyanta in Act V of the play echoes her stronger articulation of this attitude in the Mahābhārata, where she emphasizes her half-celestial origin. See van Buitenen, vol. 1, p. 169.
22. See Bakhtin, pp. 130–46, for his discussion of the representation of the 'interiority' and 'exteriority' of character and individual self in the context of ancient biography and autobiography in Greek and Latin.
23. See Vishvanātha, chapter 6.
24. See Mishra, pp. 44–45.
25. As a character-type, a jester is a clown, buffoon, or 'fool', who brings humour, laughter, playfulness, irreverence, and

foolishness to a situation, in order to entertain; in a literary work, his antics are harmless and diversionary. In contrast, a trickster is an entertaining character-type who, in addition, is deceptive, scheming, unreliable, unpredictable, and potentially harmful. Māḍhavya, in *Shakuntalā*, is a jester, the king's entertaining companion by occupation; whereas Mephistopheles, in Goethe's *Faust*, is a trickster.

26. See Jones, Preface; and Mishra, pp. 224–25.
27. Pollock, 'Social Aesthetic', suggests that Sanskrit theorists connect the aesthetic goals of Sanskrit literature to the organization, dynamics, and objectives of Hindu society in the classical period.
28. See van Buitenen, vol. 1, pp. 155–71.
29. Kashyapa's function in the overall plot is interpreted variously. He may be placed in Kaṇva's secondary plot; or in a tertiary incident that is integrated directly into the principal plot, and that brings together Dushyanta's and Shakuntalā's respective streams.
30. See the relevant entries in Appendix B. Also consult O'Flaherty; and Dimmit and van Buitenen.
31. See the entry on *prajāpati* in Apte; and consult Appendix B and the relevant annotations in the Notes to the Play.
32. See Dhanañjaya, pp. 57–58, on the heroine and her companions; however, he treats the latter as flat stereotypes.
33. Shakuntala's probable age in Act I is commensurate with the ages of comparable heroines in European literature: in *The Divine Comedy*, Beatrice is twelve years old when Dante first sees her; and, in Goethe's *Faust*, Gretchen is fourteen when Faust encounters her for the first time.
34. In the tragedies by Aeschylus and Sophocles, a chorus is a group of characters (common Greek citizens) who appear on the stage in masks, chant and display stylized dance-like movements, and comment on events and situations from a conventional social and moral point of view, without mimetically enacting a scene in the main action.

35. See Miller, *Theater*, p. 337.
36. See Apte's entry on *abhijñāna*.
37. Cognition is the mental faculty or process of knowing, of acquiring knowledge (including factual, empirical knowledge). It includes the capacity for sense-perception and for forming conceptions, but excludes emotion and will.
38. For some of this historical background, see Dharwadker, 'Emotion'.
39. This summary is based on the account in Miller, *Theater*, p. 336.
40. My summary is based on the *Kishkindha* and *Sundara* books of the Sanskrit Rāmāyaṇa. See Goldman, vols. 4 and 5; Lefeber, especially p. 291; and Sattar, especially pp. 373–410.

Select Bibliography

The following list contains three kinds of items: works that are cited in this book; works that I have consulted but did not have an occasion to cite; and works that readers with various interests are likely to find useful in their explorations of *Shakuntalā*, Kālidāsa, and classical Indian drama and theatre, as well as Sanskrit literature and poetics, premodern and modern South Asian and other literatures, and dramaturgy and performance. The citations of specific works in the main text of the book and in the Endnotes are in standard format, and are keyed to authors' last names and short titles (as necessary), or to titles of works (when authorship is indeterminate or unfamiliar).

The Bibliography is arranged in a single list in the order of the English alphabet, but it is annotated in order to identify and distinguish several kinds of works (Indian-language sources, earlier translations of the play, important scholarly and critical commentaries, and so on). The annotations are light, selective, and functional, and appear in brackets at the end of specific entries.

For historical information on translations of *Shakuntalā* and of Kālidāsa's works into Europhone as well as Indian languages, see Raghavan, 'Bibliography of English Translations' and 'Bibliography of Translations of Kalidasa's Works'; Schuyler; and Figueria. For more extensive listings of scholarship on Kālidāsa, *Shakuntalā*, classical Indian drama and theatre, and classical India, see the specialized bibliographies in Miller, *Theater*; and Sengupta and Tandon.

Apte, Vaman Shivaram. *The Practical Sanskrit-English Dictionary*. Delhi: Motilal Banarsidass, 2003. [Third edition in Apte's lifetime published in Pune, 1890; enlarged by anonymous editor(s) in 1965.]

Aristotle. *Poetics*. Edited and translated by Stephen Halliwell. Cambridge, Massachusetts: Harvard University Press, 1999. [Implicit reference for discussion of plot, character, theme, structure, unity, spectacle, and performance in my commentary.]

——. *On Rhetoric: A Theory of Civil Discourse*. Edited and translated by George A. Kennedy. Second edition. New York: Oxford University Press, 2007.

Arthashāstra. See Olivelle, *King*.

Bakhtin, M.M. *The Dialogic Imagination: Four Essays*. Edited by Michael Holquist. Translated by Caryl Emerson and Michael Holquist. Austin: University of Texas, 1981. [See especially the long third essay, 'Forms of Time and of the Chronotope in the Novel', pp. 84–258.]

Baumer, Rachel Van M., and James R. Brandon, eds. *Sanskrit Drama in Performance*. Honolulu: University of Hawaii Press, 1981. [Excellent collection of essays by scholars and theatre practitioners on performance in the Sanskrit–Prakrit tradition, and on modern productions of classical plays, including *Shakuntalā*. Consult Baumer and Brandon's commentary on each part of the book. For important individual essays, see Gandhi; Raghavan, 'Sanskrit Drama'; Richmond; and Vatsyayan.]

Bharadwaj, Parul. 'Shakuntalā on Celluloid: The Framing of an Archetype in Colonial and Post-colonial Hindi Cinema'. In Sengupta and Tandon, pp. 110–27. [Analysis, with stills, of two remarkable, commercially successful film versions of *Shakuntalā* by director V. Shantaram, in 1943 and 1961.]

Bose, Mandakranta. *Movement and Mimesis: The Idea of Dance in the Sanskritic Tradition*. Dordrecht: Kluwer, 1991.

——. 'Staging *Abhijñānashākuntalam*'. In Sengupta and Tandon, pp. 38–53. [A distinctive account by a scholar-practitioner of a modern production in Sanskrit–Prakrit; essential reference for theatre personnel, along with essays in Baumer and Brandon.]

Brodbeck, Simon. 'The Rejection of Shakuntalā in the *Mahābhārata*: Dynastic Considerations'. In Sengupta and Tandon, pp. 219–37. [Multilayered structural and thematic analysis of the play in relation to its epic source.]

Brown, Jane K. *Goethe's Faust: The German Tragedy*. Ithaca, New York: Cornell University Press, 1986.

Chari, V.K. *Sanskrit Criticism*. Honolulu: University of Hawaii Press, 1990. [Detailed overview of classical Indian poetics, with many technical arguments; especially helpful for scholars and students unfamiliar with the Sanskrit intellectual tradition.]

Coulson, Michael, trans. *Shakuntalā by Kālidāsa*. London: Folio Society, 1992. [English translation with: general introduction by William Radice; 'The Story of Shakuntalā from the *Mahābhārata*', translated from Sanskrit by Peter Khoroche; essay on 'Shakuntalā' by Abanindranath Tagore, translated from Bengali by Radice; '*Shakuntalā*: A Tale Retold in Pahari Miniatures' by Daljeet Khare.]

Devadhar, C.R., and N.G. Suru, eds. and trans. *Abhijñānashākuntala of Kālidāsa*. Delhi: Motilal Banarsidass, 1981. [First published 1934. Popular edition in Devanagari script with facing English prose translation; with detailed, multifarious notes to the play and tabular index of verse-forms.]

Dhanañjaya. *Dasha-rūpaka*. Edited and translated by George C. O. Haas. New York: Columbia University Press, 1912. [Classic of Sanskrit criticism from the tenth century. Haas misunderstands the term *rūpaka*, and hence renders the work's title as *The* Dasharūpa: *A Treatise on Hindu Dramaturgy*; the Sanskrit text as he edited it is still usable, but his translation is often erroneous or misleading.]

Dharwadker, Aparna, and Vinay Dharwadker, trans. *One Day in the Season of Rain* by Mohan Rakesh. Gurgaon, India: Penguin, 2015. [Translation of Rakesh's modernist Hindi play, *Āshāḍha kā eka dina* (1958), which imaginatively and incisively dramatizes Kālidāsa's life, personality, works, and literary career.]

Dharwadker, Vinay. 'Emotion in Motion: The *Nāṭyashāstra*, Darwin, and Affect Theory'. *PMLA*, Volume 130, Number 5 (October 2015), pp. 1381–1404.

Dimmit, Cornelia, and J.A.B. van Buitenen. *Classical Hindu Mythology: A Reader in the Sanskrit Puranas*. [Particularly useful for background on Vishṇu (section 2); Kāmadeva (section 3); and Nārada, Vishvāmitra, Yayāti, and Shakuntalā (section 6). Also see O'Flaherty.]

Doniger, Wendy. 'Rings of Rejection and Recognition in Ancient India'. *Journal of Indian Philosophy*, Volume 26, Number 5 (October 1998), pp. 435–53.

——, and Brian K. Smith, trans. *The Laws of Manu*. London: Penguin, 1991. [Translation of *Manusmriti*, Hindu 'lawbook' that has been normative since the epic period; canonical form dated about 300 CE. Extensive commentary, annotation, and other scholarly features. Chapters 7–8, on kings, and Chapter 9, on women, are especially relevant to *Shakuntalā*.]

Dwivedi, Rewaprasada, trans. *Abhijñānashākuntalam Nāṭaka*. Hindi translation in Tripathi, Dwivedi, and Dwivedi, pp. 311–525. [Rendering in prose and rhymed and metrical verse in modern Hindi, with extensive critical apparatus accompanying the facing Sanskrit–Prakrit text.]

'Ekphrasis'. In *The New Princeton Encyclopedia of Poetry and Poetics*, edited by Alex Preminger and T.V.F. Brogan, pp. 320–21. Princeton: Princeton University Press, 1993.

Fass, Ekbert. 'Faust and Sacontala'. *Comparative Literature*, Volume 31, Number 4 (Autumn 1979), pp. 367–91.

Figueira, Dorothy Matilda. *Translating the Orient: The Reception of Shakuntalā in Nineteenth-century Europe*. Albany: State University of New York Press, 1991.

Frank, Joseph. 'Spatial Form in Modern Literature: An Essay in Two Parts'. *The Sewanee Review*, Volume 53, Number 2 (Spring 1945), pp. 221–40.

Frye, Northrop. *Anatomy of Criticism: Four Essays*. Princeton: Princeton University Press, 1957.

Gainor, J. Ellen, Stanton B. Garner, Jr., and Martin Puchner, eds. *The Norton Anthology of Drama*. Second edition, 2 vols. New York: W. W. Norton, 2013.

Gandhi, Shanta. 'A Sanskrit Play in Performance: *The Vision of Vāsavadattā*'. In Baumer and Brandon, pp. 110–40. [An important Indian woman director's reflections on and account of staging a classical Sanskrit play by Bhāsa in Honolulu in 1974; required reading for theatre personnel.]

Gerow, Edwin, trans. *Mālavikā and Agnimitra*. In Miller, *Theater*, pp. 253–312. [English translation of *Mālavikāgnimitra* by Kālidāsa; with philological notes to the play, pp. 368–76.]

——. 'Plot Structure and the Development of Rasa in the Shakuntalā. Part I'. *Journal of the American Oriental Society*, Volume 99, Number 4 (October–December 1979), pp. 559–72.

——. 'Plot Structure and the Development of Rasa in the Shakuntalā. Part II'. *Journal of the American Oriental Society*, Volume 100, Number 3 (July–October 1980), pp. 267–82.

——. 'Sanskrit Dramatic Theory and Kālidāsa's Plays'. In Miller, *Theater*, pp. 42–62. [Useful scholarly overview; my commentary diverges from Gerow's perspective at several points.]

Gitomer, David, trans. *Urvashī Won by Valor*. In Miller, *Theater*, pp. 177–251. [English translation of *Vikramorvashīya* by Kālidāsa; with extensive notes to the play, pp. 344–67.]

——. 'The Theater in Kālidāsa's Art'. In Miller, *Theater*, pp. 63–81. [Clear summary of classical theatrical conditions and conventions, and basics of dramaturgy and performance based on the *Nāṭyashāstra*.]

——. 'Can Men Change? Kālidāsa's Seducer King in the Thicket of Sanskrit Poetics'. In Sengupta and Tandon, pp. 167–84. [Provocative, compelling new reading of masculinity, gender, and power in the play.]

Goethe, Johann Wolfgang von. *Faust I & II*. Edited and translated by Stuart Atkins. *Goethe's Collected Works*, Volume 2. Princeton: Princeton University Press, 1984.

Goldman, Robert P., ed. *The* Rāmāyaṇa *of Vālmīki: An Epic of Ancient India*, Volumes 1–6 to date. Princeton: Princeton University Press, 1984–. [A comprehensive translation of the epic with full critical apparatus and commentary, based on the Baroda edition, nearing completion; several translators.]

Goodwin, Robert E. *The Playworld of Sanskrit Drama*. Delhi: Motilal Banarsidass, 1998. [Offers a complex interdisciplinary perspective, especially in its first two chapters, 'The Playworld of Sanskrit Drama' (pp. 1–24) and 'Aesthetic and Erotic Entrancement in the Shakuntalā' (pp. 25–66); discussed in Gitomer, 'Can Men Change?']

Heifetz, Hank, trans. *Kumārasambhavam: The Origin of the Young God*, by Kalidasa. Gurgaon, India: Penguin, 2014. [Originally published by University of California Press in 1985.]

Johnson, W.J., trans. *The Recognition of Shakuntalā: A Play in Seven Acts* by Kālidāsa. [With] *Shakuntalā in the* Mahābhārata. New York: Oxford University Press, 2001. [A contemporary English rendering of the play in prose and verse, with introduction, explanatory notes, and bibliography; accompanied by a full verse translation of eight chapters from the epic.]

Jones, William, trans. *Sacontalá; or, the fatal ring: an Indian drama. By Cálidás. Translated from the Original Sanscrit and Prácrit*. London: J. Cooper, 1790. Eighteenth Century Collections Online. Gale. University of Wisconsin Madison. 5 April 2016. [Facsimile of copy in the British Library; first print edition dated 1789.]

Kale, M.R., ed. and trans. *The Abhijñānashākuntalam of Kālidāsa. With the Commentary of Rāghavabhaṭṭa, Various Readings,*

Introduction, Literal Translation, Exhaustive Notes, and Appendices. Tenth edition. Delhi: Motilal Banarsidass, 1969.

Kālidāsa. For Sanskrit–Prakrit texts, see Devadhar and Suru; Kale; Mishra; Monier-Williams, *Shakuntalā*; Narayan Ram; Somadeva Vasudeva, *Recognition*; Tripathi, Dwivedi, and Dwivedi; Tripathi.

For English translations of *Shakuntalā*, see Coulson; Devadhar and Suru; Johnson; Jones; Kale; Miller, *Shakuntalā*; Monier-Williams, *Sakoontala*; Rajan; Ryder; Somadeva Vasudeva, *Recognition*.

For English translations of other works, see Gerow, *Mālavikā*; Gitomer, *Urvashī*; Heifetz; Reddy; Ryder.

For Hindi translations of *Shakuntalā*, see Dwivedi; Mishra; Rakesh; Singh.

Kaul, Shonaleeka. 'Pleasure and Culture: Reading Urban Behaviour through *Kāvya* Archetypes'. In *Ancient India: New Research*, edited by Upinder Singh and Nayanjot Lahiri, pp. 254–81. New Delhi: Oxford University Press, 2009. [Analysis of 'urban men and women . . . as social and sexual beings' in late epic and early classical periods.]

Lefeber, Rosalind, trans. *Rāmāyaṇa*. Book Four: *Kishkindhā* by Vālmīki. New York: New York University Press and JJC Foundation, 2005. [Revised version of prose translation in Goldman, Volume 4, now with facing Sanskrit text in Roman transcription.]

Liu, Siyuan, ed. *Routledge Handbook of Asian Theatre.* New York: Routledge, 2016. [A handy, though uneven, source of information on Indian theatre in all historical periods and all genres. The most useful contributions are by Aparna Dharwadker, on modern theatre, pp. 243–67; Kathy Foley, on puppets, pp. 177–201; Arya Madhavan, on dance, music, traditional performance, pp. 97–101, 131–34, 480–85; David Mason, on costume, make-up, stage, theatre architecture, pp. 202–06, 222–25; Farley Richmond, traditional theatre, pp. 9–30; and Anita Singh, on gender performance, indigenous performance, pp. 413–17, 437–42, 456–60. These items in the handbook are not listed separately here.]

Mahābhārata. See van Buitenen.

Manusmriti. See Doniger and Smith; Olivelle, *Manu's Code*.

Martin, Richard P. *Myths of the Ancient Greeks*. New York: New American Library, 2003. [Handy reference for comparison with Doniger; Dimmit and van Buitenen.]

Miller, Barbara Stoler, ed. *Theater of Memory: The Plays of Kālidāsa*. Translated by Edwin Gerow, David Gitomer, and Barbara Stoler Miller. New York: Columbia University Press, 1984. [Excellent anthology of translations, with scholarly commentary; individual items are listed here under the three contributors' names.]

——, trans. *Shakuntalā and the Ring of Recognition*. In Miller, *Theater*, pp. 85–176. [English translation of *Abhijñānashākuntala* by Kālidāsa. With informative commentary and notes to the play, pp. 333–43.]

——. 'Kālidāsa's World and His Plays'. In Miller, *Theater*, pp. 3–41. [Useful critical overview, in a historical and cultural perspective.]

Mishra, Yadunandan, ed. *Abhijñānashākuntalam of Mahakavi Kālidāsa, Based on the Nirnaya Sagar Edition*. Varanasi: Chaukhamba Orientalia, 1987. [A trilingual work, with Sanskrit–Prakrit text, Sanskrit translation of Prakrit passages and complete Sanskrit commentary on the play, and Hindi prose translation and full critical apparatus in Hindi; with introduction and critical and interpretive notes. The play-script follows the twelfth Nirnaya Sagar edition of 1958, critically edited by Narayan Ram with Rāghavabhaṭṭa's fifteenth-century Sanskrit commentary on the play.]

Mitra, Pramadā-dāsa, and J.R. Ballantyne, trans. *The Mirror of Composition, a Treatise on Poetical Criticism*. Banaras: Motilal Banarsi Dass, 1956. [Reprinted from the Bibliotheca

Indica edition of 1865. A painstaking prose translation of Vishvanātha's *Sāhitya Darpaṇa* [1384], using a text prior to Kane's critical edition of 1910; now dated because of its Victorian diction, but still very useful for scholars and students without access to Sanskrit. See Vishvanātha for editions used here.]

Monier-Williams, Monier, ed. *Shakuntalā; or, Shakuntalā Recognized by the Ring, a Sanskrit Drama, in Seven Acts, by Kālidāsa; the Devanagari Recension of the Text.* Hertford, England: Stephen Austin, bookseller to the East-India College, 1853. [Historically, the second major critical edition of the Sanskrit-Prakrit text (after Otto Böthlingk's 1842 edition), with literal English renderings of the verses and extensive critical and explanatory notes; the common reference for all subsequent editions of this recension.]

——, trans. *Sakoontala or The Lost Ring; an Indian Drama Translated into English Prose and Verse, from the Sanskrit of Kālidāsa.* Varanasi: Indological Book House, 1961. [Originally published in Hertford, England, by Stephen Austin, bookseller to the East-India College, in 1856; fourth edition, 1872. Historically, the first literary-scholarly translation in English (accompanied by extensive notes) based on a critically edited Devanagari text of the play, which displaced William Jones's 1789 prose rendering of an unedited text in the Bengal recension.]

Narayan Ram (Acharya 'Kavyatirtha'), ed. *The* Abhijñānashākuntalam *of Kālidāsa, with the Commentary of Rāghava Bhaṭṭa.* Twelfth edition. Mumbai: Nirnaya Sagar Press, 1958. [My English translation of the play is based on this critical edition of the Devanagari recension, which appeared just over a century after Monier-Williams's 1853 edition, and represents the cumulative work of several generations of Sanskrit scholars.]

O'Flaherty, Wendy Doniger, trans. *Hindu Myths.* London: Penguin, 1975. [Handy, wide-ranging sourcebook on Hindu mythology, with extensive scholarly guidance. Especially useful for sections on Brahmā, Indra, and Vishṇu and his incarnations. Also see Dimmit and van Buitenen.]

Olivelle, Patrick, ed. and trans. *Manu's Code of Law: A Critical Edition and Translation of the* Mānava-Dharmashāstra. New York: Oxford University Press, 2004.

——, trans. *Saṁnyāsa Upanishads: Hindu Scriptures on Asceticism and Renunciation*. New York: Oxford University Press, 1992. [With important scholarly introduction on asceticism; more useful for scholars than general readers and theatre practitioners.]

——, trans. *Upanishads*. Oxford: Oxford University Press, 1996. [Introduction provides very good overview of Vedic texts, religion, rituals, and social and historical contexts.]

——, trans. *King, Governance, and Law in Ancient India: Kauṭilya's* Arthashāstra. New York: Oxford University Press, 2013.

Pollock, Sheldon. *The Language of the Gods in the World of Men: Sanskrit, Culture, and Power in Premodern India*. Berkeley: University of California Press, 2006. [Comprehensive historical, theoretical, and interpretive account of the Sanskrit–Prakrit world in a global context; specialized, but essential for scholars and advanced students.]

——. 'The Social Aesthetic and Sanskrit Literary Theory'. *Journal of Indian Philosophy*, Volume 29, Numbers 1–2 (April 2001), pp. 197–229.

——. 'Sanskrit Literary Culture from the Inside Out'. In Pollock, *Literary Cultures*, pp. 39–130.

——, ed. and trans. *Rama's Last Act* by Bhavabhūtī. New York: New York University Press and JJC Foundation, 2007. [Sanskrit text and facing English translation of *Uttararāmacharitam*, an important late-classical play in discussions of Sanskrit–Prakrit drama and poetics.]

——, ed. *Literary Cultures in History: Reconstructions from South Asia*. Berkeley: University of California, 2003. [Excellent general reference on Indian literatures, ancient to modern; especially useful for Pollock's Introduction and his essay, 'Sanskrit Culture'.]

Puchner, Martin. *Stage Fright: Modernism, Anti-Theatricality, and Drama*. Baltimore: Johns Hopkins University Press, 2002.

Raghavan, V. 'A Bibliography of English Translations of Sanskrit Dramas'. *Indian Literature*, Volume 3, Number 1 (October 1959–March 1960), pp. 141–53.

——. 'A Bibliography of Translations of Kālidāsa's Works in Indian Languages'. *Indian Literature*, Volume 11, Number 1 (January–March 1968), pp. 5–35.

——. 'Sanskrit Drama in Performance'. In Baumer and Brandon, pp. 9–44. [The best historical, conceptual, and practical overview of ancient and classical Indian theatrical culture and performance traditions.]

Rajan, Chandra. *The Loom of Time: A Selection of Plays and Poems by Kālidāsa*. New Delhi: Penguin, 1989. [Offers verse translations of two long poems, *The Gathering of Seasons* and *The Cloud Messenger*; and prose and verse translation of the Bengal recension of *Shakuntalā*. Includes an informative general introduction and helpful editorial resources. The main reference for the play in translation for contributors to Sengupta and Tandon.]

Rakesh, Mohan. *Shākuntala* [by] Kālidāsa. New Delhi: Rashtriya Natya Vidyalaya, 1999. [Originally published in 1966. Premier postcolonial Hindi literary translation of the play; with brief introduction, no notes. Close rendering, but classified as a *rūpāntara* ('formal transformation') and not as a *bhāshāntara* (literal translation).]

——. *One Day in the Season of Rain*. See under Dharwadker and Dharwadker.

Ramanujan, A.K. 'The Ring of Memory: Remembering and Forgetting in Indian Literatures'. In Ramanujan, *Uncollected Poems and Prose*, edited by Molly Daniels-Ramanujan and Keith Harrison, pp. 83–100. New Delhi: Oxford University Press, 2001. [A basic discussion of memory, perception, and cognition and their interrelations, with a brief analysis of *Shakuntalā*, based on Miller's translation.]

——. *The Collected Essays of A.K. Ramanujan*. Edited by Vinay Dharwadker. New Delhi: Oxford University Press, 1999. [Thirty essays on general themes, epic and classical poetry, postclassical and modern poetry, and folklore; excellent general reference on Indian literature and culture.]

Rāmāyaṇa. See under Goldman.

Reddy, Srinivas, trans. *Malavikagnimitram: The Dancer and the King* by Kalidasa. Gurgaon, India: Penguin Books, 2014.

Richmond, Farley. 'Suggestions for Directors of Sanskrit Plays'. In Baumer and Brandon, pp. 74–109. [Very good essay by scholar and practitioner, with rare photographs of modern productions of Sanskrit plays on the international stage. Rich in practical detail; essential reading for theatre personnel.]

Ryder, Arthur W., trans. *Shakuntala and Other Writings* by Kalidasa. New York: E.P. Dutton, 1959. [Originally published in 1912. The translation of *Shakuntalā* is in prose and rhymed, metrical verse, but the 'poetic' diction is now outdated. Based on the Bengal recension in Pischel's edition of the play, discussed in Rajan's Introduction.]

Sahni, K.C. *The Book of Indian Trees*. Mumbai: Bombay Natural History Society; New Delhi: Oxford University Press, 2000. [Informative source on several species mentioned in the play: for example, *ashoka*, banyan, *shamī* (under *khejri*), mango, sandalwood.]

Santapau, H. *Common Trees*. New Delhi: National Book Trust, India, 1995. [Originally published in 1966. Guidebook covering several trees mentioned in play, especially *ashoka*, banyan, mango.]

Sattar, Arshia. *The Rāmāyaṇa* by Vālmīki. New Delhi: Viking, 1996. [Useful one-volume modern English version of the epic for general readers.]

Schuyler, Montgomery, Jr. 'The Editions and Translations of Shakuntalā'. *Journal of the American Oriental Society*, Volume 22 (1901), pp. 237–48.

Sengupta, Saswati, and Deepika Tandon, eds. *Revisiting* Abhijñānashākuntalam: *Love, Lineage and Language in Kālidāsa's Nāṭaka*. Foreword by Romila Thapar. New Delhi: Orient Blackswan, 2011. [Informative, stimulating, and wide-ranging collection of recent essays that analyse the play textually and contextually; see especially the individual contributions listed here under Bharadwaj; Bose; Brodbeck; and Gitomer.]

Singh, Raja Lakshman, trans. *Shakuntalā nāṭaka*. Agra: Sahitya Ratna Bhandar, 1964. [Singh's first Hindi prose translation was published in 1863; his second Hindi translation, with prose in Khadi Boli and verse in complex metrical and rhymed dialect forms, appeared in 1889. This modern edition reprints the latter. A remarkably meticulous, lively, imaginative, and dramatically sound rendering of the Devanagari recension, with each verse footnoted with a prose paraphrase.]

Somadeva Vasudeva, ed. and trans. *The Recognition of Shakuntalā*. New York: New York University Press and JJC Foundation, 2006. [New edition and English rendering of Kashmir recension; with scholarly apparatus, but lacking in literary quality.]

——. 'The Inarticulate Nymph and the Eloquent King'. In Sengupta and Tandon, pp. 185–205. [Unusual, complex, philological discussion of the play's themes, centred on the Kashmir recension.]

Stein, Burton. *A History of India*. New Delhi: Oxford University Press, 1998.

Swarup, Vishnu. *Garden Flowers*. Fourth edition. New Delhi: National Book Trust, India, 1988. [Particularly helpful on jasmine, lotus, and water lily.]

Tagore, Rabindranath. 'Shakuntalā'. Translated by Sukanta Chaudhuri. In Tagore, *Selected Writings on Literature and Language*, edited by Sukanta Chaudhuri and others, pp. 237–51. New Delhi: Oxford University Press, 2001.

Thapar, Romila. *Cultural Pasts: Essays in Early Indian History*. New Delhi: Oxford University Press, 2000. [Omnibus edition of over fifty essays by Thapar; excellent discussion of historical background to Kālidāsa and the play.]

——. *Shakuntalā: Texts, Readings, Histories*. New York: Columbia University Press, 2010. [Original Indian edition published in New Delhi by Kali for Women in 1999. Very influential in the critical reinterpretation and revaluation of the play across disciplines in the early twenty-first century; required reference for general readers, specialists, students, and theatre practitioners alike.]

Tripathi, Mithilaprasada, Rewaprasada Dwivedi, and Sadashivakumar Dwivedi, eds. *Complete Works of Kālidāsa*. Third edition, 2 vols. Volume 2: *Nāṭyakhaṇḍa* [Plays]. Ujjain: Kālidāsa Sanskrit Akademi, 2008. [An alternative critical edition, based on various Devanagari manuscripts, including one at Houghton Library, Harvard University (date not given); with the Sanskrit–Prakrit text (*Abhijñānashākuntalā-nāṭakam*) and Rewaprasada Dwivedi's prose-and-verse Hindi translation (*Abhijñānashākuntalā Nāṭaka*) on facing pages (pp. 311–525), and with an extensive critical apparatus.]

Tripathi, Shrikrishnamani, ed. *Abhijñānashākuntala of Mahākavi Kālidāsa*. Third edition. Varanasi: Chaukhamba Surbharati Prākāshan, 1984. [Edition of the Sanskrit–Prakrit text with parallel Sanskrit and Hindi commentaries, based on the Bengal and Devanagari recensions. I mostly consulted the Introduction, pp. 1–74; and the Dramatis Personae.]

Van Buitenen, J.A.B., ed. and trans. *The Mahābhārata*. 3 vols. Chicago: University of Chicago Press, 1973–78. Volume 1: *The Book of the Beginning*. Volume 2: *The Book of the Assembly Hall* and *The Book of the Forest*. Volume 3: *The Book of Virāṭa* and *The Book of the Effort*. [Meticulous, annotated translation of the critical edition of the epic, with scholarly commentary; incomplete but indispensable. My specific references are to Volume 1, which contains the original *Shakuntalā* narrative, pp. 155–71.]

Vatsyayan, Kapila. 'Dance or Movement Techniques of Sanskrit Theater'. In Baumer and Brandon, pp. 45–66. [Concise, accessible, and informative account of classical Indian theory and practice of movement, mime, gesture, and facial expression in theatrical performance.]

Vishvanātha Kavīraja. *Sāhitya-darpaṇah* [1384]. Edited by P.V. Kane. 1910. Downloaded from http://www.southasiaarchive.com, at University of Wisconsin, Madison, 19 October 2015. [My reference is primarily to the sixth *parichchheda* or part of this work, the text of the 337 verses (*kārikā*s) of which appears in Kane's Appendix E, pp. 61–109. See Mitra and Ballantyne for English translation of earlier Sanskrit text.]

——. *Sāhitya Darpaṇa*. Edited by Satyavrat Singh, with Hindi Commentary and Notes. Varanasi: Chowkhamba Vidyabhawan, 1963. [Edition with extensive critical apparatus; for specialists in Sanskrit and Hindi. See Mitra and Ballantyne for English translation of earlier Sanskrit text.]

Wolpert, Stanley. *A New History of India*. Fourth edition. New York: Oxford University Press, 1993.

Copyright Notice for Theatre Practitioners